10-20-19

To Hilly
I Love you — You
Crazy Woman!
thanks For Your Support
Sally
(C.M. Castillo)

THE PAGES OF Adeena

A NOVEL

C. M. CASTILLO

iUniverse

THE PAGES OF ADEENA
A NOVEL

Editors: Laurie Shoulterkarall and Doris Strieter
Original Cover Art: Satish Prabhu

Certain characters in this work are historical figures, and certain events portrayed did take place. However, this is a work of fiction. All of the other characters, names, and events as well as all places, incidents, organizations, and dialogue in this novel are either the products of the author's imagination or are used fictitiously.

iUniverse books may be ordered through booksellers or by contacting:

iUniverse
1663 Liberty Drive
Bloomington, IN 47403
www.iuniverse.com
1-800-Authors (1-800-288-4677)

ISBN: 978-1-5320-7641-1 (sc)
ISBN: 978-1-5320-7640-4 (e)

Library of Congress Control Number: 2019907765

Print information available on the last page.

iUniverse rev. date: 06/29/2019

To Kris, the girl without a filter

CONTENTS

PART I

PART II

Part

I

CHAPTER 1

Summer–1952

Addie Kahlo walked through the front door of the small apartment she shared with her cousin Rachel and threw her hat toward the coat rack in the corner, missing it completely. Rolling her eyes, she muttered, "One of these days I'm going to hit that darn hook dead on." As she bent to retrieve her hat off the floor, she took a quick look around the cozy living room, briefly wondering where Rachel had gone. Shrugging, she grabbed a Coke from the ice box, plopped down on the sofa, and pulled the new leather journal from her handbag, smiling excitedly as she slowly flipped through the empty pages outlined in gold. She couldn't wait to fill it with her thoughts and dreams. There was something cleansing about journaling, she thought; it always made her feel lighter afterward, like having just gone to confession, but without the religious part.

Sitting back comfortably on the sofa, Addie adoringly smoothed the soft mustard-colored leather book with her fingers, smiling as she recalled how, at the age of eight, she announced to her parents that one day she would be a famous writer. Having just read *Alice in Wonderland*, she had decided she could write like that and immediately began jotting down ideas and storylines at every opportunity. Now, as the early afternoon sun warmed her face, she contemplated her long-ago decision and chuckled at her youthful arrogance. But, her desire to be a writer hadn't wavered; she was certain that becoming an author was her future. Sighing in contemplation and bathed in the warmth of the sun shining through the small front window on a lazy Saturday afternoon, she settled in to write.

Addie Kahlo - Personal Journal, June, 1952

I'm going to be a writer. It's who I am. I think from the first moment

I understood the concept of reading, that the words on a page could conjure magic and adventures, I was in love with books. As a kid I loved to read about princesses and kings, villains and heroes. These were images I could only experience through the pages of the books I loved. I suppose I have always lived in two worlds. They couldn't be any more different. In my real life I live here in Chicago with my parents, two brothers, and my best friend/cousin, Rachel. I love my life here. Rachel and I live together in the downstairs apartment of my parents' building. Yeah, we're pretty lucky. I think we're the only teenagers who have our own place.

I was born in Chicago on August 10, 1934, four years after my brother Tony and two years after my brother Danny. By the time I turned eight, I knew I loved to create fiction. I was writing my own plays and performing them in one-woman shows on the back porch of our parents three- flat. Mom and dad figured it was better than playing in the street, so they were ok with it.

Growing up on the south side of Chicago in the late 40's and early 50's endowed me with a great love for my family, the neighborhood, and city life in general. On the west corner of 18th and Cornelia, across the street from Stanley's Deli, is The Angel, our family-owned night club. The Angel opened in 1936 and was named for the sleepy little town of Puerto De Angela, a coastal haven on the Gulf of Mexico and the birth place of my great-grandparents. My father and several aunts and uncles own and operate The Angel. The club is very popular with the locals and the multitudes of service men who come up from the Army and Navy bases scattered throughout Illinois and Indiana.

It is now the summer of 1952, and in September I begin my senior year of high school. I'm very excited! Even though I am a bit of an extrovert amongst my family, I can be unusually quiet and shy with new people, and there are always new kids at the beginning of a school year. I wish I were like my brothers and cousins, who all tend to resonate serious swagger, have loud laughs and loads of confidence. I think I am a good actress, though, and can easily pretend to be like them—but I never feel as if I am. I suppose I've always felt a little bit different from my brothers and cousins, and because of that I have always dreamed of living a different life.

Recently I have discovered the authors, artists and activists of avant-garde turn-of-the-century Paris. I read everything and anything I can find; I think it is my new obsession! The first time I read the autobiography of Alice B Toklas by Gertrude Stein I needed more, like an addiction. I became enthralled, excited, and have, quite literally, fallen in love with not only her writing, but with the era. How wonderful must it have been sitting in a café in Paris chatting with Gertrude Stein and sharing recipes for pot brownies with Alice B Toklas. I imagine discussing politics with F. Scott Fitzgerald and listening to the jazz of Josephine Baker and Flossie Mills on the Champs-Elysees. Another favorite of mine is the writings of I.A. London. I've fallen in love with his poetry. How amazing would it have been to meet him, as his poetry touches my soul with its imagery and prose. If I didn't already know in my heart where my desires gravitate, I think I would be in love with him. I can hardly wait to go off to college so I can immerse myself in learning all that I can about my favorite authors, artists, and socially-conscious heroes of the surrealist movement. My goal is to one day travel to Europe, perhaps live in Paris, and make my living as a writer, like my heroes.

Addie closed her journal with a flourish, yawned, and looking around the room was surprised to see early evening shadows as the afternoon sunlight dimmed to twilight. Turning to the clock on the wall, she realized that she had lost track of time. She stood up from her cozy spot on the couch and lifted her arms for a long languid stretch, happy with what she had accomplished today. Her favorite English teacher had told her that keeping a personal journal is necessary for all writers, and she was excited that she found it so fun and easy to do. Hearing the front door swing open, she turned to see Rachel walk in carrying a brown paper bag in her arms; the telltale sounds of beer bottles clanged together as she placed the bag on the table in the small bright kitchen.

"Hi Ad, whatja doing?" Rachel asked as she emptied her shopping bag of beer and milk. Turning, she looked at Addie who once again was plopped sleepily on the couch, "Oh no, Ad, please put down that book and get ready. Mickey and his friend Alan are picking us up in less than an hour and you're not even dressed!" Addie sighed, craning her neck to look at her cousin Rachel who stood with her hands on her hips and an exasperated look on her pretty face. Her deep brown eyes sparked with indignation and impatience as she waited for Addie to respond.

"Rach, why do I have to go?" Addie whined. "Can't you and Mickey go without me? I'm not up for going out tonight." Addie lifted her stockinged feet onto the coffee table and leaned back with an exaggerated sigh, eyeing Rachel with a pleading look.

3

Groaning heavily, Rachel rolled her eyes. "Addie, sweetie, we discussed this. You agreed to the double date. Mickey said Alan is looking forward to meeting you, and we talked about this like a million times!" Addie cringed at Rachel's now-shrill voice and groaned. She knew Rachel was right, and after all, she did promise.

"Okay, okay Rach, I'll get dressed, but don't get your hopes up. I am not going to be dating this Alan guy. I have college to think about. I don't know why you insist on trying to set me up all the time. I am not interested in dating anyone right now."

Rachel turned to Addie, "Look, Ad, I'm only trying to help you. You know you haven't dated in ages. It's time to get back on the horse."

"What!? It really hasn't been ages. Take that back! Get back on the horse? What does that even mean?" Addie huffed out playfully as she jumped off the couch and walked toward the bathroom to prepare her bath. "You and Mickey can just date this Alan guy if you like him so much." Addie winked mischievously at Rachel and closed the bathroom door just as Rachel threw a sofa pillow at her head.

"So, Adeena, I've really been looking forward to meeting you. Rachel can't stop talking about you, and I feel as if I know you already." Alan's genuine pleasure at meeting her was evident in his warm smile. Feeling a bit awkward, having never been on a blind date, Addie gave Alan what she considered her friendliest smile. "Rachel tells me you're a writer. That's pretty sweet. What do you like to write about?" Addie shifted her surprised gaze to Mickey and Rachel as they encouragingly nodded in Alan's direction, waiting for her to jump into the conversation. Caught off guard, Addie was at a loss for what to say, so instead she smiled politely and nodded.

Clearly deciding that Addie had lost her ability to speak, Mickey jumped in to help her out. "Yeah, Alan, my man, Addie always has her head in a book. She like lives it night and day, right, Ad? She's going to be a famous writer one day if her determination has anything to do with it. Seriously, if she's not reading, she's constantly pecking on that typewriter of hers or writing in her journal, all serious looking. Isn't that right, Ad?"

Addie visibly colored and looked back at Alan to gauge his reaction to

Mickey's description of her. To her surprise he had a sweet sincere smile on his face. She noted he was quite handsome; his eyes were large liquid pools of soft chocolate brown that any girl would find dreamy. He had dark wavy hair distinguished by a prominent widow's peak which she thought was quite striking. He was also tall and well-built. She realized that he must be a serious athlete to be so fit. Watching him, she could only read his sweet smile as being playful, and she realized with a slight shock that he was genuinely interested in meeting her and hearing about her writing.

This realization made her sigh a little bit with a feeling of regret since she was not physically attracted to him, despite his good looks and sweet smile. She hated disappointing anyone, but she knew that there was little to no chance that they would be the adorable dating couple that Rachel hoped they'd be.

"Please, call me Addie," she finally offered, pulling herself away from her thoughts when it became clear everyone was waiting for her to join the conversation. "I enjoy writing fiction. Mickey's right. I'm going to be an author." She added enthusiastically, "It's the premise of being able to create my own characters, guide them through the development of their personalities, and then send them off on any type of adventure I can imagine, that is just so thrilling to me." Addie smiled up at Alan, excitement evident in her voice, knowing that she simply couldn't help her enthusiasm when she spoke about her writing.

Alan asked a few pointed questions about her writing, and his deep brown eyes watched her while she responded. She searched his face for any sign of boredom or polite disinterest, but only noted sincerity. Addie decided she liked Alan Nackovic. His genuine good-natured personality put a whole new spin on her interest in him. He was so sincere and attentive to her that Addie could almost believe him to be some kind of kindred spirt. She just didn't want to date him, but being his friend was something she knew she did want.

Addie lay comfortably in her bed that night thinking over the evening's double date. She smiled when she thought of Alan. He had been the perfect gentleman, opening doors for her, looking intently at her as she spoke as though every word she said was the most amazing thing to come out of anyone's mouth. Still, there was something about his demeanor. It was as though he was conspiring with her, as if his chivalry was for the benefit of Rachel and Mickey. This realization left Addie curious, and she looked back at the evening with more thought. At one point, after a particularly funny story Mickey was telling, she could have sworn Alan was about to slap her in the back like she was a track buddy who had just told a funny story. Instead, at the last minute, he had put his arm around her shoulder. She chuckled to herself. She thought he should have slapped her on the back. Rachel would have been horrified.

Placing her hands behind her head, Addie allowed her eyes to adjust to the darkness of her bedroom. A soft breeze billowed the light blue curtains her mom had hung just last week. Closing her eyes, she let her mind drift, as it often did, to the real reason she worked so hard to avoid dating. She hated lying to Rachel, but she saw no other way. She pursed her lips thinking about all the excuses she had made—too much homework, school was too important, or all the boys at school were too immature. Thinking about it now, she saw her excuses as being pretty pathetic. So far, thank god, no one other than Rachel had really questioned her about her lack of dating interest.

Addie sighed heavily. The truth was that she had no interest in dating boys. It was so simple, yet not simple at all. She had known for a while now that she wasn't interested in boys as anything other than friends. Thinking back, she recalled how, at the age of fifteen, she recognized that she was way more interested in girls. The realization had frightened her. She didn't want to be different, but she knew that she was. Closing her eyes, she visualized that moment when she understood the truth about herself.

The epiphany had come to her as a shock; she had actually been astonished, and even a little traumatized. Not because she was ashamed of who she was; no, she had just simply had no idea up until that moment. She had been oblivious to the obvious, telling herself that all girls on occasion admired other girls or found them attractive. But eventually she had to acknowledge that the daydreams that entered her thoughts when she noticed an especially attractive girl at school were surely not what other girls dreamed of. Nor could she deny the crushes she had on glamorous movie stars. She was sure Rachel didn't find Kim Novak sexier than Frank Sinatra like she did. No, she liked girls. She was attracted to girls, and that was that. Lying in bed she questioned what it was about females that she found so appealing.

Yawning, Addie told herself to go to sleep. None of her questions or contemplations about who she was, why she was the way she was or why she found women so fascinating were going to be answered tonight. Before she closed her eyes to sleep, she thought of Alan again. She knew Rachel was encouraged by how well they had gotten on. She realized that Rachel would probably try and set up another double date because she and Mickey were always trying to set her up. Addie smiled. They were sweet, but dammit she wished they'd stop. Finally allowing her over-active brain to settle, she had one last thought before she drifted off. Right now, it was enough knowing that she accepted herself. It gave her strength, knowing that despite acknowledging who she is, it was better than living with confusion and doubt.

CHAPTER 2

Rachel opened the back door and leaned out to shake the dust off the small area rug she held in her hands while Addie busied herself cleaning out the icebox. "Addie, I just don't understand why you won't come out with us on Friday. Alan really likes you, and you seemed to like him that day we all went out. What changed?"

"Nothing has changed, Rach. Honestly, I do like him He's a nice guy, but I just don't like him in the boyfriend kind a way. Oh yuck, what is this stuff in this container? I'm throwing it away." Addie had her head in the icebox attempting to figure out what mystery items they needed to throw out before they grew legs. Tossing the mystery container in the trash, she sighed and leaned against the kitchen counter. "I'm sorry, Rach, I'm just not there yet. I have a lot on my mind right now. You know my folks can't afford to pay for college, so I have a little over a year to secure scholarships that will help cover some of the cost."

Rachel turned toward Addie, showily breathed a deep sigh, and gazed at Addie with big hurt, blinking eyes. Addie knew that look. "Oh no you don't! Stop that!" Addie laughed, "You know I can't say no to you when you give me those puppy dog eyes. Look, okay I'll go out with Alan this Friday on a double date with you and Mickey, but understand I am only doing it for you. And maybe because he's nice and I think I can be friends with him." Rachel screamed and ran toward Addie, throwing her arms around her and encircling her in big hug while all Addie could think was that this was all a big mistake.

Friday night came sooner than Addie had hoped, and as she checked herself out in the full-length mirror while dressing for her date with Alan, she couldn't help but feel like a fraud, and it was not a good feeling. Speculating that she'd need to fend off invitations to dinner and the movies from Alan over the next few weeks until he got the hint she wasn't interested made her weary. Closing her eyes, she thought of Rachel who was thrilled at the notion of the two of them dating. Alan was Mickey's friend and Rachel loved the idea of the four of them double dating. Christ, Addie thought resignedly, how do I get myself in these messes? It looks like I will disappoint Rachel again. I just hope this will be the end of her crusade to find me a boyfriend, because it's exhausting. At least when I go off to college, she won't be able to set any dates up long distance, not that I'd put it past her to try.

"It's really good to see you again, Addie." Alan's voice was soft as they walked to the concession stand to pick up Cokes and snacks. Turning to acknowledge him, Addie saw a playful smile dance across his face. She returned his smile, feeling awkward and uncomfortable. She shouldn't be here, she thought to herself. Turning away from him, she stared straight ahead and cleared the lump she suddenly had in her throat.

As they continued to walk in silence, her thoughts drifted to planning Rachel's demise. "I just cannot believe," Addie told herself, "that she did not tell me that this fiasco of a double date would be at the drive-in movie theater across town! I should have walked home as soon as I realized. Why do I always give in to her!? Because she gives you that pathetic puppy dog look that always does you in that's why." Ugh! The internal dialogue she was having with herself was starting to give her a headache.

Hearing Alan mention how nice the weather was, Addie realized that he was doing his best to start a conversation. Clearing her throat, she clumsily took the cue. "Yeah, it's a nice night. Ah...it's really good to see you again too, Alan." He chuckled softly and took a pack of cigarettes out of his shirt pocket and offered her one, she declined. She decided she needed to tell him immediately, before things went too far, that she wasn't interested in dating him. She was starting to feel like a fraud. This was their second date, and she didn't want to give Alan the wrong idea; it was best to nip it in the bud. Turning to Alan, she put her hand on his arm and stopped their slow momentum toward the concession stand. "Listen, Alan, I..."

"No, Addie, it's okay, really. You don't need to spell it out for me, I totally get it. You don't really want to date me, and that's okay."

Momentarily taken aback by his directness, she pressed on. "Alan, listen please. It's not that I don't find you attractive or I don't think you're interesting. It's just that I am not interested in dating anyone right now." Alan's eyes watched her as she spoke, and she could see that he was waiting to hear more. "You see," she continued, "I have plans. I mean we're going into our senior year of high school this fall, and my plan is to go away to college and study journalism after graduation. Dating right now is just not smart. I have too much to accomplish in the next year to get prepared, and dating will get in the way."

Alan looked at Addie as she awkwardly pleaded her case. "It's fine, Addie, really. Can I be honest with you? I actually don't really want to date you either."

The surprise on Addie's face was unmistakable. "Wait, what?" Addie stopped talking and stared at him wide-eyed. "I mean, really, what's wrong with me?" Alan raised his eyebrows, clearly amused he softly chuckled. Blushing from her ridiculous response, she tried to recover. "Uh, so why did you agree to go out with me then?"

Shrugging his shoulders, Alan grinned. "Probably for the same reason you agreed to go out with me. Our friends pushed us into it." Addie looked up at Alan with amusement and smiled, feeling a real sense of relief and a little bit silly for her momentary outburst of indignation. She noted that Alan looked relieved too. He smiled back at her, his soft brown eyes shining.

Addie shook her head. "Wow, just wow." Now that she was off the dating hook, she felt a great sense of relief. "So, do you think that we can be friends?" she asked with real sincerity.

Alan smiled broadly and nodded. "I'd like that." Taking a deep breath and blowing it out loudly, she nodded. Suddenly she felt excited about hanging out and seeing the film. It was a modern romantic musical starring Fred Astaire, Jane Powell, and Peter Lawford titled *Royal Wedding*. She had heard other kids at school discussing the movie, and everyone said that it was really good. Besides, she had a secret crush on Jane Powell. Addie found her adorable, sometimes daydreaming during algebra class that they were dancing together in the moonlight. Turning to Alan again, this time with an open earnest smile, she reached out and linked her arm through his and gestured toward the concession stand. She felt blissfully relieved and knew she could now enjoy Alan's company as a friend with no other expectations.

Walking back to their spot, Addie saw Mickey and Rachel setting up lawn chairs in front of the car. "Hey, you guys, this is perfect," she said. "We have hotdogs and Cokes. I don't know about you guys, but I'm starved." Alan walked to the trunk of the car and pulled out a couple of blankets that Rachel and Addie could use since the night was chilly.

"Ah, thanks, Alan," Rachel said sweetly. "See, Addie, what a gentleman Alan is?"

Addie snickered at Alan, and he batted his eyes at her, which prompted a burst of laughter from her because his action was so unexpected. Settling in, Addie looked up at the clear sky, feeling as though a ton of bricks had been magically removed from her shoulders. This is nice, she thought, no girlfriend expectations, thank God! She was enjoying watching Jane Powell dance across the screen when Rachel announced that she and Mickey were going to sit in the car since it was getting a lot chillier. Addie sneaked a peek at Rachel, and sure enough, Rachel was giving her that look that said she needed to stay outside the car with Alan. It was fine with her, she thought as she cringed. She certainly didn't need to hear the two of them going at it in the back seat of the car. Alan turned to Addie and shrugged, knowing exactly what Rachel and Mickey were up too.

"Hey, Addie," Alan said, "Come sit next to me. We can share the blanket and cuddle." He winked at her, and she knew immediately he was teasing her for Rachel and Mickey's benefit. She rolled her eyes and walked over to sit under the blanket with him as Mickey and Rachel scrambled into the backseat of the car.

Watching the movie and stuffing her face with popcorn, Addie was mesmerized by Jane Powell. Turning briefly to Alan to see if he was enjoying the film as much as she was, she nearly choked on her popcorn. She couldn't believe what she was seeing. Was Alan checking out Peter Lawford like she was checking out Jane Powell? Wow, she thought. Wait, is this wishful thinking or is this really happening? Is Alan like me in that way? She stole another quick peek at him before quickly turning back to her popcorn. Good lord, she thought excitedly, could Alan like boys the way I like girls? Addie tried to relax her breathing as she was nearly hyperventilating with excitement.

Closing her eyes for a second, Addie considered the odds. I know there are others like me, but honestly, how would I know? How would I know if someone is like me? It's not like this sort of thing is discussed over the dinner table. In fact, it was against the law! Addie's mind started playing back her covert research efforts into homosexuality. As a writer, she knew research always brought results, if not answers, at least a hypothesis. She simply needed to know what the heck was going on with her. She figured research was her best option to finding answers, but tracking down any information on homosexuality was not that easy.

Addie recalled how scared she was that day she took the 'EL' to the main library downtown and slowly made her way over to the information desk. She was perspiring as though she had run a mile in 100-degree heat when she finally got up enough nerve to ask the librarian for information on homosexuality. The look she got nearly scared the bejeebies out of her. Thank god she was a fast talker, quickly blurting out that she was writing a paper for her college entry essay. After the librarian suggested that Addie should consider another topic, she walked her to a section that was mostly ancient scholarly articles and papers by the likes of Ellis and Freud.

Addie did find a newer publication from 1951 by Donald Webster Cory titled *The Homosexual in America*. She borrowed the book from the library, along with a book by Ellis, just so the librarian would not suspect anything. As she was signing the borrowed books out, she thought about how she had continued to babble to the clerk about research and essays. Nothing like the feeling of a little paranoia to get me talking like an idiot, she thought. She had gone home, locked herself in her room and devoured the books from beginning to end. She needed to know why her feelings were different from other girls and why she wasn't attracted to boys.

Addie soon realized she wasn't going to find the answers she was hoping for. The books, it turned out, were specifically geared to homosexual men. However, overall, she believed that the ideas Cory penned were plausible. He appeared to argue toward the normalcy of the psychology of the homosexual. Despite the book not providing any direct answers, it opened her eyes to counter-theories on homosexuality. In addition to Cory, she found information referencing new studies which were emerging and being debated in scientific circles. These studies offered arguments that attraction to one's own sex is not a mental illness, but possibly a biological trait.

This gave Addie pause as she read. Granted, these theories were controversial, but they still offered her a sense of hope. She also found that there are plenty of writings, documented throughout history, that offer glimpses into the lives of same-sex relationships. According to several articles she managed to find, same-sex attraction had been around for as long as humans have.

After reading all the information on the subject she could find in the library, Addie decided that she had to be okay with her own theory, that homosexuality was simply just another form of love. She knew it was a simplistic theory, but nothing that she read had anything to do with the type of person she was. She didn't understand why she was the way she was, but she knew she wasn't a bad person. She couldn't agree with the religious arguments against it or society's hate and fear. How could she? She had herself to use as an example.

Thinking long and hard about it, Addie realized that society's fear and disgust with homosexuals was a much bigger issue than anything she could figure out at this point. So, she let it go for now, more assured that even though she felt no shame about who she was, she knew the consequences could be very bad if anyone found out. Besides, she thought, my sexuality is no one's business but my own.

Addie brought her thoughts back to the drive-in movie and Alan sitting next to her. She watched him. She thought he seemed mesmerized with Peter Lawford. Could he really be like her? She was excited, thinking that if he liked guys like she liked girls they could talk about it with each other. Addie really wanted someone to talk with about her feelings, someone to whom she could relate and confide in. It would be pretty neat if Alan saw the world through the same kind of lens as she did. As he comically sucked on a straw, Alan turned and looked at Addie, surprised that she was studying him so closely.

"Addie, if I didn't know better, I'd say you were infatuated with me," Alan teasingly implied as he popped some popcorn into his month. She nudged his shoulder playfully and grabbed the popcorn from his hand as she turned her thoughts back to the film.

"Alan, um, don't you think Jane Powell is fabulous?" she said dreamily.

"I mean just look how she dances across the screen. She's so beautiful." Addie swooned as she stared at the screen as if in a trance.

Alan raised an eyebrow as he watched Addie's apparent adoration of Jane Powell. "Well, yeah, I suppose she is beautiful, but she's not really my type. She doesn't do anything for me." Alan snorted and then laughed quietly under his breath. "You know, Addie," he remarked as he continued to watch her, "I think you and I may have more in common then we initially believed."

CHAPTER 3

That summer before senior year Alan and Addie became inseparable. They had bonded that night at the drive-in and soon after were always together, so much so that everyone they knew assumed they were dating exclusively and in love, which of course was about the farthest thing from the truth. But the ruse worked to their benefit. It kept their friends from trying to set them up, and it kept their parents from asking too many questions about why they were not your average hormonal teenagers.

"Alan, are you a virgin?" He and Addie were sitting in a comfortable swing on the front porch of his family's home. Over the past few weeks it had become their "go to" spot to simply relax and watch the stars. It was 10:00 on a warm late July evening. As neither one of them had really felt much like hanging out at the park with their friends, they ended up on his front porch. Alan sipped his Coke and sheepishly cocked his head toward Addie.

"What kind of a question is that, Ad?" He tried to sound offended, but his lips curled upward into a wicked little smile.

"You're right," Addie said, her cheeks visibly flushed in the soft light of the porch lamp. "I don't know why I asked," she said, feeling embarrassed.

Alan shook his head and looked at her. "No, it's okay that you asked. I'm just shocked, that's all. You and me, well, we haven't ever talked about stuff like that, so now I'm just all a flutter." He pretended embarrassment and fanned his face with his hand in a way that sent Addie into a fit of giggles, laughing so loudly that the drink she was gulping down at that moment came up her nose. She tried not to gag, but it was too late. Alan grabbed for a napkin that his mom had laid out on the small table next to the swing and tried in vain to wipe her month.

"Ewe!" she screamed, "Leave me alone. I got it!" He laughed and

15

tried even harder to wipe at her mouth. They ended up play fighting and giggling until his mom came out to scold them for acting like children. They calmed down, but Addie's inquiry remained unanswered, and she could tell that Alan was intrigued by her question. She decided not to push, so she simply sat on the porch swing daggling her legs and continuing to watch the stars.

"Um, no, I'm not." Addie turned to look at Alan. He had his head down, and even in the dim light of the porch lamp she could tell he was blushing. She was immediately taken aback.

"Wait. what? she whispered, staring at him wide eyed. Alan looked sheepish as he continued to sip his Coke.

Reaching for her hand he pulled her from the swing. "Come on, let's go. We can meet up with Rachel and Mickey at the park and talk on the way." They were silent as they began their long walk toward the wooded area of the park, the soft crunching noise of twigs and rocks under their feet the only noticeable sound. Addie took a sideways glance at Alan, waiting for him to speak. Alan cleared his throat. "Uh, I said, no, I'm not a virgin." Addie turned to look at him.

"Okay." It was all she could think to say, not really knowing if he wanted her to respond. She rolled her eyes at herself for her lack of a decent response. You're so articulate, she thought, visibly cringing. She patiently waited for him to continue.

Alan looked toward Addie, attempting to gauge her reaction. His eyebrows creased together, and Addie sensed that he was debating with himself whether to go into any more detail. She could tell that he was nervous, but she knew instinctively that he wanted to talk. Speaking without thinking, she awkwardly asked, "So, um, do you love her?" Alan gulped and Addie rolled her eyes feeling like a complete idiot.

"Oh my God!" She halted in her tracks as she grabbed his arm to stop his forward momentum. "Did I just say that?" She closed her eyes. "What a stupid question," she said, chastising herself. She continued to cringe in embarrassment even as Alan burst out laughing. With the tension in his face visibly gone, she couldn't help herself, and she laughed too. "Uh, Alan, really, don't answer that. I'm sorry, just let me shut up. I don't even know how that asinine question came out of my mouth," she said, wiping away tears of laughter.

Alan shook his head slowly. His laughter subsiding, he released a long breath. Pulling a crumpled pack of Lucky Strikes from his pocket, he watched Addie as he lit a cigarette. "It's cool, Ad. I know I kind of shocked you. But you asked and well—you know that I feel like I can share stuff with you that I can't share with anyone else, right?" Moving closer, he nudged her shoulder and looked at her with big expressive eyes. "Our friendship means so much to me, and I hope it does to you as well." Addie smiled and reached for his hand.

"Of course, it does. You're my best friend, Alan," Addie said softly, and she meant it too. She knew instinctively that they would always be this close. Alan broke out into a wide grin and his entire face lit up. As they continued their walk toward the park, they grew silent once again. Alan looked torn, as though he wanted to say more but wasn't certain that he should. She was about to ask when he spoke.

"Ad, can I be honest with you? I mean like really honest?" He looked nervous. Addie noticed a light sheen of perspiration across his brow, and he didn't look at her when he spoke.

"Alan, let's stop walking for a minute, okay?" Addie suggested. "Come on, let's sit here." She gestured to a bench which overlooked the park's small lagoon. He nodded and slowly followed her, taking a seat next to her when she sat. "Alan, you know that whatever you tell me is between us. No one else will ever hear of it, I promise." Alan saw the sincerity in Addie's eyes and he knew he could trust her. He took a deep drag of his cigarette, licked his lips absently, and sighed quietly. He turned toward Addie, surprising her with his seriousness.

"Here it is. I'm kind of afraid to say it. You promise you won't judge me? If anyone ever found out it could ruin my life. But I just need to tell someone, I need to tell you—no one else but you."

Addie looked at Alan, suddenly nervous for him because he sounded so somber, and she was worried that he was in some kind of trouble. "Whatever you share with me, said Addie, I won't judge you. You can trust me." Alan nodded.

"First, I want to tell you, Addie, that I really admire you. You're smart and confident. I mean you know what you want, and you have your sights set on it. College, a career, New York. Most girls I know only want to find a fella and get married. Oh, not that there's anything wrong with that, but you, you have that confidence and inner strength that I wish I had." Addie looked at Alan at that moment with a little fear in her heart, not quite understanding where all of this was heading.

"Alan, honestly, I'm not that strong, cause right now you're scaring me. Please tell me you're alright. I mean you're not sick or anything, or in trouble, are you? Please tell me."

Alan took another long drag of his cigarette, then threw it down, grinding it under his shoe. "Addie, here's the thing—it wasn't a girl." He said it quietly with a little bit of a tremor in his voice, but with a sternness too, like he wasn't ashamed. Addie said nothing. She knew it, of course; she'd only been waiting for him to tell her. Now that he had, now that he said probably the scariest thing on earth for any one person to say to another person, she was speechless. She thought he must be the bravest person she had ever known. She stared at him open-mouthed, ready to tell him it was all okay, but nothing came out. She knew she needed to say something, anything. But she was just too shocked that he had voiced her own secret.

Alan and I *are* the same, she screamed in her head. His admission was confirmation to her that she wasn't alone or sick. Because, if an amazing person like Alan could be a homosexual, then it might just be okay. "We *are* kindred spirits," she whispered to herself.

As Addie continued to reflect on Alan's admission, she didn't notice that he was watching her. Apparently taking her lack of response as a rejection, he stood up without another word, and quickly headed back toward the path they had just walked. His quick movements brought her back to the moment. She immediately jumped up and chased him down, grabbing him by his shirt sleeve as he tried to pull away. "Leave me alone," he yelled, hurt and pain in his voice.

"Alan! Alan, please stop. Don't leave! Do you think I wouldn't understand, that I'd hate you?" she shouted, looking at him in a kind of panic. "Alan, please listen. I understand! I do," she said with tears in her eyes, not tears of fear but of relief. "I understand because I'm like you. I'm like you, Alan!"

Addie couldn't believe she had said it. She said it out loud to somebody besides her own reflection in the mirror and the pages of her journal. She felt such a sense of release. She felt freer—she felt terrified. Alan looked at her with an incredulous wide-eyed gaze; it took him a moment to comprehend what she had just shared. His eyes glistened with tears. Addie had never seen Alan cry. But slowly, a smile appeared on his face, and he exhaled a long breath, looking to the sky with such a sense of relief that Addie had to laugh. Her heart was so full of love for her friend and she knew she would do anything in the world for him. Alan reached out and grasped Addie in a tight hug, nearly squeezing the breath out of her. His sudden joy spilled from him so quickly that Addie could hardly keep up.

"Addie, really? Really? You're like me," he whispered loudly as he lifted her and twirled her in a circle. "I want to tell you everything," he said in a rush. "I haven't had anyone to talk with, and now you're here and I can share everything! But, know this, Addie," he said, looking at her intently, "You can share your secrets with me—all your adventures and stories. I want to hear them, and like with me, it will all be just between us. We can be each other's confidants, I promise!"

Addie felt lighthearted with excitement and relief. She quickly grabbed Alan's hand and attempted to slow his enthusiasm so she could speak. He relaxed a bit at the feel of her hand, warm and strong in his own. He squeezed it gently and pulled her back toward the bench they had so recently vacated. Sitting down again, he said, "I feel liberated, like now it will be okay."

"Alan, I need to tell you, well—I don't have any secrets to share." She lifted her head toward the sky and pursed her lips. "The thing is, I'm like you in my heart and in my head, but not in practice." Embarrassment stained her face as she spoke. "I'm afraid that I haven't had the courage or even the opportunity to explore any 'adventures,' as you so shrewdly call them."

Alan watched Addie and nodded knowingly, as if saying he understood. "Addie, you know you are so very lovely. I have seen how guys at school look at you." He looked at her closely. "And," he continued, "I have also seen how a few girls at school look at you as well."

Addie looked at him in shock, "What?" she questioned, startled at his words. "No, they don't. Do they? No, Alan, you are so teasing me right now, right? No girls look at me *that* way."

Alan let out a big laugh and shook his head, "Oh Addie, I'm serious. You are just so distracted with your books and your journals that you simply don't notice. Have you seen yourself? You're beautiful. You have those gorgeous hazel eyes, long lashes and soft wavy hair, and you're tall and statuesque, kind of like those models in the magazines. No girls at school look like you. Okay, maybe Rachel looks a bit like you, but that's because she's your cousin."

Addie stared at Alan, taken aback by his observation of her. She just couldn't believe he saw her that way. She knew what she looked like; she looked at herself in the mirror every morning. She just didn't see it. At 5'8 she thought she was too tall for a girl, and her hair was too unruly and hard to manage. She did think her eyes were her best feature, though she briefly wondered how she came to have hazel eyes when no one in her family had anything but various shades of brown. "Alan, really? Are you serious? You see me that way?" she asked, still skeptical.

"Yes, I do, and I'm not the only one who does. Trust me. I'm sure the guys at school would be all over you if they didn't think I was your guy. Plus, the kids at school like you, even if you are always caught up in your books. You're nice to people, unlike some of those stuck-up girls at school." Alan grabbed Addie's hands and suddenly lifted her up from their seated position. He twirled her around and stood back, smiling at her. "You are gorgeous!" he yelled at the top of his lungs.

Addie laughed. "Stop that! You're embarrassing me!" she said even though the compliment made her happy. She grabbed Alan's hand and made him sit back down. He leaned back on the bench looking thoughtful.

Turning to her, he smiled. "Remember right before school let out in June, that girl in your science class; what's her name? You know, the cute one with the really thick glasses."

"Clare," Addie said, recalling the day he referred to and feeling a rising anger invading her thoughts.

"Yeah, Clare, that's right. Anyway, you stood up for her when that jerk from class purposely bumped into her by the lockers. He bumped her so hard her glasses flew off and she couldn't see. Everyone started laughing as she got on all fours to try and find them." Addie narrowed her eyes and recalled how that idiot had bumped Clare on purpose because she had bested him in the verbal chem exam. He thought he was so smart and superior. He was not happy that a girl had beat him. Alan continued, "You shoved him back so hard he flew right into Mr. Kikta, remember? Then you said, loud enough for the entire school to hear, "Michael Magneti, you are an ass and a sore loser!" Then you got down and picked up Clare's eye glasses and pressed them gently into her hand. She was so grateful, I thought she'd cry. But you gave her that look and a nod that kind of said, be strong and don't give them the satisfaction of knowing you care what they think. Do you remember, Addie?"

Addie's mind went back to that moment. Besides recalling how that guy was such a jerk, she suddenly remembered that she did see Alan there, though she didn't know him at the time. He watched her and nodded as though he was on her side. "He had it coming, Alan. What a jerk he was! I wanted to punch him in the face!" Her indignation was fueled again at the memory of it.

Alan grinned at her feistiness. "Well, that's when I decided I wanted to know you. But I didn't know how to approach you. I finally got the chance when I found out Mickey was dating your cousin. I kind of asked him to introduce us."

"What? But Alan, I don't understand. You aren't into girls," she whispered close to his ear, turning slightly pink.

He laughed and said, "Yeah, well I liked you and wanted to be your friend. Mickey told me you didn't date and to let it go, but I figured if I could get to know you, you'd see that I wasn't after anything but your friendship."

Addie's heart suddenly clenched as she looked up at Alan. She smiled at his handsome teary-eyed face and hugged him again, filled with feelings of relief and happiness. "We're kindred spirits, Alan," she quietly whispered. Despite her embarrassing lack of experience, she felt encouraged. She had a friend with whom she could share her secrets, a confidant. Addie realized she didn't feel alone any longer. It was a wish that she hadn't realized she believed in enough to make it come true. But it had, and she couldn't help thinking God must be okay with her and with Alan and others like them because things like their friendship just didn't happen.

CHAPTER 4

The summer was flying by. August came in with a vengeance, hot and sticky and uncomfortable. Living in the Midwest was great if you liked the change of seasons, but August could be brutally hot, just as February could be viciously cold. Addie and her friends had about four weeks before senior year began, and they wanted to take full advantage of the time remaining. Most days they hung out at the lake, a short 20-minute train ride up north. Chicago's lakefront was impressive, with miles of beachfront dotted with concession stands here and there from the north to the south side. It was also easy to hop the train to Riverview, the northside amusement park that stood about a mile south of Wrigley Field, the home of the city's beloved Chicago Cubs baseball team.

Living on the southside had its disadvantages because, in Addie's mind, most fun spots in the city were pretty much situated on the northside of town. But the trains, affectionately called the "EL" because they were elevated above the City's central district, known as the "Loop", ran throughout the city and could take you pretty much anywhere for twenty cents a ride.

The sound of the "EL" overhead made Addie wince as she walked along the busy sidewalk. It was a hot day. She had just left her apartment, yet she could feel the beginnings of perspiration under her arms as she hurried the four blocks to her family's night club. Finally reaching the steps of The Angel, she sighed and swung the main door open. The coolness of the overhead fans was a welcome relief to her heated skin. "Addie, grab that tray of glasses, will you? We'll need them for tonight's event," Joe Kahlo, Addie's father, called to her as she walked past the club's freshly-waxed oak bar. Addie's Uncle Jon waved at her as he rushed by to help his son Phil set up the club's tables with white table clothes and small vases of fresh flowers.

"Sure thing, Dad," Addie responded as she grabbed the tray of freshly washed wine glasses off the bar. The Angel was hosting a WWII veterans' event to raise money for vets who had fallen on hard times due to their war time disabilities, both physical and psychological. Addie's dad and four of his brothers had all fought in the war and were big proponents of helping out other veterans however they could. Tonight's event would be free to all veterans. There would be food, drinks, and gift bags stuffed with toiletries and much-needed clothing. Some of The Angel's patrons and local businesses had generously donated to the cause and offered their help as well. WWII was still fresh in the minds of many people, and now, with the war raging in Korea, Americans were sympathetic toward veterans as well as the new group of young men who were going off to fight.

"Addie, I'd like you and Rachel to wait tables tonight. Are you good with that?" Addie looked down at her father who was stooping, checking the lights on the small stage. His stocky frame appeared uncomfortable as he balanced on one knee, grunting while he checked the switches and plugs to ensure that all would be ready for the evening's festivities.

"Whatever you need, Dad. Honestly, I can't speak for Rach, but I know I'm open to whatever you need me to do."

"Okay kid, thanks. I appreciate the help. I mean, I know you are busy dating Alan and all," he teased. Addie smirked and shot him a look; he laughed and made a face. "What? You two are inseparable. Is Alan coming tonight?"

"Yes, Dad, you know he is. He promised to watch the door with Danny and Tony, remember? And Dad, please don't tease him about keeping me honest. You know we are just dating and it's not serious. Alan and I are both going off to college after graduation."

Joe Kahlo smiled at his only daughter. "I know, honey, but you kids are always together. Thick as thieves you two are. Your mother and I were thinking that maybe he might ask you to marry him."

"What?" Addie screamed. "Marry him? Dad! Oh, for heaven's sake! No, we are definitely not getting married. I have college to attend and so does Alan. He's going to be a building engineer. He's already submitting his applications to schools across the country. As for me, you know I've got my eye on some schools out east. I have already completed a number of scholarship applications. Hasn't mom mentioned to you that two came back stating I'm conditionally approved?" Addie babbled. "I just need to submit an essay, since my grades are good. I need to concentrate on making the best grades possible in senior year to get the funds."

"I know, honey. We were just hoping. Your mom and I aren't looking forward to you going off to college so far away," Joe Kahlo said with a despondent look on his face. Addie sighed and looked at her dad. He was being Dad, that great guy who always made her laugh and taught her the proper way to run a business. He was hoping, she knew, that she would get in the business, like Rachel and her brothers planned to do. She knew that her dad and his brothers and sisters were going to retire within the next ten years. A few of them had already done so.

The goal was to teach the kids how to keep the business running successfully and then hand the day-to-day operation over to them, with the parents maintaining oversight from a distance. It was a successful club, profitable and well-respected due to the family's philanthropic participation in the community. With the nightclub and large apartment building adjacent with retail shops on the main level, the business was a strong legacy for the families' next generation.

"Addie, Joe, you two here?" Jane Kahlo, Addie's mother, walked into the club, fanning herself with her free hand and glad to be out of the heat of the scorching sun. She looked around the empty space for her daughter and husband. Huffing out a breath, she brushed some lose damp hair off her pretty face as she enjoyed the cool breeze that the ceiling fans generated.

"We're in the back, Mom," Addie yelled out as her mother walked toward the rear of the club with a basket of flowers.

"Oh good. I'm glad I caught you here, Addie." Jane laid the basket of flowers on the crates of beer stacked in the storage room. Smiling at her daughter, she kissed her cheek. "Let's go out to the front of the club, sweetie. You too, Joe," she said, looking at them. "I think it's a good time to speak with Addie about what we discussed. Do you agree, Joe?" Addie looked at her dad with a questioning gaze, and Joe smiled back, though Addie thought his smile seemed a little sad.

As Addie and Joe walked out to the front of the club, Addie felt a growing panic in the pit of her stomach. Good lord, she thought, I hope this has nothing to do with my perceived marriage to Alan that Dad just mentioned. Shit! Addie was already racked with guilt from the ruse that they were dating. She hated the idea of having to fly by the seat of her pants by making up some nonexistent love affair between the two of them.

Addie continued her musings as she waited for her mother to settle in and begin the discussion. To date, she and Alan had been lucky, as neither of their parents had asked any personal questions specific to their relationship. They, like all their friends, assumed they were dating exclusively. A thin layer of perspiration immediately formed on Addie's face. Her stomach knotted up, and she could sense anxiety making her limbs tense. How was she going to deal with this, she worried? She already hated the lies of omission. Now it would be face-to-face lying, to the two people she most loved and respected.

Jane led the way out to the small tables next to the bar and pulled out a few chairs. Addie stood next to the chair she pointed to. "Sit," Jane said. Both Joe and Addie quickly sat, stiff and straight as if they were in some sort of trouble. Jane looked at their fearful faces and barked out a laugh as she eyed them. "Okay you two, I'm not that bad. You both look like scared mice."

Joe shivered, and with an exaggerated flourish of his hand, wiped at his brow. "God, Janie, it was almost like a flashback of boot camp." Jane Kahlo eyed him sternly but then broke out into a warm smile.

"Oh, stop Joe. You're a fool."

Addie looked up at her mom, whose warm brown eyes were full of fun. Feeling an immediate sense of relief, she relaxed and sat back, grateful when her Uncle Jon came by with bottles of ice-cold Cokes. "Janie, are you and Rosie ready for the gig tonight? You know the crowd always loves it when you and your sister get to singing, the place goes nuts for you ladies." Jane smiled at her brother-in-law. Addie could sense her mother's excitement.

"Yes, Jon. Actually, I'm here not only to speak with Addie, but also because Rosie and I are putting the final touches on our songs. She should be here any minute. We want to make sure we are on the same page and ready to woo the crowd tonight." Jon rubbed his hands together in anticipation, complimenting the duo on their talent and letting Jane know that they had an open invitation to sing at the club any time. Jane blushed, pleased with his compliments, she smiled broadly.

Once Jon left them to their small impromptu family meeting, Jane grabbed Joe's hand and they both looked at Addie with smiles on their faces. Oh no, Addie thought, here it comes. "Addie, your father and I were discussing your future."

"Uh, huh, okay," she stammered, nervous as hell thinking they were going to ask her if Alan and she are being careful.

"Well," Jane said looking at her husband. "We cashed in one of our savings bonds, and we want you to have the money to help with your first year of college," she said with a big grin on her face. "It's not much, honey, but it should help with day-to-day expenses, books and supplies."

"What? Wait, what? You want to help me with college?" Addie was fighting back tears as she looked at these two selfless people whom she adored. "Mom, Dad, really? Wow, oh my God, that is so amazing. I don't know what to say. I'm shocked—and thrilled!" Throwing her arms around both her parents in a group hug, she wiped tears from her eyes. "I thought you were going to ask if Alan and I were getting married after high school or something like that." Addie stammered as she released her parents from the bear-hug she had just given them.

Jane pulled back and looked at Addie in surprise. "Addie, where on earth would you ever get an idea like that?" Addie turned to her dad and saw him just shrug as he attempted to change the subject.

"Okay, girls," Joe announced, "now that that's done, whatja say we get back to getting the place ready for tonight." He immediately sprang from his seat and headed back toward the storeroom.

Rachel and Addie stood staring into their respective closets. Eyebrows scrunched and hands on their hips, they both wondered what outfit to wear for the evening's festivities at The Angel. Addie sighed and threw several discarded outfits on her bed. Her dad and Uncle Jon requested that they get "dolled up", as this evening was a special event, but also to be practical as they would be servers on their feet most of the night. Addie yelled, "Rach, what are you going to wear?" as she sorted through her closet for an appropriate dress.

"I don't know," Rachel yelled back, "and I'm not happy about it either, damn it! I can't believe that we gotta wear a dress tonight. It's hot out and we're going to be running around serving people. I wanna wear shorts and

Pops wants me to wear a darn dress. It's not fair!" Addie smirked, knowing Rachel was on a roll with her indignation.

"Well, there's nothing we can do about it, Rach. It is The Angel's big event, so I guess we need to do what our dads want us to do, at least for tonight."

Rachel pulled out one of her most summery dresses and declared she was wearing it because it was going to be sweltering in the club with all those people. Addie agreed and grabbed a similar summer dress to change into. "Addie, let's go on a double date Friday. Mickey and I haven't hung with you and Alan in weeks. We can go to Riverview and then grab something to eat up at Margie's. Mickey's got his brother's Chevy now. You kids can drive with us. What do you say?"

Addie felt a bit guilty because it was true that she and Alan were not seeing a lot of Rachel and Mickey. Instead, they spent a whole lot of time listening to music and talking about their future college plans and, of course, their secret. They couldn't wait to go to college and be independent adults. "Sure, Rach. Let me speak with Alan, but I'm sure he'll be all in," Addie turned and smiled at her. Rachel beamed, her big beautiful smile lighting up her whole face. Addie's heart clinched; she adored Rachel. A terrifying realization hit her a few moments later as she heard Rachel singing along to her favorite Eddie Fisher song. She would never be able to tell Rachel that she liked girls. If she did, she feared she would certainly lose her.

That evening, Rachel and Addie were busy serving glasses of beer and punch to the patrons of The Angel, who whistled and cheered for Jane and Rosie as they did their own version of Rosemary Clooney's tunes. Everyone was having a great time, the regulars as well as all the veterans and their wives and dates. Sounds of talking, laughter, and music filled the club. Earlier in the week, Addie's younger cousins had outdone themselves, filling bags with food, toiletries and other supplies to pass out to the veterans who had fallen on hard times.

Addie's mom and Aunt Rosie had stacked dozens of these bags up by the door with a sign saying, "For our heroes—Please take one on your way out." There were American flags and red, white, and blue balloons decorating the club, making it look patriotic and festive. Alan, Mickey, and Addie's brothers Tony and Danny were in charge of ensuring that each veteran got a bag. Addie thought it was neat to see how everything just all came together.

"Addie, can you get more clean glasses please? I'm running out here," yelled Rachel from across the bar.

"No prob, Rach. I'll grab the empties off the tables and go and wash them," she yelled back over the music. Both Rachel and Addie had been working for several hours, waiting tables and serving customers at the bar. Everyone was good-natured and didn't complain that they were not what you'd call professional waitresses. They missed a few orders and forgot to take others, but they did their best, and no one was left unattended. The club's hired servers were busy at the other end of the club, serving at the smaller bar and bringing out mounds of food. It was nearly midnight when things began to quiet down, and most patrons had had their fill of beer and pasta. Rachel and Addie were pretty much spent, and looked it too, with their service aprons covered in spilled beer and pasta sauce.

"Addie, I think the last of the customers are on their way out, with a little probing from Dad," Rachel announced. "Jeez I'm beat. How about you?" she groaned as she plopped down on a chair. "My feet are killing me. Do we have to clean up tonight or can we wait until the morning?" Rachel sounded exhausted, and Addie could tell she was dead on her feet.

"Go ahead, Rach, let Mickey take you home. I'm going to hang out and lend a hand closing up," Addie said between yawns.

Just then Alan walked into the room. "Addie, if you're staying, I'll stay with you," he announced as he walked across the bar carrying empties to deposit in the bin. I'm not that tired, and I want to walk you home anyway. It's too late to walk by yourself."

"Always the gentleman," smiled Rachel, winking at Addie. Addie rolled her eyes.

"Ad, your cousin Bobby and brother Tony are out back dumping the empties and checking that no one passed out behind the building," chuckled Alan as he sat down to join the exhausted group. Despite Addie's fatigue, she smiled and shook her head. She could recall that more than once the boys ended up carrying someone in who had overindulged and then had to pour coffee down their throats to sober them up before they sent them on their way.

"Great job tonight, kids," Addie heard her dad say as he and her Uncle

Jon came in from the kitchen area. "Couldn't have done it without your help. We didn't expect as many vets as showed up," he said a bit sadly. "All those fellas outta work, you'd think Uncle Sam would be more grateful." The exhausted group all looked at Joe and Jon, knowing that they believed themselves lucky, having returned from the war with all their limbs and mental faculties intact. They had the nightclub and family which was a lot more than many of those who showed up tonight had.

"It's all good, Pops," Rachel said and hugged her father Jon. "We were all happy to help. Plus, we got tips! A little spending cash doesn't hurt, right, Ad?" she said as she smiled sweetly at the group. Rachel's good humor broke the solemn mood that had suddenly appeared when Joe spoke of his comrades in arms.

"Okay you kids," smiled Rachel's dad, "off with you now—we can clean this mess up tomorrow. For now, you've all earned a rest." The group started to drag their tired bodies out of the uncomfortable chairs.

"Don't need to tell me twice, sir," piped up Mickey, "Come on, Rach. I'll walk you home. You look beat."

As everyone began to shut off lights and prepare to leave, Alan gently touched Addie's shoulder, "Hey, come on, that's our cue too. Let's beat it out of here."

CHAPTER 5

It was only a four-block walk from The Angel to Addie's and Rachel's apartment. Though the evening was still uncomfortably warm, being out of the hot alcohol- and cigarette-infused club made Addie feel a whole lot better. Exhausted and holding on to Alan's arm, more for support than affection, she felt happy. It was the kind of happy you feel when you have shared quality time with family, when you know that your efforts and participation in something have been worthwhile, when even if it was only for one night, people who have fallen on hard times could laugh, eat a good meal, and get some much-needed support.

"Alan, did you have fun tonight? I mean I know you worked most of the night, but it was fun, wasn't it, with all the music and people looking so happy?"

Smiling down at Addie, Alan held her arm gently. "Oh yeah, Ad, it was neat, hah! I can't believe what good singers your mom and aunt are. I never knew they could really belt out the tunes, and boy can they dance! I mean wow! They must have danced with a hundred guys."

"I know," Addie said excitedly. "Mom told me that when Dad was in the service, she and my aunts would work at the USO, serving food, talking and dancing with the service men. She said these men just really needed to talk and laugh. It was something my mom said they could do, you know—for the boys." Addie suddenly felt a bit anxious, almost afraid, and held Alan's arm a little tighter. "Alan, I hope this war ends soon. It's terrible to think of you and Mickey and the other kids going off to Korea." Alan didn't say anything in response, and for a second, Addie thought maybe he didn't hear her, but then he squeezed her hand tightly, and she knew he too was a bit worried. They remained quiet and in their own heads as they walked toward Addie's and Rachel's apartment.

"Addie, listen, would you be up for a little adventure? I'd like to take you somewhere." Addie looked up at Alan, and he had a hopeful look in his eyes with a hint of fun. She was so relieved that they'd switched topics just then that she readily agreed. "Good!" he said excitedly, rewarding her response with a dazzling smile and a kiss on the cheek. Addie smiled at how charming Alan could be. It didn't surprise her that there were always throngs of high school girls, and even a few older women, vying for his attention. He'd tease her and tell her she should be jealous. After all, he was a catch, and she was lucky to have him. Usually that was her clue to slap him on the back of his head.

Two days after the party at The Angel, Alan phoned. "Addie," Addie's father called from the den, "Alan is on the phone for you." Addie sat on the bed in her old bedroom in her parents' apartment playing records and daydreaming about Doris Day. She had recently watched the film, *On Moonlight Bay*, starring Doris Day and Gordon McRae, and she was smitten. Gosh, how wonderful would it be to be held in Doris's arms like Gordan McCray was, Addie thought with a smile.

"Coming, Dad!" she yelled back so he could hear her. As she walked into the den and picked up the phone, she watched her folks move into the living room to listen to their favorite radio show, though she suspected that they wanted to give her and *her boyfriend* a bit of privacy.

"Addie, hi. What are you doing tomorrow evening? Are you free?"

Addie sighed exaggeratedly. "Well," looking quickly into the living room to make sure her parents weren't eavesdropping, "No, I'm not actually. I have a date with Elizabeth Taylor. We're going shopping for a new outfit for the Academy Awards. She always wants me to look my best. Why, what are you doing?"

"Hah hah, very funny, Ad. You better be careful. What if your folks hear you joking like that?"

"I know," she chuckled, "It's just that you're the only one I can talk to like this, and I'm in a silly mood."

"Well, I hope that silly mood of yours continues through tomorrow. Remember that adventure I mentioned a few days ago? Are you up for it tomorrow night, say around 9:00?"

Addie suddenly didn't feel so silly, just excited and daring. "Alan, where are we going? Tell me," she whispered. "I can't wait. You know I have as much patience as a 2-year-old."

Alan laughed. "I'll tell you when I pick you up, okay? I promise. I'm borrowing my brother's car so we can ride in style. Oh, and wear something nice, you know, like if we were going out on a date."

The next evening Addie stood in front of her bedroom mirror scrutinizing her outfit. Rachel was out on a double date with Mickey and their friends Kathy and George, so she had the apartment to herself and was free to fret about her appearance. "Good Lord," Addie said out loud to herself, "Okay, what is wrong with me? Why can't I find something to wear?" Addie had changed outfits four times and still felt dissatisfied with her appearance. "Jeez!" She sat on her bed in her bra and girdle and sighed out loud, exasperated. "Why am I so concerned about what I look like? It's Alan, for Pete's sake, not Ava Gardner. Okay, okay," she said, trying to calm her nervousness as she threw on outfit number five. Smoothing out her dress she sighed. "You look as good as it's going to get, so just relax."

Addie gave herself the once-over again and decided that the dress she had finally settled on, a soft lavender with a cinched waist and wide cream-colored collar, showed off her long neck and small waist. It was one of her favorite dresses and one that cost her nearly a week's salary from the club. She liked that her low heeled black patent leather pumps kept her just under 5'9. Being a tall girl always seemed to get her plenty of stares. She didn't know where Alan was taking her this evening, but she knew she didn't want to stand out like a sore thumb. As an afterthought, she pinned her hair back in her best imitation of Rita Hayworth, though her hair was more of a soft auburn than flaming red.

A low whistle got her attention. "Wow, Addie, you look amazing." Alan scanned Addie's entire body with his eyes, slowly moving from the top of her head to her patent leather pumps. Addie blushed. If she didn't know any better, she'd think he was checking her out. He was right on time for their "date," and Addie's parents had come down stairs to see them off. Addie saw them come down and thought, oh no, how embarrassing. Joe stood by the door and made small talk with Alan as Addie grabbed her shawl. They didn't act this way when Tony went out on dates, she thought, slightly annoyed, as Alan helped her on with her wrap.

Even though it was summer, nights could be chilly in the Midwest, especially by the lake, so she thought it best to wear a light silk shawl just in case. She realized Alan never said where they were headed. So why did she assume they were going somewhere downtown close to the lake? God, Addie, relax, she thought to herself. You're acting like you are on a real date instead of this pretend date with Alan. She had no clue why she was so nervous. Just get a hold of yourself, she thought. She glanced at her parents standing at the door. "Bye, Mom, Dad," she said as she dashed out the door, grabbing Alan's hand. She couldn't wait to leave.

"We won't be any later than midnight, Mr. and Mrs. Kahlo," Alan volunteered, as Addie dragged him to the car.

"Be careful—pay attention to the road, Alan!" yelled Joe Kahlo as they got into Alan's brother's car and drove off.

It was a nice breezy evening, and the air flowing through the open window of the car helped to ease Addie's nervousness. Alan glanced at her as he merged into traffic. He grinned and slowly shook his head from side to side. "Okay, mister, why are you laughing at me?" Addie questioned, slapping his shoulder playfully, hoping it would wipe the shit-eating-grin off his face.

"Oh Addie, Addie, Addie, why are you so nervous?" Alan teased as they moved quickly through traffic.

Addie closed her eyes briefly and shook her head. "Am I?" she quietly responded. "Ok, yes, I guess I am, I admit it. Though I have no idea why." Addie leaned back on the seat and looked out the window at the city. What is the matter with me tonight, she thought. I feel so jittery for some reason, as if this adventure Alan is taking me on is going to somehow change my life?

"Come on, Ad," Alan said as he took her hand. "Don't be nervous. It's just a nightclub we're headed to, though it is an unusual one, I admit. But it's really just a place."

Addie turned to look at Alan, "You know that you promised to tell me what this is all about, right? So, will you now? We've been inseparable for months, and yet I have never heard you mention this nightclub. Why?"

"Okay," Alan said, briefly glancing in her direction as he maneuvered the Buick through the city streets. He took a deep breath. "Well, I've kind of known about this place for a while now. It's French. Well, it has a French name, anyway, and you gotta know a special password to get in. The password changes every few weeks, and they will only give it out a few times during the week. And if you miss it, well, then you can't get in anymore."

"Really?" Addie said, intrigued. "That sounds so mysterious. Is it okay that we go there? Do we need to be 21 or something? Why is it so secretive? Are we going to be able to get in, Alan? I don't have a fake ID. Do you?"

Alan good-humoredly laughed at her rambling as he skillfully merged into the busy traffic of downtown Chicago. "Yes, we'll get in. I have the password. But the thing is, it's different, Ad. They'll serve us and never ask for identification. I can't explain it, the atmosphere, the other guests, it's all different. You'll just need to see for yourself. We're almost there."

Alan drove to an area near the "EL" somewhere on LaSalle and steered the Buick next to an old dumpster. Addie looked around and suddenly felt a little apprehensive. The area was dark, deserted, and felt a bit sinister, like a gangster film from the 30's. She half-expected James Cagney to come out of the back alley and start shooting his Tommy gun. She rolled her eyes at herself at that last thought. As Alan slowly pulled the car into the spot and killed the ignition, she noticed the sidewalks were wet. "Hey, Alan, why are the sidewalks wet? It hasn't been raining."

Alan got out of the car, came around and opened the door for her, and then looked around. "Beat's me. Maybe they hosed down the alley." He held out his hand to help her out of the car. Addie took it forcefully, still apprehensive about the area. "Are you okay? Addie, what's wrong?", Alan asked as he helped Addie maneuver through the puddles of water that spotted the sidewalk.

"Oh, I'm fine. Why do you ask?" she answered, attempting nonchalance.

"Well for one thing, you are about to break my fingers." Addie looked down and saw that she was gripping Alan's hand so tightly his fingers looked almost disjointed.

"Oh shit! I'm so sorry." She quickly let go of his hand. "I guess this area kind of gives me the willies. Why are the streets wet? Doesn't it somehow seem darker here than downtown? Where are we, Alan?"

Alan pointed and said, "We're here, Addie. Welcome to Café du Temp."

Addie looked in the direction that Alan pointed toward and saw a door which she could have sworn hadn't been there a moment ago. The door was metal, coal black, and wider than an average door, but not as wide as the doors at the big downtown department stores. It was a heavy door, which you could tell by the bolts that outlined the frame. In the center of the door toward the top was a small window. Well, it was not quite a window, but more like a little door itself. It had tiny bolts on it as well, though anyone could see it only opened from the inside. There was no sign anywhere advertising the club, no name or emblem, or even a lamp. The only lights illuminating the door were from the street, and they were not doing a very good job of it. Alan walked toward the black door, taking Addie's hand as he did, and rapped his knuckles on it rhythmically.

The small door opened, and from where Addie stood, she could see the face of a man. Well actually, she could only see his eyes which were a striking light blue. Alan whispered something to the man, and suddenly the door opened dramatically with the noise of a loud sliding bolt. As it opened inward, the man suddenly appeared. He wasn't tall, but he held himself regally, which made him appear taller than he was. He had short dark hair, slicked back and shiny. His striking blue eyes appeared kind, as did his smile. He wore an elegant black tuxedo, and Addie thought him very handsome. She was silently grateful that both she and Alan were dressed to the nines, because if this man's tuxedo was any indication of what people in the club were wearing, well, they would certainly have been sorely out of place if they came dressed in their high school clothes. The man suddenly smiled broadly and bowed slightly, saying with a flourish of his hand, "Welcome to Café du Temp, monsieur, mademoiselle." He didn't have a French accent, though his pronunciation sounded perfect to Addie, as if he were French himself.

CHAPTER 6

As Addie and Alan slowly walked over the threshold and into the space, Addie felt her nerves relax. If anyone had asked her to describe how she felt at that moment, she would not be able too. It was almost impossible to describe the feelings she was experiencing. Her entire being felt an awakening; a beginning of something. She could not describe it any other way, but she felt her heart pounding and an excitement that lifted her. She was looking around like she had just been transported to the moon. Gazing at her with a soft smile, Alan gently squeezed her hand in his and brought her back to herself. They moved down a narrow marble walkway, dimly lit with stunning soft blue lights. Addie thought they looked like the blue of flames, comforting and warm. Café du Temp smelled slightly of clove cigarettes and flowers.

Trying to take in everything at once, her eyes widened as they entered the main club area. An elaborate stone and wood bar dominated the space. The stone was a rich marble, and the wood railings glistened as if polished to perfection. Small lights above the bar that looked like stars gave off a beautiful soft glow that was enhanced by the intricate ornate mirrors that adorned the wall behind it. To the right of the bar was a service door that swing wide as servers and waiters moved expertly through it with trays held high above their heads. Several feet from the door were a number of tall cocktail tables, covered in white tablecloths and decorated with soft-lit candles and fragrant lilacs. Addie could tell that these beautifully adorned tables held a perfect view of the dance floor and the wide stage where a jazz quartet played lively toe tapping music.

Well-dressed patrons sat at small tables strategically placed near the stage while others moved effortlessly to the music, gliding across the dance floor. At the long ornate bar were animated patrons, women and men deep in conversations and drinking champagne and martinis. Smiling bartenders were busy serving drinks and taking orders. Addie was mesmerized. Everyone looked so elegant in their sparkling dresses, jewels, and beautifully tailored suits. It was nothing like The Angel, she thought. It was nothing like anything she had ever seen. It was what she always imagined a sophisticated New York nightspot would look like or perhaps a swanky restaurant in Hollywood.

"Monsieur," said the same man who had opened the door for them, "would mademoiselle and you care for a table near the stage, or would you prefer the bar area?"

Alan looked to Addie and she immediately said, "Let's sit near the bar."

The man raised his eye brows slightly with a smile but then gestured to a tall cocktail table with two leather stools in the bar area. Their table had a perfect view of the stage. Lovely white and purple lilacs set in the center glowed in the soft light of the candle. Once they had ordered two martinis from the waiter, Alan turned and whispered to Addie, "The bar area, Ad?"

"What?" She laughed. "I like sitting here. We can see the whole of the place and people-watch. I don't want to be craning my neck at one of those little tables. It would be too conspicuous."

"I suppose that's true," he said. "I forget this is your first time here. Isn't it something, Ad? It's not that big of a space really, but somehow it looks it. It must be how those mirrors are placed, you know, to give it that illusion."

"I think you're right, Alan, because I thought it was grander too, but no, now I see that it's not as big as I first thought. How in the world did you find this place? It's amazing!"

Alan looked at Addie and winked. "I'll tell you later."

Addie suddenly gasped. "Hey, we just ordered martinis! How can we do that? We're just kids! They're going to serve us martinis? I never had a martini. I hope I like it," she whispered conspiratorially.

Alan smiled at her excitement. "I know, the first few times I came here I was terrified. I thought the place would get raided or something for selling alcohol without checking my age. Apparently, they must pay somebody off, because they never seem to bat an eye when I order a drink, not that I have ever gone overboard. I wouldn't do that...but you know."

"Okay, now I feel excited," Addie said. "I really hope I like my drink. It sounds so sophisticated to drink martinis. Don't you agree?"

As Alan and Addie got themselves situated at the small bar table, they were both very conscious that they wanted to appear sophisticated, instead of the awe-struck teenagers that they actually were. They waited for their drinks as they craned their necks, trying not to draw attention to the fact that they were staring at all of the patrons. Addie was thrilled to be there. When the drinks arrived, Addie did her best imitation of Kathrine Hepburn as she carefully sipped her martini. She nearly choked. Yuck, she thought. She had to remember not to order a martini again. It was very strong and didn't taste very good, plus it was making her lightheaded. She looked around, attempting to cover up her gaffe and noticed something that she had not initially detected when she first arrived.

All the patrons, the cigarette girls, and even the waiters at the club were fairly young. She guessed that most were older than Alan and she, but all were clearly younger than her parents. She also noticed that, other than the gentleman who had opened the door for them, no other man was dressed in a tuxedo. Aren't gentlemen supposed to wear tuxes at sophisticated swanky places liked this she thought? She read movie star magazines and noted that people were always draped in designer gowns and tuxedos, especially in the downtown clubs. Yet, as fancy as the club appeared, guests seemed to be dressed in various styles. It seemed to her that there was no real dress code. Some were dressed in smart looking suits and fancy dresses, others in furs and jewels and still others were dressed in a more casual style.

There were even a few handsome women in billowy dress pants and silk blouses. No one seemed to find it unusual in the least bit. Addie thought it was wonderful. It was as if everyone simply stepped into Café du Temp from different periods in time, because the clothes were just that different. She couldn't quite put her finger on why she felt this way. Everyone's appearance was very nice after all, but still...

"Alan," Addie heard someone call from a few tables down, pulling her out of her thoughts. "Alan, so nice to see you again. It's been awhile. I'm glad to see you back with us."

"Peter," Alan said delightedly, as he stood to shake hands with a very good-looking young man with delicate features and light brown hair. "It's good to see you too." Addie smiled, watching the two men who were obviously very fond of each other. She noted that Peter wore his hair in a style Addie has not seen before, a bit long on the top and to the side, short in the back and shaved off his neck. It was unusually becoming. His suit was cut differently from the style she had seen her brothers and dad wear. It was beautifully tailored; it had less flair on the lapels than the style of the day, and the shoulders where much more tapered than she'd seen. She considered that he must be European; perhaps this was the new style in Europe.

"Peter," Alan turned to Addie, "I'd like you to meet my best friend Adeena Kahlo. You can call her Addie. Everyone does, right, Ad?" Addie smiled and nodded. "Addie, this is Peter Harris." Peter smiled warmly and reached out his hand to Addie's. He covered her hand with both of his and gently squeezed it without shaking it.

"So nice to meet you, Addie. I hope you are enjoying yourself this evening, as the jazz quartet is rather good."

"Oh yes. I agree they're fantastic, Addie responded enthusiastically, turning her head to the stage. Turning back to Peter's warm gaze, she smiled. "It's nice to meet you too, Peter. It's my first time here at the Café, and I just think it's amazing."

"Addie," Alan continued, "Peter is the manager of Café du Temp."

Addie raised her eyebrows, "Are you, Peter? Wow. I'm sorry, you just seem so young," she said as her cheeks turned slightly pink.

Peter laughed. "Well, thank you, Addie. I'm a bit older than I look, but thank you for the compliment."

"Alan, Addie, I need to get back to my duties, but please order what you like. It's on me this evening. It was lovely meeting you, Addie, and Alan, catch me before you leave." With that Peter left them.

"Wow, Alan, look at you, palling around with the boss." She tipped her martini at him and took a tiny sip, wincing at the taste. Turning back to Alan, she noticed his deep crimson face. "Wait," she whispered, "are you blushing?" Suddenly the penny dropped. "Wow Alan...oh wow."

Alan turned even a brighter shade of red. "Addie, for Pete's sake, you're being too loud. People are going to stare."

"Nobody is staring," she leaned in and whispered, "but...oh wow, Alan." She took another drink of her martini.

"Stop saying that," he whispered tightly under his breath, still blushing but with a sparkle in his eyes. Alan grabbed a slip of paper that sat on their small table. "So," he cleared his throat, "you wanna order something to eat?" Clearly, he was changing the subject. "They have some fairly good stuff on the menu. It's kind of fancy, you know, French stuff, but it's not bad."

Addie took the hint, struggling to hold back her questions and giggles. "Sure, let's do. This martini is going straight to my head." After they finished their small plates of paté and cheeses, Addie felt less lightheaded and ready to dance. "Alan, they're playing a Nat King Cole ballad. Let's dance."

"Okay, but I'm warning you now, I only got a C in Miss Clark's dance class."

"That's not possible. She gives everyone an A. Come on," Addie said as she grabbed his hand. "I'll lead."

CHAPTER 7

"Today is the last Monday in August," Addie said as she marked the date on the kitchen calendar.

Rachel looked up from her cup of coffee and smirked, "Why are you so excited? We have to go back to school in a week. The summer just flew by, Ad. We didn't even get a chance to go to Riverview, and I really wanted to go to Riverview."

Addie laughed lightly as she poured herself a cup of coffee. "The sooner we start school, Rach, the sooner we finish. Aren't you excited? We're seniors!" Rachel gave a halfhearted smile and sipped her morning coffee as she stared out the kitchen window. Addie, sensing that something was bothering her, sat down across from Rachel. "What is it, Rach? Tell me."

Rachel shook her head. "It's nothing, really. Only that once we graduate, it'll be different, that's all. Everybody will be gone. All our friends are either going off to college or getting jobs somewhere, and well... you'll be going off to some fancy college in New York."

Addie sighed. She knew that it was going to be a big change for Rachel and for her as well. She knew that she'd miss her life here in Chicago, but for her, college was the beginning of her life as an author. "Rach, that's like months and months away. We still have a whole year left to hang out. Besides, I won't be gone forever. I promise. You know you can come visit and go to all those frat parties with me." Addie smiled and grabbed Rachel's side to tickle her.

Rachel screamed and giggled, trying to push Addie away. "Okay, okay! I give! You're right. I'm just being hormonal; I got my "friend" this morning."

Addie cringed, "Ewe, too much information." Rachel laughed and left the kitchen to get ready for the day.

Addie couldn't help being excited about starting her final year of high school. As much as she loved her family and life in Chicago, she could hardly wait to graduate and begin her college life in New York. She had applied to three universities in New York and two in Chicago. Just last week she had received her acceptance letter from the University of Chicago, and from her first choice, Vassar. Vassar was the only college she really wanted to attend, so when a telegram arrived from the admissions office of the college, she was terrified. Rachel had to open the letter for her because her hands were shaking so badly. As she stood in the kitchen holding her mother's hand, wide-eyed with anticipation, the smile on Rachel's face once she had opened and read the letter nearly made Addie faint. Instead, she screamed with happiness, throwing her arms around her mom and crying with joy.

It had always been Addie's dream to attend Vassar, study journalism, and become a published author. She had yet to hear from the other universities, but she didn't really care. Vassar was where she intended on going. She had read everything she could get her hands on about the school, and she was excited to find that one of her favorite poets, Elizabeth Bishop, was an alumnus. The University of Chicago was also a top school, with Nobel Laureates on staff and a solid reputation, but Vassar was one of the top liberal arts college in the country and was renowned for its curriculum as well as for the beauty of its campus. She had read that in the school brochures and planned on saying that exact same thing to her parents when she told them that Vassar was her first choice over the University of Chicago.

Addie knew her family really hoped that she'd attend a school in the area, but she also knew that in order to live the life she intended on living, she needed to be independent. She could never be that in the bosom of her family. Attending an all-women's college such as Vassar was a conscious choice. The idea of living on campus and meeting like-minded women who were also studying journalism, as she planned to, thrilled her. It brought to mind the promise of new friendships, and perhaps something more.

She thought about that possibility quite a bit as she lay in bed dreaming of her future.

The weekend before classes began Alan suggested that they go back to Café du Temp, and Addie had readily agreed. She was mesmerized by the hypnotic club and couldn't wait to return. That first evening when Alan took her to Café du Temp, a little over three weeks prior, was stamped in her memory. She reran it over in her mind on a regular basis. The excitement of the nightclub, the people, drinking fancy cocktails, listening to cool jazz played by real musicians, not high school kids, had simply captivated her. It was so different from anything she had ever experienced, and she absolutely loved it.

Walking into Café du Temp was like walking back in time; it fascinated her. She knew that as a writer she needed to observe and experience her surroundings. Being at Café du Temp was a perfect place to observe people. How else would she get a feel for the world around her if she didn't take advantage of a perfect opportunity when it was presented to her. She had filled up nearly a third of her journal with her thoughts and observations of this magical place, and going back there again with Alan excited and thrilled her.

As they made their way through downtown to LaSalle Street, Addie asked Alan, "When did you get the secret password? I don't recall there being any announcement about it the last time we were there." They were nearing Café du Temp, and Addie realized she was feeling that familiar sense of excitement.

"It's not really a secret password, Addie" It's more of a code, I think. Before we left that first night, you remember that Peter told me to go up to the guy who let us in. His name is Alex, by the way. Peter said to be sure to say, "A splendid evening; don't you agree, Alex? The music is spot-on." Once Alex acknowledged the phrase, he would then give me the code words to get in the next time."

"Are you serious?" Addie asked with surprise. "Who says that? Spot-on?" That sounds like something English people would say. Americans don't speak that way."

"I know! I felt kinda dumb saying it, but I figure it's a European club, right? So maybe they talk like Europeans. Anyway, after I said the words to Alex, he leaned over and whispered, "Orchids can be white."

"Orchids can be white? That's the code? You're serious, aren't you?" Addie looked at Alan incredulously. "Well, that's just so strange, but okay. So, we will be able to get into the club by saying that phrase?"

"Yep, according to Peter, and Peter is a stand-up guy. He's not going to say it unless it's true."

Alan and Addie arrived at the exact location they visited the first time they came to Café du Temp. Addie noticed immediately that the streets were once again damp. She said to herself, "Okay, this is weird. It is *not* raining." She was going to mention it to Alan, but he was already rapping his knuckles on the tiny door within the door. The tiny door opened, and Alan whispered the code to the man Addie presumed to be Alex, although she couldn't see his face. The door opened and they were led into the nightclub.

The familiar sent of clove and flowers seeped into her senses. It felt soothing, and she decided she liked it. Alex led the couple to the same two seats in the small bar area where they had initially been seated the first time they had come to the club. The waiter appeared, and to Addie's shock, he remembered her even though she had only been there one other time. He bowed slightly and said, "Good evening Miss Kahlo. It's lovely to see you back." She smiled, feeling special.

"Shall I bring you a martini?"

"No! I mean, no thank you. I think I will have some wine please, a glass of red, thank you."

"Of course, miss, and the gentleman will have the usual?" Alan smiled and nodded.

With their order taken, the waiter bowed and walked away. "Alan! He remembered that I had a martini. It's been three weeks since we've been here. How can he remember me?"

Alan shrugged his broad shoulders and smiled. "Who knows? I guess you left an impression on him," he said as he gave her a wink. "Addie, I swear I have no clue how these fellows remember everything, but they do. This place is so strange. I mean, the first time I came in, they treated me like I was one of those movie stars you're always googly eyed over. Now, they greet me like I am a big deal or something, instead of a high school kid. I mean who ever gives a bourbon to a high school kid without being worried about getting busted?"

44

Addie listened intently to Alan and knew she had similar concerns. "I know what you mean. Do you think it's because, you know...you and Peter are friends?"

"I initially thought it might be, but now I don't think so anymore." Alan looked around and leaned into Addie, so he could whisper, "Peter mentioned to me that the people who come to Café du Temp are well...here for a reason. I know it sounds kind of cryptic, but I didn't want to come across as some naive kid, so I didn't question it. But you know, I have been kind of observing, and anyone who comes in gets the same treatment, as if they're somebody special. The thing is, Addie, Peter also said that not just anyone can get in. He said that those of us who are here were meant to discover it and that Café du Temp will mean something special for each person who walks through its doors." Alan laughed and continued, "I know it sounds crazy. I mean it's a night club. But Peter looked so serious and excited, he kind of made me think it was all a good thing, you know... like we are going to find something magical here."

Addie's eyes were wide with questions, and she wished at that moment that Peter would come by so she could ask him what it all meant. She believed Alan, as she sensed it too, that they were there for a reason. But what reason? None of it felt sinister, the club nor the people they had met.

They had ordered another drink, and while they waited for their cocktails, they chatted and enjoyed the sounds of the evening's jazz. Addie noticed that the crowd appeared to be larger than the first night she came to Café du Temp. All of the tables were occupied, and it was standing room only, even at the elaborate bar. The jazz sounded smooth and sexy, and everyone appeared to be having a great time. Just as she had done the first time she had come to Café du Temp, Addie observed the crowd. She enjoyed seeing the varied styles of dress, hairstyles, and hats. There were even some guests who wore the traditional clothes of their home land: India or perhaps the Middle East, Addie thought.

She didn't see anyone dressed like her though, in a cream-colored summer sleeveless dress reaching just below the knee, with a matching shell sweater draped over her shoulders. She thought this was kind of strange, as after all, it was summer in Chicago. As she sipped her wine and watched the crowd, she wondered if anyone in this strange place noticed her or Alan.

After a few more moments of looking around, Addie finally admitted that no one seemed to be paying any attention to them. She rolled her eyes at herself for even thinking anyone would find two teenagers intriguing. She smiled now, soaking up the ambiance, a bit giddy with the reality of sitting in a grownup club. She wanted to soak in everything she saw and then write it all down in her journal. As lovely and bewitching as Café du Temp appeared, she knew it was an oddity. It was like a place from a fairytale, like an enchanted castle. Addie took another small sip of her wine and told herself to stop trying to make this a mystery to solve. She needed to relax and enjoy the evening. She sighed. "What am I looking for anyway?" she asked herself. She really didn't know.

Their waiter brought them their second drink, and Addie was grateful for the distraction. She was spending too much time craning her neck left and right. "Isn't this band cool, Addie? I think I'm getting a real appreciation for jazz. Hey look, there's Peter! Addie, do you mind if I step away for minute to go say hi? If you're uncomfortable with me leaving, I won't."

"No, I don't mind. Go ahead, I'm fine. Just don't leave me stranded here and take off with him, if you know what I mean," she winked. Alan looked appalled. Addie giggled at his shocked look of indignation. "Okay, okay, I was just kidding, I know that you wouldn't. I'm fine. Go ahead. I like the music and I have my wine."

"Okay, I won't be long. I promise."

Despite her initial indifference to Alan leaving her to speak with Peter, she felt uncomfortable as soon as he had stepped away. She didn't know what to do. Trying her best to be sophisticated and look unaffected, Addie sipped her drink. She wished she had thought to bring her journal. She could have busied herself jotting down some of her observations. The last time she was at Café du Temp with Alan she couldn't wait to get home and journal everything she had observed about the amazing experience. She knew she was lucky to have had this opportunity and didn't want to forget a single minute of it.

But seriously, she thought, how would I look jotting down notes at a nightclub? I would look so square. Addie shook her head and laughed a little at herself. She willed herself to relax again. Alan would be back shortly, and after all, she was a grown woman with no need to feel uncomfortable. Sitting up straight, she took a deep breath and turned her seat and attention to the music. She loved the music that was being played tonight. It was jazz, of course, but it was old jazz from the 20's, maybe Louie Armstrong or perhaps that band her parents had grown up listening to, Paul Whiteman and his orchestra. She always enjoyed it when they'd play that old-time music at The Angel. It always sounded so romantic. She realized the same quartet had been playing the last time she and Alan were there. They looked dapper in their white suit jackets and black bow ties.

Addie didn't know it, but she would remember this moment for the rest of her life. It would be this very moment, when she gingerly sipped her wine, alone at her small table, with the melodic sound of the jazz horn seeping through her veins like a drug. This very moment, when the light of the candles gave off a romantic glow, and the musicians' white jackets and spiffy ties added to the ambiance and magic of the evening. It was at that moment when the direction of her gaze, and of her life, changed forever.

A strikingly beautiful woman was seated at a small table for two, but she sat alone. The candle on her table flickered softy, making her eyes appear almost golden as she took a delicate sip of her drink. Her table was to the left of the stage, slightly obscured by shadow, but Addie could still see her smooth elegance and poise as she gracefully lifted her glass to her lips and watched the musicians as they played. Addie's eyes followed the line of her jaw to her long neck, and then to the soft blond waves that fell to her shoulders, in a hairstyle from a different time. She appeared young, perhaps in her early 20's, and Addie thought she must be very confident to come to Café du Temp unescorted.

Curious as to who the lovely stranger was, Addie wished she could go up to her and introduce herself. But what would she say exactly? As she considered an appropriate topic, she realized that her observation of the woman was very obvious to anyone who bothered to pay any attention. "Oh God, I'm staring at her like a complete idiot," she whispered to herself, her cheeks turning slightly pink. Just as she was about to lower her eyes to avoid the inevitable embarrassment of being caught, the woman looked directly at her. She looked straight into Addie's eyes, her amber gaze warm, interested, and with a hint of fun. "Oh no," Addie whispered, though she couldn't help but smile back in response. It was as if her brain had decided, without her permission, to plaster a big goofy grin across her face.

Addie couldn't say how long she stared transfixed, because suddenly Alan appeared and put his arm around her shoulder. Peter stood at his side. She turned to them attempting to focus and profess a calmness she did not feel. She felt flush and knew that she was blushing as she was still reeling from being caught staring at the woman. Thank heavens, it's dark in this place, or Alan would take one look at me and know something was up, she realized.

"Addie, you remember Peter."

Addie smiled, grateful now to focus on someone other than the beautiful woman at the small table near the stage. "Of course, hello Peter. Nice to see you again," she said, extending her hand to Peter's. "I'm really enjoying the music. Café du Temp is a true gem and I love it here."

"Thank you, Addie! I am so pleased to hear you say that. Our number one priority is creating an atmosphere which allows our guests to feel welcome and enjoy the experience of Café du Temp." Peter had a beautiful sincere smile, and Addie immediately felt comfortable around him. It was no wonder Alan was smitten with him. I would have been too, if I were inclined to like boys that way, she thought.

"Alan mentioned to me that you are an aspiring writer, Addie. You are in good company as many of our guests are also in the arts, including painters, writers, and even poets. If you would allow me to, I can introduce you."

Addie looked at Peter and then at Alan. "Oh, thank you Peter," she said, "but please, I don't want to impose, I..."

"Honestly, it's no imposition. I would be delighted." Addie looked to Alan, who stood just behind Peter, for help, but Alan just grinned and shrugged his shoulders.

Finally, Alan jumped in. "Peter, Addie and I haven't yet had a chance to get up on the dance floor. She loves to dance, and you should see her tango. Do you mind?" Addie gave Alan a look, thinking she could have punched him just then. Tango? She didn't know how to tango. She smiled at Peter and tried to look enthused.

Peter looked between the two of them and bowed slightly. "Okay, you two. Go ahead and skip the light fantastic. But Addie, next time you visit us here at Café du Temp be prepared to talk about the arts with many serious writers and painters. Enjoy your evening." Peter took Addie's hand

and kissed it lightly. To Alan, he leaned in close and whispered something in his ear, making Alan blush a deep scarlet.

"Alan," Addie whispered loudly into his ear after Peter left them, "what the hell?"

"What, Ad?" Alan chuckled back.

"The tango, really? And why'd you tell Peter I'm a writer? I only write for the school paper. I haven't even started college yet, nor have I learned everything I need to know before I can be a true honest-to-goodness writer! What if he introduces me to some famous person? I'm going to look like a stupid kid pretending to be a writer! How embarrassing is that going to be?" Addie crossed her arms and sat back in her chair.

"Come on, don't be sore. You're a fantastic writer. I've read your stuff in the school paper. I bet you can hold your own with anyone Peter introduces you to. Besides, he really likes you, uh, I mean us." Addie did a double take at Alan, picking up on the not so subtle reference to Alan's relationship with Peter. Sipping her wine, she conceded that Alan was being a good friend.

"Okay, maybe you're right," Addie said, letting him know she wasn't really upset by squeezing his hand. If it weren't for him, she knew she wouldn't be here having this amazing experience. She knew he always had her best interests at heart. Taking a deep breath, she looked at Alan for a long moment. Finally standing, she smiled and pulled him from his seat, "Come on you, time to dance. As usual I'll lead."

CHAPTER 8

Addie could hardly believe that this was the second time in three days that she and Alan were sitting at their small table at Café du Temp. To say that he was surprised when she suggested they come tonight would be an understatement. He had looked at her curiously, but then easily agreed without comment. What could she tell him anyway that wouldn't immediately embarrass her? Could she tell him she saw a woman with beautiful amber eyes and golden hair, obscured by shadow? Could she say that since seeing her less than two full days ago she couldn't seem to get the woman out of her mind? She hadn't a clue what she would say to Alan, because she had no idea what she was doing.

Alan made himself comfortable at their small table and perused the menu. Addie wasn't hungry but agreed to order food so as not to bring attention to her nervous stomach. When they had arrived at the club earlier that evening, Addie's eyes instinctively went to the small table by the stage. Her disappointment was palpable when she saw that the table was unoccupied. But later as she and Alan danced, she noticed the woman standing near the stage speaking with an elegant man, both of them sipping champagne. A few moments later, Addie watched as she walked to the small table by the stage.

"Uh, Alan," Addie whispered conspiratorially, "don't look, but do you see that woman sitting to the left of the stage? I said don't look!"

Alan had turned to look where Addie had indicated but quickly turned back. "Addie, how can I see who you want me to see without looking? Be reasonable."

"Oh, yeah, okay. Look, but don't be obvious. I don't want her to think we're talking about her, uh even though I guess we are."

Alan whistled low, "Wow, she's quite a looker, Ad. Who is she? Someone you know?"

"No, no one I know. It's only that, well, don't you think she kind of looks like someone who just stepped out of the past? She has that film noir look, doesn't she? Like Lauren Bacall in *The Big Sleep*? She's really attractive. I mean she has those amazing eyes, and her hair is— what?" Alan was staring at Addie with a grin on his face that went from ear to ear. "What? What?" she whispered loudly. "Do you think I'm interested in her, is that what you're thinking? Well, I'm not. I'm not." Addie blushed a deep shade of pink. She could feel her face getting hot and a drop of perspiration suddenly trickled down the front of her bra under her dress.

Alan grabbed Addie's hand. "Adeena Kahlo, you do know it's okay if you see a beautiful woman and admire her, right? I'm no expert, but that girl sure is gorgeous."

"Excuse me, sir." Both Alan and Addie jumped, startled by the appearance of their waiter. "Mr. Harris would like to buy you and Miss Kahlo a cocktail. Shall I bring you the same, or would you prefer something different?" Addie sighed, grateful that the waiter had come by just then and thankful that he had saved her from total humiliation.

Alan looked up at their waiter. "That would be great, thank you. Uh, by the way what's your name? I should have asked before. I'm Alan and this is Addie," Alan offered, a bright smile lighting up his face.

"My name is Sam, sir." Sam smiled kindly and bowed. "Very pleased to meet you both," he said pleasantly. "Another bourbon, sir, and shall I bring you another wine, miss?"

"Yes," Addie said, "another red wine. Thank you, Sam." With that, Sam left them to fill their order. Sighing, Addie leaned in closer to Alan. "Okay, I admit it. I find that girl to be very beautiful." She felt the heat of her embarrassment on her face. It was one thing to tell your best friend that you like girls, but it is quite another to actually point out a girl you found attractive to that best friend. "Alan, seriously though, doesn't she look like she just stepped out of one of those Maxfield Parrish paintings, all light and beauty? Don't look!"

As their evening progressed toward 11:00 PM, Addie watched the comings and goings of the crowd. She was thoroughly enjoying herself. As a matter of fact, she couldn't think of when she had enjoyed herself more. The atmosphere was mesmerizing, and the music was fabulous; she and Alan had danced to nearly every song. She also danced with Peter and a very nice young soldier wearing a uniform that Addie had never seen before. However, as much fun as she was having, she just couldn't stop herself from glancing over periodically in the direction of the beautiful woman at the table by the stage.

Addie decided that she had never in her life seen a more striking woman in person. Who was she? With her soft blond hair shining in the dim light of the candle and her elegant form, she could easily be a movie star or even a princess, with her one long leg crossed over the other as she sat sipping her cocktail and listening to the music. Suddenly noticing Alan's goofy grin, Addie cringed and moaned at her own silly staring. "Earth to Addie, earth to Addie." Alan snapped his fingers a few times in front of her face, bringing her back from her daydream and totally embarrassing her.

"Oh, jeez Alan. You startled me," Addie said as she took a long drink of her wine.

"Well, sweetie, unless you want that beautiful woman to have you thrown out, you should probably stop ogling her."

Addie looked surprised. "I wasn't! Was I? Oh god," she said, putting her head in her hands and moaning. "I was, wasn't I?"

Alan laughed and took a sip of his drink. "Well, yeah, maybe a little. Hey, it's okay. She's gorgeous, and she has that mysterious look going for her for sure. Hey, don't look now but I think your dream girl is eyeing you as well."

"What! No, she's not. Is she? Oh, Alan, don't tease me."

"I'm not," Alan whispered. "I saw her look your way, and she looked thoughtful. Maybe she wants to come by to say hello."

"Oh yeah right, now you're laughing at me. If you weren't my best friend, I swear I'd pop you one." Addie laughed and playfully hit Alan on the shoulder. Alan winced as if in pain and whined. "Big baby," Addie said as she pinched his cheek and laughed when he too burst out laughing.

"Excuse me." The soft elegant voice surprised them, capturing their attention. "Hello. I hope I am not interrupting. I wanted to introduce myself. I'm Isabelle, a friend of Peter," she said, holding out her hand in greeting. Both Addie and Alan were so distracted by their horseplay that they hadn't noticed that the beautiful woman had walked to their small table.

"Oh, hello!" Alan smiled and immediately took her outstretched hand in greeting. He quickly stood and pulled out a chair for the young woman. "Please join us, won't you?" asked Alan with a warm and inviting smile. Suddenly feeling shy, Addie could do nothing but stare. She felt as nervous as a mouse, though no one would ever believe that was possible, including her. Didn't her family always brag that she had nerves of steel? That wasn't the case at this moment, since all she could do was sit there with her mouth slightly open and nothing whatsoever coming out.

"I'm Alan, Alan Nackovic," Alan said as Isabelle took the offered seat. "and this lovely person sitting here next to me is Adeena Kahlo, but everyone calls her Addie." Isabelle smiled warmly as she turned to Addie. Addie lifted her eyes to Isabelle, and she had to stop herself from sighing. Isabelle was even more stunning up close, her beautiful hair laying softly against her shoulders, her skin glowing with health, light amber irises sparkling with flecks of green, and her full lips, stained a soft pink, were set in a dazzling smile.

As Isabelle's gaze connected with her own hazel stare, Addie felt a pleasant but nervous sensation throughout her body, making her heart pound fiercely in her chest. Finally, after a moment, Isabella held out her hand in greeting. "Hello, Adeena Kahlo. It's very nice to meet you. May I call you Addie?" Isabelle stared deeply into Addie's eyes with a look that Addie couldn't quite identify. She could do nothing but nod her approval as this beautiful woman named Isabelle gazed confidently at her and spoke her name.

"I do apologize," Isabelle turned, addressing them both. "I am not normally so forward as to interrupt someone's evening, but Peter and I are old friends, and he mentioned I should meet the two of you. So, I thought I'd take advantage of the opportunity to introduce myself." Addie watched Isabelle as she spoke, her clear British accent warming places in Addie's body that she didn't know could be warmed. The sound of her voice was like velvet against her skin.

"We're very glad you did, Isabelle," Alan said, "and may I say that I love your accent. You're British, aren't you?" Isabelle smiled at Alan in response and nodded slightly. "I believe you are the first Brit we've ever met, right

Addie?" Alan nudged Addie under the table prompting her to join the conversation. Isabelle watched Addie, her eyes sparkling with what Addie felt was sincere interest.

"That's right, Addie responded, quietly watching Isabelle with the same level of interest. She could feel Isabelle's curiosity in her gaze, as if she were saying, "Who are you, Adeena Kahlo, and why do you want to know me?"

"So, Isabelle," Addie said kindly. "are you a frequent visitor to Café du Temp? I have only actually been here a few times myself, but I absolutely love it." Blushing slightly, Addie continued, "There is just something about being here that makes you feel almost special. That's the way I feel anyway."

"Yes, I believe that's a perfect description of how Café du Temp makes those of us who visit feel. Please, call me Issie," she offered thoughtfully as she gazed directly into Addie's eyes. Addie thought she had never seen a more beautiful smile.

Alan looked between the two women, and then cleared his throat. "Ladies, if you'll excuse me a moment. I see Peter over by the bar. I'd like to go thank him for sending over these cocktails. I won't be but a minute." Alan smiled, bowed slightly and left to speak with Peter. Isabelle quietly laughed and shook her head.

"Well, that was subtle," Isabelle said as she watched Alan walk away.

"Excuse me?" Addie didn't quite understand the comment.

Isabelle looked at Addie again with her same warm smile and said, "Oh, I'm sorry, never mind. So, Addie, tell me, are you old enough to be drinking that glass of wine you are holding so protectively in your hand?" Isabelle leaned in closer, a flirtatious look in her eyes. Addie was momentarily taken aback by the obvious teasing but sensed no harshness in her voice, only humor.

"Well, Issie," Addie said, sitting up suddenly taller in her seat, "I am eighteen, and in my opinion, if I can legally join the military and risk my life, I can most certainly have a drink."

Isabelle laughed joyously, her entire face lighting up with her beautiful smile. "Touché, Addie Kahlo, touché."

"So, that's some crush you have."

Alan and Addie were driving home after leaving Café du Temp, and Addie was thinking about how Isabelle's eyes twinkled like a million stars when she laughed. Addie blew out a breath and turned to Alan. "Alan, do you think I'm being silly? I mean, I just met her, and we've only known her for a few hours. How can I feel these feelings I'm apparently feeling?"

Alan briefly took his eyes off the road and focused on Addie. "It's called attraction, Ad. When I first noticed Peter, I was immediately attracted to him. I didn't even know him, but I knew that I thought he was a beautiful man. Then, once we spoke and I learned what a great person he is, the attraction grew. I think kind of the same thing has happened to you with Isabelle. You saw her and immediately felt an attraction, but then, when you spoke with her and realized that she is beautiful inside too, your attraction grew."

Addie raised an eyebrow and teased, "Okay you, when did you become so philosophical?" She moved closer to Alan as he drove and put her head on his shoulder.

Alan grinned, "Anyone can see there's an attraction between you two. I could almost see the sparks flying around the room."

Addie moved from Alan's shoulder. With a hint of hope in her voice, she questioned, "Alan? So, you're saying you think Issie is attracted to me too?"

Alan smiled and responded, "Oh yeah...I definitely do."

"Alan," Addie whispered, "this isn't good. I have to finish high school and then go away to college to start my new life. I can't be attracted to a random girl I met at a random night club that I'm not even old enough to be going too."

"Addie, don't get ahead of yourself. You two just met. Besides, Café du Temp is not just some random night club. I mean, think about it. For one thing it's located in an area that shouldn't see any business, but yet the club is always full of people. Second, what other club can you and I go to, as 18-year-old high school kids, that would treat us like we're grown-ups? And you know that Isabelle isn't just some random girl."

Sighing Addie laid her head on the back of the car seat and closed her eyes. "Okay, you're right of course. Isabelle is far from random. And you are so right about Café du Temp." Addie sat up straighter in her seat and looked at Alan, eyes wide with sudden realization. "Alan, you *are* right. It's as if that place just appeared out of nowhere. I mean, did you ever really look around? It's classy, but it looks like it belongs in another time. I noticed that there are no windows, but the lighting gives the appearance of a summer evening. Also, the other patrons are always having great conversations, but the few times I overheard their discussions I couldn't understand anything they were talking about. It was as if the conversations were outside of my realm of understanding. Why would anyone talk about WWI as if they were there, but yet they couldn't be older than 30? And I heard a woman talking about organizing a group to march for women getting the vote. And what the hell is an eye phone, Alan? You never did tell me how you discovered Café du Temp. Come on, give it up."

Keeping his focus on the dark road, Alan brought back the memory of his first visit to Cafe du Temp. "You know my dad is a builder, right? Well, sometimes I help him pick up materials for job sites. Anyway, several months back I was going down to the Loop to pick up some plumbing supplies, and I decided to take a short cut up LaSalle. It was getting late, and I knew my dad would kill me if he found out I put off getting the supplies until the last minute. While I was cutting through under the tracks, my dad's car stalled. I got out to check under the hood and noticed the door."

"The door?"

"Yep, the door. It seemed strange to me, a door just there in that non-descript building with nothing else around it, and that tiny little door within the door. So, I walked up to it and tried to open it. Of course, it wouldn't open. I was just about to walk back to the Chevy when the tiny door opens up and there's this voice. It was Alex and he say's "Code?" I had no clue what he was talking about, so I told him I didn't know any code. So, he looks at me for a long minute, and next thing I know, the door opens and there he is all dressed up in that spiffy tux. He bows slightly and gestures me in. So, I go in."

Addie looked directly at Alan. "Weren't you scared? Or nervous to just walk in a place like this?"

"No, because I didn't feel anything bad was gonna happen. You know what I mean?"

Addie thought for a second, "Yeah, I do know. I felt the same way the first time I stepped through that door. It was exciting and not at all scary. How can that be? We're not children. Shouldn't we be more cautious?"

Alan looked thoughtful and nodded. "Yeah, I'd sure be mad at my little brother if he pulled something like that...anyway," Alan continued, "once I walked in, I realized I was in a nightclub. It was crowded, the jazz band was playing, and I guess I got sucked into the atmosphere. That's when I noticed Peter for the first time. He walked toward me with his hand outstretched. He was so handsome. Anyway, he welcomed me, and as they say, the rest is history."

CHAPTER 9

Lying in bed that night, Addie couldn't sleep. All she could do was think about Isabelle— her infectious laugh, her sparkling eyes, and her beautiful voice. Sighing, she knew she was smitten. Alan immediately saw through her attempts to act cool. Cringing, she hoped she wasn't that obvious to Isabelle. From her conversation with the beautiful Brit earlier tonight, she knew Isabelle was extremely bright and intuitive. It wouldn't surprise her if Isabelle was already aware of Addie's attraction to her. Alan thought Isabelle had looked just as interested. This knowledge sent delicious tingles throughout her body.

Opening her eyes wide, she blushed deeply, recognizing where the tingling was centered. She cleared her throat and turned over on her side. She told herself to go to sleep. Class began in the morning, and she couldn't be falling asleep on the first day of school. But the truth was that she wasn't a bit tired, and Isabelle's beautiful smile just wouldn't leave her thoughts. She played the evening over in her mind. After Alan had left to speak with Peter, she had suddenly felt shy and tongue-tied, but Isabelle had been so funny and kind that she had gradually relaxed. No one ever called Addie a shrinking violet, but around Isabelle this evening, she had suddenly been at a loss for words. At first, she had mostly listened, but Isabelle had slowly drawn her out until she found her voice. Then their conversation had fallen into a lovely rhythm that Addie just didn't want to end.

"Tell me, Addie, what is your wish?"

"My wish? How do you mean?"

"I am referring to your dreams, darling. You said that you are eighteen. I imagine you will go off to university as you seem the academic type." Isabelle winked, smiling to let Addie know it was meant as a compliment. "Then you will want to achieve something. I see you as a woman with a

58

plan." Isabelle took a sip of her wine and looked at Addie over the top of her glass.

"You saw all that in just this little time speaking with me?" Addie smiled and rolled her eyes, as if it was her turn to tease. Isabelle tilted her head at Addie, as if saying "Well, what is the plan?"

"You, Isabelle..., by the way, what's your last name?"

"Androsko."

"What sort of name is that?" Addie asked, not unkindly.

"It's Czech," Isabelle smiled, "Now you were saying?"

"Well you, Miss Isabelle Androsko, are very observant, because yes, I do have a plan." Addie couldn't help being excited and smiled when she thought about her dream of making a career as a writer. "It's my last year of high school, and I am going to college in New York after graduation. I'm going to study journalism; I want to be a writer."

"A writer." Isabelle looked intrigued. "What a marvelous plan. What type of writing will you do?"

"Well, I love the idea of writing fiction," Addie smiled excitedly. "The premise of creating characters, developing them, forming their personalities, giving them challenges, having them fall in love, or experience heartbreak, adventure..." Addie stopped speaking and blushed, suddenly noticing that Isabelle was looking at her intently. "Well, it's what I've always wanted to do."

Isabelle smiled, and her eyes danced with admiration for this young woman. She moved her hand in a circular motion, as if telling Addie to continue. Addie nodded, and her flushed cheeks cooled slightly. "Over the past few years I've been fascinated with the literary contributions of early 20th century authors. I've studied some of the works of Hemingway, Henry Miller, Virginia Woolf, Fitzgerald, Gertrude Stein, and others. Their writing has really inspired me. I mean I've always dreamed of being an author, but what I've learned from their writings has opened my mind to a whole new way of seeing life." Addie smiled, feeling shy suddenly. "I wish I could explain it better, Issie, the excitement I feel from what I've read."

Isabelle looked at Addie, a thoughtful expression in her eyes. "I understand, I do. I feel that way as well when I am moved by a particular author's work."

Addie's smile grew wide, no doubt in her mind that Isabelle did understand. "Issie, can you imagine having been a fly on the wall at one of Gertrude Stein's salons in Paris? It had to be the coolest experience of one's life. I mean, simply observing and listening to those brilliant artists speak of their works. Think of it, conversing with Picasso, or listening to Natalie Barney quip about the social atmosphere of the day. I've often wished I had been born during that era. It must have been so glorious to be surrounded by all that creativity!"

Addie sat back and continued, "To be there, at the early part of the century amongst all that talent, quite literally at the start of avant-garde modernism in art and literature. It must have been something." Addie was beaming with excitement and awe.

Isabelle's eyes grew as wide as saucers as she listened to Addie's excitement. Momentarily stunned at hearing Addie speak of a time and place with which she was intimately familiar as if it were in the distant past, she hoped that Addie's excitement was a suitable distraction from witnessing her reaction. Isabelle brought her glass to her lips to cover up her shock. Looking to Addie now, she couldn't help the genuine smile that creased her face when she looked at her. Isabelle thought she was beautiful, bright and charming. She suddenly had this strong desire to touch her. Moving her fingers slowly across their small table, she reached over and took Addie's hand as if it were the most natural thing to do.

Addie felt a sudden charge at the touch, and raising her eyes to meet Isabelle's, she saw an immediate darkening of Isabelle's eyes. Instinctively, she knew that Isabelle felt it too, this wonderful pull toward someone new. Addie had never experienced this thrill of overwhelming attraction for another. It was wonderful and intimately exciting.

Now lying in bed, Addie smiled as her eyes drifted closed. Her final thought before she fell asleep was that even though she had never experienced anything like what she felt tonight, she instinctively knew that Isabelle had been very tenderly and expertly seducing her.

The following day Addie sat in her first class of her last year of high school, her senior journalism class. She was glad to see there were about twenty other students in attendance, all seniors like her. She disliked small classes. She believed there wasn't enough discussion with small groups, and

Addie loved discussion and debate. Debate brought out some great ideas that the students often didn't realize they had in them.

"Addie, come sit by me." Addie turned to see her friend Maggie waving her over. Addie and Maggie had been friends since the 3rd grade. She immediately got up and moved to sit next to her in the front row. "Addie, I hear Mr. Connors is going to teach this class. He's so dreamy, don't you think? And I hear he isn't married either!"

Addie chuckled at her friend. "Maggie, he's like 40 years old! So what if he isn't married. It's not like he's going to be your date to the prom." Maggie giggled.

"Well a girl can dream, can't she? Hey, isn't Rachel taking this class? You two are usually inseparable."

Addie sighed, "She's decided to take accounting. Can you believe it, accounting? She plans on going into the family business after graduation and wants to make sure she can do the books."

"Really," Maggie squealed. "that's so neat. Rachel's gonna run a nightclub! How very sophisticated. Do you think she will let us sit at the bar and order highballs and daiquiris?"

"No, I don't think so Maggie. It will be a couple of years before that will happen. But I'm sure she will allow us to sit at the bar and order a Coke, at least when the club is closed." Maggie pouted but immediately laughed at herself. Addie couldn't help but laugh along with her.

That first full day back at school was a whirlwind of activity. Addie only saw Alan in passing, and Rachel not at all. She used most of her free periods reviewing her class schedules and skimming through the new text books that were assigned. She spent lunch with Maggie and some of the other girls, chatting about classes and the very first senior dance, the Winter Ball, in early December.

"Rach, you here?" Addie had just walked into their apartment. Classes were over for the day. All she wanted to do was drop onto the sofa, turn on the radio, and listen to music with her eyes closed and her feet up. Just as she sat down, the telephone rang. Addie reached for it just as Rachel walked in. She smiled and waved at Rachel as she spoke to her mom. "Hi, Mama. What's the hap? Yes, I know that's not acceptable English. Okay, yes that would be fine." Rachel looked questioningly at Addie as she hung both their jackets up in the hall closet. "Sure, Mom, I'll ask. Rach, you want to go out to dinner with us tonight? Dad wants to check out a new jazz band at that Italian place on Superior. He says his treat." Rachel enthusiastically nodded her head. "Okay, Mama, Rachel's in. Yeah, we will meet you out front at 7:00. Okay, bye." Addie blew out a long breath, leaned over and buried her head under a sofa pillow.

"Hey, what's wrong? You okay?" Rachel asked. Addie yawned her response, as Rachel plopped down on the couch next to her. "Well, no one told you to go out on a school night until 1:00 in the morning." Rachel laughed as she said, "I do not feel sorry for you."

Addie turned to Rachel, eyebrows raised in mid yawn, "Hey! How do you know what time I came in? Are you spying on me?" Addie teased.

"Yeah, right," Rachel said on her way to the bathroom to wash up for dinner. "All I know is that must have been some date for you to come in so late."

Now, sitting in the backseat of her parents' station wagon on their way to dinner, Addie's mind drifted to the previous evening. Her exhausted brain told her that being with Isabelle yesterday was well worth being half asleep at dinner tonight. "Hey Ad," Rachel whispered loudly, pulling Addie out of her thoughts. "Do you think we'll be able to get a glass of wine with dinner tonight? I think we look twenty-one." Rachel looked expectantly at Addie, moving her eye brows up and down.

Addie covered her mouth so she wouldn't burst out laughing at Rachel's silly face. "Don't count on it, Rach. My parents aren't going to let them serve us wine." Grinning and shaking her head at Rachel's pouty face, Addie immediately thought of the wine and the martini she had at Café du Temp, which in turn brought her thoughts back to Isabelle. It had been less than 24 hours since they had met; yet she couldn't wait to see her again. They had parted only after pulling themselves away from each other's gaze, yet neither had made any suggestions about future plans. Damn, Addie thought, why didn't I ask her to meet me again or at least get her telephone number. Inwardly chastising herself, she knew she had been too enamored with the beautiful Brit to think clearly. Sighing, she considered her options. Could she go back to Café du Temp this Saturday on her own? Alone? A single woman?

She knew that simply wasn't done. Women were supposed to be escorted to restaurants and clubs, or at the very least, go out as a group. Thinking back, she recalled seeing several women at Café du Temp who seemed to be there unescorted, including Isabelle. She distinctly remembered this because it was so out of the norm. Yet these women hadn't been asked to leave nor gawked at because they were without a man.

It suddenly occurred to Addie that Café du Temp wasn't concerned about such things. She was beginning to appreciate the club more and more by the minute. But, if she risked it and went on her own, would Isabelle be there? More importantly, would she be happy to see her? Not wanting to think too much about Isabelle's reaction to seeing her again so soon, she took a cleansing breath and attempted to bring herself back into the present. She suddenly remembered that this coming Saturday was her dad's birthday, which meant a family weekend. There was no chance of going off on her own personal adventure anytime soon.

"Ad?" Addie immediately turned to focus on Rachel. "You okay? I asked you how Alan was doing. I haven't seen him for a few weeks." Rachel looked concerned as she kept her voice to a whisper. Looking to her parents who were having their own conversation in the front seat of the car, Addie reassured Rachel that everything was fine with her and Alan. She whispered back smiling, saying that Alan was busy studying for his college entry exams and that most evenings they hung out at his house, which wasn't really a lie, but wasn't the full truth either. She couldn't help feel some guilt though, because she adored Rachel. She hated twisting the truth with her. But how could she tell her that she and Alan were not really a couple? That they were both secretly queer and using each other as a cover. The premise of admitting such a thing was impossible. She could never tell her, as it would certainly destroy their relationship. Turning to Rachel now, she covered up her concern with what she hoped was a thoughtful smile.

The Italian place on Superior Street turned out to be called Maggio's. It was a small restaurant with checkered tablecloths and great food. Rachel and Addie split a chicken Marsala dish that was fresh, tender, and piping hot, but it was the jazz quartet that got Addie's attention. Their music immediately brought to mind the musicians at Café du Temp. They even wore the same type of white dinner jackets with black bow ties. The sound was just as sexy and silky. Addie wondered if this was what all jazz sounds like. Does it always seep into your bones and break your heart?

Turning to watch her family's reaction to the music, Addie smiled. It seemed they all felt the magic of it as well. Her mother sat with her eyes closed, mesmerized by the sound, her dad was tapping his foot to the beat, while Rachel looked positively enthralled. Addie listened intently, closing her eyes momentarily as she visualized Café du Temp. There was Isabelle, smiling at her above her wine glass, with that cocky look and a challenge in her eye. God, she thought with a shiver, this can't be happening to me. I have plans.

The first week of classes flew by quickly, full of new assignments, club registrations. and catching up with classmates. As a reporter for the school paper Addie had proposed that her first assignment be to write a piece on the new cool jazz sound that was becoming popular. It was 1952, new sounds were emerging with blues and jazz influences, and Miles Davis, Chet Baker and Dave Brubeck were starting to gain momentum. Her editor thought it a fantastic idea. It didn't surprise Addie that as she got older, her favorite type of music was now jazz. She had grown up with it, as it was always played at home or at The Angel. And now, because of Café du Temp, it reminded her of her time with Isabelle.

"Addie, wait up!" Addie turned to see Alan jogging down the hall toward her. "Hi, gorgeous. Where you off to?" Alan gave Addie a quick peck on the cheek as he grabbed her books to carry them for her.

"Actually, just leaving. Care to walk me home?"

"Sure, you're my girl, aren't you?" Alan gazed down at Addie from his height of 6'2, and winked, his beautiful dimples in full view. Addie playfully smacked his arm, then took his hand in hers as they walked out of school together. They made a striking pair.

"Alan?"

"Hmm?"

"Do you ever feel guilty? I mean about you and me, pretending to be a couple?" Addie looked down as they walked, biting her lower lip, a nervous habit she could never seem to break. "Sometimes I do, Alan. I mean sometimes I want to tell Rachel everything. She's my best friend, next to you of course, but then I realize I can't. It makes me feel bad that I can't share this part of my life with her."

"Yeah, I know, Ad, I do feel bad sometimes too, especially with my folks. You know my dad gave me that man to man talk a while ago. He still checks with me to make sure we are being careful, now that he thinks you and I are together. He's always so earnest and sincere. Makes me feel like a jerk sometimes."

Addie looked at Alan now, realizing that Mr. Nackovic probably wasn't the only one who thought they were being intimate. She was pretty sure that everyone they knew thought they were doing it. "So, your dad thinks you and I are having sex?"

Alan looked apologetic and said, "I'm sorry, Addie. I didn't deny it."

Addie shook her head "No, it's okay. I'm sure everyone we know thinks that. We've been inseparable for months. I know Rachel does because she is always teasing me. I think she is a bit miffed though because I don't gossip about us like that, if you know what I mean."

Alan looked surprised. "Wow, do girls talk about that stuff too? I thought it was only the guys in the locker rooms."

Addie rolled her eyes. "You're kidding, right? I think that the girls are worse than the guys. A few months back, Rachel, Maggie, and I took some beers from the club and got drunk in our apartment. We started to talk about dating, and guys and you know, stuff. One discussion led to another, and before you know it, those two were sharing the most intimate details of "doing it" that I'd ever heard. I was so grossed out I wanted to puke." Addie cringed and shook herself with disgust. Alan cracked up laughing.

"No shit? And here I thought girls were all sugar and spice and everything nice."

Addie, who was both laughing and disgusted at the same time, shook her head. "Oh no, Alan, girls can be just as raunchy as the boys."

"Man, I had no idea. Hey, listen, Ad." Addie looked to Alan as she wiped tears of laughter from her eyes. "I just want you to know that I would never ever talk about our *pretend* relationship to any of the guys. I don't need to act like some stud and make up some BS story about you and me just to try and fit in."

Addie reached for Alan's hand. "Alan, you have got to be the nicest guy in the world. How'd I ever get this lucky to have you as my best friend?"

Never all that comfortable with compliments, Alan blushed. "Well, I think we need to thank those two walking over there." Alan pointed in the direction of two people walking up the street. "Mickey, Rachel! Addie and I were just going to Stan's to get a Coke. Care to join us?" Mickey and Rachel walked toward them, Mickey giving a thumbs up.

"We were?" asked Addie, laughing at Alan.

Grabbing Addie's hand and walking toward their two friends, Alan winked. "Yeah, we were. You buy."

CHAPTER 10

That evening Addie and Alan sat on the front porch swing of Alan's family home, listening to the crickets chirping their rhythmic song, the only sound on an otherwise quiet night. It was early September, and the first week of school was over. They sat quietly, deep in their own thoughts as they slowly rocked back and forth on the swing, Addie's head resting on Alan's shoulder.

Lifting her head, Addie turned to Alan. "Guess what? Rachel informed me today that we will be double dating for the Winter Dance in December. She's thrilled to be a senior and can't wait to do all the senior dances and parties. Believe it or not, she already set a date to go shopping for our gowns." Alan didn't say anything for a moment, just looked up at the starry evening. But then he pulled his knees up to his chin and looked at Addie.

"Do I get to wear a tux? Because tuxes are really cool. I think I'd look quite good in a tux, don't you?"

"I think you'd look like Peter Lawford in a tux, tall and handsome. I'm almost insecure walking next to you because you're so good looking."

"What?" Alan jumped off the swing and stood back, staring at Addie. "Adeena Kahlo. are you fishing for a compliment? Have you seen yourself? You are beautiful, no wait, you are beautiful and exotic." Addie put her head back and howled with laughter.

"Exotic, am I? Maybe I should throw some bananas on my head like Carmen Miranda?"

"Yes, but make sure they're peeled. And some oranges as well. Can you manage a melon up there? Your head is kinda big." This just made Addie laugh even harder, setting off Alan, who began to do his best Carmen Miranda imitation.

"God, Alan, you are a goof," Addie said as she wiped away tears of laughter from her eyes.

Alan plopped back down on the swing. "We are a pair, aren't we?" Alan said, suddenly looking solemn. "Addie, you know this last year is going to go by quickly, and then we are both off to school. What will I do without you when you go off to Vassar?"

"I feel the same way. I can't wait to start the new chapter of my life, but I don't want this chapter to end. I will miss you so much, Alan. I know I'm being selfish, but you are the only person I can speak with, bounce things off about, you know...who I really am."

"It's not selfish, Addie. We need each other to stay grounded, you know? Hey, do you want to go to Café du Temp tomorrow evening? I can get my brother's car; he owes me."

"I wish I could, but it's my dad's birthday, and the family is having a celebration at The Angel. My mom and Aunt Rosie are going to sing. I was going to invite you as my date." Addie smiled at Alan and winked. "Will you be my date, good looking?" Alan batted his eyes and giggled, pretending shyness. Addie swatted him on the head and told him to behave before she got up to go help his mother with dinner.

Saturday was busy with preparation for Joe's birthday celebration. Addie's mom Jane and her Aunt Rosie were rehearsing their songs while Rachel and Addie prepared the tables with white tablecloths, candles and flowers. "Mom, so how many family members are we expecting? I'm thinking we may need more chairs for dad's big night."

Jane looked down from the small stage and spoke into the mic, "No sweetie, we are only expecting about 25. Your father was firm about not wanting the entire clan attending. He said they would get too rowdy, and he doesn't want to have to call the cops to cart his relatives off to the pokey."

"Hah! That's about right, Aunt Janie" laughed Rachel.

Addie chuckled and looked around the room. "Then we are all good here. Rach and I have everything ready to go. Is it okay if we head home to get ready? Alan and Mickey are coming by, and we will all walk over together."

"Of course, sweetie, we will see you kids this evening."

As Addie and Rachel walked to their apartment, Addie wondered, not for the first time today, whether she and Alan could sneak out early from the celebration at The Angel and head to Café du Temp. She wanted to see Isabelle again. With any luck Isabelle would be there tonight. An added concern was that Rachel would be at her side during her dad's entire party and would want to know why she was leaving early. Though she and Alan never spoke about Café du Temp as being their secret, Addie somehow knew that it needed to be. She couldn't tell Rachel or anyone else about it. Without anyone needing to tell them, they both instinctively knew that its existence needed to stay between them.

"Rach?"

"Yeah?"

"Can I ask you to keep something between us and cover for me?"

"Oh of course, Addie, of course!" Rachel's eyes shown with excitement as if she were about to hear something delicious. "Tell me, what's going on?"

Well, Alan and I may slip out from Dad's party a bit early, so could you cover for me?"

"That's it? Rachel looked disappointed. "I mean, why do you need to leave early? Are you two going off to some other party? Why can't Mickey and I tag along?"

Addie immediately felt guilty. "Oh Rach, don't give me those puppy eyes. It's not anything like that. We just need to talk, and well, it's better to do it in private and not in front of 25 of our family members. Please, Rach, I promise we are all going to have so much fun at the Winter Dance. Plus, you've already scheduled our shopping adventure for our gowns and that will be fun too."

Addie felt bad. She knew she had been shutting Rachel out and hated herself for it. But how could she tell her about their secret? It was impossible. Addie looked over at Rachel and noted that she looked a bit less hurt at the prospect of a day shopping for party dresses. "Rach, I can't wait to go shopping with you. We can even have lunch at the Berghoff. I know how much you love it there." Finally, a small smile appeared on Rachels pretty face. Addie smiled wide and wrapped her arms around her cousin in a tight hug. "I love you, Rach, and thanks for covering for me. You're the best!"

"Yeah, yeah, yeah. Let me go, you goof. I can't breathe!" Rachel giggled as Addie held her tight, threw her head back, and laughed.

The music on the evening of Joe Kahlo's party at The Angel was festive and loud. Family members toasted Joe and congratulated him on reaching the ripe old age of 42. Alan was standing by the bar listening to Addie's mom and aunt belt out a Rosemary Clooney song when Joe walked up to him and slapped him on the back.

"Alan, son, are you enjoying yourself?" Alan turned, looked at Addie's dad and smiled. He really liked Mr. Kahlo. He was always friendly and treated Addie and his other kids with great respect.

"Oh yes sir, I am. Thank you so much for inviting me, sir!" Joe Kahlo grinned and slapped Alan hard on the back again nearly toppling him over. "Good, glad to hear it, son. "Al, may I call you Al?"

'Well sir, no ever has, but yeah, sure."

"So, listen Al, you know Addie is going off to college next year, right? Well, the misses and I want to make sure she is going to be ready and prepared for this big move. What I'm saying, son, is that we know that young people like to have fun, but..."

"Dad! Dad!" Oh, dear lord, what is he doing, Addie, who had overheard the conversation, thought nervously as she walked up to Alan and her father. "Dad, please, Alan and I are dating, that's all. He is also going off to college, so... Anyway, Dad if you will please excuse us, Alan and I are going to say hello to some of the cousins." Addie quickly pulled Alan away from her father, mortified that her dad was going to give Alan a warning about maintaining her virtue.

"Oh, good god! I cannot believe him!" Addie was beet red as she walked with Alan toward the bar. Alan was grinning from ear to ear.

"Oh, I don't know, Ad, I think it was kinda sweet that your dad was looking out for you, because as you know, I have quite the reputation." Addie did a double take at Alan and burst out laughing. "Hey, jeez, why are you laughing so hard? I could have a reputation you know...if I wanted one."

"Of course, you could, dear heart. Now, can I speak to you privately for a second?" Alan looked at Addie and nodded as he grabbed her hand and led her out to the patio.

"So, what's up? Everything ok?

"Everything's good, yeah," Addie replied. "I was just thinking that maybe you and I could get away a bit early and go have a drink at Café du Temp. I mean, if you'd like to of course."

Alan smiled with eyes twinkling, and said, "This wouldn't have anything to do with a gorgeous golden-eyed blond, would it?" Addie tried her best at acting as if she hadn't a clue what he was referring to but failed miserably. She couldn't keep the grin off her face.

"Well, yes... maybe. So, can we? Are you up to it or are you too tired?"

"Tired? What am I, 40? Of course, I am up to it, absolutely. As a matter of fact, I was going to see if I could drag you away too. Peter said that they are going to have a new jazz band tonight, and he wanted my input, god only knows why. I don't know a thing about jazz."

"Alan, are you really that dense? He wants to see you, silly. That's why he made that excuse about the band." Alan looked delighted.

So, what do you say we leave about 10:30? Everyone will be three sheets to the wind and won't even notice we're gone."

"Sure, but what about Rachel and Mick? They'll notice."

Addie sighed, the initial guilt she felt with Rachel returning. "It's fine. I spoke with Rachel earlier, and she'll cover for us."

"What!? You didn't tell Rach about Café du Temp!" Alan had something akin to panic in his voice.

"No, of course not. I just told her that you and I needed to talk, and we may be leaving early. I feel terrible about the lie, but really what choice did I have?"

CHAPTER 11

"Smashing pumpkins," Alan whispered loudly to Alex, and the black door opened with its usual ominous sound. Alex smiled and politely welcomed them as they walked into the heart of Café du Temp.

"Smashing pumpkins? What does that mean?" whispered Addie as she put her arm through Alan's.

"I haven't a clue, but that is the code I was given. Wouldn't that be the coolest name for a band ever? Addie laughed, shaking her head, as if that was the silliest thing she had ever heard.

Looking to Alan more seriously, Addie asked, "Alan? How do I get to know the code, in case I ever want to come alone?"

"Well, you only need to go up to Alex and recite that phrase I told you about, you know...blah, blah, blah spot on. Wait, alone? Addie you wouldn't come here alone, would you? I mean, why?"

"Well no, most likely not, but I have seen women here unescorted, so I don't see why I couldn't if I wanted to." Alan looked a bit leery but nodded.

"Mr. Nackovic, Miss Kahlo, lovely to see you again. Your usual table?" Alan and Addie both turned and smiled at Sam and nodded as he led them to their seats. At the same time, another waiter came by with two flutes of champagne on a silver tray. He bowed and said, "Complements of Miss Androsko."

Addie immediately felt butterflies take flight through her stomach. She turned her head toward the small table by the stage, and she felt her whole body react with excitement. Isabelle looked like a beautiful vision with the soft lights of the club glowing around her. Addie couldn't breathe. She could only smile with her whole self.

Addie wasn't aware, but when she looked toward Isabelle's table to mouth "thank you," Isabelle believed she had never seen a more beautiful smile. Addie's smile was dazzling. Isabelle took a deep breath in order not to appear so obviously smitten. She needed to tread lightly. This was dangerous, very dangerous. First of all, she was aware that she should not be frequenting Café du Temp as often as she had been.

Since she first saw Addie, she'd been there three times in three weeks. Secondly, the rules were simple: dalliances are permitted and actually encouraged, though any feelings that even hinted at going beyond simple attraction are discouraged, as they could affect the past and or the future. But, for reasons Isabelle could not comprehend, Adeena Kahlo affected her. There was just something truly compelling about the young woman that made her want to know so much more about her.

Isabelle recalled that the first time she'd seen Addie, she couldn't take her eyes off her. She was tall, with hazel eyes, long dark wavy hair and a beautiful carriage. She was stunning, like a beautiful Spanish princess. Isabelle, always the observer, noted Addie's slight nervousness and barely concealed excitement. She herself had experienced the same feelings of nervousness tinged with curiosity and excitement the first few times she had entered Café du Temp as well. Now, she was no longer curious about the varied people who walked through the doors. She knew that they were special because no one walked through the doors of Café du Temp unless they were meant too. Each individual who entered was destined to contribute something unique to the world. Isabelle still wasn't sure what her contribution would be, but she had come to accept that it would be meaningful.

Taking a sip of her brandy, she raised her glass to Alan and Addie from her table by the stage. Alan, always the gentleman, walked over to her table, bowed, and politely asked her to join them. Isabelle smiled, nodded, and took Alan's arm as he led her to their table through the thick crowd of patrons. She watched Addie's eyes as she walked toward her; they were glorious and full of excitement and curiosity.

"Isabelle, thank you for the drink, but it wasn't necessary," Addie smiled and clinked their glasses.

"But I wanted to. I am so pleased that you and Alan are both here this evening. I do so enjoy your company." Isabelle leaned in and put her elbows on the small table, thoroughly comfortable with Addie and Alan now. "It is my understanding," she said excitedly, "that a fabulously talented singer will be performing tonight. I'm new to this American style of music and quite excited to see her perform. She is said to be quite unique and destined to be a legend."

"Really, so you enjoy jazz then?" asked Addie, captivated by the silkiness of Isabelle's voice and scent of her perfume.

Isabelle smiled, "Oh yes, I adore it. It's such an impassioned sound. Don't you agree?" Addie and Alan nodded in agreement, both equally enamored by the sexy, sometimes dark sounds of jazz's fusion of blues and ragtime. "Peter also shared that she is years ahead of her time in style and talent. Her name is Nina Simone, and I am very keen to hear her sing."

Addie found herself utterly charmed by Isabelle's excitement. "Issie, why don't you join us here at our table. Both Alan and I would love to have you. Ah...I mean to have you join us." Addie was silently thankful that the club's soft lights gave off a slightly rosy glow as she was sure her face was beet red.

Alan looked at Addie with one raised eyebrow. He wanted to say something sarcastic to tease her but decided instead to give them some time alone. "Ladies, if you'll excuse me, I'm going to find Peter to say hello. I won't be gone too long." Alan quickly squeezed Addie's hand, smiled at Isabelle and moved off in search of Peter.

Isabelle watched Alan as he walked toward the stage eyeing Peter. "I think your beau is a bit in awe of our Peter. Is Alan an aspiring club manager?" Addie giggled despite attempting to act adult and sophisticated in front of this beautiful woman.

"Sorry," Addie said still giggling slightly. "No, Alan is not planning on entering the entertainment field. Actually, he is not my beau, though we are very good friends." Addie looked directly at Isabelle over her glass as she drank, waiting for her response. A hint of a smile slowly appeared on Isabelle's lovely face, and her eyes sparkled as she gently licked her lips. Addie suddenly felt flushed. It was as if Isabelle was seducing her with just a look and could read everything that was on her mind at that moment. This would have been unfortunate, as Addie was picturing Isabelle with her head thrown back and Addie's head buried in her cleavage.

"So, Addie," Isabelle said, to avoid staring at Addie's mouth, "the last we spoke you mentioned you're a writer. Tell me all about that." There was genuine interest in Isabelle's voice, allowing Addie to feel completely comfortable with speaking about her dream of becoming a published author.

"Well, I'm just a high school writer right now. I write for the school paper," Addie smiled to hide a slight blush, embarrassed to admit to this sophisticated Brit that she was still in high school. "But I'm going to study journalism at Vassar in the fall, and, as I mentioned, I write fiction. I also want to teach. Don't you think teaching is a very noble profession, Issie? I adore my high school teachers. Mrs. Bennet, my English teacher, is so inspiring and brilliant. She is very passionate about literature, and she has been to Paris. Can you imagine, Paris!? Mrs. Bennett is the one who opened my eyes to Virginia Woolf and Gertrude Stein. I will always be grateful for her mentoring. She also ..." Addie stopped suddenly, a deep flush reaching her cheeks, as she realized she had just been rambling on without taking a breath. She was mortified.

Isabelle looked at Addie with a bright smile and shook her head as if to ease Addie's flushed embarrassment. "Why did you stop talking just now, Addie? I wanted to know what else your Mrs. Bennet said."

Addie flushed a deeper shade of red. "Issie, are you teasing me? I'm sorry, I don't usually talk this much, I..."

Isabelle reached out and gently put her hand over Addie's. Addie felt that touch throughout her entire body and she could see in Isabelle's eyes that the touch mirrored her own response.

Isabelle looked at Addie intently. "No, I am not teasing you, I adore listening to others speak of their dreams and plans. I like to think of myself as a writer of sorts, and I always find great joy in being made privy to others hopes and dreams. It is, I believe, important for writers to get perspectives on others' views of the world, don't you agree? So, don't apologize darling, I am thoroughly enjoying our conversation. I am the one who asked you to tell me of your writing, was I not? Now, tell me, what sort of fiction is your love? Are you a writer of mysteries, suspense? What about romance?"

CHAPTER 12

September-1911-Paris

Isabelle Androsko sat with her dear friend Simone, dining alfresco at a small café in the heart of Paris, enjoying her coffee, and content to know that she would never tire of Paris in autumn. She adored the excitement, the people watching, the smell of fresh flowers, and that all-too-familiar aroma of clove cigarettes that everyone seemed to be smoking. Her life here in Paris was a far cry from her parents' home in London, with its proper rules and somber etiquette. Isabelle looked over at Simone, and, not for the first time, caught her breath at the beauty of her friend. She felt sad for Simone right at this moment, as she had just ended one of her many affairs, and, even though she herself had ended it, these dalliances always affected her.

"Simone, darling, how are you today? Is the fresh air and lovely morning easing your headache?"

"Yes, *mon ami,* it is very soothing, though as you know a broken heart needs more than sunshine to heal." Isabelle hid a knowing grin behind her hand as she dabbed at her mouth with a napkin. Simone's affairs tended to be many, very dramatic, and usually short-lived.

"Simone, your heart must only be slightly bruised, darling, as your relationship with this Spanish gentleman lasted such a short time."

"Issie!" Simone's eyes widened first with shock and then mirth. She could not keep the smile from her face. "Well yes, that is true, I suppose, but dear god, it was passionate!" Issie couldn't help herself and laughed loudly at Simone's breathy response. Simone laughed along with Issie, as a truer friend never existed.

"Isabelle, and what of your love life, *cheri*?" Simone inquired, as she dabbed at her smiling eyes with her own napkin. "It's been quite some time now since that terrible experience you endured with that Renee woman."

"Oh Simone, please don't. You know she was a mistake and one that I dare say left its mark on my confidence. I should have heeded your advice. You knew from the start that she was simply using me; however, I couldn't see past her sparkling green eyes and stunning figure."

Issie thought of Renee Caron and that terrible time, a little over a year past, that she, Isabelle Androsko, an independent, educated literary poet, could not pull herself away from that devious young beauty. She was but 22 years old at the time; however, Renee, all of 20, was a captivating vixen, and Isabelle had briefly thought that she might just be the one. How wrong she had been. Now, even after a year had passed, she still shied away from any type of relationship. That is until she walked into Café du Temp less than a month ago and met the enchanting Adeena. Addie Kahlo. Just her name sent shivers of pleasure throughout her body.

"Issie, Isabelle? Where did you just go, *cheri*? You looked for a moment as if you were in a trance. Oh, *mon ami*, I have seen that cryptic look on your face before. Just what are you up to? Or should I say, who are you up to?" Simone's eyes twinkled with interest.

"Please, Simone, I have no idea what you could be referring to. There is no one. I was only thinking of that terrible time and how very happy I am now that I am finally able to say that the vixen, Renee Caron, is out of my life once and for all."

"Hmm, very well, darling, if you say so. You do know that if you are up to something, I will most certainly pry it out of you. After all what are best friends for?"

Isabelle lay on her very comfortable bed that evening, visualizing Adeena Kahlo's smile. How did Simone know that she had someone on her mind and in her heart? Curse Simone and her perceptiveness, Isabelle thought with a shake of her head. That woman is too smart for her own good. Isabelle sighed and realized that it was all entirely true. All she could do was think about Addie Kahlo. She reran the last conversation they had over in her mind. Addie was such an innocent, so eager about her future and her writing. She was adorable in her excitement and wide-eyed enthusiasm. Isabelle couldn't help but get caught up in the ebullience with her. After all, she herself was a writer and knew the thrill of being published and gaining respect for one's work.

All evening Isabelle had been curious but unable to specifically pinpoint what time period Alan and Addie were from, even though she listened attentively to their conversation in the hope that it would provide her with clues. She could tell by their style of dress that it was not a time prior to her own era, as she noted the subtle details of their clothing and speech. She deduced that they could be from any time period within fifty or so years of 1911. She had dismissed the idea that they could be from too far in the future, as she had read H.G. Wells, and their clothes simply did not adhere to any preconceived ideas of what would be worn in the next millennium.

As Isabelle adjusted to the darkness of her room, she continued her musings of this evening's conversation. She closed her eyes and again saw Addie's expressive eyes when she spoke, and her smile...that beautiful smile that lit up her entire face. These images of Addie sent that all-too-familiar heat throughout her body. She felt herself shiver with desire. She opened her eyes wide at the realization that this young woman, whom she has just met, was making her feel this way. She got out of bed and opened the window to allow the cool night air to encircle her.

Isabelle stood there with her arms folded around herself. She was in trouble and she knew it. How could she feel what she was feeling for this young woman with whom she had only had a handful of conversations? "This is impossible," she breathed out loudly to no one. She should have never gone back to Café du Temp after such a long hiatus. If she hadn't, she would have never met Addie Kahlo. Sighing audibly Isabelle knew deep down that that was not true. Nothing that had anything to do with Café du Temp is random; she and Addie were destined to meet.

As the hour grew late, and most of Paris slept, Isabelle thought back to that evening when she first saw Addie. She had enjoyed a lovely Saturday with Gertrude and her mix of artist friends at Gertrude's and Alice's Salon. It had been a particularly fun evening as Pablo had teased Gertrude about the new painting she had acquired from Matisse. He knew how to get her goat, though it had taken only a few moments for Gertrude to see through his ploy. But, after the good-natured teasing, a brilliant discussion on the avant-garde modernism sweeping Paris ensued. It was a glorious discussion, and Isabelle loved every minute of it.

It was on the drive home when her driver, Jacques, taking his usual shortcuts through the semi -deserted streets, had stopped to allow a stray dog to pass, that she had seen the door. She had made him pull over immediately. Jacques had taken this short cut through Rue Moliere many times, but Isabelle had never before seen the door on this particular avenue. But that evening, there it stood; solid, and black and inviting. She knew that if the door appeared, she had to go to it. It was just what needed to be done. So, with minimal trepidation and a bit of excitement in her heart, she did. Alex had smiled and welcomed her as she walked through the now-familiar door and down the hall to the heart of Café du Temp.

Her usual table of course was waiting for her, despite the fact that she hadn't been back in close to a year. Sam brought her a cognac, and as she swallowed the smooth brandy, she felt its strong heat travel down her throat, warming her insides with its familiar fire. She closed her eyes to the beautiful sound of jazz piano and wondered why she was there. Isabelle knew that there was always a reason one finds themselves at Café du Temp. She thought she'd never see it again, yet here she was.

Isabelle couldn't say why she was chosen to be a patron of this remarkable establishment., She only knew that she was. The reason, she deduced, would make itself known in its own good time. Instinctively, she recalled how she knew not to share her knowledge of Café du Temp with her many friends. So, she never did, thinking that one day she would see Picasso, Gertrude, or Monet sipping their own drinks and conversing with other patrons, but she hadn't. She also couldn't quite understand why she never felt uncomfortable seated at a small table alone. A woman alone, without an escort, was always questionable. However, that was not the case at Café du Temp. Isabelle noted that there were often women who initially came in alone, but always seemed to find conversational companions to engage with in an interesting discussion. She herself had always met interesting people to converse with.

That evening was different. Isabelle was barely there five minutes when she spotted the young couple seated at a cocktail table near the bar. She initially thought they were much too young to be there but quickly realized that their age didn't really matter. Then, she heard the young woman laugh, and it was a magnificent sound. She looked over and stared into the loveliest face she had ever seen. The woman was beautiful, with an unmistakable glow of youth and innocence. Just as she found herself staring quite openly in the woman's direction, Peter had approached her and kissed her cheek. She smiled, pulling her eyes away from the young couple across the room. Realizing that she had missed Peter, she hugged him. He always smelled delicious. She was sure he wore some fragrance that hadn't yet been concocted in her time. "Isabelle, it is so good to see you again. You are as lovely as the flowers in a Paris spring."

"Good heavens, Peter, that is quite the compliment," Isabelle's eyes sparkled.

"But it is the truth, my darling Issie, and I've missed you." Peter's genuine smile reached his eyes, and Isabelle felt the warmth of it throughout her heart. "The last time I saw you was well over a year ago, your Paris time, of course." Isabelle smiled in understanding and then looked at Peter with questioning eyes.

"Peter, why am I here?"

Peter looked directly into Isabelle's eyes and smiled. He took her hand and sat down beside her. "Sam," he waved the server over to him, "please bring me a brandy and another for Miss Androsko. Thank you, Sam. Now my dear Isabelle, you know as well as I do that I don't have any idea why you are back." Peter sighed and smiled with a sympathetic nod. "Two years ago, when we first met, I knew that you were meant to walk through that door, but as with all who enter, I am not privy to the reasons why. I long ago accepted that we have our own journey, and this place," Peter waved his hand and slowly looked around, "is our vehicle. Why and how, I haven't a clue. All I do know is that every single person who walks through that door contributes to the world in some unique or profound way. I am only a gatekeeper of sorts, Issie.

"What I can tell you is that these contributions are varied and meaningful, though some so small and seemingly insignificant that one would hardly notice until history points to them as the catalyst that changed the world. Others are more personal, a chance encounter that changes a person's life to one of happiness. That happiness leads to children and one of these children grows up to invent a cure for a devastating disease."

"But Peter, what if I fail at whatever I am intended to do, just as I did before? Good heavens, I am not going to cure polio!" Isabelle looked wide-eyed with concern. Peter reached over and handed Isabelle her brandy.

"You did not fail, Isabelle, don't you see? You are here now. Whatever you are meant to experience or understand, or if there is an individual who is destined to cross your path...well then that has yet to happen."

Isabelle sighed, bringing back that memory of first seeing Addie at Café du Temp. Peter had said that she hadn't failed, and she instinctively knew he was being truthful. She also knew that somehow Adeena Kahlo was part of her destiny and that truth both frightened and excited her.

CHAPTER 13

"Adeena, I'm speaking to you. Are you listening?" Addie was sitting, very much in a daze, at one of the tables at The Angel, folding and refolding the same cloth napkin. She had come by to help her mother clear the remnants of the previous night's event. She turned and saw her mother gazing questioningly at her.

"Oh Mom, I'm sorry. I wasn't listening. What did you ask?"

"I asked, sweetheart, if Rachel was going to stop by and help with this mess? We need to make sure everything is ready, cleaned, and set up for tomorrow. Your father hired the jazz band we saw at Maggio's, and we already have a number of reservations. We need to make sure that the tables are ready and that the place is spotless. Do you know if she's coming?"

"Oh yeah, she said she was. I'm sorry, Mom. I was distracted." Addie couldn't help herself. All she could think about was seeing Isabelle again. Everything about that woman sent electric currents through her body. Their last conversation had confirmed it for her. She was enamored with the beautiful Brit. She was entranced, she was in lust, she wanted to kiss her, hold her and look in her beautiful eyes forever. "Jeez, get it together," Addie scolded herself as she got up from her seat and began helping to set up the club for the next evening's festivities. Just then, Rachel walked in and winked at Addie as she kissed her aunt hello and sauntered past.

Turning her eyes sharply to Rachel, Addie pursed her lips and slowly shook her head. She was jealous and she knew it. Rachel looked like she had just had sex. I want to look like that, Addie thought. Look at her, she's glowing for Pete's sake! She had never in her life been with anyone, male or female, and she wanted to... she really wanted to. She wanted to know how it felt to have that look that Rachel had on her face, and she wanted it to be with Isabelle.

"Hi there, sweetie," Rachel's singsong voice floated by in a haze of happiness. "What do you need help with?"

Addie continued to burn with envy. "Rach, you look like you just had sex," she whispered with indignation when they were by themselves.

"Well, I guess I just did," Rachel giggled behind her hand. "Oh Addie, please don't be angry with me, I know I was supposed to be here sooner, but Mickey and I just got caught up in our…uh…discussion, and before you knew it, we were…uh, you know." Addie looked at Rachel for a second eyes glaring. Then she shook her head and rolled her eyes at Rachel's obvious disorientation. Sighing, she realized she could never really stay angry at Rachel, no matter what sort of shenanigans she got into.

"So, you're sure you're not peeved at me, Ad? I know I screwed up and I'm really sorry." The girls had walked back to their apartment and were now relaxing before getting ready for bed. Rachel was in the kitchen preparing two cups of late-night cocoa as a peace offering, nervously glancing toward Addie and hoping she wasn't still miffed.

"Oh god no, Rach, water under the bridge." Addie sighed and stretched out her long body on their couch and closed her eyes. "Besides, everything got done, and our folks are not stressed about tomorrow." Rachel looked visibly relieved.

"Okay then, good. I was worried because you were awfully quiet tonight. I thought you might be really mad at me." Addie looked at Rachel and smiled, hoping she didn't look as melancholy as she felt. She wanted so badly to tell Rachel about Isabelle. She needed to talk and wanted Rachel's opinion on what she should do about her budding feelings. But, how could she? Rachel would never understand. She would be shattered, and Addie couldn't do that to her. She loved her and was terrified that Rachel would hate her if she knew she liked girls.

"Seriously, Rach, how could I ever be mad at you? I'm fine really, I am. It's just stuff on my mind about this new school year, that's all." Addie visibly cringed at her own lie, quickly taking a drink of cocoa to hide her reaction. She hated the lies she continued to tell. Trying to pull herself out of her own mood, she changed the subject and focused on making fun of Rachel's sultry entrance into The Angel earlier that day. Rachel good naturedly laughed along with Addie and was convinced by the end of the evening that Addie held no hard feelings about her impromptu rendezvous with Mickey. Smiling, Rachel skipped off to bed.

Breathing out a tired sigh, Addie got up to turn off all but one light. She sat back down on the couch cross-legged to finish up the last of her hot cocoa. Leaning back, she reran the past few weeks in her mind and thought about what she had decided to do. She would speak with Alan about going to Café du Temp solo. She wanted to see Isabelle by herself without any distractions. She needed to know if Isabelle had feelings for her beyond the flirtation they had shared. She knew she certainly had feelings for Isabelle, and if this was real, she needed to know if Isabelle felt the same.

If truth be told, Addie was terrified of her own feelings. She had no experience and nothing to compare them to since she'd never been this captivated by anyone before. All she knew was that when she looked at Isabelle something in her heart changed; it beat faster. She felt lighter and immensely happy. It wasn't simply her beauty, but also the intelligence in her gaze, the sincerity in her voice and eyes, and her gentle kindness. The tender way she touched Addie's hand; it was everything. The few times they'd been in each other's company Addie had an overwhelming urge to kiss Isabelle, to be with her, and to know everything about her. This fascination was consuming her every waking thought, and it scared the hell out of her. Instinctively she knew Isabelle found her attractive. She would even go so far as to say that Isabelle found her engaging and interesting.

Addie smiled, remembering the last time they had spoken at Café du Temp. Addie and Alan were preparing to leave for the evening. Isabelle had stepped behind her to help her on with her coat. She had stood so close that Addie could smell her perfume. She had lifted the coat over Addie's shoulders and smoothed down the material, gently gliding her hands down over her arms and lightly wrapping her own arms around Addie, hugging her. She leaned in and buried her face in Addie's neck, breathing in her scent. Addie had visibly shivered. Then, Isabelle had gently kissed Addie's cheek, looking deep into her eyes. "Until we see each other again, sweet Addie," she had whispered. "Oh god," Addie moaned and closed her eyes, remembering that moment so vividly. "Yes," she said to herself, "I need to be sure that she feels the same."

"Hey Alan, wait up!" Addie was leaving study hall to go to lunch and saw Alan coming in from the track. He was still wearing his track suit and was heading to the showers. Alan spotted Addie and waved as he walked toward her, placing his sweaty arm around her shoulders with a wink. "Ewwww, don't touch me!" Addie laughed as she threw Alan's arm off her shoulder. "Yuck!" She wiped at her shirt to remove any sweat stains Alan may have left. "You heading to lunch right now?" she asked, "though now I think I just lost my appetite. Can you join me? I'd like to talk."

"About what?" Alan asked as he leaned on Addie and put his armpit in her face. "Stop that, you jerk!" She squealed as she quickly moved out of his reach. "Go take a shower, will you? You stink! So, can you meet me in ten?"

"Sure, gorgeous, unless you wanna come in and help wash my back?" Alan raised his eyebrow and winked, doing his best Marlon Brando imitation. Addie smacked him in the gut and for the second time cringed and laughed.

"Yeah, I don't think so, big guy."

"So, Alan," Addie shot Alan a sideways glance as they walked to Stan's for a burger and Coke. Feeling a little uneasy about what she intended to say, she decided to just get it over with. "I was thinking that I'd like to go to Café du Temp this Saturday. I was hoping to get the code from you so I can get in. I know I probably should have made the effort to get it myself, but..."

"What?" Alan turned and looked down at Addie as they walked. "Yeah sure, I can give you the codeword, but seriously, if you want to go back Saturday, I can go."

Feeling uncomfortable and not completely certain what her goal was, Addie avoided Alan's gaze. "I know, but I think I'd like to go by myself this time," she said quietly. "I hope you understand."

Alan looked at Addie. Although he was not at all comfortable with her going alone, he said, "Okay, I think I get it. This has to do with Isabelle, doesn't it?" Addie nodded, hating where the conversation was going. Stopping suddenly, Alan turned toward her. "I need to be honest,

Ad. I don't really think going alone is such a good idea. You've seen the neighborhood. It's kind of deserted. And I know they serve unescorted women, but still..."

Addie sighed with uncharacteristic impatience. "I know it's creepy around there, but I'll take a taxi and have them drop me off at the door. Alex usually opens it at the first knock, so I'm sure it'll be fine. You know I really don't need your permission, right?"

Surprised at her defensive tone, Alan scoffed. "I know that, Miss Independent. Be honest with me though. Why don't you want me to go with you? Besides, what will you tell Rachel? You girls live together. If I know her, she'll insist on tagging along." Addie was becoming frustrated. She could kick herself for not getting the code when she had the chance. She didn't want to have to tell Alan her plan. All she wanted to do was go and speak to Isabelle without any distractions. Why was this so hard?

Addie looked up toward the sky as if it held an answer and decided just to come clean. She knew he wouldn't really judge her. "Okay, Alan, here it is: I want to see Isabelle and I want to see her alone." She gently bit her lip and looked up at him. "I need to know if she feels anything for me. The thing is, I think she does. The way she looks at me, it's as if she's looking into my soul. I feel something for her, Alan, something more than friendship. I think about her all the time, and honestly, I can't stand not knowing if this thing between us might be something." She closed her eyes and lifted her head, sighing with frustration.

Alan took Addie's hand and squeezed it as they continued to walk. "Of course, I'll share the code with you. I'm a dope for grilling you. Listen, before you say anything, I have an idea, so just listen. What if we tell Rachel to cover for you Saturday night? We can tell her that you and I will be going out and probably staying out late, wink wink, in case your folks question why you're not home. Then I'll drive you to Café du Temp. They got a pay phone there; I saw it. You can call me at home to pick you up when you're ready. Well, what do you think? This way Rachel will be covered, your folks won't know a thing, and I won't be sitting up wondering like some over-protective boyfriend if you got mugged,"

"You'd do that for me?" Addie was smiling from ear to ear, not for the first time wondering how she got so lucky to have Alan in her life.

"Of course, I will. Hey, you may need to cover for me one day. What are best friends for anyway, if we can't be each other's lookout? Like I said, that area is sketchy, and besides, Rachel would kill me if anything happened to you." Addie smiled at Alan, her eyes shining with affection as they walked into Stan's.

CHAPTER 14

The wind was biting. Alan ducked his head low as he rode his bike home from class, thinking for the hundredth time that he needed to get his own car. His brother Frank had his own car by the time he was eighteen, Alan thought enviously. "Yeah, but he didn't have to save for college. He's here working at Dad's business," he said out loud to no one. "Christ! It's cold as a witch's tit out here for late September." Alan's fingers were white with the cold, and they burned with the frostiness of the whipping wind. He rode faster, wanting to get home as soon as he could.

There he could sit in front of the fireplace with hot apple cider and wiggle his toes in front of the warm heat of the flames. Jeez, he thought to himself, I'm so queer! The thought made his stomach momentarily sink and fear gripped him. Then he stood tall as he sped up and the feelings quickly passed. He knew who he was, dammit! It's taken me nearly all of my eighteen years to accept who I am, he concluded. I'm not a sissy, I'm a man. Who I sleep with doesn't make me anything less.

As he neared his house, Alan reminded himself to ask Frank if he could borrow the Buick this Saturday. There was no way he was going to let Addie drive to Café du Temp alone. He could at least drive her there and pick her up. He thought about how much he admired her. She's accepted who she is with a clear mind and little fear. He knew that taking a stand and sharing her feelings with Isabelle took courage, as this was all so new for her. If there is any fear in that girl, I've yet to see it, he thought. He was worried for her though, because he knew Addie was falling in love. No one had ever looked at him the way she looked at Isabelle. That look was more than a crush; that look was love.

Alan sat in front of the fireplace with his hot cider, closed his eyes, and breathed in the smell of warm apples. "Hey punk, you look more like

Dad every day. Where's your pipe and house slippers?" Frank, Alan's older brother, laughed and teased Alan as he joined him on the floor by the fire.

"Says you, jerk." Alan put his cider down and surprised Frank by grabbing him in a head lock. "Say uncle, say uncle!"

"Okay, okay, moose! Uncle! Uncle!" Frank and Alan lay on the floor laughing.

"I may be younger than you but I'm still bigger."

"Yeah, well, you just got lucky is all. So why are you home anyway? Why aren't you out with that seriously gorgeous doll face of yours?"

Alan smirked at his older brother, then laughed good naturedly. "Addie's got homework to do, but I'm glad you mentioned her. Can I borrow your wheels this weekend? Just on Saturday. I'd like to take Addie out, you know, some place special." Frank looked at Alan with a know-it-all look. "Well little bro, I was going to drive up to Milwaukee with some of the guys to hang out, but seeing as you've got a special date, well, okay. How much is it worth to you?

"I'll wash the Buick and fill the tank."

"Deal! I can catch a ride from Hank. So, listen, little brother, you're being careful, right? I mean, I know you have these big plans to go off to college. I'd hate to see them messed up by you making your girl in the family way, if you know what I mean."

Alan wanted to laugh, but he saw how serious Frank was. He was touched by his brother's sincerity. He decided not to make a joke of it and embarrass him. "Oh, that's not anything you need to worry about, Frank. Addie and I are definitely being careful."

"Okay, Ad, there's a phone booth next to the small bar on the east side of the club. You call me when you are ready to be picked up." He looked at his watch. "It's only seven now, but I'm not going out tonight. I got a trig test on Monday and it's a bitch, so I need to study. Listen, I don't care what time you call, but call me, okay?" Alan was turned toward Addie as they sat in the Buick in front of Café du Temp. His eyes were serious, and Addie herself felt a bit nervous.

"Just don't worry. I'll call you. Anyway, I don't even know if she will be here tonight. Remember to wait twenty minutes before you leave. If she's not in the club, I will have some tea and leave. If I'm not out in twenty, you know it is safe to go home." Addie looked at Alan again. "Alan, thank you. I can't tell you how much this means to me that you're here." Addie reached out to give him a quick hug and then opened the door of the Buick and quickly walked to the entrance of Café du Temp.

Alan watched as Addie walked toward the club and rapped her knuckles quietly on the small door within a door. Once she offered the code he had given her, she immediately gained entrance. Alan couldn't help but think that this was something like one of the fairy tale books that he had read as a kid. Addie just walked through the looking glass, he thought. He shook his head to clear his brain and lit a cigarette, determined to wait for twenty minutes just as Addie had requested. He thought he might wait twenty-five, just for good measure.

Alan was thinking about some of the things that Peter had shared with him about the club when he heard a door slam somewhere, snapping him out of his musings. Ten minutes had passed without his realizing it and Addie hadn't come out. He was itching to go in. After all, he knew the code and he would be welcome. He smiled to himself. He wouldn't mind seeing Peter. But what then, spy on her? Addie would be sore. He had promised her this, and he had to show her that he trusted her judgement. "Okay, okay," he said out loud, "I need to wait ten more minutes and then leave. Addie will be fine. After all, Café du Temp is not a dive; it's special. It's not like she's going to be kidnapped or anything. Get a grip, man!" Alan rebuked himself and lit another smoke.

Taking long drags of his cigarette, Alan watched the door. He again thought about the conversation he had with Peter on that first weekend he found himself at the club. Peter had said that not everyone was invited to Café du Temp and that those who walked through the door would leave their mark on the world. He had laughed loud and hard, questioning Peter as to what he, Alan Nackovic, could ever possibly leave to the world that was of any significance. Peter had smiled warmly and drawn him in for a passionate kiss.

CHAPTER 15

Addie felt the fragile balance of her nervous energy tip toward a light panic as she walked through the door. She took a deep breath to help calm herself. This was the first time she had been to Café du Temp on her own without Alan. She wasn't sure if she was nervous because she was a lone woman in a night club or because she would be speaking about her feelings with Isabelle. Probably both, she thought to herself. Okay, you wanted to do this, so do it, Miss Brave Heart. Deep breaths, deep breaths, she reminded herself.

"Miss Kahlo, how lovely to see you this evening. Would you like your usual table?"

Sam was his customary warm self. Addie noticed that he didn't even blink, in spite of the fact she had walked in alone. Alan had said that it was likely that no one at Café du Temp would judge her, and it appeared he was correct. "Hi, Sam," Addie smiled warmly. Sam always made her feel comfortable. She noticed he was extra attentive to her this evening. She could only surmise that he knew she was nervous about being there alone and wanted her to know there was no reason to be, at least not in that regard.

Sitting at the small table, Addie took a moment to admire the beautiful décor of the club. As she looked around intently, she realized it was a mixture of styles. It was a fusion of classical and deco design. I'm not an expert, she thought, but these styles normally shouldn't go together, but somehow here they worked beautifully. She realized that Café du Temp oozed the sophistication of a by-gone era, yet, at the same time it provided a comfortable, non-intimidating ambiance with a touch of deco chic. She caught herself smiling and shook her head slightly. Jeez, I've been here at Café du Temp three times and hadn't really appreciated its décor until now. I've been too focused on the excitement of being here and on staring at Isabelle to notice anything else. "God, you are in so much trouble," she whispered to herself, quietly laughing at her own lustful thoughts.

"You have a beautiful laugh." A smoldering gaze, partially hidden by the darkness of the club, greeted Addie as she looked up.

"Isabelle." Addie's heart started beating hard and fast. "Hi. I didn't see you walk up to the table. I must have been daydreaming." Addie felt her face flush with embarrassment as she looked at her beautiful new friend. "Please join me. I'd love the company."

"Are you sure you don't mind?" Isabelle looked around to see if Alan was near. "I don't want to interrupt your evening with Alan; I only wanted to stop by and say hello."

Addie cleared her throat and felt the familiar butterflies swarming in her stomach as she glanced toward Isabelle. She stood and gestured toward the other seat at the small table. "No, please join me. Alan is not with me tonight. I actually...well, I came alone." Addie couldn't help but laugh a bit at her own nervousness.

Isabelle looked at Addie and teasingly raised an eyebrow in quiet surprise. She then slowly sat down on the offered seat. "Really? Alone, Miss Kahlo? How very cosmopolitan of you." Isabelle smiled and continued to look at Addie with an intense gaze as she called Sam over to bring her a cognac.

"You're teasing me, Issie," Addie said, not at all offended, and laughed low in her throat.

Isabelle acknowledged the tease and laughed lightly. "So, tell me," Isabelle inquired as she made herself comfortable, "why are you here alone this evening? I hope you and Alan did not have a row." Isabelle had a concerned look on her face and waited for Addie to respond.

"A row?" Addie sipped her tea, trying not to let her hand shake as she brought the delicate cup to her lips. Realizing that Isabelle was alluding to her and Alan arguing, she quickly responded, "Oh no, not at all. Alan had a lot to do this evening. He's actually studying for an important exam this coming Monday. Anyway, I wanted to come, and well, here I am." Her knees were quietly knocking together under the small table, and she silently prayed that Isabelle wouldn't hear them.

Isabelle looked entirely pleased at Addie's response, "I am very happy to have run into you then. I was hoping that I would; it's lovely to see you again." Isabelle's eyes burned bright as she continued to watch Addie, whose cheeks flushed pink. Addie wasn't used to having the attention of a beautiful woman.

"I was hoping I'd see you too. I... ah..." Lifting her cup, Addie raised it toward Isabelle. "Shall we toast then to our new friendship?" Addie clinked her cup with Isabelle's glass and took a delicate sip of her tea. "You look amazing tonight Isabelle. You have the most beautiful clothes. Honestly, they look gorgeous on you. You're gorgeous," she said softly, eyes bright with admiration for the stunning woman sitting across from her.

Addie could feel her face once again burning from embarrassment, but she simply couldn't help express her admiration. She knew Isabelle could see her shyness and her embarrassment at being so vocal in her observation of her. She was painfully aware that every emotion showed on her face. She hated that she was so terrible at hiding her feelings. But Isabelle didn't seem to be embarrassed by the compliment. She simply smiled a bit shyly and continued to look at Addie. Feeling bold, Addie leaned forward and asked, "Isabelle, do you have a boyfriend?"

Isabelle's eyes widened at Addie's question. The sip of her cognac went down her throat the wrong way and immediately she began to cough. Addie, not knowing what else to do, jumped up and began to gently pat her on the back. "Oh Issie, I'm sorry. I didn't mean to startle you with my asinine question. I swear sometimes I don't know why I say the things I do. Please forgive me. You don't need to answer that, and it's none of my business." Addie continued to pat Isabelle on the back as her coughing fit subsided.

When Isabelle could breathe again, she began to laugh, which brought on another fit of coughing. "Oh Jeez, what's wrong with me?" Addie said miserably. "Are you okay? I have no idea why I asked that." Addie looked at Isabelle with concern.

"It's quite alright, Addie. Honestly, you just took me by surprise. Your directness is refreshing. There is no pretense for you, is there?" Isabelle gently wiped at her eyes, clearing the tears that pooled there from both her coughing fit and laughter. She took a sip of the water that Sam had quickly brought her when she began to cough and then lifted her head and focused her gaze directly on Addie. Addie smiled with an embarrassed tilt of her head. Clearing her throat, Isabelle waited a moment before she spoke, "No, I don't have a boyfriend." Gazing at Addie she said, "You are a wonder, aren't you, Addie Kahlo? An adorable, splendid wonder."

Briefly closing her eyes, Addie lifted her head and sighed as she listened to the melodious sound of the jazz horn. The melody was soft and deep. Though she was unfamiliar with the piece, its haunting sound penetrated her soul as if it were part of her, as if she belonged to it. Slowly opening her eyes, she saw Isabelle watching her from across their small table. In spite of her nervousness, Addie felt thrilled and daring as she gazed at Isabelle over her glass. "I'm very happy that it's just the two of us this evening," Addie said softly, "I love being with Alan, but it's nice just being here with you right now."

Lifting her drink to her lips, Isabelle regarded Addie with a teasing smile. "Are you flirting with me, Miss Kahlo?" Addie's eyes went wide and her expression changed from calm to slightly flustered. Reaching out, Isabelle gently touched Addie's hand. "It's alright, darling. I like it."

"You, you do?" Addie whispered and tilted her head. This flirtatious banter over cocktails in the soft light of a beautiful nightclub was all so new to her. She desperately did not want to misstep, but she wanted to know more about the woman who sat across from her. Isabelle slowly answered with a nod and an amused twinkle in her eyes. Addie cleared her throat. "So," Addie started, "tell me something about you."

Isabelle took a sip of water, her eyes never leaving Addie's, as she reached for Addie's hand where it lay next to her barely touched glass of wine. Addie swallowed. The feel of Isabelle's soft fingers on her was perfect. She slowly turned her own hand, so her palm was in contact with Isabelle's. Feeling daring, she gently wrapped her fingers around Isabelle's, bringing their hands together in a soft embrace. This feels amazing, she thought.

Isabelle looked down at their entwined fingers and gently smiled. "So," she started, "you already know I'm from England. England is quite different from the States, you know. It is very proper and conservative, at least the England I come from," Isabelle said, brows furrowed slightly. "My family is from London now, but as I mentioned, my surname is Czech. My grandfather came to England to make his fortune when he was very young and ended up starting a family there. I was born in Derby, which is a about two hundred kilometers from London. I went to school in Paris, fell in love with the city, and decided to make it my home."

Feeling slightly self-conscious, Addie softly bit her lower lip. She felt like a kid next to Isabelle even though she sensed Isabelle was only a year or two older. She'd never been anywhere other than where she lived. "Wow, just wow. I haven't ever gone anywhere." She looked up from their entwined hands and shook her head. "I've never been out of the Midwest. Going to school in Paris must have been amazing."

Sensing from Addie's shy response that she was a little bit in awe of her travels, Isabelle squeezed Addie's hand. "You know, Addie, London is not so far from Paris. Traveling there is similar to you traveling to one of your different states; it's not such a huge endeavor. It only seems this way because it is in a different country from what you know, and of course, it is Paris." Addie nodded and rolled her eyes playfully, realizing that Isabelle could see that she was a little bit awestruck. She was grateful that Isabelle wanted to put her at ease.

What a life Isabelle must lead, Addie thought. She's traveled to so many places and now lives in Paris. One day I too will see the world, she told herself. Suddenly it occurred to her, *she lives in Paris, thousands of miles away.* "Isabelle, you live in Paris?" Addie said through her suddenly tight throat. She could not help the deep disappointment in her voice. Quickly sensing Addie's concern, Isabelle half smiled and slowly nodded yes.

Addie swallowed, breathing deeply to steady her increasingly erratic heart. She felt her entire body deflate. Refocusing and trying to not let her feelings show, she asked hopefully, "Are you here as an exchange student or for work?" The hope obvious in her voice, she waited and watched as Isabelle took an agonizingly slow sip of her drink. The realization that she and Isabelle might not be able to explore whatever this was that they were feeling for one another brought a profound ache to her heart.

Isabelle felt the sudden despondency resonate from Addie, more than saw it. She wanted to reach out, enfold her in her arms and ensure her that this was only the beginning of their friendship, and that for them, there could be so much more. She craved to tell her that she already felt so very much for her and that they could somehow work through this. She wanted to tell Addie to trust her. She rationalized that, if they were ever going to have more than what they shared here and now, she would need to explain to Addie what *this* was, but how?

How could she explain something that she herself could not yet completely understand? She had no doubt that she could open Addie's eyes to the impossibility of Café du Temp, but she was fearful that her explanation would frighten Addie away, if she even believed it. Her only hope was that Addie would accept the impossible, as she herself had accepted it over two years ago.

Isabelle thought of Simone and how she would have knocked her in the head for being so blasé in her initial approach to Addie. What was she thinking, flirting and wooing the young woman without any real thought to the consequences? With feelings of real regret, she accepted that she hadn't been thinking of anything but herself. Then, quickly, much too quickly, she recognized that she felt more, that she wanted more with Addie. It was a truth that she initially did not want to admit to herself, as their circumstances were impossible. But she understood that she had no choice in the matter; one's heart does not ask permission to feel for another. Looking at Addie now, she saw so much in her eyes—trust, trepidation, hope and disappointment. She also saw something more, and that something more spurred Isabelle on. She wanted Addie to know that she was here, at Café du Temp, because she was destined to be. She hoped that they could discover together what that meant for both Addie and for herself.

"Addie," Isabelle said as she gently touched Addie's cheek and felt the softness of her skin. She looked into her eyes and her breath caught; Addie's gaze was sweet and so inviting. "I promise you, you will not be rid of me so quickly," she said with more feeling then her words could express. Yes, I live in Paris, but I am here now where I want to be, sitting at Café du Temp with you."

Addie felt a small sense of hope upon hearing Isabelle's words, but her natural cautious nature kept her from being overly optimistic. "Is it enough for us now to learn more of each other," Isabelle asked, "and perhaps see where our new friendship may lead?" There it was. Addie felt the unmistakable pull of their attraction for one another. To her great relief, she instinctively knew that it was more than a simple flirtatious dalliance. She knew that Isabelle felt it too, this pull to know her better.

Looking over her glass as she sipped her drink, Addie watched Isabelle's quiet contemplation. She could feel her attraction, and something more, something deeper. She wanted to ask Isabelle what she was feeling, but felt it wasn't the right time, not yet. For now, she was encouraged, knowing that she and Isabelle were connected. Her initial disappointment in finding out that Isabelle had a life in Paris had been momentarily dispelled.

Sensing an acceptance in Addie's gaze and demeanor, Isabelle allowed herself to relax. Tilting her head slightly she smiled and said, "So, Addie, tell me more about you. I'd like to know more about you."

Addie grinned slightly and nodded. "Okay" she said. "Well, I feel as if I'm just beginning my true life," she volunteered contemplatively. "My adult life, I mean. It's like an adventure I have waited a long time to start." She smiled shyly at her own description of her feelings. "I've known from the time I could read that I was going to be a writer, and perhaps a scholar as well. I love learning and I love teaching. I could see myself opening the hearts and minds of students to the beauty of literature. Yeah," she said almost in a whisper, "I think I can be a scholar." Reaching for her drink, she waved her hand suddenly in a light matter of fact way. "After all, it is 1952 and women can be scholars. Do you agree, Issie? Do you believe women can be scholars?" Isabelle smiled adoringly at Addie's enthusiasm as she nodded her agreement.

Addie smiled and took a drink of her wine as she looked around the club. She was happy, happy to be there at Cafe du Temp sharing her dreams with Isabelle. "Anyway, my parents are supportive of my choices. I'm fortunate in that sense.

Isabelle listened intently, desperately trying to hide her shock at what Addie had said. The date 1952 sailed through her brain and spun in circles in her mind. Dear god, she thought, Addie comes from over 40 years in the future. An American from Chicago, and an American from 1952! She suddenly felt lightheaded. She breathed in deeply and took a big gulp of water. She looked at Addie with an affection that pierced her heart and a kind of wonder for this young woman from the future. The open innocent look of joy that Addie gave Isabelle as she spoke left no room for doubt. This soft-spoken, sincere, bright young woman named Addie Kahlo made her heart sing. Isabelle wanted to know her and to know everything about her. As she willed her pulse to slow its frantic pace, she realized she held the same emotion and adoration in her heart for Addie as Addie held in her eyes for her.

"Isabelle?" Addie watched Issie's face go from amused and interested to slightly serious. She immediately thought Isabelle may not be feeling well. Her concern was real as she reached out her hand and gently touched Isabelle's cheek. "Isabelle, what is it?" Isabelle leaned into Addie's hand and smiled.

"It's nothing." Isabelle sighed as she looked to Addie and asked, with a bit of hesitation and a slight quiver in her voice, "Do you like me, Addie? I like you, I like you very much." Addie felt her pulse quicken as she knew what Isabelle was asking. It was a question that asked more than the words could express. Even with the slight fear she felt of the unknown and her nervous excitement, making her words a jumble and less than eloquent, Addie wanted Isabelle to know that, yes, she liked her. She liked her very much. But for now, all she could do was acknowledge this simple truth with a brilliant smile that reached her eyes and a firm nod of her head.

They regarded each other with a shared understanding and acceptance, Addie looking at Isabelle and Isabelle looking at Addie, and for that moment, it was as if no one else existed.

Suddenly, there was another person. "Pardon me, ladies. Would either of you care for another drink?" It was Sam, and his words brought them out of their daze of mutual admiration and desire. Isabelle shook her head, then smiled and looked at Sam.

"Sam, could you please bring our bill? Miss Kahlo and I will be leaving for the evening."

Addie raised an eyebrow and asked, "We're leaving? May I ask where we are going?"

Isabelle moved closer, making Addie's head spin with the scent of her perfume and the feel of her closeness. "Addie," she quietly whispered, "I want to share some things with you." Addie, sensing something thrilling, looked intently at Isabelle as she spoke. "It may be a bit unbelievable ...rather inconceivable actually, but will you trust me?" With a nervous energy born of her sense of adventure as well as her desire to know this woman, Addie nodded yes and put her trust in Isabelle.

CHAPTER 16

Isabelle stood, and reaching for her wrap, placed it around Addie's shoulders. It was heavy satin with small beads delicately woven into the fabric and intricately sown along the seams. It had a long fur collar that was soft and smelled faintly of jasmine, just like Isabelle herself. Addie had never seen anything like it. It was long and reached down to her ankles. It made her feel as if she was being lovingly wrapped in a warm blanket. "Please keep this on, as it will deter any questions, and it will keep you warm." Addie had no clue what Isabelle was talking about. It was a beautiful early fall evening in Chicago, and anywhere Isabelle intended to take her would not require such a heavy wrap.

Isabelle took Addie's arm in hers and walked with her to the corridor that led to the exit out of Café du Temp. Addie felt the excitement of something new and daring. "Addie, let's check with Alex to ensure the code has not changed, as you will require it once you return."

Addie knew this of course and immediately thought of Alan, "Oh, I need to telephone Alan. He is going to pick me up this evening. We made arrangements, and he actually drove me here." Addie looked at Isabelle, a bit embarrassed. She suddenly felt like a child and did not want to appear like one in front of Isabelle. But Isabelle didn't seem to mind at all.

"Of course, there is a telephone down the hall. Why don't you ring Alan and tell him you'll be ready to leave at midnight? That will allow plenty of time for us to explore and return in time for Alan to meet you." Isabelle gestured toward the hall where the telephone booth stood.

As Addie walked toward the telephone booth, she positively radiated excitement. Isabelle liked her as she herself liked Isabelle. She could hardly believe it! She was thrilled and excitedly awaited whatever adventure Isabelle had in mind. But she also knew Alan would be concerned, so she had to make certain he understood and trusted her to be back outside of Café du Temp by midnight. Midnight, Addie thought, like Cinderella. She quietly laughed at herself and moved quickly into the telephone booth.

Alan picked up on the second ring, his voice was a whisper, "Addie, hi. It's still early. Is everything okay? Are you ready for me to come fetch you?"

Addie bit her lip and said, "No, actually Isabelle wants to take me somewhere. I wanted to telephone early to let you know I will be back by midnight. You can pick me up in front of Café du Temp then."

Alan sighed into the telephone, "Addie...midnight? Are you sure about this?"

Surprised at his response, Addie felt defensive and put off by his attitude. "Well, Alan, honestly no, I'm not at all sure. But I want to go with her. I trust her and am very sure she will bring me back to Café du Temp at midnight as she promised."

"Okay, okay." Alan was concerned and tried not to sound foreboding but felt compelled to warn her all the same. "It's just that you know as well as I do that Café du Temp is different, which means the people who frequent it are also different."

Addie sighed, and again felt a defensiveness rear up within her. "What are you saying, Alan? That I shouldn't trust those who we meet here? Remember we...you and I, are part of Café du Temp as well. Should Isabelle not trust me, should she be worried about me?" She trusted Isabelle and wanted Alan to understand and trust her as well. She was hurt and slightly offended that he questioned her judgement.

"Hey, don't be sore. I'm sorry, I guess I'm just concerned. We don't know that much about what goes on there, you know? You'll be careful, right? Anyway, I'll be at the club to pick you up at midnight." Addie realized Alan was only concerned for her, and this awareness allowed her agitation to immediately melt away. In its place, she felt a tenderness toward him. She loved him, and he only wanted to protect her. She knew she shouldn't be upset about his concern.

"Alan, I'm sorry for being so defensive. You're right, of course. I need to be very careful, but please trust me." Addie desperately wanted Alan to understand.

Alan smiled into the telephone. "Hey, we are each other's cover. I've got your back Addie. I'll see you at midnight," he said, sounding brighter.

Addie hung up and walked back toward Isabelle who was waiting for her at the door.

"Hi," Addie said shyly as she grabbed Isabelle's hand and gently squeezed it, "I'm ready. Alan will be here at midnight so that gives us a few hours. Where are we off to, another club?"

Isabelle looked at Addie, nodded, and took a deep breath. "I know a lovely little café where they have fabulous coffee and teacakes." Isabelle held Addie's arm and with determination led Addie through her door. Isabelle's heart was pounding through her chest. She couldn't believe what she was about to do, but every instinct in her said this was right, and Isabelle always trusted her instincts. Still, she'd never brought any person through her door before. She silently hoped Addie would believe what she was about to see.

The first real sense of being someplace completely unfamiliar came as Addie walked across the threshold of Cafe du Temp onto the street. She felt a chill in the air and immediately noticed that the familiar smells of Chicago were no longer present. There was no scent of the lake as the strong winds blew in from the east, no distant harsh smell of Fulton Market, with its mounds of rotting fruit and vegetables, and no choking fumes from the busy traffic of downtown Chicago.

The air smelled like flowers and something else she couldn't identify, horses perhaps. The pavement under her feet was wood, and as appeared to always be the case around Café du Temp, damp. Instinctively she knew she was no longer in Chicago. There was a slight fog surrounding them, but she could still see the unfamiliar streetscape. This most definitely was not Chicago. A foghorn sounded in the distance and horse hooves clomped nearby.

A fear gripped her, and she fleetingly thought she might be losing her mind or experiencing some type of breakdown. She held tight to Isabelle's arm and looked to her with questioning eyes; but she could not resist scanning her surroundings more thoroughly, and the shock of what she saw made her reconsider a breakdown. She thought she might have died and was somewhere in transition to another plane of existence. Then, just as she was about to spiral into a panic, she felt Isabelle take her hand and hold it tightly, leading her through the unfamiliar streets. Isabelle's tight grip brought her back from her panic, and she allowed herself to be led.

Afraid to speak too loudly, Addie whispered, "Isabelle, where are we? I don't understand. This is not Chicago." They stopped suddenly. Addie looked around again, and she simply could not believe what she was seeing. This was not possible. The streets were lit by gas lamps that barely illuminated their surroundings. There were women walking in long frilly dresses, wearing hats adorned with feathers and flowers. Men wore suits of striped tweed, their heads covered by bowlers, and many carried canes. There were horse-drawn carriages that clattered through the streets which they shared with cars that she had only seen in museums. She could only stare transfixed, her mouth open, amazed at the impossibility of what she was seeing before her. It was a slightly chilly evening, and Addie instinctively wrapped the garment Isabelle had given her tightly around her shoulders. As Isabelle led her through what appeared to be a square, Addie twisted and turned her head, attempting to take in everything around her.

Despite her fear, Addie's mind was quickly taking in the smells, the sounds, and the scenery of this impossible place. It's Paris, her mind reasoned. It couldn't be anything but...but how? How can I be in Paris, and in what time period am I? As if to confirm her assumption, looking up, she nearly fainted. There was the Eiffel Tower, looming majestically into the sky. She took in a deep breath and stared wide eyed, mesmerized by this mammoth of a monument. She turned and looked at Isabelle, confusion and shock in her eyes. She needed to know what was happening to her.

Isabelle watched the kaleidoscope of emotions play out on Addie's face as she led her through the Champ de Mars to the small café near the Seine. She had to give Addie credit; she was holding up well. She briefly recalled her own reaction to learning that Café du Temp was a portal that guided its occupants to unknown destinations. She herself had fainted.

"We're here," Isabelle announced to Addie as she gestured her into a small café beautifully lit with candles in colored vases. As Isabelle led Addie through the door, Addie felt the warmth immediately sink into her chilled bones. While she felt marginally better, she still felt like she was in a dream. Isabelle led her to a small table near the window and pulled her down in the seat opposite her. *Deux cafés, s'il vous plaît,* Isabelle announced to the server as he came to take their order. She turned to Addie and explained, "I asked him to bring us two coffees."

"Yeah, I got that," Addie quipped, rubbing her eyes as if trying to wake up. "Isabelle, please, tell me what is happening. Where are we? Am I losing my mind? Wait," Addie suddenly looked at Isabelle with wide eyes. "Did you slip me a mickey? I've never taken drugs, but I hear that they have some pretty bizarre effects. Please tell me you drugged me. I won't be sore."

Isabelle thought Addie looked so adorable in her shocked confusion at that moment that she couldn't help but scoot her chair over and throw her arms around her to hug her tightly. "Oh Addie. No, darling, I haven't drugged you. But I know you deserve an explanation, and I suppose I am the one designated to give it to you. The thing is, sweetheart, I don't know the entirety of it. You see, I only know bits and pieces. I myself am still, well…finding my way. But I will share everything I know."

Their server brought their coffees, hot and steaming, along with some pastries that Isabelle said were called *croissants*. Addie breathed in the aroma as she brought the delicate porcelain bowl up to her lips with shaky hands and carefully tasted the delicious brew. Isabelle watched her. In the hazel of her irises, reflecting the light from the candle on the table, Addie's eyes were wild with questions. Isabelle felt such a tenderness for her, wishing she could spare her the shock of what she was about to share with her.

"Listen," Isabelle said tenderly as she reached for Addie's hand and held it. Addie looked around, aware that they were not in the safety of Café du Temp, but in a very busy café. It was clear that no one was paying them any attention, so she relaxed and held tightly to Isabelle's hand as she waited for her to explain.

Isabelle took a calming breath. "Addie, do you believe in things you can't tangibly hold in your hand? That there are realities that we, as humans, have yet to understand and accept? I ask this because I need you to believe in this," Isabelle commented as she waved her hand indicating their surroundings. "You are not losing your mind, nor are you drugged. This is real. Like myself, you have been given an incredible opportunity." Addie looked like a deer in the headlights as she waited for Isabelle to continue. She thought of science and religion and how they were often at odds in their explanations of the realities of the world. Perhaps, she supposed, they're both right. Addie nodded, waiting for Isabelle to continue.

"Two years ago, as I was returning home from an evening out here in Paris, a door appeared. Well, I should say that I saw the door where there had not been one before. Like with you and Alan, it called to me. I was curious and excited. Once I walked through that door, I soon realized that Café du Temp was different. I know you felt it too. I saw it in your eyes that first evening we met. Well, I fell in love with it, the music, the atmosphere, the mystery. I suppose I was a bit of a lost soul who had found a home.

After I met Peter, we quickly became close. He took me under his wing and shared with me the true nature of Café du Temp." Addie looked questioningly at Isabelle. How close were she and Peter, she thought, her stomach tightening with dread? As if Isabelle knew Addie's concern, she immediately clarified, "Peter and I were never lovers, sweetheart. He prefers the more masculine sex, as I think you know." Addie, blushed, as Isabelle gently squeezed her hand.

Isabelle continued, "Peter explained to me that Café du Temp is a kind of portal. Those of us who are allowed to enter will, in some way, leave our mark on the world. He said that the significance of one's destiny cannot be understated. Each contribution, no matter how seemingly insignificant, will have a profound effect on the destiny of others. It appears that Café du Temp is a guide for those of us who have somehow veered off course. Its power is that it gently guides us back to our destiny." Isabelle breathed deeply, as if attempting to quell her own nervousness. "Honestly, I don't understand it all myself, but Addie," Isabelle looked deeply into her eyes, "I truly believe that you and I are destined to know each other."

Addie was doing her best to absorb everything Isabelle had just shared. Despite the implausibility of what she had heard, she could see that it was true. All the signs were there—being served alcohol despite their age, the eclectic mix of people, and her table always being available despite how crowded it always appeared to be. Then, there were the various conversations she had overheard that never appeared to make sense, the sudden appearance of the door, and, of course, Paris.

"Isabelle," Addie said as she continued to hold tightly to Isabelle's hand and looked directly at her. She was terrified to ask, but knew that she needed to know. "Are those of us who come to Café du Temp from different periods in time? It's just that some of the conversations I've overheard seem so strange to me, as if I have no point of reference. And the clothes, people's clothes, our clothes, they're different from Peter's and yours."

Issie?" Addie's eyes were wide and questioning, and a little afraid. Unshed tears pooled and threatened to fall. Her face was flushed, and her unspoken question lay heavy between them. "Issie, when are you from?"

Isabelle's mouth formed a small sad smile. She looked directly at Addie and whispered, "This is my home, Addie, Paris, 1911." Addie fainted.

CHAPTER 17

The subtle feel of a tender kiss on her forehead and gentle fingers smoothing her hair brought Addie back. She opened her eyes to see Isabelle looking down at her with concern. Her head hurt. She slowly blinked her eyes open as the fog began to lift from her brain. She gradually realized that she wasn't at The Angel or with Rachel. She was with Isabelle at a café somewhere in Paris in 1911. "Oh god," she moaned. She attempted to sit up too quickly, and feelings of nausea seeped into her stomach and throat. "Oh, I feel awful. What happened?"

"Shh, it's alright, Addie. You'll be alright, but be still." Isabelle held a small glass next to Addie's lips and placed a cool damp cloth on her forehead. Addie took a small sip of the offered drink. The strong liquid slid down her throat, immediately warming her stomach and slightly easing the nausea. Addie's eyes darted around the room. She saw a frightened looking waiter standing next to Isabelle, as well as an older gentleman dressed in a dark suit with a stiff bow tie. As Isabelle looked down at Addie with concern, the man said something in French. Isabelle responded to him while gently moving her hands through Addie's hair. "God, what the heck happened," Addie whispered, as Isabelle helped her sit up.

"Are you alright, Addie? Are you dizzy?"

"What happened, Isabelle? Did I faint? I fainted, didn't I? Oh god, I've never fainted before." Addie slowly sat up and saw that she was in a small room with an overstuffed couch, a wooden chair and desk. It must be an office, she thought. I've fainted and they've carried me to this office. She closed her eyes again and tried to think, but it was all so impossible. Everything was impossible, yet here she was. She sighed again and looked up wide-eyed toward Isabelle and waited for an explanation.

Isabelle turned from her and spoke again to the older man. Addie had to steady herself as she listened to the beautiful sound of Isabelle speaking French. Both the waiter and older gentleman bowed slightly and left the room, closing the door behind them. Once they were gone, Isabelle reached for Addie and put her arms around her, holding her close. "Oh Addie, I didn't mean to frighten you. I'm so sorry, I just didn't know how else to tell you. Do you remember what we discussed before you...well, fainted?"

Slowly, Addie pulled back from Isabelle's embrace and stared at her. "Yes, yes I remember." Looking at Isabelle now, the implication of where she was at that moment made her head spin, and she felt she might faint again. "How could I not," she said, holding her forehead, suddenly feeling emotional and a little bit afraid, "Iss, is it true? Are you from 1911? No, don't tell me! Of course, it's true! But how can this be happening? I don't understand any of this." Addie looked frantically around and then turned back to Isabelle whose face was rapt with compassion and concern.

"Iss," she said, on the verge of tears now that the reality of their situation became clear. "I've just met you and I want to know you, but how can I when... If this is real, I am a lifetime away!" Addie looked at Isabelle, tears of frustration stinging her eyes, her voice soft and full of emotion. "Iss, I can't lose you so soon. I simply can't."

Isabelle nodded and looked into Addie's eyes, "No, Addie, we won't lose each other. I won't allow it, not for a minute," she said with determination in her voice. "Sweetheart, I don't believe that our meeting was happenstance. It means something, it means something to the both of us. Where we are now, in our lives, this has to be a part of the reason we are here, together." Attempting to regain her composure, Isabelle pulled back from Addie while reaching out to tuck a loose curl behind her ear. "We'll figure this out, we will. I promise we will." Gently wiping the tears from Addie's eyes, she smiled. "Do you trust me?"

Addie held tightly to Isabelle's hand. Steeling herself, she sat up straight and nodded. "Yes, Issie, I do trust you," she softly replied.

"Good, that's good." Isabelle blew out a relieved breath. "But first, let's make certain you are alright. Here, let me help you stand up. Are you able to walk?" She looked to Addie, who stood on unsteady legs, "My grandmother's apartments are only a short walk from here. We should go there. We will be able to speak more in private. You can rest and when you are ready, we'll talk through everything." Addie nodded, and with the help of Isabelle, walked toward the café exit. *"Merci beaucoup,"* Isabelle called out to the café owner as she led Addie out into the chilly evening.

Addie immediately felt her head clear as the cool evening air hit her body. The nausea subsided and she felt more like herself, calmer after the emotional panic of a few moments ago. Looking around, the sight of Paris 1911 felt surreal. Taking a cleansing breath, she knew that she desperately needed to understand why she was a part of this strange world.

"It's not far; we're nearly there." Isabelle felt Addie's apprehension as she quietly led her toward an iron gate that was adorned with elaborate wrought iron roses and delicate and ornately designed butterflies. Entering the property, Addie looked up at the building wide-eyed. It was enormous. Does her grandmother live here by herself she thought? The size and the grandness of it immediately brought to mind the type of manor houses common in gothic novels, but she had never seen anything like it in person. She was speechless as she was led through a large foyer to what Isabelle called the music room. True to her initial impression, Isabelle's grandmother's home was grandiose and elaborate. A fire was lit in the fireplace. Big comfortable stuffed chairs were scattered throughout while a velvet couch with bright colorful pillows adorned one side of the room. A grand piano, with its rich polished wood and intricate markings, was the focus of the room.

While Addie scanned the space, mesmerized by the stateliness of it, there was a knock at the door, and, of all things, a butler entered. Addie knew her mouth must be hanging open, but she couldn't help herself. He looked as if he'd just stepped out of the pages of a gothic novel, with his dark suit and perfectly trimmed beard and hair. Addie nearly laughed from the absurdity of it, but stopped herself, guessing that Isabelle would not be amused. "Good evening, Mademoiselle Androsko. Is there anything I can bring for you and your guest?"

"Good evening, Andre. No, but thank you. We are fine and please feel free to retire for the evening."

"Thank you, Mademoiselle. Have a good evening." As Andre exited the room, Isabelle turned and smiled sheepishly at Addie.

Addie's eyes followed Andre as he left the music room. "Uh...okay, now I know I've lost my mind. Isabelle, are you a princess or countess or whatever aristocratic English women are called?"

Isabelle laughed lightly and shook her head as she gestured to Addie to sit by the fire. "This is my grandmother's home. She is in London, and I stay here on occasion. I own a small apartment nearer to the Louvre, which I assure you it is nowhere as extravagant. As for Andre, he has been with the family since before I was born. Does he make you nervous?"

"Oh no, it's not that. Well, actually, I've never experienced anything quite like this before. I live in a three-flat in the basement apartment with my cousin Rachel. This is...I'm speechless."

Isabelle sat back on the lounge, crossed her legs and sighed, and looking directly at Addie, she smiled. "Well, you have every right to be speechless. I'll let you in on a little secret," she whispered, "When I first learned of Café du Temp and its unique abilities to move one through time, I fainted as well." Chuckling, she considered her next words. "It took me days to come to terms with it. I am still often at a loss for words to describe it or explain it. I'm sorry I had to tell you the way I did, but I felt that if I didn't first show you...if you didn't see it all with your own eyes, you wouldn't believe. I hope you can forgive me."

Addie stood up and walked over to sit next to Isabelle. She watched her for a moment, struck by her sincerity and gentle kindness. Addie reached for her hand, and Isabelle grasped Addie's tightly. "Forgive you? There's nothing to forgive. I came with you of my own free will. I honestly don't understand how being here with you, in Paris, is possible, but I am here. It's magic, Issie. I feel like Alice from Alice in Wonderland, opening the door to another world, or," she said with a smirk and a shake of her head, "I just might really have a brain tumor."

Isabelle squeezed Addie's hand and laughed at her flippant remark, making Addle chuckle despite the seriousness of their situation. Looking at Addie with tenderness, Isabelle lifted her hand and gently kissed her palm. The feeling of Isabelle's soft lips touching her skin sent a powerful current through Addie's entire body. Taking in a quick breath as she looked into Isabelle's gentle compelling eyes, she wanted so badly to reach out and kiss her at that moment. She had never kissed another woman before, and the excitement of the possibility made her eyes widen and her heart race. Before she could get up her nerve to move closer, Isabelle did. She lightly touched Addie's cheek with her hand and brought their lips together in a sweet gentle kiss.

Addie's heart beat frantically in her chest, her lips tingled, and she could taste the sweetness of Isabelle on her mouth. The kiss was even better than she had dreamed. Driven by the look of tenderness mixed with desire on Isabelle's face, she moved closer and tentatively brought her mouth to Isabelle's once again. She parted her lips and let her tongue slide slowly into Isabelle's open mouth. As their kiss deepened, she couldn't help the groan of pleasure that escaped her. Isabelle's grip brought her closer still, and she heard her release a soft sigh. They parted at the same time, staring and still holding on to one another. Isabelle spoke first. "I've wanted to kiss you from the first moment I heard your beautiful laugh. When I looked toward the sound, it was you. You were so lovely at that moment that I could not take my eyes off of you. And now, well, now that I know you... you're so much more."

The longing in Isabelle's voice moved through Addie like a cool breeze on a hot day, welcoming and utterly satisfying. She knew that anything she could possibly say at that moment would be inadequate. Overcome with feelings she couldn't verbalize, she laid her forehead on Isabelle's shoulder. Breathing in her scent, she sighed as she tentatively moved to kiss Isabelle's neck, then the strong plane of her jaw, and finally, her mouth. Sensations she had never experienced before coursed through her as their kisses became more insistent. Addie could feel Isabelle's heart pounding against her own.

After several long minutes, Addie had to pull back. Breathing heavily, she held Isabelle's shoulders and looked into her eyes. She needed to be certain that the feelings she was having, feelings of desire, deep admiration, and trust, were reflected in Isabelle's own eyes. And they were, they *so* were. Every emotion Addie was feeling was reflected back in the beautiful tender look that Isabelle was giving her. Smiling shyly, she reached out and tenderly caressed Isabelle's cheek. She didn't yet understand how or why she was here in Isabelle's Paris, but she did know that she was falling in love.

Addie felt smooth warm fingers stroking her forehead as she slowly opened her eyes. She looked up to see the most beautiful face she'd ever seen looking down at her. Her head was on Isabelle's lap. Smiling, Isabelle leaned down and gently kissed Addie softly on her forehead, "You fell asleep. How do you feel?"

"I fell asleep? Seriously?" she said, closing her eyes and feeling the heat of a blush form on her face. "How embarrassing." Isabelle laughed lightly, leaned down and gently kissed Addie's soft lips. The feel of Isabelle's mouth on hers sent a thousand butterflies cascading through her stomach. She reached up and pulled Isabelle to her, deepening the kiss. She had never experienced anything so wonderful. Isabelle's response to her kisses was eager and passionate. Addie could feel heat in her core and the unmistakable tingling of arousal as Isabelle hands gripped her waist. Isabelle's eyes never left Addie's as she gently maneuvered their bodies so that Addie lay beneath her. As Isabelle pressed her soft lips to Addie's once again, Addie could feel the firmness of Isabelle's breasts against her own, immediately sending bolts of desire through her entire body. The sound of Isabelle's frantic breaths coursed through Addie as she tried to control her own breathing. She was desperate to make love to her, to feel her soft warm skin against her own as they explored each other's bodies. She was ready, she had never been so ready. Her mind couldn't connect to anything but this exquisite woman pressing her body against hers. She could feel Isabelle's moist lips on her throat and hear her ragged breathing as she tasted Addie's skin. It was amazing! Addie felt amazing. And then, it was gone.

Isabelle suddenly halted, shocking Addie out of her desire-infused euphoria. Looking at Addie, Isabelle sighed deeply as if suddenly realizing something utterly disappointing. Running one hand through her tussled blond waves she smiled roguishly and then tenderly kissed Addie on the lips, gently lifting herself from Addie's grip and off of her body. Addie groaned at the sudden loss of Isabelle's touch and gave her a questioning look. "Addie," Isabelle whispered, touching Addie's cheek, "I adore you. I promise you we will have our time together, though right now I'm afraid we must get you back." Turning her head to the clock above the fireplace she smiled sadly. "It's half past 11:00, and we need to get you to the door by midnight so you can get back to your own time."

As Addie tried to focus on Isabelle's words, she opened her eyes wide and looked a bit bewildered. She was so disappointed she could have cried, and if truth be told, she was still entirely aroused. She wasn't ready to go. She wanted to stay right where she was, in Isabelle's arms. As her mind began to clear she reluctantly acknowledged that Isabelle was right, she must get back to the door and to her own time. Lying on the couch sulking and disheveled, she halfheartedly allowed Isabelle to help her up and then giggled when Isabelle embraced her and planted gentle kisses on her eyes, nose, and cheeks. She smiled with affection as Isabelle lovingly smoothed down her hair and straightened her dress. Once they were both presentable, Isabelle led them from the warmth of the cozy room to the front steps of the house.

The evening was chilly, and she was glad she had Isabelle's warm wrap covering her. To Addie's continued surprise, Isabelle's driver appeared, and they both stepped into the rear seat of an automobile that Addie had only seen in old films. It was a short ride toward the Seine to the location where they had last walked through the door. Addie feared the door wouldn't be there, but just as quickly thought, would having to stay here with Isabelle be such a sacrifice? The thought thrilled her. She shook her head and hoped she would not have to deal with anything as life altering as that just yet. She leaned her head on Isabelle's shoulder and savored the feel of being so near to her. She felt secure in the knowledge that Isabelle's feelings for her were just as real as her own.

"There, there it is, Addie!" The car stopped abruptly; they were within a few feet of the door. It was 11:45 and Addie needed to go.

"Iss, I... Please tell me we will see each other again." Addie held tight to Isabelle's hand as she waited for her reply. She couldn't lose Isabelle so soon after finding her. Closing her eyes, she breathed deeply attempting to calm her racing heart.

"Yes," Isabelle said as she watched her. "Addie, open your eyes and look at me." She reached up and gently touched Addie's cheek. Staring into Addie's questioning gaze, she made a promise. "Yes, darling, we will see each other again. I promise you. We will see each other again very soon."

CHAPTER 18

Addie watched the lights of the city speed by as she sat silently next to Alan. As promised, he had been waiting for her, a Lucky Strike dangling from his lips, in his brother Frank's maroon Buick, the radio playing an old song by Frank Sinatra. Staring out the passenger side window, she knew that her feelings were all over the place. She was happy and relieved to see Alan, but also numb and feeling confused about leaving Isabelle. Good god, she thought, now that I'm back, was all of that real? Reaching up she lightly touched her mouth and remembered the perfect softness of Isabelle's lips. An intense wave of feeling overcame her. Is this love? She closed her eyes and shivered, picturing the desire in Isabelle's eyes and feeling that same desire flow through her even now.

"Addie, you're a million miles away. What happened?"

Turning to look at Alan, she quickly decided to tell him everything. She desperately needed to talk to someone. "Alan, can we drive somewhere, maybe to the lake? I really need to talk." Still reeling from the shock of her experience with Isabelle, her hands shook slightly and her stomach felt off. Breathing deeply, she was soothed by the memory of Isabelle's kisses as they held each another in the parlor of Isabelle's grandmother's house. She trusted Isabelle, and despite how incredible it all appeared, there was no doubt in her mind that she had somehow been transported to Paris, 1911.

"Yeah, sure." Alan's voice sounded concerned, but he didn't push. He knew that she'd tell him in her own good time. Alan drove toward South Shore. He knew of a nice stretch of beach there, and at this time of year, and at night for that matter, he was sure there would be no one around. As he pulled into a secluded parking area, he glanced at Addie; she looked somber and a million miles away. The beach was deserted, and the chilly wind was biting as they stepped away from the Buick. Alan quickly went

113

to the trunk and pulled out a blanket. He put the blanket around Addie's shoulders, and they walked to a small section of beach looking out to Lake Michigan. As Alan guided her toward some driftwood to sit on in the sand, Addie stared out at the lake, black except for the lights of the city across the water.

"Where do I even start?" Addie whispered. She continued to look out at the dark vastness of the lake as Alan patiently waited for her to continue. "I'm in love with her, Alan. I look at her beautiful face and expressive eyes, and there is no one else in the world. Tonight, she invited me to visit her life, and Alan...it was impossible. It was like a fairy tale, and I was Alice, walking through the looking glass."

Alan looked at her questioningly but said nothing as he put his arm around her. She leaned her head on his strong shoulder, grateful for his company and friendship. They sat that way for a few minutes, both of them listening to the sounds of the waves hitting the shore and the faint noises of the city. She breathed deeply, taking in deep gulps of chilly air and sat up. "Alan, do you remember when we first started to go to Café du Temp and we thought it was strange, in a good, not scary way, but different?"

Alan nodded and thought back to his first visit, "Yeah, I remember how mesmerized I was when I first entered. You know, Addie, you're the only one I ever told about it. It was like I had to share it with you. Like you had to experience Café du Temp too. Wow... I just realized that. Isn't that crazy?"

"Yeah, well that's an understatement." Addie turned toward Alan and looked at him. "Alan, Isabelle took me to her family home...her home in Paris, 1911 Paris." Alan just stared, apparently waiting for the punchline. "Oh Alan, I'm in love with a girl who is from 1911 Paris." Addie sighed deeply, suddenly feeling exhausted she closed her eyes and pressed a palm to her forehead.

"Ad, what are you saying? Alan pulled a cigarette out of his shirt pocket, cupped his hands against the wind and lit it, taking a deep drag. "So, you're telling me that you were somehow magically transported back in time to Paris or something?" Huffing out a nervous laugh, he looked at her. "I think you're pulling my leg. Come on...what's this about?"

Addie lifted her head, tired and desperately wanting him to believe her she reached out and clasped his wrist in a vice like grip. "Listen to me,

Alan. Think about this before you decide to not believe me. Think about what Peter said to you, the strange conversations we've heard, the clothes we've never seen before, the table that is always conveniently available for us whenever we walk through the door, and the strangest thing of all, that we never feel the slightest urge to tell anyone else about Café du Temp. We are never tempted! Don't you see, Alan? Café du Temp is some kind of mysterious gateway that only certain people experience." Addie looked at Alan, praying that he would believe her. She needed for him to believe her.

Alan searched Addie's eyes for any hint of pretense but all he saw was a desperate truth and a trace of fear. She released his wrist and he stood up suddenly and began to pace the small area around the beach where they sat. He took another deep drag of his cigarette before looking back to his friend.

"Okay, tell me what happened, everything you can recall." Addie released the breath she hadn't realized she was holding. "Do you believe me? Alan, please say you believe me." Alan sat back down next to Addie and looked at her and knew instinctively that he did. He did believe her.

"Yeah, it all sounds crazy but yeah, I believe you."

Addie threw her arms around Alan and hugged him. "Thank god... thank god."

Alan flipped away his dying cigarette and immediately lit another. "Ad, listen, I need to tell you something. I didn't tell you before because I guess I didn't want to believe it, but I think I also met someone from a different time. It was that first evening I was at Café du Temp. Peter introduced us. Nice guy, older than me, but still young, you know? He introduced himself as Eddie, Eddie Rickenbacker. I noticed right off that his suit was tweed and his collar almost looked like it was made of something like cardboard. He wore a bowtie.

"Anyway, he said he was a pilot and that he would be going to the front in a matter of days. I... I didn't get it, you know? The front? But, before I could ask, someone caught his attention and he smiled at me, shook my hand, and said 'God speed' to all of us and then he was gone. That whole evening, I was curious. This guy was just so different. I even thought about it the next day, so at dinner that evening I asked my dad if he ever heard of anyone named Eddie Rickenbacker. Do you wanna know what my dad said? He said Eddie Rickenbacker was a WWI flying ace who was awarded the Medal of Honor in 1918. So, do I believe you Addie? Yeah, I'm afraid that I do."

When Addie opened the door to her apartment it was nearly 3:00 a.m. She and Alan had talked for hours, going over everything they could recall specific to Café du Temp. Everything and anything that could help them understand how they came to discover this unusual place. Now as she slowly crept into her room and undressed, all she wanted to do was sleep. She was both physically and mentally exhausted, but lying in bed she couldn't stop her brain from rehashing the evening's events. Now all she could think of was Isabelle and what they had shared tonight. The touch of her soft lips, the feel of her breasts against her own, the beautiful words she whispered to her as she held her. "God, I'm in love with her, I'm in love with her," she muffled into her pillow.

Exasperated, Addie flung back her blankets. She knew she wasn't going to sleep anytime soon. She got out of bed and quietly walked to the kitchen to make herself a cup of tea. Sitting in her cozy living room, she thought of the events that had taken place this evening—Café du Temp, Isabelle, Paris, 1911, confiding in Alan. She tried to wrap her mind around it all, willing herself to accept the impossible. She thought about Alan and his own experience with the pilot. Surely that lends credence to her own experience, she told herself. Thank god he believed her. She could see on his face and in his eyes that he knew everything she said to him was the truth. But she also saw the concern, even a little fear, and she couldn't deny she felt that fear too; not only fear of the improbability of Café du Temp and what it all meant, but fear of her feelings for Isabelle and what their meeting each other meant to her future.

"Hey, sleepy head! Wake up! Did you sleep here all night?" Addie slowly opened her eyes to see Rachel looking down at her. She groggily realized she must have fallen asleep on the sofa.

"Rach...morning." Addie smiled at Rachel, happy to see her, a normal person in a normal world. "I guess I did. I got in kinda late and for some reason I couldn't sleep." Addie stretched out on the cozy sofa and yawned. "You made coffee," she said as Rachel handed her a cup and sat on the sofa.

"Yes, I did. Now spill the beans. I know you were out with Alan until after 2:00, because Mickey dropped me off at 2:00 and you were nowhere in sight." Addie looked up at Rachel and raised an eyebrow.

"Well, yeah, it was late when he dropped me off, but honestly we just hung out and that was it."

Rachel rolled her eyes and laughed, "Yeah right! So, if that's true, how did that little love bite on your neck get there, if all you two did was talk?" Rachel's smile was sarcastic and fun, and she couldn't wait to hear the details.

"What?" Addie jumped up and ran to the bathroom to check herself in the mirror. "Oh god, Isabelle," she whispered as she stared at the small red mark on her throat. She slowly closed her eyes and shivered, remembering in detail how that mark made its way to that very tender spot.

"Well, Addie, come on. You two are sleeping together, aren't you? Spill!" Rachel stood in the doorway, staring at Addie with a goofy smile on her face. Addie quietly grunted, not knowing how she would handle this one. She'd have to deal with it later, but right now she needed coffee.

"Your move, Ad." The two friends were sitting in Alan's family's screened-in front porch playing chess and drinking Cokes. "Mom wants to know if you're staying for dinner. Can you?" Addie took a drink of her Coke and nodded yes. She was concentrating on her next move and trying to figure out how to tell Alan that they were sleeping together.

"Alan, uh...don't have a cow, but I told Rachel that you and I were having sex. Your move."

Alan coughed up his Coke and whistled loudly as he shook his head. "So, I finally got lucky with my girl, have I? So, how was I?" Addie looked up at Alan who was staring at her like the Cheshire Cat. She couldn't help herself, and she burst out laughing. "I'm sorry, Alan, she said between bursts of laughter. I don't mean to laugh."

"Yeah, yeah, yeah, Ad. You're a real comedian. Alan tried to look insulted, but his grinning face was a dead giveaway.

"Clearing her throat, Addie looked across the small chess board to

Alan. "So, Sunday morning Rachel noticed...uh...a mark on my throat that I did not realize was there. Stop smirking or I'll stop talking. Okay...good. Anyway, she grilled me on our relationship. She knew I got in really late and assumed that you and I were doing it. I didn't confirm it, but I didn't deny it either." Sighing heavily, Addie ran her fingers through her hair. "I hate lying to her, Alan. It feels wrong, but still I can't bring myself to be honest with her. I don't want to lose her."

Nodding, Alan stood. "Come on, Ad. Let's take a walk. Grabbing her hand, he led her out toward the path to the park.

Kicking a stone on the path, Addie breathed out a long breath. "You know that Rachel has her whole life planned out, right?" Addie said as they walked. "She will graduate from high school, marry Mickey, help run the family business, and probably have a brood of kids too."

"What's this about, Ad? Are you jealous? Alan looked at Addie as if challenging her.

"What? No! I'm not jealous," she huffed out. "That has never been the life I dreamed of for myself. You know better than most that I have much different plans. I've never thought of marriage. I could never marry. You must know that."

Putting his arm around Addie as they continued their walk, Alan looked down as her. "I know. I happen to feel the same. Honestly, I think marriage isn't in the cards for either of us. Unless we marry each other." Addie looked up at Alan's silly grin and laughed lightly, the ridiculous suggestion breaking their solemn mood. "You are such a goof."

CHAPTER 19

"Throw the ball to first base, Rach! First base!"

"ECKKKK! It has mud on it," screamed Rachel as she flung the baseball wide of first base, sending it out into the dugout area. Addie was pitching and fell on the mound laughing hysterically as Rachel who, playing shortstop, screamed that she thought there might be poo on the ball.

"Oh, for Pete's sake, honey," cried Mickey. "That's not poo, it's wet sand. Time out," yelled Mickey as he jogged over to Rachel, who stood pouting she frantically attempted to wipe wet sand off her pedal pushers. Addie was still laughing at Rachel as she jogged over to Alan, who was the game's catcher.

"Oh my god, Alan, our Rachel is such a girly girl. Look at her over there, hugging Mickey as he tries to console her for throwing the ball in the dugout." Alan laughed too and grabbed the baseball from Addie's hand as he walked with her over to sit on the bench while the game was in time out. "Oh, this is a hoot," said Addie as she wiped the afternoon sweat off her forehead. "I love this game, but I think watching Rachel play is my favorite part. Look at her, my poor girl!"

"Yeah, Mickey's a saint for putting her in the game. He knows she can't play a lick, but I guess it's either put her in the game or have your girlfriend mad at you for like a month." Addie giggled, knowing that was the truth. Poor Rachel loved baseball, but she was just about the worst player in the world, though Addie gave her points for her determination and spunk.

The game ended with Mickey's team losing 5 to 4, fair and square. It was their weekly co-ed baseball game. Just like last week, when Mickey, Alan, Addie, Rachel and the rest of their team creamed their opponents 10 to 2, there were no hard feelings. Both teams had enjoyed the competition and it was the losing team's responsibility to pay for Cokes at Stan's diner after the game. Addie, Alan, Mickey and Rachel sat at a table near the jukebox as Perry Como's smooth voice filtered through the diner.

"So, did you see that Schrik's Hardware is already decorating their windows with Halloween stuff?" asked Mickey with a mouth full of burger.

"What? Already? Its only October first," Rachel complained. "Gosh, I can't believe how time is flying. Before you know it, we'll be graduating. Just think, Addie, in about a year you'll be off at college." Rachel stole a fry from Addie's plate.

Addie looked at Rachel and raised her eyebrows, "Rach, we just started senior year. Don't freak me out by sending me off to New York already."

Rachel reached out and grabbed Addie's hand. "I'm sorry, Addie, but you already know how I feel about your leaving. I'm just excited about graduating. Pop says I can start at the club right after graduation. I'm going to help with the books, and I may even manage the servers...once I get a little more experience."

Addie squeezed Rachel's hand and smiled. "I know, honey, you're going to be an amazing night club manager." Rachel beamed. Mickey rolled his eyes at the two cousins who were smiling at each other over their Cokes. "Okay, girls, quit all the lovey dovey stuff before I gag." This got everyone at the table laughing.

After lunch, Alan and Addie walked back to her apartment, quietly lost in their own thoughts. Once they reached Addie's apartment, Alan sat on the stoop and Addie immediately joined him. "Okay, Alan, what's on your mind? You've been quiet this entire walk back."

Smirking, he said, "How do you do that?" Addie just stared at him waiting for him to continue. "Ok, well everything's changing. I guess I just realized it today when Rachel brought up graduation. We're all going to be starting our new lives in about a year. Adults with responsibilities. It's nuts. Just a few months ago I couldn't wait to graduate. Now...I guess I kinda like things the way they are" Lighting a cigarette, he sat back and took a deep drag.

"I'm trying not to think about it myself." Addie half-smiled as she looked at Alan. "Before Café du Temp and meeting Isabelle, I couldn't wait to graduate and go off to New York for school. Well, now I... I don't know what I want. I'm entirely conflicted." Her voice giving away her sadness.

Alan sat up and turned to look at her, "Hey, I'm sorry, Ad. I'm a dope, I shouldn't have said anything."

"No, it's alright." Addie grabbed his hand and squeezed it, offering a sad smile. "In about a year, Alan," she said, repeating his words. "It doesn't seem like nearly enough time."

That night, despite feeling exhausted, Addie couldn't sleep. Her head was full of thoughts of college in New York, Café du Temp, and most of all Isabelle. How had she gone from being ecstatically excited about attending school in New York to falling in love with a woman from 1911 Paris? The idea of it was so far out of the realm of her understanding that if she hadn't experienced Café du Temp for herself she would not have believed it possible. But by some cosmic action she had experienced it, and now she had no doubt that Café du Temp and its extraordinary existence in her life had everything to do with her future.

CHAPTER 20

"I need to go back again, Alan." Addie sat on the porch swing at Alan's and looked down at her sneakered feet swinging her legs back and forth. She hadn't been back to Café du Temp in nearly two weeks. Not since Isabelle had shocked her by taking her to her home in Paris.

As much as Addie believed that Café du Temp was indeed everything that Isabelle revealed to her, she still struggled with what it meant for her and for her future. Over the past two weeks she wrestled with her feelings. Should she go to Café du Temp, be with Isabelle and risk a broken heart when the inevitable happens or should she return to her normal pre-Café du Temp world? Just when she had thought she had come to a firm decision, she'd change her mind. Each day that passed held the same gut-wrenching uncertainty, but yesterday, after another fitful sleepless night, a definitive clarity had emerged. Isabelle and Café du Temp where now a part of her life for a reason. She had to go back to discover what that reason is.

Sitting on the porch step cleaning dried mud out of his track shoes, Alan looked up at Addie. "When are you thinking of going? I can probably get Frank's car and pick you up."

Addie looked down at Alan and smiled. "I know you can, but I don't want you to have to change your plans. I'm going tomorrow. I'll go alone, and I can always have Peter call me a cab. Thanks though. That's very thoughtful, but it's enough that you're covering for me with Mickey and Rachel."

Alan looked at Addie and decided he needed to say what was on his mind. He knew there'd be a chance that she would be upset, but felt he had no choice. Standing up from his spot on the porch step he moved to sit next to her on the swing, "Ad, I know you probably know this, but I gotta say it." Addie looked at Alan. Seeing that he looked uneasy, she sighed and braced herself for what he was about to say.

"It's an impossible situation. You do realize that, right? I don't know how this shit happens, this time travel stuff, but I believe it. I believe Café du Temp is everything Peter and Isabelle say it is. But Ad, how you feel about Isabelle, it can't work. Don't you see that? Honey, she's from a different world, a different time." Huffing out a frustrated breath, he said, "I don't want to see you hurt, Addie, and following through with this is going to get you hurt."

Despite his soft voice and careful delivery, his words were still difficult for Addie to hear. She knew what he said was most certainly true, but her heart still held out hope that another outcome was possible. Every night since her inconceivable trip to Paris, she could think of nothing but Isabelle. She missed her voice, her smile, and her touch. Their seemingly accidental meeting at Café du Temp had to be more than random; it had to mean something. She was certain of it.

Addie looked up at Alan's concerned face, and feeling the emotion and uncertainty of her situation overwhelm her, she felt the tears spilling from her eyes. Alan immediately reached out to put his arms tightly around her.

"Ad, don't cry. I'm sorry. I didn't mean to upset you."

Addie threw her arms around Alan and laid her head on his shoulder, quietly sobbing. "No, it's okay, Alan," she said, shaking her head to let him know it wasn't his fault. "I know what you're saying is likely the truth. I guess hearing it from someone else just...well, it just made it more real." Sitting up and wiping her eyes, she felt marginally better. "Alan, despite what we know, I still need to go back. I can't allow my fear of being heartbroken stop me from learning why Isabelle and Café du Temp are now part of my life."

Alan looked at Addie with wonder, "I have to give you credit, Ad. I don't know if I could do what you're doing. I'm not in love, but even so, I'm still not ready to take the step of looking for my purpose. I mean... why *I am* part of Café du Temp. I suppose we all move forward at our own pace, and I guess I'm just not ready yet. Does that make sense?"

Addie wiped her tears and sighed. "Yeah, it does. I think when you're ready to find out why you are part of that world, you'll move forward. And I promise you, when it's your turn, I'll be here for you too."

Addie's taxi pulled up to the area on LaSalle Street where the door normally stood, and she prayed that it was still there. She recalled one evening at Café du Temp, not too long ago, where she had talked with a young woman named Emilia. Emilia had said that sometimes the door wasn't where it had always been, that it sometimes vanished. This frightened Addie because she didn't doubt for a minute that this was possible. Nothing regarding this place seemed impossible, especially after her experience traveling to Isabelle's Paris. Curious, Addie had then asked Emilia how she could know such a thing. Emilia said that a friend had discovered whatever he was meant to, that he knew instinctively where his path needed to lead, and after that, he could never find the door again.

She had asked Emilia how she could possibly know this if she had never seen him again after he had left Café du Temp? Emilia's cryptic response was that he had left her a message in a painting he had created and that was how she knew he had succeeded. The painting was now on display in the Metropolitan Museum of Art in New York. Addie, taken back, vowed one day to go see the painting by this now famous painter. She wisely decided not to ask any more questions for fear of fainting from hearing the answers.

Addie breathed a sigh of relief when she saw the now familiar black door. She had been more than a little unnerved by her recollection of that specific conversation with Emilia and had feared that the door wouldn't be there. Shaking off her nervousness, she paid the cabdriver and calmly exited the cab. She shrugged as she observed the always wet pavement and dark corners. With determination in her step, she walked to the door and rapped her knuckles purposefully. Her heart raced at the thought of seeing Isabelle again.

"Good evening, Miss Kahlo. Your usual table?" Addie smiled at Alex as he led her through the ornate hall. "Yes, Alex, that would be lovely, thank you." Alex returned her smile and led Addie through to her table near the bar. She was not at her table more than a few minutes when she sensed Isabelle's presence.

Addie felt such a wave of relief crash over her that she had to close her eyes and calm her racing heart. "Isabelle," she breathed out quietly, "will you join me?" Addie stood and gestured to the chair opposite her. She immediately noted that Isabelle appeared unsettled and not her usual assured teasing self. Addie realized that Isabelle was cautiously watching her, hesitating for a brief moment before she slowly moved to sit. Addie felt Isabelle's hesitation like a slap. But what had she expected? She knew that she needed to explain her disappearance over the past two weeks; she owed Issie an explanation. She was suddenly more concerned than nervous, and the look of anxiety and confusion in Isabelle's eyes moved her to speak.

Addie reached for Isabelle's hand and gently enfolded it in her own. Isabelle did not pull away, filling Addie with relief. Isabelle closed her eyes and shook her head slightly. When she opened her eyes and looked up at Addie her eyes held a gentleness and sadness that took Addie's breath away. "I wasn't sure...," Isabelle cleared her throat. "It has been nearly two weeks. I thought...I thought you perhaps changed your mind. I thought you might not come back."

Addie pursed her lips, lowered her head and nodded. "I'm sorry, Isabelle. I'm so very sorry. I know that my actions have been selfish. I wanted to come back." Addie's eyes were sincere as she looked at Isabelle. Her emotions suddenly overwhelmed her, and she breathed in deeply. "I...it has been difficult for me to come to terms with everything that has happened. I hadn't realized how profoundly affected I would be by discovering that you live in Paris twenty-three years before I was even born. I needed some time alone to try and understand why I'm now a part of this." Addie looked around to emphasize Café du Temp.

"I'm sorry that I...." Addie sighed and gently smiled at Isabelle. "In the end, I realized I had to come back, Iss, because you're here. Because you have quickly become important to me. It's as simple as that. I've missed you."

Isabelle closed her eyes, exhaled with relief, and slowly nodded. When she looked at Addie, she saw a sincere and powerful truthfulness in her eyes. Addie had missed her, and even though they hadn't said it aloud to each other, Isabelle knew that Addie was in love with her. She could see it in every part of her regard for Isabelle and in the adorable crooked half-smile that was all Addie. Isabelle mentally shook herself, a small smile creasing her lips. She held tightly to Addie's hand and simply beheld her beautiful girl. Her heart was filled with relief and joy that Addie had come back, that she had made her own decision to return. Isabelle wasn't always so certain about decisions she herself had made. She knew that on more than a few occasions her choices were questionable, but not this, not her feelings for Addie Kahlo. No, she could not be more certain that she was in love with her. Addie had very quickly become the most important person in the world to her. She had sworn to the heavens above that if Addie would have her, she would love and cherish her with all her heart, and that she would be there for her always, supporting her and helping her achieve her dreams and goals.

"I'm so happy that you've come back," Isabelle whispered, needing to touch her. She gently caressed Addie's cheek. Addie looked deeply into Isabelle's eyes and nodded, her own heart pounding in her chest at the realization that Isabelle's feelings mirrored her own. "Addie, will you come with me now?" Isabelle asked, a slight creasing of her brow the only clue to her nervousness. Addie smiled and her eyes shown a brilliant hazel. "Yes, Iss, I'd like that very much."

Isabelle walked arm in arm with Addie through the streets of 1911 Paris. It was only Addie's second time there. and her admiration for the beautiful city was still very new. She gazed around as a child would at a carnival, filled with excitement and wonder. Isabelle couldn't help but be taken with Addie's delight. She loved the look of astonishment and joy on Addie's beautiful face. Addie was naturally inquisitive, and her thirst for everything and anything about Paris filled Isabelle's heart. She enthusiastically answered all of Addie's questions as they walked through the cobblestone streets toward her grandmother's apartments.

"Would you like some tea? It's rather chilly in here, don't you think?" Isabelle rubbed her arms as she walked over to the fireplace. "I can light a fire. Are you hungry? I can have some canapes made for us." Addie sat, her legs crossed Indian-style, in one of Isabelle's grandmother's very comfortable chairs, watching Isabelle. She noticed for the first time that Isabelle appeared nervous. Thinking her nervousness was adorable, Addie looked at Isabelle and reached out her hand. "Issie, can you stop pacing and sit with me please?"

Isabelle turned and stared at Addie for a moment, rolling her eyes at herself. She smiled shyly, and, taking Addie's offered hand, she walked the short distance to sit next to her. Addie uncrossed her legs to make room for Isabelle on the large chair and turned toward her as she sat down. "Issie," Addie smiled and gently kissed her palm. "Honey, why are you so nervous? It's only me, Addie, the overly inquisitive American sitting here in your grandmother's humongous parlor." Addie giggled when Isabelle huffed out a breath and laughed.

"Oh Addie," Isabelle said as she reached up and brushed a lock of hair off Addie's forehead. "I'm just so happy you're here," She placed her arms around Addie and squeezed her tightly. Addie hugged her just as fiercely, and then, pulling back slightly, she touched Isabelle's lips gently with her thumb, watching as Isabelle's pupils grew darker. Unable to resist the urge, she leaned in and kissed Isabelle softly on her mouth. The sweetness of their kiss filled Addie with desire, and she moaned low in her throat as Isabelle deepened the kiss. She could feel Isabelle's heartbeat and hear her own soft moans. Pulling back from their kiss, she held tight to Isabelle, placing her head on Isabelle's shoulder, and sighed.

Holding Addie in her arms, Isabelle couldn't help the smile that she knew graced her face. Pulling back slightly, she gazed at Addie, enchanted, her heart filled with so much love she feared it might burst. "You know, darling," she said as she placed a wayward auburn curl behind Addie's ear, "it is rather chilly in here. What do you say we have a fire and a cup of tea?"

Once the fire blazed in the hearth and the tea was served, the room felt cozy and warm. "Addie?"

"Hmm?" Addie had her eyes closed and was snuggled comfortably with her head in Isabelle's lap while Isabelle soothingly ran her fingers through her hair.

"I think we should talk, don't you?" Addie looked up at Isabelle, her eyes wide with anticipation, and nodded. She reluctantly sat up from her comfortable position on Isabelle's lap. "How about a sherry," Isabelle said. "Do you enjoy sherry?" Addie stood up and stretched her 5'8" frame.

"I don't know. I've never had it before. Is it sweet? I like sweet," she said with a wink.

Isabelle shook her head and laughed. "You know, darling, you're not as shy as I initially pegged you as."

Addie chuckled as she reached up for the offered glass. "Issie? How tall are you?"

Isabelle turned to Addie curious as to why she asked. "I'm a bit over 180 centimeters, and with heels, phew, likely taller than any other woman in Paris!"

Addie grinned, "Hmm...that's about 5'11". Well, I think you look like a goddess, a tall, strikingly beautiful goddess." Isabelle turned to Addie. Smiling, and without so much as a word, she took Addie's sherry and gently set both of their drinks on the side table. Turning, she reached for Addie. Pulling her into her arms, she kissed Addie deeply, their tongues swirling and teasing. Addie was breathless with desire as she pulled Isabelle close. She moved her mouth down Isabelle's jaw, kissing the smooth soft skin of her throat. She couldn't get enough of her. Making her way to Isabelle's mouth again, she shivered as her tongue sought Isabelle's, the kiss deepening as both women felt the unmistakable power of their passion for each other.

"Addie," Isabelle whispered breathlessly next to Addie's ear, "darling, I know we must talk about what is happening, but all I want to do right now is make love to you. Will you sweetheart? Will you allow me to make love to you?" Addie's heart was pounding fiercely as she felt an overwhelming yearning for this beautiful woman in every cell of her body. Isabelle moved her mouth slowly to Addie's neck, placing soft wet kisses down her throat to the top of her breastbone. Addie released a soft groan as Isabelle seductively opened the top buttons of Addie's dress while slowly moving her head lower to kiss the smooth firm breasts that she had so skillfully exposed. Addie gasped at the delicious sensation of soft kisses and the gentle but firm hands caressing her. She moaned, pulling herself closer to Isabelle when she felt the sweet sensation and throbbing pressure of her need grow between her legs.

"Issie." Addie could barely catch her breath. "Issie...I've never..." Isabelle lifted her head and looked lovingly at Addie. She saw the desire in Addie's eyes and something more. She saw a sweet shyness, and she saw love. Gently, Isabelle took Addie's hand and kissed her palm. She heard Addie whisper, "Yes...I want to be with you, more than anything." Isabelle briefly closed her eyes, emotion as well as uninhibited desire clutching at her heart. She knew that she was in love with this beautiful young woman. Still gently holding Addie's hand, she slowly led her upstairs to her room.

Isabelle's room was like Isabelle, feminine, elegant, and beautiful. Tall, ornate leaded- glass doors were open to a long balcony as a soft breeze billowed the delicate white curtains that hid the room from the outside streets. The breeze brought a welcome reprieve to Addie's overheated skin. Faint sounds of music from a nearby restaurant could be heard just above the sound of the city. Isabelle closed the door behind them and slowly reached for Addie, gently kissing her hair, her lips, and her cheeks. She led Addie to the large ornate bed, where Addie slowly seated herself. Isabelle watched Addie closely. Bending to her knees in front of her, she held her hands and gently kissed them as she looked up at her. She carefully removed Addie's shoes and then, unhooking her stockings from her garter, she slowly removed them. Isabelle stood and unhurriedly lifted Addie to a standing position, and with the tenderest of movements cupped Addie's face and leaned in and kissed her deeply. Addie's entire body reacted, a sort of electric shock went through her, and she clung to Isabelle, overwhelmed with the feel of her.

"Addie, is this alright, darling?" Isabelle whispered. "Please tell me if I move too quickly or if...you want to stop, or if I do something you don't like. I want you to be absolutely comfortable." Addie quietly laughed, and despite her nervousness, she pulled back to look at Isabelle, who to Addie's utter surprise, looked more terrified than Addie herself felt.

"Issie, I know...I know this is my first time, but I want this. I want this with you, and honestly I am so very ok with not being comfortable." Addie's heart was beating so loudly that she was certain Isabelle could hear it. Isabelle nodded and grinned, quite pleased with Addie's steadfast determination.

Isabelle's desire was immediate. The look in Addie's eyes washed away any trepidation that she was moving too quickly. This felt right, this felt so very right. Isabelle caressed Addie's cheek and leaned in for another passionate kiss. She slowly began to undo the unopened buttons of Addie's dress. Once undone, she slipped her warm hands under the material and removed the dress, allowing it to fall to the floor. Then, just as slowly, she undid the buttons of her own dress and allowed it to fall at her feet. Stepping out of it, she reached over and helped Addie out of her slip, her gentle eyes never leaving Addie. Slowly and meticulously she took Addie in, mesmerized by her youthful beauty, her smooth honey colored skin clothed in nothing but a bra and panties.

Isabelle touched her own heart with a trembling hand as she watched Addie with eyes full of desire and love.

Addie had never been undressed by anyone before, and she found it to be overwhelmingly titillating. It was all she could do to keep her breathing in check as she watched Isabelle's slow seductive dance. When they were both completely undressed, Addie's breath hitched as her own eyes took in Isabelle's naked body. Addie thought Isabelle was the most beautiful person she had ever seen. The look of desire in Isabelle's stare was so arousing it nearly brought Addie to her knees. As if in a dream, Addie felt rather than saw Isabelle's hand guiding her down onto the large ornate bed. She watched as Isabelle slowly straddled her, her eyes never leaving Addie's. Lowering herself carefully on top of Addie she held her close. Both women groaned deeply at the contact of their bodies. The feel of this beautiful woman, her smooth heated skin, soft curvy hips and firm breasts was everything Addie had envisioned. Her heart pounded, not only with desire but also with an unbelievable tenderness and love. Addie wrapped one long leg around Isabelle's hip as they explored each other's body with soft caresses and gentle kisses.

Addie, fueled by the love she felt for this woman and the unbelievable feel of her body pressed against her own, moved through their foreplay with no fear or shyness. Feeling the pull of desire reach her core, she allowed herself to move without a thought to her inexperience; she simply allowed her body to follow its natural desires.

"Addie, my love, tell me, is this alright?" Isabelle asked breathlessly as she moved her soft demanding lips to Addie's breasts, tenderly licking and sucking her hardened nipples as her hands moved freely to caress Addie's hips and thighs.

"Oh god Iss, yes, yes," Addie whispered breathlessly as she arched her back and moaned. Shock waves coursed through her body at the delicious sensation of Isabelle's gentle sucking. Isabelle slowly and deliberately moved her palm down the length of Addie's long smooth body to the flat plain of her stomach, kneading her flesh with her fingers as she lowered her hand toward Addie's soft curls. "Oh god," groaned Isabelle when she felt the slick wetness of Addie's desire between her legs. "You're so wet, so very wet." Isabelle's heart pounded as the trembling of her own body made her aware of her own building excitement. She could hardly believe that she felt herself close to climax. She told herself that she needed to control her own release as she wanted this first time for Addie to be all about her pleasure.

Despite her own passion threatening to overtake her, Isabelle was mesmerized by the feel of her beautiful new love. Pulling herself from her persistent attention to Addie's erect nipples, she sensuously kissed along Addie's body until she reached her mouth once again. Whispering words of adoration, she kissed her deeply. Moaning with desire when she felt Addie's tongue, as desperate as her own, she held tight as Addie's legs moved sensuously over her thighs and backside. Without any thought other than to please her lover, Isabelle moved eager fingers to the velvet smooth folds of Addie's sex. With a gentle touch to Addie's soaked clit, she marveled in the feel and scent of her as she slowly drew small circles with her fingertips. Feeling the wetness coat her fingers, she sighed as Addie released a deep groan of pleasure while gripping Isabelle's strong back.

Isabelle could sense that Addie was close to her release, and the sounds of her arousal encouraged Isabelle, as well as exciting her. When she felt Addie was ready, she held her close and slowly entered her, tenderly pushing her way into the depth of Addie's warm wetness, and curling her fingers, she felt Addie's sex tighten around her. Suddenly, Addie let out a loud gasp. Pumping her hips, she groaned loudly, bringing her body closer to Isabelle. "Ohhhhh god! Oh god! Issie, deeper, please go deeper!"

The fevered cries of Addie's excitement sent Isabelle to heights of bliss that she didn't think possible, and she entered Addie with the full force of her fingers. As she held tightly to Addie, she rocked their bodies, thrusting in and out, all the while whispering words of adoration and love. At the feel of Addie clamping herself around her fingers, Isabelle lifted her head. Bringing their mouths together, she kissed Addie passionately. "Come for me my love, don't hold back, let yourself feel it," she whispered in Addie's ear as she lavished attention on Addie's throbbing sex.

Suddenly Addie's head flew back, and she released a loud fevered groan as her body went taut. "Ohh! Oh, god!!!" She shook in Isabelle's arms as her orgasm overtook her. Feeling her own impending release seconds away, Isabelle quickly but gently reached for Addie's hand and guided it to her own throbbing sex. Kissing Addie deeply, she climaxed violently as Addie entered her, and they held each other in a tight embrace.

Addie lay in Isabelle's arms; one hand lay gently on her hip, the other playing with her hair. Entranced by the feel of Isabelle's smooth naked body, she gazed up into her beautiful soft eyes. She couldn't stop looking at her; she was stunning, flushed from their lovemaking, disheveled golden hair framing her face, soft amber eyes shining with mischief and satisfaction. Addie felt like she was the luckiest woman in the world. So, this is what it feels like to make love to the person you love, she thought to herself. Now I get it. Now I understand.

"Issie."

"Yes, baby?"

"Did I... was I ...did I please you?" Addie looked up at Isabelle, eyes bright with a mixture of shyness and hope. Isabelle could not help but find Addie's gaze adorable. She pulled her closer, and lifting her chin, gently kissed her lips.

"Oh, my darling, you have totally overtaken my senses. I am ecstatic and sated. You, my young beauty, are amazing, thrilling, sweet, charming, and so very beautiful," she said as she kissed Addie sweetly on her lips.

Addie giggled softly with relief, blushed, and then blew out a long breath. Cuddling close she looked at Isabelle. "I was crazy nervous, Iss. But gosh, I... well..." Falling back on the bed, she looked up at Isabelle, and an almost serious whisper tinged her voice as she looked deep into Isabelle's eyes. "I have never felt anything so wonderful. I knew it would be wonderful because it was...you." A sweet shy smile grazed her lips as she reached out and caressed Isabelle's cheek.

Isabelle's breath caught, and there was so much love for her reflected in Addie's eyes that she felt her heart swell with happiness. Then, to her astonishment and embarrassment, she began to tear up with emotion, releasing a soft cry.

"Iss," Addie raised herself on her elbows immediately. "Issie, what's wrong? Did I say something to upset you?" Addie's brow furrowed with concern as she reached to gently wipe the tears from Isabelle's face. Isabelle released a deep breath and shook her head. "Good god, I can't believe this. Bloody hell," she said as she sniffled and sheepishly smiled at Addie. "Darling, do you understand that I am supposed to be the experienced one? The more knowledgeable older lover who guides you through your first sexual experience? Yet here I am blubbering like an infant because I am so besotted with you. I positively adore you!" Isabelle shook her head, unbelieving that she was still tearing up and couldn't seem to stop while Addie smiled broadly and wrapped her arms around Isabelle, completely and utterly smitten.

"Issie?"

"Yes, my love?"

Isabelle looked down at Addie whose head lay on her chest and whose hand was lightly caressing her stomach. The emotion of a few moments ago seemingly overwhelming her, she tried to calm herself by breathing deeply. "You are so very beautiful, Iss, so amazingly kind. I want to know everything about you...I mean...I want to know you, and I want you to know me." Looking up at her with a soft hopeful gaze, Addie reached for Isabelle's hand. Then, blushing deeply, she slowly closed her eyes and buried her head in the comfort of Isabelle's warm neck. "Oh god," she sighed, "I sound like a kid, don't I? A naïve smitten kid." After a moment she lifted her gaze back to Isabelle. "It's just that, gosh, I wish I had the words."

Wrapping her arms around Addie, Isabelle breathed in her scent and gently kissed her forehead. "Shh, it's fine. I understand what you're feeling, I do." Sitting up suddenly and looking at Isabelle, Addie's eyes filled with emotion. She felt certain and strong, more certain then she had ever been. "Isabelle, I want to tell you...I need to tell you, I'm in love with you. I'm so in love with you." Addie continued to watch Isabelle for what felt to her like an eternity but was, in actuality, less than a moment.

Isabelle slowly closed her eyes. The tears that she was finally able to stop a few minutes before, spilled again. She brought her hand to her mouth, covering a soft sob. Opening her eyes, she nodded and looked at Addie with deep love. "Yes Addie, I'm in love with you too. I love you so very much."

⸙

Addie opened her eyes to darkness; the soft white curtains were still as no breeze entered Isabelle's room. As she lay content in Isabelle's sleeping

133

arms, she thought about their declaration to each other. She could hardly believe it. Isabelle loved her as she loved Isabelle. She couldn't stop smiling. After their conversation, they fell back into bed, making love for hours. She swooned with the memory of how she had brought Isabelle to orgasm numerous times and how she herself had turned out to be more sexual than she could have ever imagined.

"Are you awake, baby?" Isabelle whispered as she stirred and yawned, tightening her arms around Addie lovingly.

"Yes," Addie responded, burrowing her face into Isabelle's neck, "and I know I need to be leaving soon, but I don't want to go."

Isabelle heard the disappointment in Addie's voice and acknowledged that she felt the same. "I know, baby, I don't want you to leave either, but we both know you must."

Addie sighed, "I know, Iss, but when will we see each other again? I don't know if I can stand to be apart from you for too long. Is that wrong? Am I being too clingy?" Addie suddenly felt she was being too clingy.

Isabelle chuckled softly and hugged her, "No, darling, you are not being clingy." As she continued to chuckle an idea suddenly popped into her head. "Addie, today is Wednesday is it not? I believe your Wednesday is the same as my Wednesday, true?"

Addie thought for a moment and agreed. "Yes, isn't that funny, Iss. We have the same days, but different years...I wonder why that is?"

"I don't know, darling." Lifting an eyebrow, Isabelle bit her lip in contemplation. "There is so much about Café du Temp that is a mystery. I often wonder if we will ever know more than what it allows us to know." Gazing at Addie introspectively, she sighed. "Perhaps how it's mysteries intertwine in our lives is all we are meant to know." Isabelle smiled at her own enigmatic thoughts, as if they were silly ramblings. "What do you think, Addie, do you think I'm being too cryptic?"

"God no, Iss. I happen to agree with you. I believe we all experience *our own* Café du Temp. I mean, our own individual journey. Each time I enter its doors I feel as if each interaction, each detail of my experience is somehow part of my reason for being there. Does that make sense?" Isabelle watched her attentively and drew her brows together in thought.

"Yes. Yes, Addie, it makes perfect sense. I believe you've described it brilliantly!" She said excitedly, "We each have our own path, our own journey. Such as you coming here to my Paris. Do you see, darling? This," Isabelle continued, as she waved her arm gesturing the expanse of their surroundings, "is part of *your* journey." Addie smiled brightly as she kissed Isabelle's cheek, letting herself hope that they were right and that their journey would be traveled together.

CHAPTER 21

The air was heavy with humidity for so late in the day. Addie briefly wondered if she should have worn her sleeveless dress instead of the long-sleeved blouse and long slacks she had thrown on. She and Alan were walking toward the park to meet with Rachel and Mickey. The boys had a flag football game scheduled with some guys from a rival school, and she was meeting Rachel at the park to cheer on Alan's and Mickey's team. As they walked, there was an easy silence between them, Alan tossing a football in the air and Addie daydreaming about yesterday evening with Isabelle. She couldn't keep the smile from her lips as she reran their day together in her mind.

After a fabulous afternoon of making love, they had lain in bed nibbling on fresh fruit and cheese while they talked, each open and sharing everything from their childhood memories to their dreams of writing. Addie had never been so open with anyone, but it was so easy with Isabelle, as her eager attentiveness and sincere interest spurred Addie on. In turn, Isabelle was just as giving. Addie was fascinated by Isabelle's childhood in London. She smiled as she had pictured a beautiful ten-year-old Isabelle playing soldiers with her cousins in her family's gardens.

They had even touched on their feelings about what Café du Temp meant to their future. Their tentative words about its presence in their lives were a revelation that they had both silently agreed to put on the shelf, for now.

Later, after another hour of lovemaking, Isabelle had smiled broadly when she took Addie in her arms and asked her if she would accompany her to a party the following Saturday. Addie couldn't contain her excitement. She had thrown herself into Isabelle's arms and ended up toppling them off the bed onto the rug. They had laughed so hard that it took Addie a

136

good ten minutes to get up off the floor. Addie shook her head and smiled at the memory.

"Alan, Isabelle invited me to a party this coming Saturday." Alan stopped tossing his football and looked at Addie. "A party? What kind of party?"

"I don't really know, other than it's dressy, so I'm assuming it's like a cocktail party." Addie suddenly laughed out loud. "I was so excited about her inviting me that I didn't think to ask what sort of party it is. God, I'm hopeless." Addie beamed at Alan, happy to be able to share her excitement with him.

"Hmm," Alan mused, rubbing his chin, "So, do you think that you and Isabelle would want a handsome debonair man-about-town to escort you?"

Addie laughed good naturedly at Alan's attempt at tagging along, "Hmm. Why, do you know one?" Addie said, smiling at his silliness. They both chuckled as they continued their walk to the park.

"So, Ad, I'm actually going to Café du Temp tomorrow night. Peter mentioned the last time I was there that he would kinda like it if I came by this week. Are you up for joining me?"

Addie turned and squinted at Alan as the sun hit her eyes. "I'd love to, but Rachel and I are going shopping tomorrow to look for those dresses for the fall dance and then grab dinner. I really haven't spent much time with her, and I can tell she's excited about the two of us going out and having some girl time."

Alan bent close to Addie's ear, and teasingly said, "Really? Well, you already shared with me that you had plenty of girl time last night."

Addie screamed, and laughing, slapped at Alan's shoulder. "Alan! Oh my god, you're embarrassing me. Why did I even say anything to you?!" She laughed and shook her head.

Addie reached out and grabbed Alan's hand, holding it loosely in her own, smiling happily at him as they walked. She didn't know what she'd do if she didn't have Alan to talk with. She was grateful to have his friendship. He turned and smiled at her as they continued their walk.

"I'm happy, Alan." A sweet smile graced her face as she beamed at him. "I can hardly believe that Isabelle feels the same for me as I feel for her. She told me she loves me. Alan, that beautiful amazing woman loves *me*, Addie Kahlo. I think I must be the luckiest woman in the world."

Turning to Alan, her happiness quickly turned to concern. Seeing his stoic expression, she frowned. Her concern making her defensive, she asked, "What are you thinking, Alan? Tell me. You haven't said a word for a full five minutes. I know you, and I know when you have something to say. So please just spit it out."

Tossing his football in the air, Alan sighed, "Addie, come on."

"Come on what, Alan? Do you think we're wrong, that we're being naïve? Tell me, do you think Issie and I are making a mistake? Believe me," she breathed out, attempting to reign in her defensiveness, "we are both painfully aware that we come from different worlds, and if we are to have a future together, we must make some decisions."

Alan looked at Addie, shocked and not quite believing what he had just heard her say. "A future together? Addie, do you hear yourself? You can't possibly believe... I mean...well that this will work. Honey, you are from two different worlds! You hardly know each other. Are you so sure that this isn't more than a fling?"

Addie furrowed her brow and looked at her friend, surprise obvious in her expression, "A fling? Is that all you think this is?" she said, hurt by his brash words, "I thought you understood. I told you that I love her, and I know she loves me!" Addie started to quickly walk away, hurt and angry at Alan's words.

Alan immediately reached for her, wanting to explain himself. "Addie, wait. Please don't go. I'm sorry. I didn't mean that the way it came out." Addie felt tears sting her eyes. She couldn't help the hurt she was feeling, but she was determined not to cry. "Shit, Ad, I'm sorry. Please don't cry."

Addie wiped at her eyes. "I'm not crying, dammit! Why are you being such a jerk, anyway?" Addie turned toward Alan, obvious hurt in her eyes. "What Isabelle and I have, what we feel for each other is not temporary, Alan. We didn't set out to fall in love, but we did. I cannot believe that what we feel is not real. I won't believe that, not ever." Addie stood rigid and took a deep breath, feeling suddenly shaky as she wrapped her arms around herself and tried to calm her anger and hurt feelings.

Alan felt awful for what he had just said. His response was a kneejerk reaction to her words. He never wanted to hurt Addie, but knew he couldn't just stand by and watch her heart be broken. He believed that any future she wanted with Isabelle would be impossible. He was worried for her and for the pain this relationship with Isabelle would eventually cause her. He bent down, picked up a stone and tossed it as he contemplated what he would say next. He looked at her seriously. "I'm so sorry, Addie. You know that I love you. I didn't mean for my clumsy words to hurt you. The thing is, I *do* believe you. I do believe that you and Isabelle are in love. But, as your friend, I need to be the one to say, be careful, think hard about what you want and what you are willing to give up. This is a perfect scenario to get hurt and hurt bad."

Addie frowned at the words Alan just uttered. "Hurt? Do you think Isabelle would knowingly hurt me? Because I trust her and..."

"No, I don't think that she would knowingly hurt you, Addie. But I think, in the end, she will. She'll break your heart, and you might just break hers too. Listen to me." Alan put his hands on her shoulders and looked at her intently. "You are both from different worlds, *literally from different worlds*. I know you. You won't leave your world, and if Isabelle is the person I think she is, she won't leave hers either. Honey, there is no future in that. I'm sorry."

Addie shallowed the lump in her throat and looked up at Alan solemnly. "I think I want to go home, Alan, if you don't mind. Tell Rach I'll see her at the apartment."

Alan reached for Addie's hand, "Let me walk back with you, Ad. The guys won't mind if I'm a few minutes late." She looked up at him and nodded.

They walked silently back toward Addie's apartment, each thinking their own thoughts. She knew that what Alan said about being hurt was an all-too-real possibility. But she was so in love with Isabelle that she had completely avoided discussing it with her at any great length. It seemed every time they attempted to talk about their different worlds, they fell into each other's arms. She knew they were both avoiding a discussion because the idea of being apart was too painful to think about.

A feeling of dread made itself known in Addie's stomach, and she wished at that moment that she could be with Isabelle. She wanted to hold her and feel that strength of their love. She needed that reassurance so desperately right now. Turning to look at Alan walking next to her, she saw that he looked miserable. A tenderness came over her, and she reached for his hand. Thinking suddenly about his and Peter's situation, she realized she had never asked him how he was coping with the strangeness of being with someone from a different world. Maybe he was confused too, and just as afraid as she was. She suddenly felt selfish because she never asked how he was dealing with it all.

"Alan, what about you? I know I don't ask, but... are you okay? Are you being careful with your heart?" Addie's look was sincere, and she wanted to be there for Alan as he had always been for her.

A small smile creased his lips. "Well, it's a bit different for me, Ad. I, well...I'm not in love with Peter, and I know he's not in love with me. We like each other, and for us that's enough right now. You know, Addie, I can accept that there is a reason why we, you and I, are part of Café du Temp. I mean, finding out that our future was off-course somehow and that destiny stepped in to set us on the right track has opened my eyes to never outright denying the seemingly impossible. I believe that everything that is happening to us is real and that it means something. It means something to our future."

Looking at Addie now, he smiled sheepishly. "I should have said that before jumping all over your case about you and Isabelle." Addie looped her arm in Alan's and held it closer as they continued on their walk. "I can't pretend I know the answers, Ad. I don't even think Peter knows. I think he is simply following his own road just like the rest of us. But I am secure in my belief that destiny will guide us toward the path that we are meant to follow. I have to believe that, because otherwise, why are we part of this curious world of Café du Temp?"

Addie smiled, turned to Isabelle, and sighed dramatically. "There are too many dresses to choose from, Issie." When you suggested that I wear one of your dresses to the party I had no idea you were a clothes horse." Addie stood barefoot in her slip in front of Isabelle's wardrobe, feeling overwhelmed. "I don't know what to choose, Issie. You pick something, please. Though honestly, I'm not sure any of these will fit me, since you're taller." Addie turned and smiled at Isabelle who was leaning against the door frame, watching her. Isabelle slowly walked over to where Addie stood and wrapped her arms around her waist.

"Whatever you choose, darling, will be stunning on you. As a matter of fact, I venture you wouldn't need to wear anything other than the slip you have on now, and you will be the most beautiful woman at the party."

Addie rolled her eyes to the ceiling and laughed. "Are you flirting with me, Miss Androsko?" she asked. "Cuz right now, I need your good fashion sense more than your adoration."

Isabelle smiled playfully and winked. "Yes, love, I think I am." They both laughed. Addie turned in Isabelle's arms so that she was facing her and placed a soft lingering kiss on Isabelle's lips. "Hmm, that's nice," Isabelle whispered as she responded to Addie's kiss and then moved her mouth down Addie's sensitive neck.

"Umm," sighed Addie as she moved more securely in Isabelle's arms, savoring the delicious feel of Isabelle's soft lips on her throat. She was starting to feel that all too familiar sensation throughout her body whenever Isabelle paid her extra attention.

"You smell like sunshine," Isabelle whispered. She was ecstatically happy; she could not get enough of her beautiful girl.

Reluctantly pulling back from Isabelle's kisses, Addie sighed, nervous about what she would wear to the party. She wanted to look her best and make Isabelle proud. "Issie," she pleaded, "please pick something out for me. I have no clue what I should be wearing. It's all different to me, and I want to look my best for you."

Isabelle noted that Addie did look a bit panicked at the prospect of having to choose an outfit from her extensive wardrobe. Unwrapping her arms from around Addie, she walked over and pulled a large box from a shelf. "Well, my love, as this party is your first adventure in Paris, I think it calls for something all your own." Addie looked curiously at the box, wrapped with a red bow, that Isabelle had laid on the bed. Addie looked at Isabelle questioningly. "For me?" Isabelle encircled Addie's waist with her arms, once again placing a soft kiss on her forehead. "Yes, my beautiful girl, for you."

Addie reached up and caressed Isabelle's smooth cheek. "Oh Iss, you always make me feel so special. You didn't need to buy me anything, honey. I'm sure any of your beautiful dresses would be fine." Addie hugged her tightly. "Thank you, baby," she whispered in Isabelle's ear. Lifting an eyebrow, she grinned mischievously. "You know, Iss, I wouldn't say the party this evening is my first-ever adventure with you." Addie smiled shyly at Isabelle and blushed, a bit embarrassed by her own flirting.

Isabelle looked absolutely shocked at Addie's flirting and laughed, gently shaking her head. Looking down into Addie's sparkling eyes, she spoke softly with a seriousness that made Addie's heart pound. "Addie, please know that my heart, my mind and my body adore you; my love for you is genuine. I'm so happy that we have found each other."

Reaching up, Addie gently placed her hand on Isabelle's cheek and leaned in, kissing her deeply. After a moment, Isabelle sighed and moved her own hands through Addie's silky hair as she once again moved to place gentle kisses down Addie's throat. Addie closed her eyes, letting the amazing sensations of Isabelle's touch run through her body. "Isssssssie... don't you want me to open my present?" Addie could barely speak, the excitement she was feeling at the touch of Isabelle's lips was all she could focus on. "Later, my love. Right now, I have something else in mind," Isabelle replied.

The late afternoon sun cast long shadows across the floor as they lay in bed, naked, and satisfied after a passionate afternoon of lovemaking. Addie lay comfortably with her head on Isabelle's chest, her eyes closed and her hand making small circles on Isabelle's flat belly. A strong breeze blew the white curtains, making them appear as if they were dancing to the music from the streets of Paris, two floors below.

"Issie?"

"Hmm?"

"I love you."

Isabelle lifted her head off the pillow and gently kissed the top of Addie's head, holding her lips still for a moment, breathing in the scent of her. "I love you too, sweetheart," she whispered into Addie's hair.

"Iss?"

"Yes love?"

"I'm so happy being with you. I've never felt like this before. You know, my cousin Rachel, who is also my best friend, is in love. She and Mickey have been together since sophomore year. She always looks so happy, and I just didn't get it. I mean, I have never felt like that before for a boy, so I didn't understand, and I really wanted too. But now, now I feel what love is, with you." Addie looked up into Isabelle's intense eyes and smiled shyly.

Isabelle looked down at Addie's sweet face and held her tighter. "I'm not an expert on love, darling. I'm a few years older than you, and, in the past, I thought that I might have been in love, but I wasn't. I know I wasn't, because nothing has ever felt as right as you and I do. I love you, Addie, and I am as sure of us as I have ever been of anything." Isabelle kissed Addie's forehead and brushed a lock of hair that had fallen over her eyes behind her ear.

Addie thought her heart would burst with the love she felt for Isabelle and the bliss she was feeling about their declaration of love for each other. Lying in this woman's arms was where she knew she was meant to be. But, despite her happiness, she could not help the fear that crept into her heart with the realization of their situation. The sudden appearance of it made her shiver with dread. Isabelle felt Addie stiffen, and Addie knew that she felt it too. Addie held tight against Isabelle's body, never wanting to let her go.

CHAPTER 22

Addie stood in front of the full-length mirror, mesmerized by her own reflection. She just could not believe the person staring back at her was actually her. She wished she had had her Brownie camera so she could take a photo. "Holy moly! I look...I look..." Isabelle walked around Addie, adjusting a hem here, a sleeve there, and finally she stopped and stared, captivated by the vision before her.

"You look absolutely gorgeous, that's how you look!"

Addie was in shock. She felt transformed by the costume she wore. The light silk burgundy floor length gown clung to all her curves. Long elegant sleeves with tiny pearls woven into the fabric at the wrists covered her arms. The bodice was lined in the same small pearls and showed just a hint of her ample cleavage. Her smile couldn't be any wider. It was Saturday night, and she was dressed for an evening in Paris in 1911. She simply couldn't stop saying wow and staring at her dress. Isabelle was enchanted by Addie's 1950's dialect, which she found adorable.

"Wow, indeed my love, wow, indeed." Isabelle circled Addie, her eyes sparkling with excitement as she placed a sweet but firm kiss on her painted lips. "Honestly, Addie, if this weren't such an important evening we would not be going anywhere," Isabelle whispered as she gently kissed Addie's neck. Addie moaned, and she could feel that delicious sensation that worked its way through her entire body any time Isabelle touched her like this. "Umm, right...right. I need to stop right now," Isabelle said. "The car will be here very shortly." Addie just giggled.

As they approached the automobile idling in front of the house, Isabelle reached for Addie's hand and gallantly assisted her into the car. Isabelle couldn't help but be excited about showing Addie her world. "I am going to show you my Paris tonight, Addie. I want you to see the things you've dreamed of, the music, the art, and the poetry of the city. You will meet the most interesting people, darling." Leaning over so that she was but a mere inch from Addie, she softly whispered, "Darling, let us allow ourselves this beautiful night before we speak of serious things." Addie searched Isabelle's eyes, nodded, and smiled.

It had been well over a week since, after a particularly passionate afternoon, they broached the topic of their different worlds and what that meant for a future together. They had both fumbled painfully through impossible options and ended up in tears. Addie had asked Isabelle to give them more time because they were both too emotional to speak with any level of rationality. Isabelle had readily agreed. When she came to visit Isabelle today, she felt she was ready to consider the possible outcomes, or at least as ready as any one person could possibly be in a situation such as theirs. But Isabelle wanted them to enjoy their evening together without that serious discussion at the forefront of their thoughts. It was Isabelle's turn to ask for a little more time.

As Isabelle's driver took them through the streets of Paris, Addie sat anxiously on the edge of a soft leather seat, nervously gripping Isabelle's hand. "Darling, are you alright? Is anything wrong?" Addie turned and looked at Isabelle. "What makes you think anything is the matter? I'm perfectly fine, excited really," offered Addie, a bit too loudly.

Isabelle snickered and put her arm around her. "Darling, it's only a party. I promise you will be fine, and may I say, you will be the most beautiful woman in attendance."

Addie sighed, "Ugh. Okay, I admit it, I'm nervous. I'm terrified I'll say the wrong thing. As you are painfully aware, I don't speak 1911."

Laughing, Isabelle said, "You will be fine, I promise you. So, Miss Kahlo from 1952 America, you simply must relax. I am the one who should be nervous. After all, I will be escorting the most stunningly beautiful woman to this evening's festivities, which is quite nerve wracking." Isabelle lifted her brow and winked.

Addie smiled, rolled her eyes and crossed them, making Isabelle laugh. "You do realize, Issie, that you are going to give me a swelled head if you don't stop saying things like that," Addie said, placing a quick kiss on Isabelle's lips.

The car stopped in front of a tall building that looked oddly familiar to Addie, though she couldn't recall where she had seen it. The huge structure was adorned with ornate stone foliage over the entryway, and an impressive black wrought iron gate dominated the front of the building. As she waited for Isabelle's driver to open her door she froze. She suddenly remembered where she had seen this particular entryway before. It was in a book in her literature class. "Isabelle....Holy Mother of God! This is 27 Rue de Fleurus!"

Isabelle quickly turned to Addie, who appeared to be about to faint. "Addie, what's happening? What's wrong?" Addie was doing her best not to hyperventilate. She closed her eyes and forced herself to breathe as Isabelle looked on, concerned. Keeping her eyes closed for several moments, she worked to slow her breathing and was finally able to calm herself down.

Slowly opening her eyes, Addie looked at Isabelle and reached for her hand. Realizing she had alarmed her, she wanted to reassure her that she was fine. "I'm okay, honey, really I am. I'm sorry if I startled you. I'm well, just slightly flipping out right now," she said, clearing her throat.

"What? What's going on, darling?

Smiling broadly, Addie reached out and encircled a surprised Isabelle in a fierce hug. "Thank you, Issie, thank you from the bottom of my heart for this." Pulling back from a curious smiling Isabelle, she finally let her in on what had her so shocked. "Well, if I'm right, I think I'm about to meet *the* Alice B Toklas and *the* amazing Gertrude Stein. I may also be able to see firsthand the paintings of Picasso, Matisse and Cezanne. I might even get a chance to speak with the likes of Ezra Pound, Natalie Barney, and every other brilliant innovator at the dawn of the avant-garde modernist movement!"

Isabelle's relieved smile broadened, finally understanding what had Addie so out of sorts. "Darling, please don't do that to me again, or I will certainly be... what did you call it, *flipping out,* as well. Oh, and we will need to chat one day about your absolute adoration of Alice and Gertrude. You will need to educate me on all the fuss you make over them. But, for now my love, we must get moving. One does not keep Gertrude waiting."

꜒꜑꜓

"Isabelle! So happy that you've graced us with your presence this evening, dearest." Simone, Isabelle's closest friend, moved toward Isabelle and Addie as they were ushered through the door by a stern-looking petite woman who took their wraps. Simone leaned close and kissed Isabelle on both cheeks, giving her a little hug.

"Simone, you're here! I thought you had another engagement tonight," exclaimed Isabelle, quite pleased to see her dearest friend.

"Oui, I did, but when Alice mentioned to me that you were bringing a guest, well let's just say, I was curious." Isabelle rolled her eyes at Simone's playful teasing. "And, who do we have here?" Simone moved her teasing eyes to Addie, who stood nervously next to Isabelle. Taking in Addie's stunning appearance, intense hazel eyes and slightly anxious posture, Simone smiled warmly.

Addie noted Simone's playful curiosity, but also saw a genuine smile and sincere kindness in her gaze. "Simone Fabre, I'd like you to meet Miss Adeena Kahlo. Darling, this is my dearest friend, Simone." Isabelle smiled brightly as she introduced the two most important women in her life to one another.

"*Tres content de faire votre connaissance*, Mademoiselle Kahlo." Addie smiled at Simone with interest.

"Wow, I wish I knew what you just said, because it sounded beautiful." Simone looked at Addie amused and laughed heartily.

"Isabelle, she's fabulous!" Addressing Addie, Simone explained, "I said that I am pleased to meet you, Miss Kahlo. Now I need to ask, does Isabelle refer to you as Adeena, or is there something playful we can all call you?" Addie smiled openly. She immediately liked Simone; she was fun and clever. Addie thought her stunning as well, with her thick rich ginger hair, deep grey eyes, and aristocratic carriage.

"Yes, my friends call me Addie, so Simone, I would very much like it if you called me Addie." Simone gave Addie a brilliant smile and a gentle squeeze of the hand, "Splendid. Addie it is." Isabelle beamed at her two companions pleased to see genuine affection. Then she surprised Addie by taking her hand and walking her over to a number of other guests who were milling around the salon. Addie tried not to appear too mesmerized nor stare. However, she simply could not help but admire and be in awe of all the amazing artwork that hung on the walls. There were paintings, drawings, and etchings displayed from the floor to the ceiling on every wall.

The room was crowded with overstuffed chairs and books. Guests congregated in small groups, chatting and laughing as they enjoyed their cocktails and cigarettes. Addie held Isabelle's hand tightly as they made their way toward a stout woman who appeared to be holding court with a small mix of admirers. Next to her was the petite woman who had taken their wraps. Isabelle paused suddenly and playfully winked at Addie then walked them both closer to the small group who appeared to be engaged in a heated debate.

"Now tell me, will all this commotion result in one of those lovely paintings being ripped from the wall and thrown to the floor as happened a few weeks past?" Isabelle quipped to the group with smiling eyes. The group turned to look at Isabelle and a few laughed heartily. The stout serious looking woman glared at Isabelle, and it was all Addie could do to not hide behind Isabelle's skirts.

"Hmm. Isabelle, sweetheart, you know as well as I do, I will not risk destroying any of these paintings if there is a potential for a profit in a few years." Isabelle laughed at the woman's words, and the woman responded with a hearty laugh of her own as she quickly embraced Isabelle and kissed her on the cheek.

"Issie, my darling, I am so happy you are here," the woman said between snips of laughter. "Pablo is debating with me on the merit of Cezanne's last piece. I find it a perfect example of cubism, and I believe that he will one day be recognized as one of the best artists of post-impressionism. Your thoughts?"

Isabelle sighed and looked at the group as they appeared to be waiting with bated breath for her response. "Now Gertrude, you must allow me some time to absorb the work, and then I can offer my opinion," Isabelle responded as she studied the painting in question with a searing gaze.

"Hah," laughed the woman. "Issie, are you sure you are not a politician? You have an amazing ability to deflect questions to keep yourself from having to take sides." The woman laughed loudly and touched Isabelle's cheek in affection. Clearly, thought Addie, they are good friends, because the woman's face radiated pure joy as she laughed and hugged Isabelle.

Isabelle turned to Addie and gently moved her forward to face the stern looking woman with the kind eyes. "Gertrude, Alice, I'd like to introduce you both to someone very special, Miss Adeena Kahlo. Addie, these are my dear friends, Gertrude Stein and Alice Toklas."

Addie thought she might faint again. She could not believe she was meeting *the* Gertrude Stein and *the* Alice B Toklas. She willed herself to speak, though at this point she believed that anything she said was not her fault. "I'm very happy to meet you both. I... I just love your amazing home. The art displayed is breathtaking. I am so pleased that I am here. Thank you both for having me."

Alice smiled and warmly took Addie's hand and held it in both of hers, "Well, we haven't had you yet, my dear, but we are very pleased to make your acquaintance, young lady. Welcome." Isabelle rolled her eyes while all Addie could do was blush, smile and nod.

Gertrude took a sip of her drink and looked at Addie as if she were scrutinizing a potential painting purchase. "Miss Kahlo, are you an artist?"

Addie quickly looked at Gertrude wishing she could say yes. "Ah, no, Miss Stein, I... I like to think of myself as a writer."

'Hmm, too bad. Leo and I are always on the lookout for talented young artists. Is your writing any good?"

Addie was flabbergasted. She knew she needed to quickly formulate a sentence in response, as the intimidating Miss Stein was awaiting her answer. "Ah, yes. I believe it is, Miss Stein."

Gertrude looked at Addie with teasing eyes and suddenly laughed. "Excellent, young lady! I look forward to reading some of your work, and do call me Gertrude. You know, Isabelle dearest, you must introduce this lovely girl to Henry and Natalie, though they can be a bit roguish, so one must be careful."

Isabelle laughed heartily. "As can you, my dear Gertrude." Isabelle winked at Addie, letting her know she was just being teased.

"Adeena Kahlo, your name dear, it is quite unusual. Are you Spanish like our dear Pablo here?" Addie turned to look at the young man to whom Gertrude was referring and realized it was Pablo Picasso. Addie smiled at the young man and turned back to respond to Gertrude.

"Actually, my father's family is from Spain and Germany, and my mother is a mixture of Mexican and Native American, so I suppose you could say I am multicultural, of which I am rather proud." Addie smiled and lifted her drink to Gertrude.

Gertrude clinked her glass with Addie's and returned her own genuine smile. "As you should be, Miss. Kahlo. I am pleased you could join Isabelle this evening. Our girl is quite the author herself, and I dare say her poetry is astonishing, although, as I've mentioned to her on more than one occasion, one must be in love to do poetry justice. Perhaps now," Gertrude lifted her head to look at Isabelle and winked, "she will be inspired." Isabelle's smile was genuine as she looked from Gertrude to Addie. Addie could feel heat rise up her throat and knew she was blushing.

Addie sat next to Isabelle, clutching her hand and smiling from ear to ear. They had just left the Steins' salon and were heading back to Isabelle's grandmother's apartments. "Did you enjoy your evening, darling?"

Addie looked up at Isabelle nearly swooning her response, "This was the second-most amazing night of my life. You know the first," she whispered shyly. "Thank you, thank you for giving me this amazing experience, Issie." She threw her arms around Isabelle's neck and lavished several playful kisses over the entirety of her face. Isabelle laughed and leaned forward, touching Addie's cheek with affection as she brought their lips together for a slower more passionate kiss.

Addie moaned low in her throat as Isabelle's tongue danced with her own, the sweetness sending her into a daze and the intensity bringing heat to her body. "So, Miss Kahlo, when must I give you back to 1952?" Isabelle whispered as she nuzzled Addie's sensitive neck. Addie could barely speak, she was so absorbed into the feel of Isabelle's kisses.

"Ah...actually I thought I'd stay the night, that is, if you want me to." Isabelle pulled back from Addie with a huge grin on her face

"All night, really?" she asked. Addie smiled up at Isabelle, and her smile took Isabelle's breath away.

"Yes, Issie...all night long."

"Ummmm," Addie sighed breathlessly as Isabelle's body molded to her own. "You feel amazing." Addie couldn't get enough of the feel of Isabelle's firm breasts against her own and the warm soft curves of her hips as they pressed to her body. They were lying in Isabelle's bed chamber, thoroughly overwhelmed with each other and frantic in their lovemaking. Isabelle slowly moved over Addie's body, kissing and nipping at her sensitive skin as she gingerly made her way to Addie's hips and then her soft inner thighs.

Writhing with breathless anticipation, Addie moaned as Isabelle gently spread her legs to reach the silky softness she now knew so well. Gripping the headboard tightly, Addie gasped, completely undone by the feel of Isabelle's tongue as it licked and sucked her swollen clit. Her breathing now labored, she allowed herself to be completely taken over by her arousal. She could think of nothing but Isabelle between her legs. Lifting her hips to give more of herself to her lover, she cried out as Isabelle licked and sucked, seductively dragging her tongue slowly across Addie's warm, wet sex.

Addie closed her eyes tightly and allowed herself to bask in the feel of Isabelle's mouth, pleasing her. Rhythmically moving her hips as Isabelle delved deeper with her tongue, her entire body could feel the beginnings of her impending release. As her breath became more erratic, and Isabelle's tongue more demanding, she felt herself falling over the cliff. She arched her back and could not stop the loud groan and whimpered scream that escaped as her release took hold. She grabbed onto Isabelle's shoulders and rocked as her orgasm smashed through her. Finally, after several moments, she was still. Isabelle moved up Addie's body slowly and held her in her arms, gently kissing her forehead.

Addie held tightly to Isabelle. Smiling and chuckling softly, she sighed, "Issie, you are going to give me a heart attack. I swear you have no idea what you do to me, but promise me you won't ever stop."

Isabelle grinned mischievously and cuddled closer with Addie, kissing her again and holding her in her arms. "Well my love, you do the same for me. You are a little vixen, aren't you? No sooner did we walk through the door and you were dragging me to my rooms. I didn't even have a chance to offer you tea." Addie looked at Isabelle incredulously and broke out in an uproarious laugh. Isabelle smiled, and she too started to laugh. After a few moments, they laid back and relaxed, content and satisfied in each other's arms.

"I love you, Isabelle. I can't say it enough."

Isabelle kissed Addie softly. "I know that you do, darling. I love you too." They held each other gently as the quiet of the early morning lulled them to their own troublesome thoughts. Without so much as a word they held each other a little bit tighter, each knowing that they would soon need to talk about their future and whether they would live it together or apart.

CHAPTER 23

Awakened by the rumbling of her empty stomach, Addie stretched her long limbs and yawned. It was dawn, but the room was still softly lit by the light of the moon. Smiling to herself, she was happy to see that she had hours and hours before she had to leave for home. They had fallen asleep in each other's arms, exhaustion finally overwhelming them after their night together. Turning to look at Isabelle next to her, she expected her to be asleep, but smiled with surprise to see that Isabelle was watching her, a sweet smile creasing her face. "Issie...you take my breath away," she whispered.

Isabelle's smile grew as she reached out her hand to brush a few wisps of hair out of Addie's eyes. She scooted closer and gently kissed Addie's soft lips, "Hungry?" Addie nodded, embarrassed by the continued grumbling of her stomach.

"Maybe a little. I didn't eat much at Gertrude's. I was too nervous," she admitted.

"Well then, what do you say about going downstairs and seeing what's in the ice box. I think there are some cold cheeses and fresh fruit there. Interested?" Addie smiled and nodded her head, quickly jumping out of bed. Isabelle watched her gather her long hair into a messy bun. "Hmm, you look mouthwatering standing there completely nude in the soft light of dawn. If I were a painter, I'd paint this memory. You are absolutely glorious."

Addie turned toward Isabelle and pursed her lips, turning slightly pink. "What's this? Are you being shy, baby?" Isabelle gently teased. "After the way you exhausted me last night, there should be no shyness left within you, darling." Isabelle laughed, seeing Addie turn a deeper shade of pink. Reaching for her silk robe that hung over the wing chair, she walked over to Addie and gently placed the garment over her shoulders. "Here you go, my darling. Wear this and we will go down and get something to eat." She kissed Addie on the lips and walked over to her wardrobe for another robe.

"Yum, this is good," Addie mumbled at she ate crisp apples and cheese, washing it all down with hot tea. They sat in Isabelle's large kitchen which was illuminated by a small kerosene lamp resting in the center of the large wooden table. "I like this, Issie, eating by lamp light in nothing but our robes after an amazing night together," Addie smiled happily as she bit into a slice of apple.

Isabelle lifted her eyebrows in response and winked. "Yes, it's great fun, isn't it? I feel so relaxed, and having you here makes it perfect." Isabelle reached across the table and placed her hand on Addie's. Taking a deep breath, she suddenly looked contemplative. "You know, love, we will need to talk about what's happening. You realize that, right?" Addie looked across the table at Isabelle and nodded. As much as she did not want to talk about their particular predicament, she knew they needed to if there were going to be any chance for them to be together.

After finishing their breakfast Addie reached over and turned down the light of the lantern. Each thinking their own thoughts, they made their way to the parlor where Isabelle stoked a fire until it caught and filled the room with its warming glow. She turned and looked at Addie, who sat comfortably on the overstuffed couch with her arms wrapped around her legs and her head resting on her knees. Sighing, she felt her heart clinch when Addie smiled at her.

"Hi," Isabelle said softy as she made herself comfortable next to Addie.

Addie raised her head and smiled at the beautiful woman with whom she had fallen head over heels in love. "Hi yourself." she whispered, taking hold of Isabelle's hand. Rubbing her thumb softly over Isabelle's palm she said, "Tell me your story." She looked up into Isabelle's eyes. "I know you were born in England and that you're Czech." Smiling, she bent and placed a soft kiss on Isabelle's palm. "I know that you're beautiful, gentle, funny, and kind, but I don't know how you came to know Café du Temp. Tell me what you believe it means to you...to us."

Isabelle took a deep breath and breathed out a sigh. "I see you like to get right to the heart of things."

Addie grinned, "Yeah, I'm kind of like that, especially when I'm nervous."

Isabelle looked intently at her. "Are you nervous then?"

"Yes, aren't you? I'm terrified actually. I don't want to lose you, Iss, the thought of it petrifies me."

Holding tight to Addie's hand, Isabelle nodded. She couldn't deny that she felt the same. "Remember when I first brought you through my door and into Paris?" Addie nodded, not interested in making any jokes about her fainting. "I know it was an astonishing shock to you. I'm sorry, darling, but it was the only way I knew to prove to you that this is real. Because I believed, as I do now, that you and I were meant to meet, and I desperately wanted you to believe it too."

Addie looked at Isabelle, her hazel eyes appearing larger. "Iss, I'm almost afraid to say it, but are you saying that you believe you and I are each other's destiny?" Addie's heart was beating hard as she waited for Isabelle's response.

"I do," Isabelle admitted with certainty in her voice. "Addie, I don't believe you are aware that I was first introduced to Café du Temp nearly two years ago." Addie was mildly surprised that Isabelle had known of Café du Temp for that long. She looked at Isabelle, eyebrows raised, but allowed her to continue without interruption. "When the door first appeared, I was immediately captivated by the magic of my experiences. Peter...dear Peter, well, he took me under his wing, explaining to me the reason why only certain people are allowed to enter. At first, I found his explanation incredible and honestly quite impossible to believe, but I soon realized that his story was not a fantasy. My own experience proved it.

I have interacted with so many incredible people from different walks of life and from different periods in time while visiting the Café, that I would be a fool not to see the reality of its existence. But at twenty years old, I was not nearly as mature as you are at eighteen, my darling." Isabelle reached over and caressed Addie's cheek. "I grew restless and impatient for something to happen for me. In hindsight, I realize that I thought some sort of epiphany was going to suddenly guide me to my destiny." Looking sheepish, Isabelle shook her head. "I was so selfish, Addie. I thought I was there to become a famous and celebrated poet."

Addie gripped Isabelle's hand. "Oh Iss, you will be, honey. You're still young, and you have a lot of living ahead of you."

Isabelle smiled. "See, you're so much more mature than I was at your age." Addie smiled and asked her to go on, wanting her to continue her story. "Well, when that didn't happen, I stopped visiting Café du Temp, writing it off as a farce. I think I was a bit angry, and of course, disappointed that I didn't immediately become famous. Even though I knew deep down that it was real, and I was led there for a reason."

After a few minutes of silence, Addie stood and began to slowly pace. Isabelle watched her. "So, you didn't believe that you had found your purpose, and therefore you became frustrated and I guess...simply quit?"

Isabelle closed her eyes and nodded. "Yes, that is exactly what I did. Not the smartest move I've ever made, I must say."

Addie watched Isabelle and felt her heart clinch at the look of regret in her eyes. Slowly walking to Isabelle, she knelt in front of her. "Iss...don't be disheartened, honey. It's all okay," she smiled. "I'm sure the cosmos doesn't hold it against you."

Isabelle looked down at Addie's gentle smile, took her hand, and grinned. "God you're precious. I also think you're correct," she said with conviction. "I suppose, like everyone who experiences the Café, I needed to understand how I fit in, but, unlike everyone, I did not have the patience to wait to find out. Eventually, I willed myself not to look for the door, and I thought I had succeeded, that is, until that first evening I saw you and Alan. By then, it had been well over a year since I had been back. Then one evening as I was returning from an event, I saw the door. I knew I needed to walk through it. I can't explain it, but I simply knew it was what I had to do." Leaning back, she sighed and reached up to rub her eyes with the heels of her hands. Tilting her head, she raised her gaze to Addie, who now stood watching her in quiet contemplation.

"When I first saw you Addie, I couldn't take my eyes off you. It wasn't only that I found you incredibly beautiful. There was more, a familiarity, a bond, which felt warm and sweet, and oh so safe. I think I loved you already. It quickly dawned on me that you were the reason I was there again at Cafe du Temp."

"Oh, Iss." Addie whispered as she quickly closed the distance between them. Taking Isabelle's hands in both of hers, she gently kissed them and held them to her heart. Her eyes wide with emotion and tinged with wetness, she nodded and smiled, "I believe that it's not a *thing* that happens to those of us at Café du Temp that guides us toward our path, or our purpose. But it's *the people* we meet there...the relationships which we form that help to guide us."

"Yes, Addie, that is exactly what I'm saying," Isabelle said excitedly. "Who we meet there, at Café du Temp, and how we interact with them guides us and helps us find our direction. You understand. I knew that you would."

Lost to their own thoughts neither spoke. Addie watched the fire and Isabelle, eyes closed, rested her head on the back of the couch. After a few moments without movement, Addie asked, "Iss? Honey, what are you thinking?"

Isabelle peeked open one eye and smiled over at Addie. Suddenly, playfully grabbing Addie, she pulled her down to her lap and brought their lips together in a passionate kiss. "Addie, you trust me, don't you?" Addie touched Isabelle's face with affection and nodded yes. "Darling, I believe with all my heart that you and I were destined to meet and are meant to be together. Things just don't happen randomly at Café du Temp; every encounter has a profound purpose." Looking intently at Addie she said what was in her heart, "I don't understand yet how this will happen for us, my love, but I promise you, this time I will have the patience needed to ensure that it does. I won't quit because I simply can't lose you."

Addie looked up at Isabelle, her eyes soft with love. She reached out and pulled Isabelle closer for a gentle kiss. Sighing softly, she released Isabelle's mouth. "Issie...I can't lie to you, I'm frightened. We're from different worlds, and that reality is such a profound barrier to our life together. But I *also* can't lose you. I just can't. I promise you, Iss, however long it takes, I will be patient too. I will wait forever for you if that is what it will take for us to be together. I want to spend the rest of my life with you."

Isabelle smiled, eyes moist with tears. "I want that as well, Addie, more than anything in the world."

CHAPTER 24

"So, nice weekend?" Alan asked, turning toward Addie, moving his brows up and down, and grinning like an idiot. They were relaxing on Alan's porch swing, enjoying a lazy Sunday afternoon. It was chilly for the first day of November. Usually the temperature would still be relatively comfortable, but even though the sun was in full bloom, the wind was bitting. Addie looked at Alan, and planting her feet on the swing, she placed her arms around her knees to help ward off the chill. She shot him a sidelong glance, knowing very well that he was teasing her.

"There's no saving me, Alan. I am body, heart, and soul in love. The best weekend of my life." Addie could not help the smile in her voice.

Alan poked Addie in the ribs. "Yeah, I bet. You should see your face. You look like the cat that got the cream."

She turned to Alan and bit her lip, thinking that she wanted to talk more about what she shared with him earlier. He too was a part of Café du Temp just as she and Issie were. She needed to know his take on what he thought it was all about. "So... what we talked about earlier, what do you think? Do you think Isabelle and I are right about how folks find their purpose, or direction? God, I don't even know what to call it?" she said shaking her head.

Alan sat back and put his hands behind his head thinking about what Addie had shared, how she and Isabelle believed that the people you meet at Café du Temp somehow influence your decisions, thus guiding you, perhaps unknowingly, down the right path toward the direction you should've been headed all along. He could see it... anything was possible now. Ever since he stepped into Café du Temp, nothing was the same for him.

He looked at Addie who waited expectantly for him to respond. "Yeah,

Ad, I think you girls are right. I agree because, well, I know that it's Peter who helped me see what I have always known, but have just been too scared to see it as a reality." Sitting forward, he smiled at Addie, happy now to be sharing his new future with her. "Ad, I don't want to get into the building business like Frank and my dad. I never wanted that. I kinda just went along thinking I had no choice. What I really want to do is study architecture. I want to design new structures. I want to be an architect, like Frank Lloyd Wright or Philip Johnson. It's what I've always dreamed of doing.

Addie grinned at Alan, happy to see him so excited. "Alan, that's so great. I'm really happy for you. I know I have never seen you too enthusiastic when you talk about working with your dad's business. I guess now I know why. So, have you talked to your dad about what your new plans are? I know he expects you to join the business after college."

"Yeah, well I'm actually planning on speaking with him pretty soon. I need to get moving on switching schools and declaring a new major." Addie asked him how he thought his dad would take the news. Alan turned and looked at Addie and grinned. "Yeah...I have no idea. But I need to talk with him. I don't want to hurt my dad, but I need to be honest with him."

Addie jumped off the swing and hugged him, "I'm happy that Peter has been able to help you realize what you really want to do with your life." Holding tight to Alan, now she wished that it could all be as simple for her. It wasn't and she had no idea what to do about it.

Sitting in English lit, Addie doodled in her binder. The class had just begun, but in her mind, she was dragging her tongue across Isabelle's collarbone, enticing soft whimpers of need from her beautiful mouth. The ringing of the class bell snapped her back to reality. She tried to focus, but it was no use. She was miserable. She hadn't seen Isabelle for nearly two weeks, and she missed her desperately. She thought about the note she'd given to Alan to deliver. She had been ill with the flu for the last week and could not meet Isabelle since she was too sick to get out of bed. Alan had planned to meet Peter at Café du Temp a few days after she got sick, and he had promised to make sure that Addie's note was delivered. She was fairly certain Isabelle had received it, but that hadn't made the past two weeks any easier. She needed to see her.

Addie thought back to the evening before they parted; they had agreed to meet at Café du Temp that Thursday for dinner, neither wanting to be apart for too long. "How did nearly two weeks pass so quickly," she thought unhappily.

"Miss Kahlo?" Uh oh, Addie thought as she looked up at her instructor. She was not at all prepared to respond to any questions. "Miss Kahlo, can you provide your opinion, please?" Addie's eyes opened wide. Oh shit, she thought, she had no clue what the discussion was about. "Your opinion, Miss Kahlo, on Hemingway's…" RINGGGGGGGG! "Okay class, chapters 15 through 20 for the quiz tomorrow, so please come prepared," her instructor said, looking directly at Addie. Quickly leaving the classroom before she could be cornered by her teacher, Addie knew she had messed up. She wasn't pleased with herself. She had to get an "A" in this class, as her scholarship depended on it. She realized she needed to focus.

"Addie! Wait up!!" Addie turned and saw Rachel jogging down the hall toward her. Rachel breathed heavily as she put her hand on Addie's arm. "Whew! You're fast! I could hardly catch up to you. Why are you in such a hurry anyway?"

Addie looked at Rachel and sighed. "Sorry, Rach, I'm so out of it today. I really need to cram for this quiz tomorrow in English lit; I want to get to the library so I can spend as much time there as possible before it closes."

Rachel smiled brightly. "Ad, you are the smartest person I know, You'll be great!"

Seeing Rachel's smiling face and honest eyes, Addie suddenly felt like crying. She wanted so badly to confide in Rachel. She wanted to tell her she was in love and scared because everything was so complicated. Feeling the emotional tension of the past two weeks getting to her, she reached out and hugged Rachel tightly.

"Hey, hey are you okay?" Rachel hugged Addie back and then held her at arm's length to look at her. Attempting to pull herself together, Addie braved a small smile and nodded as she sniffed back tears.

Rachel watched her skeptically. "Are you sure you're ok, Ad? Addie nodded again, squeezed Rachel's arm affectionally, and quickly headed toward the library.

CHAPTER 25

Sitting at her usual table by the bar, Addie sipped a cup of hot tea. Sam had brought her a selection of appetizers, but she couldn't eat because her stomach was too knotted up with nervous excitement. She looked at her watch for the third time. It was 3:00 pm on a chilly late November day. She had briefly wondered if it was as chilly in Isabelle's 1911 Paris as it felt in 1952 Chicago. When Addie first arrived, Peter had greeted her with a kiss of the hand and a warm smile, helping her to feel marginally less anxious. He had also assured her that Isabelle had received the note Alan delivered. Now, as she scanned the many doorways that seemed to dominate Café du Temp, she waited and hoped that Isabelle would soon arrive.

Mixed sounds of various horns fought for dominance as Addie lifted her head. The jazz quartet was warming up for their first set of the evening. It was now nearly 5:30, and she had been sitting, drinking cup after cup of tea for well over two hours. She realized that she would burst at any moment if she didn't use the bathroom soon. Sam had come and gone, removing the appetizers that she had not touched.

Addie breathed out a heavy sigh and checked her watch once again, finally acknowledging to herself that Isabelle was not going to appear. She was so profoundly disappointed that she could not stop the heavy flow of tears that spilled from her eyes. After several moments, she pulled herself together and called Sam over to phone for a cab. She felt drained and decided she'd go home and lie down for a little while. She'd come back tonight; perhaps Isabelle would come by later in the evening. She would leave a message with Peter to let Isabelle know that she had been there.

Before leaving, Addie decided she'd better use the bathroom. After all those cups of tea, she wasn't certain she'd make it home without an accident. As she walked out of the ladies' room, a strong gentle hand reached for hers and held it. Addie felt faint with relief, as she gazed at Isabelle's beautiful face. Throwing her arms around Isabelle, Addie kissed her lips, her cheeks, her hair. She simply couldn't get enough.

"Iss, god I've missed you. I was so afraid that you were done with me. But you're here. You're here." Isabelle gently wrapped her arms around Addie in the dim light of the walkway and kissed her deeply. All thoughts of Isabelle being angry melted away as Isabelle's tongue slipped into her mouth, mixing with hers. The soft sweet taste of her kisses made Addie's knees weak. She'd never been this happy to see anyone as she was to see Isabelle. "Addie," Isabelle whispered in her ear, "will you come home with me now?"

Addie pulled back to look at her and saw the desire in her eyes, as well as the unmistakable depth of her love. "Yes," whispered Addie. "I'd go anywhere with you, Issie, anywhere."

In Isabelle's rooms, a fire blazed in the hearth. It was already dusk, and with the curtains drawn, the flames provided the only visible light. Isabelle held tightly to Addie's hand as she led her into the room and closed the door behind them. She immediately backed Addie up against the door, taking both her hands and raising them above her head as she dragged her tongue across the curve of Addie's neck. Addie's eyes closed, and a ragged moan escaped from her throat. Isabelle's mouth was exquisite, and every gentle kiss, every drag of her tongue held Addie in rapture. Isabelle's kisses became more aggressive with need as she lowered Addie's arms and reached for the zipper on Addie's dress, pulling the garment up and over her head in one swift motion. She looked deeply into Addie's eyes, and darkened irises full of need looked back at her as she lowered herself to Addie's taunt nipples, gently nipping and sucking through Addie's bra.

Addie's head flew back and pressed against the door as she nearly fell to her knees with desire. Isabelle reached behind her and quickly unclipped Addie's bra than moving her warm fingers down her body she removed Addie's panties. Standing in the firelight, now nude except for the clip she wore in her hair, Addie watched raptly as Isabelle removed her own clothes, her breath catching with anticipation and her heart racing as each garment was slowly discarded. Isabelle's eyes smoldered as she reached out and guided Addie to her, pressing their warm bodies together she kissed Addie deeply.

Addie watched with hooded eyelids as Isabelle straddled her, moving her clit seductively over Addie's sensitive wet sex. Addie gasped with pleasure as Isabelle moved against her. The sensation of Isabelle's sex against her own brought Addie to heights of bliss that she thought impossible. As their rhythm synced, their deep moans of pleasure overtook them. Isabelle leaned down and gently caressed Addie's face. "Do you know how very much I love you, Addie Kahlo?" she whispered. "So very much." Addie thought her heart would explode as she reached up and brought Isabelle's mouth down for a searing kiss.

Isabelle moved Addie's long hair away from her face and whispered in Addie's ear, "Do you trust me?" Addie could only nod her response as she lay in ecstasy, loving the feel of Isabelle's body. Isabelle gently maneuvered her body so that Addie was now straddling her. "Baby, I want you to move up so that I can kiss you, down there. "Addie opened her eyes wide. "Issie,...? Won't I hurt you?" 'No, darling, you won't hurt me. It will feel wonderful, I promise." Addie smiled, and slowly but carefully moved up the length of Isabelle's long strong body. Once she was where Isabelle wanted her, Isabelle reached up and caressed her breasts as she gently kissed Addie's inner thighs, slowly moving her mouth toward Addie's glistening mound.

Addie thought she would pass out she was so completely aroused. The feel of Isabelle's mouth on her clit, gently licking and then sucking, was exquisite, and when her tongue entered her, she breathed out a deep groan of pleasure. As her organism built, she couldn't stop herself from calling out. "Oh Issie! Oh god, Issie! Yes!" Addie held tight to Isabelle, riding out a climax that seemed to last forever.

Breathing hard, Addie slowly moved down the length of Isabelle's body into her arms. Both deliciously spent and satisfied, Addie kissed her lover's neck as she laid in her arms. Isabelle held her tightly and rubbed small circles on her back, basking in the feel of Addie's soft skin as she held her. Breathing heavily, Addie reached up and kissed Isabelle, first on the mouth, then on her cheeks and then on her neck again. "I've missed you so much, Iss. I love you, my beautiful girl," she whispered through a haze of emotion. Every cell in her body told her this was right, that the love they had for one another was right.

Isabelle lay on her side next to Addie, watching her sleep, her soft snoring the only sound in the room. Gazing at her, her heart was full of love. She reached out to gently brush a lock of hair from Addie's forehead. Sighing to herself, she knew she was enchanted. She had never felt for anyone the way she felt for Addie. Once Addie woke, Isabelle knew they needed to talk. She had been frantic when she hadn't heard from her these past few weeks. Receiving the note that had been passed to Peter saying that Addie was ill had only increased her concern.

Isabelle hadn't realized that not seeing Addie would affect her so much. She had been frantic with worry. Without any method of communication, Isabelle had no idea how seriously ill Addie was, and that frightened her. This incident had brought the reality of their different worlds into sharp focus. She knew they would need to face these differences and somehow not allow them to dictate their future.

Addie's eyes slowly opened to see Isabelle watching her with a gentle smile. "Hello, sleepyhead. You were snoring," Isabelle teased as she leaned down and kissed Addie softly on the lips.

"Snoring, really? No, I wasn't...was I?"

Isabelle grinned. "Yes, but it was so cute." Addie rolled her eyes and smiled.

"So how long have I been asleep?"

Isabelle propped herself up on her elbow, still looking at Addie, "Only about an hour or so. You apparently needed it, love. Are you still very tired?"

"No, I'm good." Addie stretched and turned on her side to face Isabelle. Looking at her tenderly, she touched her cheek. "I'm so sorry, Iss...so sorry. I never meant to not contact you for two whole weeks." Addie's apology was so heartfelt that her emotions took over and tears appeared in her eyes.

"Oh darling, please don't cry. It's alright. I know it wasn't done purposely." Isabelle soothed, pulling Addie into her arms.

Addie sat up, pulling herself out of Isabelle's arms, but reaching for her hand, she held it to her heart. "No, no, Iss. I promise it wasn't. I caught the flu, and my mother, well, my mother refused to allow me out of the house for over a week. I'm embarrassed to tell you this, because I'm not a kid...but, anyway, then, once I was better, because I had missed a week of classes, I needed to catch up. My scholarship depends on me keeping an "A" average. And because I am the editor of our school paper, I missed some deadlines, and I needed to work through that, and..."

"Shhhh, it's fine darling, it's fine. You're here now and that's what matters." Addie looked at Isabelle, desperately wanting to believe; that now that she was there everything would be fine.

"Iss, you're being awfully quiet. Are you okay?" They were sitting comfortably in the parlor, enjoying tea and some little cakes that Isabelle knew Addie liked. At the sound of Addie's voice, Isabelle turned and offered a timid smile.

"Am I? I hadn't realized." Addie watched her skeptically, knowing she had something on her mind. Standing suddenly, Isabelle began to pace. Addie watched her movements with growing anticipation.

"It's only that...this incident has brought me back to reality." Isabelle walked to the fireplace and warmed her hands over the grates.

"What do you mean, brought you back to reality?" Addie moved to the edge of the couch, trying to hold back her growing panic.

Isabelle moved toward Addie, quickly closing the space between them. Reaching for Addie's hand, she lifted her from the couch. "Come, love, come sit with me by the fire and drink your tea."

"Well, okay, but please tell me what you mean. I'm starting to panic." Isabelle looked contemplatively at their entwined hands and sighed.

"Sit," Isabelle said. Addie sat and took a sip of her tea while she waited for Isabelle to speak.

"The first day when you did not come to Café du Temp, I didn't think it was for any other reason than you could not get away. I was disappointed of course, because I love you, but I wasn't concerned. Then, once several days passed without a word, I began to worry. I realized I had no way of contacting you. I couldn't stay at the Café for days hoping for you to appear, or even seek out Alan to find out what had happened to you. I wanted to know where you were, what had happened. I felt helpless." Addie listened intently, an underlying sense of guilt and trepidation began to seep into her heart, but she didn't interrupt.

Isabelle came to sit next to Addie, biting her lip as she looked at her. "I began to doubt myself. I started to think that perhaps I wasn't sweeping you off your feet the way you had done to me." Isabelle laughed low in her throat, shaking her head, "I was feeling a bit insecure, I think, which is something that has never happened to me. It was quite the surprise."

"Iss, that's not true. I'm totally swept off my feet. I can barely stand." Addie reached across the small table to take Isabelle's hand in both of hers.

Isabelle chuckled and said, "I don't feel that way anymore, honey. I know you love me. It's only that I was frustrated because there was no way to reach you. The gravity of my inability to contact you really brought to mind how very different our lives are. Once Peter had passed on your note from Alan, the relief I felt was short-lived because I desperately wanted to go to you and help nurse you back to health, but I could not."

Addie pursed her lips together. She sat silent, fearing she might cry, the enormity of their situation beginning to sink in. She knew exactly what Isabelle was feeling. Understanding Isabelle's frustration and concern wasn't difficult because she often felt the same way.

Isabelle placed her palm under Addie's chin, moving her face so Addie was looking at her. "Darling, none of this is your fault. It's not. It's only the reality of our different worlds that is at fault here. Don't you see?" Isabelle gave Addie a sad defeated smile.

It was several moments before Addie said anything. She simply didn't know how to respond. "Iss...what do you think we should do?" she finally offered in a contemplative whisper.

"That's just it, darling. I don't know. Though I imagine all we can do is live our lives as we have been doing, with the exception of perhaps being more cognizant of how we communicate across our different worlds."

A great sense of relief immediately flooded through Addie at hearing Isabelle's words. She was panicked that Isabelle was about to suggest that they stop seeing each other, that their different worlds made it too difficult. Sensing Isabelle watching her closely, she gave her a half smile, swallowing her relief. "Iss, do you think we should speak with Peter about us? Maybe he has some insight. Surely there have been others who have fallen in love and..."

"I don't know, darling. I know that we spoke before about seeking him out for some answers, but I have a feeling he will only tell us, in his Peter sort of way, that we must follow our own path, wherever it may lead us." Addie reluctantly nodded her agreement.

Isabelle stood and lifted Addie up off the couch. "Love, it's still quite early. You don't need to leave yet, so let's go to Café Annis. I think it would be a very pleasant thing to do. Quite honestly, I could do with a nice glass of wine right about now, and a light meal would do us good." Addie looked up at Isabelle, acknowledging that, for the moment, their conversation was over.

She knew that they had come to an obstacle in the road. Their different worlds had left them both feeling vulnerable. Addie was certain that she would never willingly leave Isabelle, yet the realization that they may not be able to stay together was an all too real possibility.

"I'd like that, Iss. Dinner would be great."

CHAPTER 26

6 Months Later

It was May 15, 1953, for Addie and May 15, 1912, for Isabelle. In an unusual bit of synchronicity, Springtime in both of their respective worlds was gloriously warm and sunny. Isabelle had decided that Paris in the Spring was something that Addie must experience. The weather had finally turned pleasant, and she thought it a perfect day for them to enjoy a walk. Over the past several months they had become increasingly more in tune with each other. Gone was Addie's initial awkwardness and shyness with Isabelle.

The open honesty, love, and desire they shared brought out a strength and confidence in Addie that, if possible, endeared her even more to Isabelle. In turn, Isabelle's quiet beauty, poetic talent, and loving attentiveness swelled Addie's heart with a love she had only read about in books. So, on this pleasant early spring day, they dressed and ventured out into the bright crisp morning. They strolled through the scenic park, the air brisk and the sun shining, happy simply being together.

Isabelle shared her poetry with Addie as they walked. She had become quite inspired since she and Addie had found each other, and her poetry, which came from deep within her heart, burst with joyous prose, love, and a sort of brilliance that had always been there in her mind and heart, but, she realized, had to her amazement only required Addie to release it.

"So, I must say that seeing you today is a lovely gift. I love when you surprise me like this."

Addie turned to Isabelle and grinned, winking as she placed her arm in hers. "I couldn't wait to see you, Iss. I just wish that I could stay the entire day, but I need to get back by 6:00 as I have a tutoring session at seven. This young boy that I'm working with is so earnest, you should see his determination." Addie smiled, thinking of Henry's scrunched-up button nose as he worked out a sentence. "I'm telling you, Iss, he will ace his English exam tomorrow if I have anything to do with it!"

Isabelle nodded and grinned. "I love seeing your excitement when you talk about your tutoring. It truly is a wonderful thing that you are doing, darling. Tell me, do you love teaching as much as I believe you do? You seem so passionate about it."

Addie thought about it briefly and knew the answer immediately, "Yes, I do love it. It gives me such a charge when they understand the written word. To be able to help someone is just so satisfying, opening up a child's mind to the amazing worlds of literature, poetry, and history, and seeing their eyes light up in understanding, well...it's just so satisfying."

"Well, Miss Kahlo, I'd say that if your passion has anything to do with it, you'd make a splendid educator. Is this something you've ever considered? I know that your dream is to be a published author, but there is no law that says you cannot do both."

"Hmm, I guess I never really considered it, but if I'm to be a struggling author, I will need to support myself somehow, won't I?"

"Indeed." Isabelle smiled and squeezed Addie's hand. "So, I hope today's visit is not in place of our weekend plans." Addie looked wide-eyed at Isabelle as they continued their walk. "What? No, not on your life, sister! I've been looking forward to spending an entire weekend with you for months. I'm excited." Addie held tighter to Isabelle's arm. Isabelle laughed loudly at Addie's colorful vocabulary.

Grunting noticeably, Addie released Isabelle's arm, looked down, and furrowed her brow in concentration. She was trying desperately to continue their walk with some semblance of grace and not step on her day dress. "Good lord, Iss, how do women walk in these dresses? Not only are they long, but they're tight. I have a long stride and I feel as if I'm walking like a mummy."

Isabelle snickered at Addie's grumbling, "Well, if it's any consolation, other than dressing for Gertrude's party, we can spend our entire weekend wearing nothing at all."

Addie whipped her head around to stare at Isabelle. Cheeks flushed pink, Addie grinned from ear to ear. Isabelle, not missing a beat, smiled mischievously and winked. As they neared the end of their walk, several children ran by, hoisting kites. Stopping to watch as the wind took the colorful triangular objects high into the sky, Addie was enchanted. She loved being here in Paris with Isabelle.

Sitting on a park bench, Addie held her face up to the sun and smiled. How curious, she thought, to be so content doing absolutely nothing. It's unbelievable. Feeling the warmth of the sun on her face, a thought crossed her mind, and not for the first time, she could see herself living here in Paris with Isabelle. The thought forced a lump in throat. What about her dreams of college? Could she really give that up to be with Isabelle?

"Addie? Are you out in the cosmos again, love?"

Addie turned and smiled, thinking that the sun shining on Isabelle's hair made her look like an angel. Swallowing the lump in her throat, she said, "Just daydreaming a little." Isabelle grabbed Addie's hand and squeezed it. "So, Issie. I still can hardly believe that Gertrude asked about me and suggested you invite me back this Saturday. That's unbelievable; it's Gertrude Stein, for heaven's sake! I'm shocked she noticed me at all, much less remembered me."

"Yes, darling, she noticed you, and she noticed me noticing you," Isabelle laughed. "Saturday will actually be special. I wanted to surprise you, but I'm too excited, so I'll tell you now." Addie raised an eyebrow in curiosity. "Do tell."

Isabelle was absolutely giddy with excitement. "Well, I have been asked to do a reading of my poetry at the party."

"Oh, baby, that's fantastic! Tell me everything. I want to hear all the details." Isabelle gently bit her lower lip, a habit that never ceased to send heat to areas of Addie's body, that made her squirm.

"Come along, love. I want to buy you a new hat to go with that lovely dress we had you measured for, and after that, I'll tell you all the details... in bed." Addie quickly moved off the bench and started walking; she didn't need to be told twice

Addie was editing the final article for the next edition of the school paper, and she thought it was a good one. The theme was "Is activism alive in post WWII America?" It was written by a new student, Steven

Keller, who had transferred from New York. Addie liked him. He was a little intense and really passionate about his politics, but surprisingly, though usually serious, he had a great sense of humor. He had Addie in stitches with his witty take on the school cliques and eccentric teachers. He was a good writer too, and she admired that. He liked her writing as well. She had shared with him a number of short stories and essays that she had compiled in her portfolio. He gave her good feedback and shared his opinion; she liked his honesty.

Addie had enjoyed working with him these past semesters. When he had asked her out on a date, it took her by surprise. She didn't get any inkling from him that he was attracted to her, but since Isabelle, she never noticed whether boys liked her or not. She was a bit disappointed that he had asked her out. She had thought they could be friends, but now it probably wouldn't work. Plus, she had Alan, and she could only handle one pretend boyfriend at a time.

"Addie, what time are you leaving? Wanna walk home together?" Rachel leaned against the door of the school paper's small office, waiting for Addie to respond.

"Oh, hi Rach. Yeah sure, I should be done in about ten. Can you wait?" Rachel skipped into the office and plopped herself down in one of the small chairs across from the old wooden desk where Addie was busy putting the final touches on the next edition.

"So, how's it looking this month? Last month's edition was really cool. I loved all the photographs of the winter dance."

Addie chuckled. "You just liked it because it had that great photo of you and Mickey in it."

Rachel beamed. "Yeah, it was neat. Mom cut it out and put it in a frame for me. It will be on our bookshelf when you get home." Addie laughed out loud and shook her head. "So, are you helping Pops and your dad Wednesday at the club?"

"What's Wednesday?" Addie asked as she continued to set up the lay-out.

"What's Wednesday? It's the day that the Jazz Notes will be playing at the club, remember? Pops and your dad expect a big crowd. Apparently, it was a real coup to get them. They asked us if we could help with the hosting."

Addie looked up to the ceiling and sighed, noticeably agitated. "Oh shit, I forgot. Yeah, okay. I can help. I just need to rearrange some stuff."

Rachel looked at Addie for a moment and grabbed her hand. "Hey, Addie, listen, stop for a sec." Addie turned and gave Rachel her full attention.

"What?" she snapped.

Rachel's eyes opened wide, shocked at Addie's defensiveness. "Hey, don't be upset. I just want to know if everything is okay. You've been so busy these past months, with school, the paper, taking all those college exams. I just wanted to ask how you're doing, that's all and um...ask about Alan."

Addie let down her guard. She knew she was on edge, but that didn't mean she should take it out on Rachel. "Rach, I'm sorry. You're right, it's been crazy these past months. I feel like everything is happening at once, and there's just not enough time. I mean, can you believe we will be graduating in a little over a month?" Addie was not only thinking about graduation and college, but also the inevitable parting of her and Isabelle. She had no idea how she would do it. How could she leave her to go off to New York? The idea of it was unbearable, and the nearer the time came the more withdrawn and unhappier she became.

Rachel smiled at Addie. "I know," she said excitedly, "Pops really wants me to start at the club right after graduation. He says that since I'll be in charge of waitstaff and ordering and stuff, I need to know the ins and outs of the business."

Addie looked at Rachel's excited face and wanted to cry. Instead she smiled and hugged her. "Rach, you are going to do great. I just know it," she said as she held her.

"As a matter of fact, you should be very proud of yourself. There aren't very many women who manage night clubs; you're going to be one of the first. I'm so proud of you, honey."

Rachel breathed out nervously and replied, "Well, I still have to train and probably won't be managing for at least another year, but yeah, I'm so excited. This is my dream, Addie, and gosh, its actually coming true!" Addie couldn't help herself; she sniffed back tears as she hugged Rachel again.

"Addie? Hey, why are you crying?" Addie desperately wanted to tell

Rachel about Isabelle, how she was in love with her and how happy they were together. She wanted to share with her that she was scared, terrified really, that the time was soon approaching when she would need to decide if she would stay with Isabelle or leave for New York. She didn't know which it would be. It was a heartbreaking decision, and she didn't know how she would manage.

Addie looked to Rachel with red teary eyes, knowing she couldn't say a word about it. "Everything's good, Rach, she said as she tried to get herself together. "Alan and I are good. Yeah, we're doing great."

"Hey, hot mama," Alan said, as he looked up from his project and drew out a long whistle as Addie walked into his garage studio. It had been several days since her meltdown in front of Rachel. She had cried herself to sleep that night. Now a few days later she felt a bit more in control of her emotions.

Addie laughed loudly. "Oh, shut up! Stop trying to make me blush. It won't work."

Alan joined in, laughing loudly. "Yeah, well you look pretty blushed to me right now. What's going on? Seriously, you look great." Alan was sitting at the drafting table that he and his dad had set up in the garage loft. He loved it there. It had a great view of the park through the large picture window, and the light was good.

"I'm hosting tonight at The Angel. Dad and Uncle Jon are trying out a new jazz band, and it looks like they sold a ton of tickets, so Rachel and I are helping out. What are you working on?" Addie leaned over to look at Alan's drawings.

"Oh this, Miss Kahlo, is my senior project that I was telling you about. It's my design for the new playground over at Dvorak Park, that is, if they ever decide to make a new playground. See here? The entire perimeter is padded with rubber instead of cement or pebbles. This way, if a kid falls, he won't crack his skull. Also, see these swings? They're also made of rubber instead of wood. They have these belts to hold the babies in, so they won't fall through."

"Alan, this looks fantastic! How did you come up with this? I've never seen a playground like this." Addie looked to the drawing and then back to Alan, awestruck. "You haven't even started college yet. Wait 'til you do; you're going to make a brilliant architect!"

Alan blushed and looked down at his feet. "So, the other day I talked with my dad and told him I didn't want to join the family business, that I wanted to design stuff and be an architect." Addie sat down on one of the crates that doubled as a chair. Giving him a concerned look, she waited for him to continue.

"Anyway, he was so pissed I thought he'd slug me. You should have seen him, Ad. His face turned bright red and his fists balled up. He started yelling, saying that he planned on having Frankie and me take over the business. He had it all planned out."

"Oh Alan, I'm sorry."

Alan shook his head. "No, actually it's okay. I know my dad, and he was mad, but once he calmed down, I jumped in and explained what I wanted to do. I showed him my ideas for the playground. He looked at them kind of surprised. He even asked what material I was thinking of using for the merry-go-round seats. After I showed him everything, he got quiet, then just walked out."

Addie was concerned for Alan as she watched him with his cherished drafting pencil in his hand. "Is he still helping you pay for school?"

Alan blew out an exasperated breath. "I don't know, Ad. If he decides to not pay, I'll figure it out. But one thing is for sure. I felt more like a man than I ever had. I stood up for myself, and that means everything."

The gig at The Angel was exciting, but exhausting. So many people had shown up that Addie and Rachel hardly had time to use the bathroom. Mickey had just dropped them off at home, and once they walked in the door, Rachel grunted her goodnight and went straight to bed. It was nearly 2:00 in the morning. *Thank god I don't have an early class tomorrow,* Addie thought. *At least I get to sleep in.* Yawning, she put on her pajamas and crawled into bed, sighing deeply at the comfort of stretching out in the quiet of her room. She was physically tired, but her mind held too many thoughts to stay settled.

Addie thought of counting sheep, but that idea came and went. As she became comfortable, she closed her eyes and thought of the past several days, specifically of her conversations with Rachel and Alan, and how, to her utter surprise, they had somehow moved passed her, looking to their future, a future that was certain and exciting.

Wishing she was as confident about her future as Rachel and Alan were, she thought about Café du Temp and how it was supposed to help guide her, but everything was more confusing than ever. She contemplated how Café du Temp had introduced her to the love of her life and how her entire world had tilted on its axis for her after meeting Isabelle. She was so conflicted. If truth be told, she wanted it all: her future as she had envisioned it before meeting Isabelle, and now she wanted Isabelle too. She couldn't imagine life without her now. It was impossible.

God, how Addie wished Isabelle was with her now. She craved her. It wasn't even so much about physical desire. Her heart ached for her. Running her hands through her hair roughly, she wanted to scream. She wasn't so naïve that she blinded herself to the inevitable truth. She had to decide. Her life here in *her own* world with school and family or a new life in 1911 Paris, with the woman she loved. It was an impossible decision.

Fear and heartache gripped her as she thought of losing her family and her dream of attending Vassar. Equally as devastating would be leaving Isabelle. The thought brought actual physical pain, and her heart felt heavy with despair. "Oh God," she prayed, "please give me the strength and wisdom to do what is right, because I can't decide, I just can't." Tears fell from her eyes to her pillow and, after many minutes, she finally allowed sleep to take over.

CHAPTER 27

It was late afternoon. They lay in each other's arms, a fine layer of sweat between them. Addie lifted her gaze to Isabelle; her eyes were closed, and a sweet smile creased her lips. She didn't want to be any place but where she was right at that moment. "Tell me, Issie," she said softly, "you promised you'd tell me. I want to hear all the details."

"Hmm, yes, I did say I would tell you everything, didn't I?" Isabelle yawned. "But you need to give me a few minutes to recover from your youthful exuberance." Addie smiled and hugged her. "Oh, you act like you are such an old lady. You're only 23 years old!"

Isabelle reached over and tickled Addie's stomach, sending her into waves of giggles. "Hey, stop that, you." Addie laughed. "Issie," she said pleadingly. Isabelle laughed too and wrapped her arms around Addie.

"Alright, alright I'll stop. It's just that I love to hear you laugh. You have such a wonderful laugh, deep and rich and sexy." Addie laughed hard at Isabelle's description. Sighing heavily, Isabelle laid back on the pile of pillows they had, in their passion, tossed around the bed.

"Addie," she said, suddenly contemplative, "before I met you, I had the most difficult time putting pen to paper. It was as if my creativity was trapped in my head, and no matter how hard I tried, it would not be released. But now, since you and I have been together, I feel so inspired. My thoughts and words come together." Addie sat up on the bed crossed-legged and held Isabelle's hand as she listened intently.

"Words just seems to pour out of me now, and I have to write everything down. Do you understand? I don't believe I have ever been this energized and happy with my poetry. It had been a struggle. However, since you and I have met, I find myself being freer, as if the happiness I have found with you has freed my creativity." Isabelle gazed at Addie and smiled. "You,

Adeena Kahlo, are the reason. Do you know that? You, my love, are my muse."

Addie looked at Isabelle wide eyed with surprise. "Your muse...me? I... really? Wow, just wow." Isabelle reached over and placed her hand on Addie's cheek. "Yes, Sweetheart...wow indeed."

The quiet tranquility of the warm bath lulled Addie's eyes to close. She had never known that two women could take a bath together, and she never imagined that it would feel so delicious. The sweet smell of lilacs rising in the steam from the heated water was heaven, as was leaning her body against Isabelle's full breasts. Isabelle's head was resting against the back of the tub, and her eyes were closed. Neither spoke, but simply lavished in the serenity of the bath and the smell of lilacs on their skin.

Isabelle kissed the top of Addie's head sweetly, prompting her to open her eyes. "About Saturday's salon, darling," Isabelle confessed, "I'm embarrassed to say that I am a bit nervous about sharing my poetry among so many great writers and artists."

Addie turned her eyes to Isabelle. "Issie, your poetry is brilliant. This will be a wonderful opportunity for you to showcase your work for those who can appreciate your talent, *and* this reading will most likely help to get your poems published." I am so excited for you! Isabelle's brow creased with thought as she gently moved Addie and pulled herself up to get out of the tub. 'Hey! Where are you going?" Addie watched her as she gracefully glided across the room, her nude body glistening as she reached for a towel.

"Addie, you're right, of course. This could become something. This could be the opportunity I've longed for," she said as she slipped on her silk robe. "Get up and out of the tub, darling, quickly." Addie stood, and Isabelle placed a towel over her shoulders. "But uh, I thought, you know, we could cuddle some more." Addie grinned seductively.

Isabelle looked at Addie from head to toe. Smiling, she bit her lip. "Later, darling. Right now, we must pick out the most smashing outfits for tomorrow's soiree.

Addie sat looking out the window of Isabelle's automobile as it glided down the busy Paris streets. She was dressed to the nines and wrapped in a beautiful long fur-lined shawl to ward off the chilly spring evening. She turned from her wide-eyed wonder of the city to where Isabelle sat, quiet and beautiful. The sight of her took Addie's breath away. She was stunning and elegant, her beauty regal with a cool air of confidence.

"You know if you continue to look at me that way, I just might need to have Andre turn the Peugeot around and take us back home."

Addie laughed lightly and shook her head. "Sorry, I can't help it. You're stunning." Isabelle smiled and reached for Addie's hand. "Are you nervous, Iss? You know that there is absolutely no reason to be. Your poetry is magnificent and your talent amazing."

Isabelle held tightly to Addie's hand, "Thank you, darling. Your being here means the world to me. I am a bit nervous though, but that's only because I don't want to disappoint Alice and Gertrude. They have so much faith in me."

"Well, it's well-earned faith, honey. They believe in your talent, as do I. You'll knock 'em dead!" Isabelle laughed appreciatively. She could not help but be caught up in Addie's enthusiasm as the car pulled up to 27 Rue de Fleurus.

Once they made their way through the door of the salon, Alice took their wraps. Addie looked around and noted that the party was in full swing. Even though she had already attended a few gatherings at Gertrude and Alice's, she still had a difficult time wrapping her brain around the fact that she was here, literally hobnobbing with the likes of the most celebrated artists and writers of the early 20th century.

Addie thought about her own dream of writing fiction. She knew instinctively that she could not share any of her work with them, as she was not from their time; she knew the rules. However, in some kind of weird photosynthesis, she had absorbed their words, their ideas, and their philosophies from the many conversations she had participated in. She felt humbled in their presence and knew that, no matter her future, she would always cherish these impossible memories.

"Addie? Are you in the cosmos again, darling?" Addie turned to see Isabelle smiling at her. "I'm sorry, Iss, did you say something?" Isabelle touched her cheek affectionately. "I said, darling, would you like to meet Natalie Barney?"

Addie's eyes shot open, "What? She's...she's here?"

Isabelle smiled and nodded yes. "Come along. It's rather crowded this evening. Let's see if we can make our way to her."

There were so many guests milling around that they could not see the other end of the room. Just as they were about to make their way across the parlor, Alice approached them. "Isabelle, I do apologize for not greeting you properly when you first arrived. I'm so very pleased to see you, my dear, and you as well. Addie. Welcome." Addie reached out and pumped Alice's hand a bit too hard. Alice smiled.

"Isabelle, we are quite excited to hear a bit of your most recent work this evening. Thank you so very much for agreeing to share your poetry with us." Alice leaned in to whisper to Isabelle, "You know, my dear, some of our guests can be quite the critics. However, Gertrude and I are certain that you will win everyone over. We would not have asked you to do a reading if we thought otherwise." Alice pulled back and smiled. "Well, I had better greet our other guests, or you know who will not be pleased. Do help yourselves to refreshments. I must also check on the ladies in the small parlor. If you'll excuse me." Addie watched her leave, mouth slightly open in awe. There goes Alice B Toklas, sauntering away in the haze of history, thought Addie. Isabelle laughed and gently nudged Addie out of her haze of hero worship.

"Isabelle!" Isabelle turned and was immediately engulfed in the arms of her dear friend Simone. "Issie, darling, how grand to see you! Where have you been, dear? I thought you might have decided to sail off somewhere and neglected to invite me." Isabelle was released as Simone leaned to kiss her on each cheek.

"Simone, you know very well I've been here in Paris. We only just had lunch a few weeks ago," Isabelle said, laughing as she returned Simone's affectionate greeting. "Simone, you remember Addie?"

Simone stood back and took in Addie from head to toe before she reached out to clasp her hand. "Of course, Addie, how very lovely to see you again, *cheri*." Addie smiled at her greeting, feeling a bit as if she were under a microscope in biology class as she clasped Simone's elegant hand. Simone winked mischievously, and her eyes went to Isabelle, "Well, dear Isabelle, now I know how you have been occupying your time, with this lovely creature no doubt."

"Simone! Really dear, must you be so crass? Addie, please just ignore Simone. She likes to tease."

Addie didn't blush, but she could feel a trickle of perspiration sliding down between her breasts. "Oh, it's ok. Uh, I mean, it's fine, really. After all, it's true."

Simone gave Addie a genuine smile. "I like you, Addie Kahlo," she said. "Now come along, my lovelies, and let's go mingle with all these fabulous people. Oh look, there's Pablo with that glorious mistress of his. Perhaps we should consider purchasing something of his, as it very well may be worth something someday."

The Sunday morning after Gertrude's and Alice's soiree, Isabelle, Simone, and Addie sat enjoying coffee at a small café on the Champ de Mars. The weather was once again bright and sunny, though the chilly wind stopped it from being a perfect spring morning. Simone closed her eyes, facing the bright sky, and smiled. "I adore this glorious sunshine! Isabelle, I need to ask dear, where did that come from yesterday?" Opening her eyes and looking to Isabelle, her grey eyes were sharp and curious. "I don't believe I have ever heard such inspired poetry from you before. It was quite astonishing."

Simone's gaze remained focused on Isabelle as Addie watched both women. Isabelle lifted her coffee and took a delicate sip before she turned her eyes to Simone with a playful expression on her face. "Are you saying, Simone, that all my previous work has been subpar?"

Simone threw her head back and laughed. "Now sweetheart, you know I am quite blunt, but not rude. This is why you adore me, is it not?" Isabelle grinned and shook her head as she took another sip of coffee.

Addie watched the two friends banter, enjoying their snarky playfulness. She sipped her own coffee and watched Isabelle over her cup. She took a deep breath and gently blew out the air from her lungs. No one sips a coffee quite like Isabelle, Addie thought. She closed her eyes momentarily to reel in her hormones. Listening to Simone, she thought of yesterday's reading at the Steins. Isabelle was spectacular. Her voice beautifully sensuous and fluid, she captured the hearts and imaginations of all those present with her brilliant poetry. Every word, each verse, each couplet was delivered with such passion that the imagery projected was palpable.

"She was spectacular, wasn't she, Simone?" Addie excitedly said as she looked proudly at Isabelle, who winked at Addie with a smile. Addie suddenly stood and cleared her throat, eyes sparkling as she turned to look to both women, who now watched her with amusement:

> *The flutter of a heart in love mirrors the movement of a dove's wings*
> *The feel of a kiss is the rumble of thunder on a stormy night.*
> *Can you feel it, can you hear the thudding of the heart in love?*
> *For no other part of you makes that sound.*

"Bravo, darling! You recite beautifully." Isabelle laughed heartedly and clapped. Bowing slightly, Addie smiled broadly.

"Did you notice, Simone, that no one could take their eyes off her?"

"Yes *cheri*, I did notice. I was one of them," Simone said, as she moved her gaze back to Isabelle. "Isabelle, you do realize that I know Jacques Manard? He and I are quite friendly. I'd like to set up a meeting."

Isabelle looked at Simone quizzically. "Simone, what are you saying?"

"I'm saying that something has changed in your work. It was good before, lovely actually, but it lacked something. I don't know... but what I heard, what we all heard last night, was brilliant. Jacques is a superb literary agent, and I think he would disown me as a friend if I allowed your talent to slip away to another."

Isabelle sat up straight in her chair and looked intently at her friend, "Simone, are you serious? Monsieur Manard is a genius with new talent and is, quite possibly, the most desired literary agent in Paris. You've never offered to set up a meeting in the past."

Simone turned to Addie who was watching the entire exchange with excitement and something akin to awe. "Addie, Isabelle apparently trusts you without question. Look at my face, dear. Do you see any pretense in my expression? Could you please assure your darling Issie that I could not be more serious?"

Addie glanced at Simone and nodded her confirmation. She reached for Isabelle's hand, "Issie, this is your dream, honey."

Isabelle gently closed her fingers over Addie's and smiled, "Simone, let's set up that meeting."

Isabelle was sitting on the chaise in her elaborate bedroom suite drinking a sherry and watching Addie quietly and solemnly packing up her weekend bag. "Addie, baby,...tell me, what is it?" It was an early Sunday evening and Isabelle had wanted Addie to stay longer, but she had declined, as she needed to get back home to prepare for class the next day.

"I don't want to leave," Addie quietly said as she stuffed her toiletries into her bag. "I... I hate leaving like this. One of the most exciting things in your life happened to you this weekend, and I need to leave. I always need to leave, when all I want is to stay here with you!" She haphazardly threw her clothes into her bag, frustration and misery evident on her face.

Isabelle quickly moved to where Addie stood, and wrapping her arms around her she held her tightly. "Sweetheart, listen to me. I want more than anything for you to stay. You know that I do. But you're right, you know? You have classes in the morning."

Addie pulled back slightly from Isabelle's embrace. She nodded, and her smile was sad. "I'm sorry. I'm being ridiculous." Reaching out, she touched Isabelle's cheek before moving to continue her packing. But Isabelle grabbed her hand and pulled her to her again. Addie's eyes became red, tears threatening but not falling, as she allowed herself the comfort of Isabelle's embrace. She reached up and placed a sweet kiss on Isabelle's mouth. "I'm nearly done here. I suppose I'd better head out."

"Wait, I don't want you to leave like this. Talk to me darling."

Addie shook her head. "It doesn't matter. Will I see you next week?" she asked, "I'm sure I can be here Saturday, unless you have other plans, then I..."

"Saturday is perfect. You know that I have no other plans when it comes to you. I want you to come Saturday. I want you here with me." Addie grinned at Isabelle's directness. "Addie, please tell me what's this about. I'm concerned, you look so sad."

Addie picked up her bag and averted her eyes, "Is Andre ready? I can wait out front for him."

"Yes," she sighed, "I informed him earlier today that you'd be needing him at dusk." Isabelle walked Addie to the front foyer, periodically turning to look at her, neither of them saying anything.

"Oh wow, he's out there already. Okay, I guess I should leave."

"Addie," Isabelle felt uneasy, "Wait, I can't stand to see you like this. Talk to me." Isabelle held Addie's shoulders, trying to get her to look at her. Addie put down her bag and looked up at Isabelle. She couldn't stop her tears from falling now; the sweet concerned look on Isabelle's face was breaking her heart. She reached out and hugged Isabelle with a fierceness that communicated volumes.

Addie clung to Isabelle as she sobbed. "I love you, Iss, I love you so much, but I don't know how we will survive this, this supernatural magical craziness we are part of. I'm scared. I can't lose you. Time is going by too quickly. It will soon be time for me to leave for school in New York."

Isabelle held Addie as she sobbed, desperate not to let her go. She wanted to keep her there with her forever. Her own tears fell as she accepted that Addie was right, that their time together was quickly coming to an end. She knew that if she asked, Addie would stay with her here in Paris, here in 1912. But then what? Addie could never be happy without her beloved family and Alan and her own dreams. No, she couldn't do that to her. They held each other for a long time, both overcome by the seemingly hopelessness of their situation.

CHAPTER 28

"What's wrong?" asked Alan.

"Nothing's wrong. What makes you think anything's wrong? A person can't pull weeds out of their mother's garden without you thinking something's wrong?!"

"Hmmm, well, for one thing, you're pulling the flowers out too, along with the roots and half the yard." Addie sighed exasperatedly and looked at the pile of yanked out snapdragons mixed in with crabgrass and dandelions. "Oh shit, shit, shit!" She leaned back on the grass, looking at Alan, surrendering any pretense of composure.

"Ad, come on, give me your hand. Get up and take a break. I brought us some Cokes and Twinkies, your favorite." Alan shook the bag of snacks in front of Addie's face. "In a bit, I'll help you clean up this mess." Addie nodded in defeat and sighed, allowing Alan to help her up off the ground and lead her to the wicker chairs on her mother's small backporch. Once seated, Alan handed Addie a Coke and she took a long thirsty drink. "I wish this were a martini."

Alan laughed. "Hah! You don't even like martinis, remember?" Addie turned and looked at her mother's small garden. Her mother loved her garden. She shook her head remembering how she had promised her that she would water and take care of her beloved flowers while her folks were in San Antonio for a few weeks. She failed. Not only did she not water the flowers, she had now absent-mindedly yanked them out.

"Addie, listen, don't worry about the garden, we'll get it cleaned up."

Addie shook her head, on the verge of tears. "But I ruined it! Look!" she said, pointing miserably at the small pile of ruined foliage. "I can't do anything right, dammit!"

"Hey!" Looking concerned, Alan asked, "What's this all about? I know it's not the garden. Come on, you know you can talk to me. We know each other's secrets." Alan smiled and gave her a quick wink. Despite her misery, she smiled at his silliness. But quickly her mood grew dark, and the tears that had been threatening all day began to fall.

"Alan, I'm scared," she volunteered as she dabbed at her swollen eyes with the back of her hand.

"Of what? Tell me," he asked gently as he pulled his handkerchief out of his pocket and handed it to her.

Addie took a drink of her Coke and leaned back on the chair. "We graduate in three weeks. In less than three months I'm supposed to be taking the train to New York to start my first year at Vassar. My folks cashed in one of their savings bonds to pay for my first year in the dormitory. I already have my classes picked out and scheduled. I've even signed up for the college paper as part of my mentorship."

"Okay, so it all sounds great, but..."

Addie suddenly jumped up off the chair and began pacing. "I can't go, Alan, I can't. I don't know my purpose! Don't you see?! Why don't I know my purpose? With Peter's help, you found the courage to do what you want. Isabelle, my sweet Isabelle, is now getting recognized for her poetry. Even Rachel! I mean even Rachel, who doesn't know a thing about Café du Temp, is gloriously happy. She is going to be one of the first female managers of a night club in Chicago. How cool is that? That's not only it, Alan." Addie was now sobbing. "How can I leave her? How can I go off to New York to college and leave Isabelle?" Addie sat down on the chair, tears streaming down her face. "I love her, Alan. I love her."

Addie opened her eyes and looked up at the clear evening sky. There were a few stars twinkling, though most were obscured by the city lights. She and Alan had walked to the park after she broke down in tears. Now, they lay on the grass looking up at the sky. They were holding hands, and Addie could feel the strength of her companions support and the friendship that she was certain would always be there.

"Let's go to Café du Temp tomorrow night." Alan turned toward Addie and rested his chin on the palm of his hand.

Addie turned to look at Alan "What? Why?"

"Well, we haven't been there together in a while and maybe Peter will have some insight. He's amazing, you know? I mean he helped me, and maybe he can help you too. What do you have to lose?" She looked at Alan, uncertainty clouding her thoughts, but she soon realized she didn't have anything to lose.

Addie hadn't been to Café du Temp on a weekday in months, as she and Isabelle had arranged to meet there at specific times on the weekends. They'd usually order lunch or a cup of tea and talk about their week, enjoying the atmosphere that only Café du Temp could provide. Then, Isabelle would smile and place a shawl or coat around Addie's shoulders, and they'd walk through her door to her world.

Now, as Addie walked through the long ornate hall which led to the main club, she realized that she hadn't spoken to Peter for any length of time in months. The only time she recalled speaking with him was the one or two times he had stopped by to greet her and Isabelle. She felt uncomfortable about asking for his advice now. After all, what could she really ask?

As Addie expected, she and Alan were escorted to their usual table. They ordered drinks and settled in to listen to the jazz quartet that was playing some current tunes as well as some of the old standards. Despite her melancholy mood, once seated, she felt a sort of calmness soak into her body. She loved the tranquil atmosphere of Café du Temp and the jazz that always seemed to seep into her soul. "It's nice being here with you, Alan. Thank you. Coming tonight was a good idea." Addie lifted her wine and clinked her glass with his.

"The music is good tonight," Alan said, winking as they toasted.

Addie grinned and said, "The jazz is always good here. Remember the first time you brought me? God, I was so excited and scared. I thought we were going to be busted for underage drinking. If I only had known." Smiling, she slowly shook her head.

"Alan," Addie sighed. "About speaking with Peter, perhaps I shouldn't. I think we're supposed to figure things out for ourselves, you know. How about we just enjoy the music and..."

Alan reached across the small table for Addie's hand. "Ad, you've got nothing to lose. Come on, try and relax."

Addie looked at Alan and nodded her agreement. Attempting to move the subject away from her own issues, Addie shifted the discussion. "So, tell me about what's happening with school. Did you complete all the paperwork to switch to the Illinois Institute of Technology? I know your dad is still on the fence about you switching to architecture, but at least you know your parents will be happy you're staying in Chicago."

"Yeah, everything is done, but damn, Ad, what a pain in the ass everything was. Honest to god, thank heaven for Mom. She was a real champ for keeping Dad reined in. I thought he'd walk out of the registrar's office a few times. He's not the most patient guy in the world."

"But, it's all okay though, right? Everything is set? I mean you will be studying architecture, just like you've always dreamed of doing."

Alan grinned broadly, his entire face shining with happiness. Addie jumped up from her seat and gave him a fierce hug. "I am so proud of you," she whispered in his ear, and she meant it with all her heart.

"Okay you two, what did I miss?" Peter walked toward them just as Addie broke off their hug.

"Peter! Hello. I was just congratulating Alan on being accepted to the Illinois Institute of Technology. I am so proud of him. Alan is following his dream!" Addie could not help but brag a little about her friend. Peter couldn't have looked more pleased. Reaching for Alan's hand, he shook it enthusiastically and pulled him in for a hug.

"This definitely calls for a celebratory toast. Sam, could you please bring us bottle of Veuve Clicquot and three glasses? We are celebrating!"

Alan smiled at Peter and clasped his hand on his shoulder, "Peter, I just want to say thank you." The look of affection and gratitude was clearly evident in Alan's eyes.

"Alan, you've always known you'd make the choice that was best for you. I simply helped put things in perspective, that's all." Alan shook his head smiling and breathed a huge sigh of relief, choosing to accept Peter's praise without further comment.

"Hey, you two," Alan said, quickly looking at both Addie and Peter. "Can you give me like five minutes? I wanna make a quick call to my brother Frank. I have his car tonight, and I'd just like to check in with him." Addie squinted at Alan, knowing exactly what he was up to.

"Oh sure, no problem," she responded. "Peter and I can catch up."

Peter gave Alan a wink and a smile as Alan headed toward the phone booth in the rear of the club.

Addie felt awkward. She was not as close to Peter as Alan or even Issie were. She quickly scanned her brain for some safe topic as her apprehension about asking him for help still made her uncomfortable. "So, Peter, new haircut?" Addie cringed as soon as the words left her lips. New haircut, really? She couldn't look at him. Peter eyed Addie with a playful grin, and she suddenly burst out laughing. "Oh, good god, I can't believe I just said that. Honestly, Peter, my social interaction skills are normally better than this."

Peter laughed along with Addie, and once they caught their breaths, he looked at her with sincere admiration and affection. He cleared his throat and raised his glass of champagne focusing on her. "Adeena Kahlo," he began, and she looked at him with a sort of wonder. "Cheers to you, sweet Addie; your gentle, compassionate heart and marvelous gift of insight into the power of the human spirit are your strengths. They will help define your destiny and ultimately, your happiness."

Addie stopped midway to clink glasses with Peter, and her eyes filled with tears. "Peter, I..."

Peter held Addie's hand and smiled, "Addie, allow me to toast to your future. It will be magnificent." Addie clinked glasses with Peter as tears slipped from her eyes and her heart pounded in her chest.

It was nearly midnight when Alan pulled up to Addie's apartment building to drop her off. She had said nothing on the entire ride home. As if he knew that she needed the silence, Alan hadn't attempted to make small talk. But now it had been five minutes of sitting with the car idling, and Addie had still made no move to open the car door. Alan shifted in his seat and looked at her as Addie continued to just stare quietly into space.

"Addie, did you get bad news? Is that what this is about? Come on, say something. I know you want to talk. We've been sitting here for five minutes, and you haven't made any attempt to leave. Come on, what is it?"

Addie turned and looked at Alan with a sad smile. "I know now what I need to do. The problem is, I'm not certain it's what I *want* to do."

Alan looked at Addie curiously, "What did Peter tell you? Did you explain to him about you and Isabelle, and...?"

"No, that's just it. I didn't say a word to Peter about Issie and me, about my confusion concerning my future, or about how terrified I am to have to make this impossible choice. I didn't say anything, but yet I am certain he knew, he knew it all."

"But I don't understand. You still haven't told me what he said to make you believe he knows."

"He toasted me."

"What? He toasted you? Like clinking glasses and saying nice words about you, like that?"

"Yes, just like that."

"It must have been some toast. Do you remember it?"

"I'll remember it for the rest of my life, word for word and the sound of his voice as he said it."

"Well come on, you're killing me here. What did he say?"

"He said, "Adeena Kahlo, cheers to you, sweet Addie; your gentle compassionate heart and marvelous gift of insight into the power of the human spirit are your strengths. They will help define your destiny, and ultimately your happiness." Then, when I attempted to question him, he said, "Addie, allow me to toast to your future. It will be magnificent.""

Alan continued to look at Addie, his brow creased in contemplation, "Wow. So, do you have any idea what he meant by his toast?"

"Yes, I do. It means I need to trust my own instincts, and whichever path I choose, that decision will lead me toward the future I was truly meant to live."

CHAPTER 29

At this moment, Addie wished that she was drinking something stronger than tea. She was trying to control her breathing, attempting not to appear upset, so that Isabelle wouldn't see the disappointment that was so present in every cell of her body. She felt like crying, and it took everything in her not to burst into tears. She closed her eyes before allowing herself to speak again. She and Isabelle were sitting in a café on the Left Bank, on an evening full of stars. There were musicians playing and people were everywhere. The atmosphere was full of the joy of Paris, yet at this moment she was anything but joyous.

Addie looked down at her meal, which she now had no desire to eat. "I had hoped you'd make an exception this time, Iss. It's my graduation, and I want you to be there." Addie was terribly disappointed, and despite her best efforts, she was teary-eyed as she looked up at Isabelle. Isabelle took a sip of her tea and gently placed her cup on the table. She looked down at her hands momentarily, not wanting to see the hurt in Addie's eyes. Seeing the pained look on Addie's face nearly broke her heart.

"Addie, do you remember what we spoke about, what we both agreed upon?"

Addie looked at Isabelle. Of course, she remembered. Did Isabelle really think she'd forget? They had just made love, and Addie was lying in Isabelle's arms. They were talking about Café du Temp, always seeming to refer back to the fairytale place whenever they found themselves contemplative. Isabelle shared with Addie what Peter had told her when she first learned of Café du Temp's special influences. Peter said it is possible for guests to visit the past, but they should never visit the future. Addie was still not sure why. She and Alan had thought that visiting the future

189

would somehow give the person an unfair advantage when they returned to their own time.

"Yes, I remember," Addie said, her response tinged with tears, disappointment, and anger. "Of course, I do, but I thought...Oh hell, I don't know what I thought! Forget I asked. It's just a silly graduation from high school. Why would you even care to go to something like that?" Addie turned away from Isabelle and tried in vain to wipe the tears from her eyes. "Isabelle, I think I'd like to go. Can we please leave? I'm sorry, but I'm not hungry any longer." Isabelle took a deep breath and nodded, calling for the bill. Once the waiter approached, Isabelle asked him to secure them a cab for the short ride back to her Grandmother's apartments.

Isabelle watched Addie silently sulk as she looked out the window of the cab. All she wanted to do was take her in her arms and hold her, tell her that she would go, that she was proud of her and wanted to see her accept her diploma, but she couldn't. She couldn't go to Addie's world because, if she did, she would never be allowed to come back to her own.

She felt like kicking herself. How could she not share that important piece of information with Addie? She felt foolish and selfish. She needed to tell her. She thought back to when Peter explained to her that there were rules at Café du Temp that must always be followed. One of rules was that one can always visit the past but never the future. Most of those who found themselves at Café du Temp never ventured to the past. Like Alan, they found their way to their destiny in their own time. She wondered what cosmic alignment had guided her and Addie to meet and fall in love when they were from different worlds.

Isabelle and Addie walked out to the small private garden adjacent to Isabelle's grandmother's home after the cab had dropped them off. Addie lifted her head and breathed in the scent of flowers. She loved it there. It was a smaller version of the many beautiful gardens sprinkled throughout Paris, with an abundance of flowers, shrubs, and trees. There was a small foot bridge decorated with stone animals and fairies that brought to mind the story of Mary Lennox in The Secret Garden, one of her favorite books as a child.

"You're angry with me," Isabelle said, her voice a mixture of pain and sadness.

Addie did not response nor did she look at Isabelle. She wanted to bask in the calming scent of the garden for just a few minutes more while they walked to the gazebo that served as one of the focal points of the small beautiful space. Once they reached the gazebo, Addie moved toward a solitary bench and seated herself quietly, taking a deep breath and blowing it out slowly. "No, Issie, I'm not angry. I think I was at first, but no, I'm not any longer." Isabelle moved to sit next to Addie and reached for her hand, pulling it to her lap and holding it tightly as if she were afraid Addie would flee.

Addie turned to Isabelle. "I'm just disappointed," she said a bit wearily. "I know that when you first brought me to your Paris, you told me that you could never come to my world. I didn't question it. I didn't understand it, but I accepted it. I accepted it because I was falling in love with you." Addie reached up and gently caressed Isabelle's cheek, a despondent smile creasing her lips. "I foolishly thought that it was a choice, and that you would eventually concede to a visit or two," Addie looked intensely at Isabelle. "But, it isn't a choice, is it?"

Isabelle lifted Addie's hand and slowly kissed her palm, and then she held Addie's hand in both of hers. "That's the thing about this, Addie. It *is* a choice." Addie looked questioningly at Isabelle, waiting for her to explain. Shaking her head gently, Isabelle's eyes became red, and Addie saw the beginning of tears forming. "But it is not a choice that I can make. You see, darling, Café du Temp allows one to visit the past, but if one steps into the future...," Isabelle sighed, her eyes moist with imminent tears, "they cannot return to their own time."

Addie's eyes opened wide at the realization of what Isabelle was telling her. "Never? They can never return? So, you're telling me that you never had any intention of visiting my world," Addie said, the shock apparent in her voice.

"I...it would have required a commitment to the future. I'm so sorry, Addie. I should have told you." Isabelle lowered her head for just a moment, then lifted her eyes to Addie. Addie saw deep love, sadness, and remorse. "At the beginning, I was so selfish I thought that it didn't matter. You never questioned it, but later, once I realized that I was falling in love with you, I was afraid to tell you. I thought the limitations of our relationship would frighten you away. I was afraid of losing you."

Addie's mind slowly absorbed Isabelle's admission. Trying to take in the kaleidoscope of surprise, hurt, sadness, fear, and betrayal she was experiencing, she turned away from Isabelle, unable to respond. This world she had stumbled into, with its infuriating cryptic messages and magic doors to different worlds, was simply too much. For a brief moment, she wanted to run, run back to the day that Alan had told her about Café du Temp. She wished for a moment she'd said no. No, she did not want to experience this adventure. Then she could have continued on with her every day average life, never having met Isabelle Androsko.

But turning back to look at Isabelle, that fleeting bit of regret dissolved as quickly as it surfaced. The love in her eyes, love mixed with sadness, fear and tears, nearly broke Addie's heart. No, she could never regret meeting Isabelle. In a thousand years of pasts and futures, she would never regret it. She reached up and gently kissed Isabelle's trembling mouth. "I love you," Addie whispered as she kissed Isabelle. "I love you, Issie." Isabelle moved into Addie's arms, gently sobbing with relief at Addie's words. Addie held her tightly as she sobbed, Addie's own tears falling as she thought of their uncertain future.

Their lovemaking that night was desperate, rough, tender, full of frantic words of undying love and soft sounds of ecstasy as they gave their whole selves to each other, physically and emotionally. In the early hours before dawn, they lay awake, snuggled together under cool white sheets, listening to the predawn sounds of the city. They had talked openly, and with an intense sadness, about the future. Addie would be leaving in less than three months for New York to begin her new life at Vassar. Isabelle would be where she was, here in 1912 Paris. She was attracting a lot of interest in the literary world, and much had been planned around her debut volume of poetry.

The soft sound of chirping finches outside the window alerted Addie to the early morning. She lay with her eyes open, head resting on Isabelle's warm bosom. She heard and felt the soft rhythm of Isabelle's heart as she slept. Breathing in her scent, Addie closed her eyes and imprinted her smell into her heart and mind. As she watched the early morning sun make its way across the room, she raised her head slightly to check the small clock on the fireplace mantel. She felt numb and heartbroken at the same time. If it were possible to do so, she thought she could die of a broken heart.

CHAPTER 30

Addie leaned against the door, holding her glass of punch, smiling, and admiring the singing duo. Her mother and Aunt Rosie were belting out "I've Got the World on a String" by Frank Sinatra, no doubt choosing the song as a tribute to the graduates.

"Hi, honey. Are you enjoying your party?" Addie's father put his arm around her shoulders and gave a gentle squeeze. She knew he was proud of her, but she also knew he was sad that she would be leaving for college in a few short months. Addie looked at her dad and felt the tremendous love that emanated from him. She adored her parents. They had always been exceedingly supportive, and they trusted her without question. The worry of ever disappointing or hurting them brought a lump to her throat and a knot to her stomach.

"Yes, very much, Dad. Thank you so much for having this party for us. It's wonderful."

Joe Kahlo beamed at his girl and looked slightly embarrassed, as he was not one for mushy stuff, as he had frequently told her. "Well, I think your mother had more to do with setting it all up. It gave her and your Aunt Rosie an opportunity to get on stage again. They've been practicing that Sinatra song for weeks." He chuckled and took a long drink of his beer.

Addie laughed with him and kissed him on the cheek. "I love you Dad."

"Addie! Come dance with us," yelled an exuberant Rachel, as Mickey twirled her on the dance floor.

Suddenly, a strong yet gentle hand grabbed her wrist. "Come on Ad, let's you and I show these two how it's done." Addie looked up at a smiling Alan, so handsome in his new suit.

"I would be honored," she said with a big smile, radiating the love and affection she held for her best friend.

As Addie danced and laughed with her family and friends, she felt happy. Happy to be so fortunate to have these amazing, caring people that she so loved in her life. The only person missing who could make this perfect was Isabelle. The sadness she felt for not having Isabelle there with her, celebrating her big day was, for the moment, held at bay. She consoled herself with the knowledge that they would soon be together and that she planned on spending every free moment with Isabelle that she had remaining before college.

cl—୭ͻ

"I'm never going to see you again, am I?" Addie turned from her packing and looked at Rachel with a combination of sadness and amusement.

"What? Don't be silly. Of course, you'll see me again. I'm going away to school, not to the moon." Addie put down the books she was sorting and came over to sit next to Rachel on the sofa. She put her arm around her and gave her a gentle squeeze. "Rach, you know I'll be back at the breaks, and how fun will it be for you to come up to New York to see me. You know you can, anytime you want."

Rachel looked at Addie and shrugged her shoulders. "I know, but it's not the same. Dammit, Ad, I'm used to having you around here being a pain in the ass!" Addie laughed loudly and kissed Rachel on the cheek.

"I know Rach, but you'll be so busy running the club that you won't have time to ever miss me."

"That's not true, Ad. Oh, I know you spend every weekend with Alan, but we always meet up during the week for breakfast and stuff. And look who will be in your room, my bratty sister Roxanne!" Addie laughed again, shaking her head at Rachel's complaining. Rachel took a deep breath and stood. "Okay, okay I'll stop, but it's not easy with you going away, that's all I'm saying."

Addie felt it just as much as Rachel. She was going to miss her terribly and the rest of her family as well, but this was part of growing up and realizing her dreams. She needed to do this. She wanted to do this. She couldn't allow herself to feel guilty or sad right now. She was going to college, and she was going to study journalism, her dream. It had always been her dream. It was difficult enough, she thought, leaving her family, but the constant reality of leaving Isabelle filled her with a despair that flooded her heart. She told herself that she needed to be strong.

Taking a deep breath to help rid herself of the dread she felt, she reached out a consoling hand to Rachel. "Hey, what do you say we finish up here and walk over to Stan's, and I'll buy you breakfast."

Rachel sniffed and smiled at Addie. "Okay, sounds like a plan, but fair warning; I'm starving, so you better have enough money."

After breakfast, Rachel walked over to The Angel to meet with Addie's father and her dad to discuss waitstaff scheduling and food prep. The Angel did not serve gourmet meals. Their menu was more like comfort food, but the food was fresh and tasty, and the waitstaff were well-trained and loyal. The waitstaff loved working for the Kahlo family. The family had always been respectful and fair to their employees, and Rachel knew she would be as well once she took over.

Later that day, sitting in her room sorting through knickknacks, books and journals, Addie considered what to take and what to leave behind. Anything left behind would be boxed up and put in the basement storage area. Her bedroom would soon belong to Rachel's younger sister Roxanne. Just as she finished boxing up the last of her high school yearbooks and other memorabilia, the telephone rang.

"Hey gorgeous, plans tonight?"

Addie smiled into the telephone, "You know, Alan, it could have been Rachel who picked up the line."

Alan sniggered. "Nah, she's at the club. I just dropped Mickey off there to meet her cause his car is in the shop. So, do you have plans?" Addie didn't, but her heart wasn't into doing anything that evening except sitting down with the pile of forms and other materials she received in the mail from the college. Ever since her and Isabelle's futile efforts to figure out a way to stay together had ended without a solution, she'd been unmotivated to do much of anything. All she could think of was Isabelle, seeing her, being with her, staring into her beautiful eyes, and kissing her endlessly. She was exhausted by the constant realization that she was losing her, and it was an effort to put on a brave face for her family and friends.

"Ad, you still there?"

Addie snapped out of her musings and sighed. "Listen Addie, just come out with me for a while. I have Frank's car, and we can take a drive to the lake. It'll be good for you to get some fresh air, and well, I'm here you know? We can talk." Addie suddenly teared up. She was embarrassed that these days she seemed to cry at the drop of a hat, and it always seemed that Alan was there, trying to bring her out of her sadness.

"Okay Alan, maybe your right. What time are you picking me up?

A small carnival was setting up along Montrose harbor; the carney workers were listening to Tony Bennett sing "From Rags to Riches" on their RCA as they stocked the booths with stuffed animals, cotton candy, and balloons. "Addie...," Alan said sympathetically.

Addie looked over at Alan as they walked along the small beach on the picturesque lakefront. "Don't, Alan, please don't say anything or I may start crying again, and I'm so sick of crying." Addie blew out a long breath and lifted her eyes to the early evening sun. "I love Chicago in the summer. I'm going to miss it when I leave." She looked to Alan again and reached for his hand. "And I will miss you, my always gallant, brilliant, sarcastic, supportive "boyfriend"." Alan smiled playfully and batted his eyelashes.

On the drive back home, Addie fell asleep leaning her head on Alan's shoulder. He moved one arm around her as he expertly steered with the other. He couldn't help but feel concern, as Addie hadn't been the same these past two months. She'd lost weight, and she'd been subdued and less apt to laugh. She spent a great deal of time alone, writing in her journal, and when she wasn't writing, she spent nearly every waking hour with Isabelle. Alan knew of course that it had everything to do with Isabelle.

They were ending, and Addie couldn't see any way through or around it. Alan truly believed that her heart was literally breaking. He knew that Addie was a strong woman, bright and independent. To be what they were, homosexuals, you had to be. You couldn't allow society, with its puritan beliefs and hateful laws, to strip you of your self-worth, your strong belief in your right to live the life you were meant to live, even if that meant you had to live it in secret.

He didn't doubt in the least that Addie still possessed the inner strength that allowed them to be resilient in a world that shunned their kind, but still he fretted. He'd never seen his friend like this, and he couldn't help his disquiet.

CHAPTER 31

"Alice has requested your company at tomorrow evening's salon. It appears, sweetheart, that you have made quite an impression on Pablo. He shared with Gertrude that he finds the lovely young American quite outspoken and forward thinking, his words."

Addie and Isabelle were having lunch in the garden, sipping red wine as they sampled bits of warm crusty bread, brie, and fruit. Addie looked up to Isabelle, and her breath caught. Isabelle was a vision in the sunlight with her hair appearing almost golden and her amber iris's sparkling. Her smile, as she gazed at Addie, was full of adoration and gentleness. Addie's efforts to appear strong as their parting approached was betrayed by the sadness in her eyes.

"I'm not going," Addie said in a trembling voice, almost a whisper. She didn't know that she was going to say it at that moment. These words had been lingering in her heart, unspoken for months as she went through her daily life preparing to leave for New York. She didn't know that she would voice them, but she did. She had pushed them to the back of her mind since the day, no, since the moment she knew she was in love with Isabelle. But now she didn't regret it. She knew all along she was never going to willingly leave her.

"Addie?" Reaching for her glass, Isabelle stopped. She visibly swallowed and looked at Addie with wide eyes. She knew of course that Addie was not referring to tomorrow evening's salon. "What are you saying?" Isabelle asked, needing to hear the words again. Addie turned toward her, and with her heart thumping in her chest, she reached for Isabelle's hand. "I said, I am not going."

It was too much. Everything Isabelle had wanted since Addie came into her life was right in front of her. All she needed to do was say yes. Yes, that she wanted Addie to stay with her, to stay with her forever. And Addie would. Addie would give up everything for her, her family, her dreams, and her world. Isabelle knew this as indisputably as she knew her own name. She wanted so badly to say yes, to throw her arms around Addie, and hold her for eternity. But, how could she? How could she so selfishly take everything away from her?

Isabelle stood and slowly walked toward the house. Addie watched her, incredulously. She watched as Isabelle calmly opened the glass doors to the parlor and walked in without a word. Addie blinked and then jumped up from her seat and ran to the house, fear and confusion filling her with dread. As she reached for the door knob, she saw that her hands were shaking badly. She took a deep breath in an attempt to calm herself before walking in to the parlor.

Addie looked around, momentarily panicked. At first, she didn't see Isabelle, but then, there she was, sitting at the ornate grand piano. Isabelle began to play Ravel's "Pavane for a Dead Princess," a piece that Addie had fallen in love with the very first time she had heard Isabelle play it. Addie listened intently for several minutes. Slowly walking to Isabelle, she lowered herself to her knees next to the bench and gently reached for Isabelle's hand. "Iss...what is it, honey? I don't understand. Talk to me, please." She could hear the fear and confusion in her own voice, and she willed herself to give Isabelle time to speak.

Isabelle turned toward Addie, reached out, and gently touched her cheek. Tears pooled in her eyes as she encircled Addie with her arms and pulled her close. After some moments, she pulled back and gently brushed aside a few loose hairs that had fallen in Addie's eyes. In a trembling voice Isabel said the words that she knew would break both of their hearts. "No, Addie, I can't let you do that. You cannot stay. You need to go."

Addie's breath caught. She was so shocked at Isabelle's words that all she could do was stare. She stood up in a rush, initially to stop the waves of nausea that suddenly took hold of her, then to catch her breath. She felt as though someone had punched her in the stomach. "What?" she whispered as she stood back staring at her. "No, Iss, you can't mean that, please."

"Addie," Isabelle started. "Yes, I do mean it. God, I wish I didn't!" She stood and moved quickly toward Addie, reaching for her hand. Addie moved back from her touch, staring at Isabelle, heartbreak and anger evident as she stared wide eyed at Isabelle. "Oh, Addie, don't you see, darling? You must go to New York! This is everything you've wanted, everything you dreamed of. Leaving your family and abandoning your dreams can't possibly be your future!"

Addie couldn't believe what she was hearing. Isabelle was telling her to leave. With tears streaming down her cheeks. she took a sharp breath as the realization of Isabelle's rejection sunk in. Building anger warred with her breaking heart. She wanted to scream, to scream and scream and scream until she passed out or died. So, she did. She screamed at the top of her lungs, "No, you can't send me away!" She stood, sobbing, great deep sobs of pain and heartbreak. Isabelle rushed to her and tried to hold her, but Addie pushed her away. "No! You don't get to hold me anymore! Don't touch me! I've been such an idiot, believing that you love me!" Addie paced and shook her hands in an effort to calm herself.

"Addie, please listen to me! Allow me to explain," Isabelle cried out as she tried again in vain to reach out for Addie. She herself was beyond consoling, but she told herself she needed to make Addie understand. "I love you, Addie. I love you! Please believe me, oh darling I never lied to you!"

Hearing the desperation in Isabelle's voice, Addie turned to look at her with tear-filled eyes. Her heart immediately clinched with compassion at seeing Isabelle so distraught. She wanted to run to her. Isabelle looked inconsolable. Her face was blotched and teary. Her hands shook as she tried to wipe her own tears, and her breathing was labored. Addie stood, silently watching her, her own arms wrapped around herself as if trying to not fall apart. She felt numb and wholly exhausted.

Needing to sit, Addie plopped onto the cushioned loveseat that stood but a foot from her and brought her knees up to her chin, covering her eyes with her hands. She was shaking as if chilled, and her head pounded. It was a moment or so before she heard Isabelle speak. Looking up when she heard Isabelle's shaky voice, Addie watched as she attempted to gather her composure. Her heart broke a little more, seeing that Isabelle appeared just as devastated as she herself was.

It had been only a few moments, but it felt an eternity as Addie watched Isabelle pace the length of the room, seemingly struggling for what she wanted to say. She looked miserable, Addie thought. She couldn't stand to see the woman she loved in so much pain. "Issie...please, tell me honey," she said softly, her quiet words trembled slightly as she attempted to steady her own voice.

Isabelle's face was pale, and her eyes red from crying, but Addie could see her steel herself as she gathered her strength. Walking to the loveseat, she sat down next to Addie and gently reached for her hands, holding them tightly she leaned down and gently kissed each palm.

"Do you remember when we first met?" she asked tenderly. Addie nodded, and despite her pain, allowed a small smile to make its way to her lips. "You were so excited about your dreams of becoming an author. You spoke of going to university and of helping mentor others. You said you loved to teach. Your voice was filled with excitement for your future, and you looked so happy." Addie listened and was about to interrupt, but Isabelle stilled her so she could continue.

"During this time that we've been together, I've learned of your deep love for your family, your cousin Rachel, and of course, Alan. I could never selfishly ask you to give up your family and your future. Don't you see, you'd never truly be happy, sweetheart? There would always be that missing piece of your life."

Addie's eyes searched Isabelle's, and the love she saw reflected back to her brought fresh tears to her eyes. She didn't think she could be any more devastated, but hearing Isabelle's selfless words of truth nearly brought her to her knees. She knew that no matter how much she loved Isabelle, she would be miserable without her family and the opportunity to achieve her dreams. There would always be a piece of her heart missing. She closed her eyes and softly nodded, acknowledging that what Isabelle said was the truth. But still, she couldn't bear the thought of life without her.

"Issie, I love you, and..."

"And I love you, Addie. Don't you see, darling? You have never asked me to give up my home, my dreams, to come and live with you in your America." Addie's eyes widened and she suddenly knew what Isabelle was trying to tell her. "Why? Addie, why have you never asked me?" Addie couldn't speak, "Tell me, Addie. Why?"

Addie's throat felt dry, and she choked back a cry. "Because I love you too much to ever ask you to give up your home and your dreams," she whispered, her own admission making her eyes sting.

"How then," Isabelle responded, "my beautiful sweet girl, can I expect you to give up yours?

Addie lay awake in Isabelle's arms, the place she felt the most loved. They were both exhausted from crying, from the pain of their imminent parting, and from the sheer emotional toll they knew was coming. Addie held Isabelle tightly, taking in everything about her, the shape of her ear lobes, the feel and weight of her breasts as they rested on her own, her fresh scent that reminded Addie of summer. It was unbearable, this ending of their relationship, but they both knew it was inevitable. They were, quite literally, from different worlds.

"I have something for you, sweetheart," Isabelle whispered in Addie's ear. Addie opened her eyes, following Isabelle's movements as she lifted herself from Addie's arms and walk to her dressing table. There she picked up a small velvet pouch and brought it back to their bed. When she handed the pouch to Addie, she blushed. Addie sat up, and with questioning eyes, watched Isabelle. After a moment, she looked down and opened the small bag. She took in a breath of surprise and looked back at Isabelle, who was smiling from ear to ear. In the pouch lay a delicate silver and amber rose, held on an equally delicate silver chain. The rose's amber color reminded Addie of Isabelle's eyes, bright and full of fire.

"It was my mother's. It meant the world to her, as she received it from her mother when she went off to school in Switzerland. My mother was one of the first woman from her community to go to university. It was quite the accomplishment. When I was preparing to leave for university, she gave it to me as a symbol of success and of her love. Now, as you go off to your adventures at Vassar, my darling, I want you to have it as a symbol of my love for you. I am so very proud of you, Addie Kahlo, so very proud." Addie thought she couldn't cry any more tears, but they came, hard and inconsolable, as she held Isabelle, the love of her life, in her arms.

Part

II

CHAPTER 32

May 1964

"Alan! It's so good to see you after all these months!" Alan smiled and gave Addie a huge hug.

"God, woman, it's good to see you too. Looking as gorgeous as ever I see."

Addie playfully pinched Alan's cheeks. "Look who's talking. Every woman in this restaurant is salivating at the sight of you." Alan laughed. Addie and Alan were meeting for dinner in a small Italian restaurant in the Morningstar neighborhood of Manhattan. The restaurant, trendy but quaint, was less than a mile from where Addie was a professor of journalism at Columbia University. "I'm so glad you could leave your meeting early. I know how busy you've been with this new project. Let me look at you," Addie said.

Alan stood back a foot and put his hands in his pockets, mimicking a model posing for a photo shoot. Addie laughed again and squeezed Alan's hand as they walked over to their reserved table. Once they were situated, Addie ordered a martini. Noting her order, Alan raised an eyebrow and ordered his own drink, a gin and tonic. "A martini, Ad? If I recall, you detest martinis."

Addie grabbed Alan's hand and gave him a wide grin. "Well, I've learned to love them now, although only on special occasions, such as seeing my dearest friend. So, tell me, how long will you be in town? Rachel phoned me yesterday, and she mentioned that you might actually be here in New York for at least a week this time. Is this true?"

"Well, yes. Actually, with this new collaboration, I may be coming up to the Big Apple a lot more regularly for the next several months."

Addie took a sip of her martini, "I know I like the idea of you being here more often, but there aren't any problems with the project is there?"

"Oh no, everything's fantastic actually. The firm is being very accommodating with their designers, and it looks like the new Chicago building will break ground right on schedule. There are some environmental specifics I will not budge on, while the board is saying that the changes are not necessary, though, I'm fairly certain that their gripes are a ploy to get us to lower our costs. We can work through it; I am not allowing them to cut environmental corners here. In the long run, this new building will be a first of its kind. Perhaps a bit pricier to build, but ultimately much less costly to operate."

Addie watched her friend as he spoke with excitement about the new Chicago project but thought he looked a bit worried as well. "Okay, out with it. What's wrong?" Addie looked at Alan with her head cocked to one side and her eyes boring into his.

He laughed, "Hah! You know me so well. Okay, Michael isn't too happy about me going off to New York as often as I might need to."

Addie leaned in slightly to keep their conversation from being overheard by the other diners. "Alan, surely he must understand how important this is to you? Michael has always been so supportive of your career. Did something happen?"

"Oh god no. You know Michael. He's fine. Since we purchased the new place, he's very excited about fixing it up. He can hardly wait to have me design the addition, which by the way, will be perfect for his parents. They will have their own space and entrance, and we will be sharing a gorgeous yard space. Ad, the best thing is that, with Michael's parents cohabitating with us, well there shouldn't be any nosy neighbors questioning the living arrangements. I mean what's there to question? The distinguished Dr. James Cinto and his lovely wife, Professor Maggie Cinto, two of the most respected professors at Northwestern, share a home with their son and nephew. That's the story anyway, if anyone asks."

"Oh Alan, really? Are you and Michael alright with that ruse?"

"Honestly, Ad, yes," Alan smiled and leaned in so that only Addie could hear him. "Here's why; Michael and I love each other. We want a home together, with our two beautiful collies, Lucy and Ethel. We want to have a nice house with a garden and a yard for the girls to run around and chase rabbits in, and we want to stay in the Midwest. Chicago is home, Addie." Addie looked at Alan, lowering her eyes briefly, knowing he was referring to her infrequent visits back home to Chicago. "And Michael's folks adore me, and I adore them. It's perfect."

Addie smiled and nodded, "Well, if that suits the both of you, then I am very happy for you. I think it's wonderful that you and Michael have found each other. Listen, mister, there'd better be a guest room in this neighborhood paradise of yours. I do plan on visiting and taking full advantage of this utopia."

Alan nodded, "Of course! You're family. You're always welcome." Alan momentarily looked at Addie with something akin to sadness but quickly covered up his expression was a smile.

Addie reached up and touched his cheek. "Listen you, do not start. I know that look. No feeling sorry for me. I am perfectly fine."

Alan grinned, "Well yeah, I know you're fine. Look at you. You're a goddamned knockout!"

Addie blushed and laughed out loud. "Oh my god, stop that! Cursing does not suit you, but thank you for saying that," Addie said, as she dabbed the tears of laughter from her eyes. "Christ, I've missed you," she said.

"And I've missed you...we all have." Addie suddenly pulled back and took a drink of her martini.

"Alan," she sighed, "please." She knew this argument. Alan, Rachel, and her parents, they all wanted her back home in Chicago. She knew her visits were few and far between. The guilt she felt for distancing herself from those who loved her made her defensive and she knew it.

Alan watched Addie as she sipped at her martini with her head slightly lowered and an unreadable look on her face. "Addie, look at me."

Addie sighed, and after a moment, she lifted her eyes to Alan, her lips pressed together in a slight frown. "Alan, what do you want me to say to you? My life is here...in New York. I have a career here, you know? The career I was so keen on having. Don't you know I'm a successful novelist? And a respected educator?" Alan reached out and held Addie's hand, the sarcasm lacing her words were not lost on him.

Just then their waiter came by to take their order. Addie looked down and reached into her handbag, pulled out a cigarette and lit it. Alan looked to the waiter, "Ah, yes. May we both have the special, please, and another round," Alan said, gesturing at their nearly empty glasses, "Thank you."

Alan shifted in his seat and reached for Addie's hand again. She did not pull away. "Addie, you're upset. I'm sorry, I had no intention of upsetting you."

Addie took a deep drag of her cigarette and exhaled slowly. "No, I am not upset," she said sounding defeated.

"Yes, you are. You only smoke when you're upset."

Addie stubbed out her cigarette and looked at Alan. "Tell me, did my family ask you to speak with me? Perhaps knock some sense into my thick skull? Tell you to see if you can talk me into moving back to Chicago and giving up everything I've worked for here in New York?"

Alan did not take the bait. He sat and took a small sip of his drink while he waited for Addie to calm down. Addie watched him patiently wait for her, just as he has had done so many times before over the years. She closed her eyes and shook her head gently, "Yes, I suppose I am upset." She sat quietly for a moment, taking in his kind handsome face. She knew why she was upset, and it wasn't about Alan or her family. "It's been over ten years, ten long years Alan. I have a life here. Everything I have strived for, career, success, friends, and respect, I have earned here in New York. Yet I feel a void. I feel like a part of my heart is missing." Addie shook her head and raised her questioning eyes to Alan. "Why can't I move on?"

CHAPTER 33

Addie paid the cabbie and walked into her apartment lobby. Just as she did every day, she checked her mail slot, dug in her purse for her keys, and pressed the elevator button. When the doors slid open, Andrew, the elevator operator, greeted her with his usual friendly smile. "Evening, Miss Kahlo. A hot one tonight, ain't it?"

Addie smiled back. "Hi, Andrew. Yes, it's quite warm out." Addie couldn't muster up much of a conversation with Andrew tonight as she silently rode up to her 10th floor apartment. Andrew tipped his cap and the doors slid open. Addie smiled at Andrew and let herself into her apartment. The silence was deafening. Normally, the quiet after a busy day at the university was a welcome reprieve, but tonight it simply felt lonely.

Walking into the small comfortable living room, Addie threw her bag and hat onto the coffee table, slipped off her heels, and looked around her cozy apartment. She had loved this place when she first rented it five years ago. She had spent many hours decorating it just so, shopping for days for the right lamp, throw pillows, and curtains. It was her home and it suited her tastes. Everything was just as she liked it. Then why, suddenly, did it feel like a prison? She sighed and verbally chastised herself. "For crying out loud, Addie! Stop it!" She shook her head as she walked over to turn on the radio. A solemn Patsy Cline song played. Addie left it on, feeling as if it fit her mood perfectly. Seeing Alan this evening and talking about home had reopened the wound that was Isabelle, and she felt drained.

Over the years, the ebb and flow of her life had become manageable, even happy. Isabelle and their all-consuming love for one another had been gently put away, locked in the depths of her heart. It was the only way she could go on. Her melancholy only surfaced at times such as now, when missing her family and home, brought the painful memories to the forefront. Realizing she would not get any sleep tonight, she decided to make tea and review some of her students' essays. She had days to go over them, but she thought the task would help her focus on something other than her melancholy.

Forty minutes after she started to review the first essay, Addie realized that the task was futile. She put down her pen, picked up her now-cold cup of tea, and walked out onto her balcony. This was her favorite part of her apartment. The small but private space was perfect for stargazing and watching the city. Seated on her lounger, she looked to the sky. "I miss you so much, Issie, so very much," she whispered to the heavens. Reaching to her throat, she gently touched the amber rose neckless that Isabelle has gifted her so long ago. "Wherever you are, I want you to know that I will love you forever. I've never stopped." Addie closed her eyes, tears of heartache and loss flowed down her cheeks, and with the tears came the memories.

September 1953

The train had just pulled into Grand Central Station, and passengers were bustling about, preparing to disembark. Addie looked at the letter in her hand. She was to meet a Mr. Jamison who would be transporting the new freshmen on a shuttle bus for the three or so hours to Vassar College. She had met a number of other freshmen on the train, and while they were all excited, nervous, and enthusiastic about getting settled into their new college life, Addie felt only numb. Thank god, she thought, I have no more tears left or I'd be bawling my eyes out right now. It was the third Monday of September, the first week of registration and classes.

In her mind, Addie reran the last time she'd seen Isabelle. It was the Sunday before last. She vividly remembered the heartbreaking goodbye and the look of utter misery in Isabelle's eyes. She had taken a taxi home from Café du Temp and silently went into her room, turned out the lights, pulled back the bedspread on her bed, and laid down as if to die. She knew she was on the verge of hysteria. She wanted to scream and cry and throw things across the room.

Never in her life had she felt such pain and loss. But, in the end, she had simply cried. She cried for Isabelle, she cried for herself, she cried for the unfairness of their situation and the loss of their love. She cried and she cried. She cried until her head ached, her nose was raw, and there were no tears left to cry. She remembered Rachel continuously knocking on her door, concern and worry in her frantic pounding.

Addie finally allowed her in, but only after Rachel threatened to call her parents. Strangely, Rachel didn't pry. She simply stayed with her, a strong silent force, within reach and there for her. After several days of not eating and staring into space, Addie attempted to steel her misery out of the fear that her family would begin questioning her about what was wrong.

"Adeena Kahlo! Adeena Kahlo!" Addie felt a tug on her sleeve, and a voice jarred her out of her reverie. "Isn't that you? Aren't you Adeena Kahlo?"

Addie suddenly realized her name was being called, and looked down at the diminutive girl tugging on her sleeve, and answered, "Yes! Here, I'm here!"

"Good, that accounts for everyone. Okay, young ladies, my name is Mrs. Cockney. I am accompanying Mr. Jamison as your chaperone for the trip back to Vassar. The drive will take several hours, so be prepared to be uncomfortable, as this is not a Greyhound bus. Quickly grab your bags. Mr. Jamison will bring your heavier suitcases and place them on the upper racks. Quickly, girls We don't have all day!"

Addie looked down again at the petite girl who stood by her side. Addie thought she must actually be from the East Coast because she totally had that cool trendy sophisticated look going for her. Her hair was jet black, straight, and cut just above her neck. Her dark eyes looked nearly black, yet held a sparkle that promised a sarcastic wit. "Boy, she sure is a crabby ass, isn't she?" the girl whispered out of the side of her mouth. "I hope I don't get her as a professor or instructor." Addie couldn't help but giggle at the girl's flippant words.

"Hi," Addie said. "I'm Addie Kahlo. I'm sorry I didn't catch your name."

The girl smiled up at Addie and stuck out her hand. "Pleased to meet yah. I'm Grace, Grace Chung."

Addie smiled and shook her hand. "Very happy to meet you, Grace Chung. Well, we better get moving before Mrs. Crabby Ass gets after us."

Addie was surprised at how easily she had acclimated to college life.

Her crammed class schedule and her duties at the school paper kept her busy while her new friendship with Grace Chung blossomed. She was happy being with Grace. Her easy manner, sarcastic sense of humor, and daring exploits endeared her to Addie. Grace would sneak in beer and set up poker games with the other girls, usually winning most hands. Addie had secretly surmised that Grace was a card shark and laughed as she, more often than not, walked away with the other girls' weekly allowances. She enjoyed their easy friendship and secretly believed that Grace had some type of sixth sense. She always seemed to know when to ask questions and when to leave well enough alone. She never pried into Addie's life, and that suited Addie just fine.

The first year at Vassar was a mixture of excitement and misery for Addie. She loved being a part of such a prestigious college. Her grades were stellar, and she received a number of accolades from the staff and fellow students for the articles and commentaries she'd written for the school paper. But, as much as she loved her life at school, she couldn't stop the constant ache in her heart. Isabelle was never far from her mind or her heart. As if to shield her own pain and loss, she found herself making excuses about coming home during breaks.

Addie couldn't bear to be in Chicago, knowing that she'd be desperate to hurry to Café du Temp, return to Paris, and run to Isabelle's door to find her. But it was not possible. Isabelle had set the tone for their parting. As difficult as it was for them both, Addie knew that Isabelle was right. They *were* from different worlds. Isabelle's life was in Paris 1912, and Addie's was now at Vassar in 1953.

Addie opened her eyes with a start. She had been dreaming. It was a dream that she had not had for a very long time, but one that always stirred a longing deep in her heart, a longing for the feel of the woman she had never stopped loving. She breathed in deeply, and looking around sleepy-eyed, she sighed. She had fallen asleep on her balcony in her lounger. She looked at her watch and saw that it was well past 3:00 a.m. She slowly got up and made her way to her bedroom. She stripped off her dress, bra, stockings and panties, and laid down on the cool sheets. She rarely slept in the nude, but tonight was different. Tonight, she needed a release. She laid back on the soft pillows and closed her eyes. In her mind she conjured up the beautiful vision of Isabelle that she had kept safe in her heart. She visualized her soft golden hair, her expressive blond eyebrows, and her beautiful deep expressive eyes that held so much feeling and love.

In her mind, she heard Isabelle whispering the sweet words of love that she so often did as she nipped at Addie's sensitive neck. Addie began to pant as she slowly touched her own breasts, squeezing and teasing her sensitive nipples. She arched her back and trembled from the feel of Isabelle slowly pulling herself on top of her and lowering her body until their breasts touched and their legs entwined. The warmth of the memory of Isabelle's body swept through Addie's mind, and she could almost feel their soft moist curls touch. The memory was a sharp jolt of erotic feeling, and Addie moved her own hand between her legs. She felt her wetness and visualized Isabelle's sexy, naughty smile as she lifted her eyes to wink at Addie before slowly dragging her tongue along Addie's clit. Addie took in a sharp breath and moaned out Isabelle's name. "Issie, oh Issie, please!" She began to slowly circle her own wetness, putting pressure on her most sensitive area. As her arousal escalated and her breathing became erratic, she opened her smooth folds and plunged her finger deep inside, screaming Isabelle's name as she climaxed.

It was several minutes before Addie opened her eyes. Sweat fell from her breasts and trickled down her sides as she lay spent and exhausted. "Oh god," she said to herself. "I can't continue to live like this. I can't." Tears welled in her eyes and her heart felt heavy with loneliness. "Oh Issie, I love you, but I can't keep alienating myself from my family, friends, and my life in Chicago. I need to go home. I want to go home."

CHAPTER 34

"What the hell do you mean, you're going to submit your resignation? Are you insane, woman?" Grace Chung fumbled through her enormous handbag for her cigarettes. Finding a single Chesterfield, bent but otherwise intact, she lit it and took a deep drag. Addie watched her friend of ten years and smiled. She knew Grace would hate the idea.

"Grace, listen before you go off the deep end. I want you to know that I have submitted my resume to the University of Chicago and Northwestern, both excellent institutions. I have no intention of simply resigning before securing another position. I may be eccentric, and this may appear to be a bit spontaneous, but I'm not a fool." Grace took another drag and looked at Addie through thick dark lashes, her eyelids tinged a deep purple. Addie thought Grace had that whole beatnik persona down pat. She was stunningly cool.

"You're not eccentric, Addie. You have a broken heart. That's entirely different."

Addie sighed. "Grace."

Grace shook her head, dragging deeply on her Chesterfield as she watched Addie through squinted lids. "Okay, please tell me what's going on. I promise to listen and not throw poorly timed innuendos around." Addie couldn't help herself; she laughed loudly at her friend, knowing that that was exactly her M.O.

The women were sitting on a bench in Central Park eating their lunch of hot dogs and Tabs. Addie, with her striking physique, was dressed in a royal blue form-fitting sleeveless dress with matching shell thrown over her shoulders, her hair up in a stylishly messy bun. Grace, as was her norm, was sporting an all-black chic beatnik look. The day was cool, but the sun warm.

"Grace, you are a shot of joy to my soul," Addie continued to laugh. Grace winked and took a drink of her Tab. "See how you speak, Addie? No one speaks that way except you. You're like a nineteenth century poet. You're brilliant, and you belong in New York, not in some backwater farm community. I'm told," Grace said with a straight face, "that there are cattle drives through the streets of downtown Chicago."

"Grace that is absolutely untrue...I think. I'm kidding! Chicago is not a back-water farm community, you east-coast snob. But yes, cattle are housed in the Chicago stockyards. However, they are not roaming the streets. My family lives nowhere near them." Grace laughed so hard she nearly spit out her drink. "Okay, okay, I digressed. I promised I wouldn't give you a hard time and, just like that, out came involuntary snarkiness." Grace wiped her month with her napkin and shifted around to make herself comfortable, ready to hear what Addie had to say. "I'm listening."

Addie sighed, "I miss my family, I miss my friends, I miss..."

"Is that it?" Grace looked at Addie questioningly. "You can always visit them. It's not as if they live in China!"

"No... no, of course that's not it." Addie shifted her position on the bench to look directly at Grace. She took a deep breath. "Alan was in town last month on business. While he was here, we spent a lot of time catching up. Once he went back home to Chicago, I realized that I missed it...my life there. I miss my family and my friends. Honestly, Grace, to my utter shock, I unexpectedly realized that I was homesick." Addie cocked her head and looked at Grace, debating what to say next. "Grace, I adore New York. It has been my training ground, my teacher, my surrogate home. Its fast-paced worldliness has guided and nurtured my achievements. But now," Addie placed her hand on her heart, "I need to go home. I need to heal and then I need to move on." She looked around and gestured with her hand. "It won't happen here in New York, Grace. Being here is avoidance."

Grace took another drag of her cigarette and looked directly at Addie. "Addie, listen. I don't need to remind you, but I will. You are the youngest female professor at Columbia, one of the most prestigious universities in the United States. You are an author, celebrated for your novels, essays, and articles. You are respected, admired, on everyone's guest list, and goddammit, you are hot as hell! Do you realize how many humans you have clamoring after you? Are you saying to me that you want to leave your life here in New York to go back to the south side of Chicago? Is that what you are telling me?"

Addie sat still, looking at Grace with a confidence and determination that she felt was long overdue, "Yes, that is exactly what I am telling you."

Grace took a final drag of her cigarette and stubbed it out under her black ballet-slippered foot. She looked up at Addie and smiled sadly. "Shit, I knew it was only a matter of time before we'd be having this discussion. I also know there is no way in hell I could change your mind. Well then, I suppose I'll need to throw you a going away party. You know how Simon loves parties. And all our friends will kill me if I send you off without a proper goodbye." Addie hugged Grace tightly. "Shit, Addie, I'm going to miss you, but I do understand. I really do. Listen," Grace pulled back holding Addie's shoulders. "I need to say something." Addie was about to interrupt but Grace held up her hand and looked at her closely. "No, allow me to say what I need to say before I become too emotional." Addie looked at Grace and nodded her agreement.

"When we met, ten years ago as wide-eyed freshmen, well, you were wide eyed. I was immensely cool." Addie rolled her eyes. "Anyway, I digress. I knew immediately that you were someone special. You had that spark, that hungry look that said that you wanted to go places and achieve great things. Well, look at you now. You *have* succeeded. I never doubted it for a minute, Addie. I admire you so very much and am so proud to be your friend."

"Oh Grace..."

"No, I need to finish this before I start bawling. Anyway, I also knew that you were sad. There was a loneliness about you that, if people didn't look closely enough, they would miss. They'd miss it because you have always been so damn strong, giving, and kind. But I saw the sadness in your eyes. Then, that day when we were sloshed over too many martinis, you told me about Isabelle." Addie suddenly closed her eyes and tried to turn away. "No, Addie, please allow me to finish. You were so cryptic, not revealing much, but enough to allow me to see your broken heart, and I put two and two together. It all made sense to me then. Your sadness was the result of losing someone you loved. Then when you met Katie, well I had hoped that she could make you happy. I think she did for a while. I'm sorry that it didn't work for you, Addie. I very much wished it would have."

Addie's eyes began to turn red and tears pooled on her lids. "It wasn't Katie's fault, Grace. She was wonderful, she just wasn't..."

"Shh Addie, I'm not judging you. You must know that." Addie nodded yes. "I suppose what I am trying to say, in my awful fumbling way, is that I know why you are doing this. I know that you are ready to go home and move on with your life, and that is a wonderful thing. I hope that you find what you've been searching for, Addie. You deserve happiness."

Addie looked at Grace and smiled sadly. She felt blessed to have Grace Chung in her life. She knew she would never take for granted her open-minded, thoughtful, and sincere friendship. So, in that sunny New York minute, any New Yorker walking by would have seen two young professional women sitting on a park bench, clinging to each other, alternately laughing and crying, each holding a half-eaten hotdog.

CHAPTER 35

August 1964

Since making the decision to move back to Chicago, Addie could hardly keep the excitement of her move from overwhelming her. She was happy and felt confident that moving back to Chicago was the right decision. She had been able to secure a position at the University of Chicago in less than two months, primarily due to the success of her novels and academic articles. However, it was with some sadness and regret that she had submitted her resignation to Columbia. As soon as she had decided to resign, she spoke with the head of the department, who was shocked and put off by the short notice.

Addie understood the university administration's concern. They would need to fill her position quickly. As the head of the humanities department, and in the process of implementing her new teaching method, she could not fault their uneasiness. She hadn't wanted to leave on bad terms; on the contrary, she had a great fondness for Columbia, and she intended to stay in contact with many of her colleagues.

To help smooth over their dismay, she had agreed to work with her now former colleagues on the implementation of her teaching program. She also agreed to return as a guest lecturer. This seemed to help resolve the majority of the issues, and she felt comfortable knowing that she was leaving on a positive note.

Addie shared her surprise with Grace at the quick follow-up that she had received after submitting her resumes to the universities in Chicago. After weighing her options, she had decided to accept an offer from the University of Chicago in Hyde Park. Grace had laughed loudly at Addie's surprise and had said, "Well, of course, they all want you, Addie. You are immensely qualified. You've won several prestigious awards, and you are a best-selling author. It would be a coup having you on their staff as a professor. They're probably salivating right now, dreaming up their new recruitment pamphlets. I can see it now, study at the University of Chicago where you can be taught by the highly talented and successful Professor Adeena Kahlo. I wouldn't doubt it if they asked you to pose for the cover as well." Addie threw a kitchen towel at Grace. They were in Grace's kitchen making cookies with her four-year-old daughter.

Addie laughed out loud now, thinking of Grace and feeling a heavy sadness in knowing that soon she would be unable to simply hop a cab to come over for a quick visit. She would miss their coffee outings and lunches. Come to think of it, she would miss quite a lot of her life in New York. After all, she had spent ten long years here. But, the idea of going home now felt immensely comforting. She couldn't wait to see Rachel and Mickey and their five-year-old twins. Rachel and Mickey had opened a successful club and restaurant that had received rave reviews for both its menu and the cutting-edge musical entertainment. Her parents were semi-retired now and finally traveling, just as they had always dreamed.

Addie's brothers Tony and Danny were running The Angel with the help of their cousins, and according to all the updates from the family, The Angel was just as successful as it had been when her dad and Uncle Jon ran it. It was the quintessential neighborhood nightclub lounge, a fun and relaxing space for the locals and service men and women. Yes, Addie was finally going home, and despite her trepidation at being back in the same city where she knew Café du Temp could still be located, she felt optimistic.

"Hello?" Addie had run up the stairwell where she was storing boxes to be picked up by the movers, to grab the ringing telephone in the kitchen.

"Addie? Why do you sound out of breath?"

"Rach! Hi! Well, I just ran up the stairs to answer this call, that's why. How are you?"

"Oh, I'm good! I'm calling to give you a heads-up. The guest count for your welcome home party has grown to 150. I know you said you wanted something small, but you know your folks, and well.... we have something like a thousand people in the family. I couldn't say no."

Addie laughed. She got it; their family was huge. "It's fine, Rach. Oh, I heard from Alan. He will definitely be there, and he's bringing Michael. So, add two more to the guest list.

"Will do. Oh Addie, I'm so happy you're moving home! We all have missed you so much. Little Addie can't wait to see you. You know she already says she wants to be a writer like her auntie. She's been drawing pictures for her new book. Purple elephants and pink cows. Apparently, it will be a psychological thriller." Addie laughed hard into the phone. After a moment she said, "Rach, thank you. I'm touched by the welcome home party you and Mickey are throwing for me. At first, I had hoped to sneak in unnoticed, but now I'm really looking forward to seeing the entire family. Tell me, will our moms be singing? Please tell me they're singing."

Addie heard a giggle on the other end of the line. "Well Ad, be careful what you ask for. I heard them practicing 'Downtown' by Petula Clark." Addie laughed so hard she nearly peed her pants.

Addie smiled as she stood gazing out the window of her office at the multitude of students and staff going about their busy day. Some were running to classes, others were reading as they sat on the grounds in the sunshine, still others were holding heated debates as they walked, cigarettes in hand, gesturing wildly. She sighed deeply, knowing that she'd miss it all. She had built a life here, but at what cost? No, it was time to stop hiding. She needed her family and her friends. She was ready to go home. Smiling, she steeled her resolve and turned to continue her packing, just as her office phone rang. "Alan! Hi. I didn't expect to hear from you until early next week when you get into town." Alan was rushing out of his office in Chicago to catch a flight to New York.

"Actually, I'll be there tonight. Apparently, the designers want to go over some final prep specs for the site, and they asked me to come in for a last-minute meeting. I should be done by 5:00 and I thought I'd check to see if you are free for dinner. I'll be leaving tomorrow morning."

"Actually, that sounds fantastic, but come over to the apartment. I'm packing and would prefer to order in if you're up for it. I can pick up a bottle of that wine you like."

"Sounds like a plan. See you around 6:30?" Addie agreed, and they said their goodbyes.

She smiled as she continued to pack up her books, humming a popular tune she had heard recently. "Excuse me, Professor Kahlo?" Addie looked up at her teaching assistant Martha, who was helping with the transition, moving files and setting up guest lecturers for Addie's classes until the university could find a replacement.

"Yes, Martha, what can I do for you?" Martha came in and closed the door. "Professor, you have a visitor. I explained to her that she needed to make an appointment, but she looked rather.... anxious, so I told her I'd see if you were available."

Addie was thoughtful for a moment and wasn't sure who it could be. "Well, why don't you send her in." Addie stood near her book shelf, boxing up her personal books and sorting them out from the university's volumes, when she heard a familiar voice.

"Hello Addie."

Addie quickly turned from her work and saw the beautiful face of Katie Lloyd. She looked just as lovely as ever, her expressive brown eyes smiling at her. She had a petite stature and was positively stunning in a smart fashionable teal suit. Addie smiled. "Martha, thank you," she said as she continued to look at Katie.

"Yes, professor." With that, Martha walked out of Addie's office and closed the door.

Addie and Katie stood looking at one another for a moment until Addie gestured for her to sit. "Katie," Addie said with genuine warmth, "this is a surprise. How are you? It's been a while. You look wonderful." Katie smiled, and the dimple on her left cheek made Addie catch her breath. Katie was stunning.

Katie sat in the offered seat and removed her hat, gently placing it on Addie's desk. She looked at Addie, her demeanor giving away her nervousness. "I heard through the grapevine that you resigned and are moving back to Chicago. I... I hope you don't mind, but I wanted to come by to say goodbye." Addie watched her former lover as she crossed her beautiful legs and tried to get comfortable in the uncomfortable office chair. Addie walked over to her desk and pulled out her own chair, moving it next to Katie's so that she was sitting opposite her. She crossed her own long legs, raising an eyebrow as she smiled at her.

"Well it seems news travels quickly in our circle."

Katie chuckled. "Yes, it seems so. As soon as the news was out, our friends couldn't wait to tell me that you were leaving New York."

Addie shook her head and pursed her lips. "Katie, I'm sorry. I was at odds about telling you."

Katie leaned in and took Addie's hand. Holding it gently, she gave Addie the sweetest of smiles. Addie held tightly to Katie's hand. They were good together once, and, in her own way, Addie loved Katie. But she wasn't in love with her, not like she was with Isabelle. "Addie, you don't owe me an explanation. We're not together anymore. You were not obligated to tell me. There is no need to feel guilty about this." Katie took a deep breath and sighed. "I just wanted to come and say goodbye. God knows I'd wrestled with the idea when I heard the news, but in the end, I decided that it was what I needed to do."

Addie looked at Katie and felt a gentleness toward her. "Oh Katie, I'm sorry..."

Katie shook her head and put her finger to Addie's lips. "Please, don't. Don't you dare apologize again. Addie, you never lied to me. You were always honest. You told me that you couldn't love me the way I needed to be loved. I... well, I was just so sure that I could change your mind."

Addie held on to Katie's hands. "I do adore you, Katie. You know that. You are an amazing, intelligent, and beautiful woman. Anyone would be lucky, hell...more than lucky to have your love and affection."

Katie's eyes welled up, and she tilted her head, "But not you, Addie. The one person I wanted more than anyone, I couldn't have."

Addie lowered her head and closed her eyes. "Katie," she said barely above a whisper. "I'm sorry I couldn't be who you needed me to be."

Katie cleared her throat and the tears that pooled on her eyelids were quickly wiped away. "Listen, Addie, let's not regret the things that we'll never be able to change, okay? We had some amazing times, didn't we? Let's remember that." Katie sat up straight and smiled. "Our goodbye should not be sad. I came by because I simply couldn't leave without seeing you off. I want you to know that I hope that you find everything you are looking for. I know…well when I heard you were leaving New York, I knew you were finally ready to go home. I was happy for you…I am happy for you."

Addie smiled with tears in her eyes and held tightly to Katie's hands. "You made me so happy for so long. I…"

"Shh, Addie. It's okay. You made me happy as well. The memories we have are good. They're happy memories. You were always honest. I knew in my heart that you didn't belong to me. I'm sorry it took me so long to let you go."

"Oh Katie, don't."

"No, listen." Katie said clearing her throat and suddenly seeming less melancholy. "I've met someone." Katie's eyes lit up, and her smile produced that beautiful dimple Addie always found intoxicating. "She's a detective with the New York City Police Department."

Addie's eyes opened wide, and she let out a soft chuckle. "Oh Katie, finally someone who owns her own set of handcuffs," Addie said suggestively.

Katie put her head back and laughed loudly. "Addie, you know me too well."

Addie laughed and threw her arms around Katie, hugging her tightly. "Thank you, thank you for coming to say goodbye. It means so much to me that you did."

After they had said their goodbyes, Addie knew it was very unlikely that she would ever hear from Katie again, even though they had both agreed to write and keep in touch. Katie had loved her deeply and passionately, but no matter how much Addie tried to give that same level of love and passion back, it was not possible. In the end, Addie had been the one to break it off, with her lover reluctantly acknowledging that to keep trying would be futile. It broke both of their hearts. Addie knew how Katie felt, of course. She was heartbroken. She knew because she had experienced the same heartbreak when she lost Isabelle.

Addie walked over to her office window and looked out at the campus. She saw Katie walking briskly as she exited the campus grounds. She closed her eyes and silently prayed that Katie would find her happiness. She smiled. Maybe it would be with this New York police woman. "Now, wouldn't that be something," she said to herself as she turned back to her packing.

Addie sat staring off into space. "What's the matter?" Alan said with exasperation, realizing she wasn't listening to him in the least. "Do you know how many times I have asked you that over the years?" He sighed as he poured Addie a glass of Zinfandel. Addie looked across the couch at Alan, lifted an eyebrow, and stuck out her tongue. He shook his head and took a sip of his wine. Alan had flown in that morning, and they were now sitting in Addie's living room finishing up their dinner of pizza and wine.

"Yes, I know, dammit." She took a healthy drink and set down her glass. "Katie came by to say goodbye this morning," she said a bit distractedly.

"And that made you feel?"

Addie quickly looked at Alan and laughed. "Okay, you. Stop playing therapist. I won't have it, I tell you!"

Alan lifted his glass and smiled "Well, how *did* it make you feel to see her again, seriously?"

Addie sighed. "Sad, guilty, regretful, aroused." Alan nearly spit out the sip he had just taken. Addie laughed now, because she could totally be herself with Alan. "Well, she looked stunning, and I have always found her intoxicating. So yes, a small part of me wanted to say goodbye in a more intimate way. Is that so wrong? Anyway, I would never do that to her. I care too much about her. I want her to be happy, so I could never allow that to happen." Addie stood and began to pack up her record albums as Alan took a big bite of his pizza slice.

"Do you regret breaking it off with her? You two were together, for what, three years?"

Addie didn't have to think about her answer. "Yes, a little over three years and no, I don't regret it. She deserves better, more than I could ever give her."

Alan sat contemplatively for a moment, then stood and stretched. Yawning loudly, he reached for a small stack of albums and began looking at the covers. Alan smirked and began placing the albums in boxes. "Shit,

Ad, this music sucks. You have show-tunes here," he said, grimacing at the covers.

She laughed, "I thought *gay men* were supposed to love show tunes." Alan howled with laughter as he lifted his glass in a toast.

225

CHAPTER 36

Addie's flight landed at O'Hare Field in a rainstorm. The plane had to circle the area for an additional thirty minutes due to traffic and weather. By the time she got off the plane she was exhausted. Yet, despite the hassle of the delay, once she set her feet firmly on ground she felt a sense of calm. She was home.

Waiting for her at the gate were her mother, father, brothers, and Rachel and Mickey. They held up a large sign, clearly made by the children, that proclaimed, "Welcome Home, Addie". Addie waved frantically when she spotted it and ran toward her family. Tears, hugs, and words of welcome home were shared among the entire group.

That night, after a big family dinner and kisses goodnight from her parents and brothers, Addie sat with a well-deserved glass of Chardonnay on Rachel's and Mickey's front porch swing. Mickey was putting the kids to bed, and Addie was grateful for the time alone with Rachel. "How do you feel, after this whirlwind of these last few months?" Rachel asked, taking a drink of her wine.

Addie turned from her stargazing to look at Rachel. "I'm tired...but it's a good tired."

Rachel raised her glass, "We're happy to have you home, Ad." Rachel's smile was huge, and Addie could feel the warmth generating from her cousin as they toasted.

She smiled and leaned back on the porch swing, looking up at the sky again and said, "I'm sorry it took so long to come home, Rach."

Rachel took a sip of her wine and waited for Addie to continue. "Thank you for letting me stay here until my apartment is available in October."

"Of course. I'd be upset if you stayed anywhere else," Rachel smiled

"You are always welcome. You're family...more than family. You're my closest friend."

Addie frowned, feeling guilty for hiding so much of her life from Rachel for so many years. "Rach...there is so much about me that you don't know. So much I want to tell you and never have... but..."

"So, tell me."

Rachel looked at Addie, and neither said anything for a moment. Then, Rachel stood up and closed the door leading to the house so that they had total privacy. Addie watched her as she grabbed the bottle of wine and poured them both a healthy amount. She continued to follow Rachel with her eyes as she sat down, picked up her glass and took a long drink.

Rachel cleared her throat. "I know, Addie," Rachel said once she placed her glass down. Addie almost didn't hear her, as she had said the words so quietly.

Addie swallowed, the color draining from her face. She suddenly felt a tightness in her entire body. She knew it was her fight or flight response. She wanted to run. Instead, she stared. She stared at Rachel, waiting for her to continue, but Rachel said nothing. She simply sat and took a small sip of her wine this time. Addie closed her eyes and whispered, "Rach... what are you talking about?"

"I know about Isabelle."

"Oh god," Addie blanched as she covered her face with her hands. She closed her eyes as fear and humiliation gripped her. Panicking, she thought, oh god, who else knows? Do my parents know?

Rachel turned toward Addie, reached over and gently removed her hands from her face. "Listen to me," she whispered sternly. "I know you. I've known you all my life. You're strong, good, and kind. Do you think that I could stop loving you? Stop being proud of who you are, all you have achieved, simply because you are different from me?"

Addie opened her eyes and stared at Rachel, wide-eyed and visibly shaken. She simply could not believe this was happening.

"I owe you an explanation," Rachel said, "and you may not like it, but I owe it to you all the same. First, I'm going to preface it with a disclaimer."

Addie looked at Rachel, confused. "What? A disclaimer? What do you mean? I don't understand."

"Wait, please. I need to say this, and I don't want to lose my nerve."

Addie nodded slowly, whispering her approval to continue. Rachel shook her hands and blew out a breath. "We were still in high school, senior year actually," Rachel visibly swallowed as she continued, "and I may have read one of your private journals."

"What?" Addie looked incredulously at Rachel.

"I know, I know...but we were teenagers, Ad! And I promise, it was only one journal, just one. You have hundreds! I was just so worried about you! There was obviously something really wrong, and I thought reading your journal would help me understand what it was. I'm so sorry, Addie."

"Oh god," Addie couldn't think of anything else to say as she sat wide-eyed and stunned.

"Addie, listen to me. I didn't read the entire journal, just the bits about meeting Isabelle at some club you went to with Alan. And a bit more about how you two felt about each other," she offered more quietly.

"Oh god, oh god, oh god."

"Will you please stop saying that and hear me out!?" Addie's head shot up at Rachel's outburst, and she swallowed hard. But she nodded slowly and tried desperately to calm herself.

"Once I had read it, I felt terribly guilty for invading your privacy. Christ knows, the shock of finding out that you're a lesbian stopped me from being any more of a busybody. Anyway, I won't lie, honey. I was terribly upset that I found out the way I did. I was also scared for you, scared that you would be ostracized. God knows I had no clue what it all meant. All I knew was that people who are homosexuals were shunned and hated. I didn't want that for you." Addie stared at Rachel, still unable to speak, eyes red and hands trembling. Rachel reached for Addie's hands to stop them from shaking. She held them gently in her own.

"Addie, you were then and are now my family, my cherished friend, closer to me then my own sister. Right before you left for college, I almost told you I knew. I was so worried about you, because anyone with a brain could tell you were heartbroken over someone. I wanted to comfort you and tell you I was there for you. I wish I had, Addie. I'm sorry I never did. I'm sorry I was not brave enough to comfort you."

Addie looked at Rachel, relief and shock evident in her stare. Lowering her head, she sniffed back tears. She was so touched by Rachel's heartfelt apology and non-judgmental acceptance. She realized she was seeing a part of Rachel she had never bothered to notice. Rachel was strong, non-judgmental, accepting, and loyal.

Addie sighed deeply. 'I don't know what to say, Rachel. I'm...I don't know what I'm feeling right at this moment."

"Do you forgive me?" Rachel asked hesitantly.

Addie's gaze was disbelieving. "Forgive you?"

"Yes, for reading your private journal, for not being brave enough to comfort you when I knew you were heartbroken, for not telling you I knew you were lesbian. I know about Alan too." Addie stood and slowly began to pace. Then she stopped and turned to Rachel.

"So, you're saying that you knew that Alan and I were a ruse?"

"Yes, but not until after I read your journal, of course. Then I put two and two together. You and Alan were much too alike to be a couple. You were more like best friends. I have to admit I was a bit jealous for a while because I always saw us as best friends. Anyway, the thing was that Alan didn't look at you the way Mickey looked at me, and you didn't look at Alan the way I looked at Mickey. I knew you two weren't in love, though honestly, it wasn't until a few years after you left for Vassar that I realized that Alan was also gay. He started to bring 'friends' over for dinners and softball games. For a while I wasn't certain, because I admit I had this preconceived notion of what homosexual men were like. Alan did not, does not, fit the stereotype. But when he and Michael met, wow! The way they looked at each other, well their love for each other was unmistakable."

Addie, who had been pacing the entirety of the front porch, came back and sat down hard, suddenly feeling drained. "Have you told Alan that you know? What about my parents? Oh God, do they know?"

"No, Ad. I haven't spoken to Alan about it, though I'm certain he realizes that we know. He has Michael. How could he not see that we would suspect they were together? But who Alan loves doesn't change how we feel about him. Michael is Alan's family, and we love them both. As for your folks, no, I haven't told them. I didn't think it was my place to say anything. I haven't said anything to anyone other than Mickey."

Addie took a healthy drink of wine and looked at Rachel, still a bit numb, but now calmer, knowing that Rachel accepts her for who she is. "I'm relieved...that you know. I hated lying to you, though you have to know that this is something I have been terrified to share. I was scared to death to tell anyone. I still am, if I'm honest. It's not an easy life to lead, Rach," Addie said quietly, half to herself and half to Rachel. "I could... Alan and Michael, we could lose everything if we were exposed. I hope you know that this is not a choice. It's simply who we are and who we have always been."

Rachel sat and watched Addie as she spoke. She could see the weariness in her eyes and hear it in her voice. She wished that she could make it all better for Addie, for Alan and Michael too. She wanted to wave a magic wand, eliminating all the bias, hatred, and fear that the world held against those who were different. But she was not a foolish woman, and she knew the prejudice existed and it was dangerous. She would never risk exposing the private lives of her family and friends to anyone. Rachel reached over, grabbed Addie's hand, and squeezed it gently.

After a moment, a thoughtful smile creased Addie's face. "Rachel Kahlo Strieter, you are really something, you know that?"

Rachel grinned and chuckled lightly. "Does this mean you forgive me?

"There's nothing to forgive," Addie said softly.

"Can I ask you something, Ad?" Addie nodded without hesitation. "Is Isabelle the reason you've stayed away for so long? You don't have to answer."

"No, I want to, I... yes, I love Isabelle very much. When we parted, I thought I'd die. She is my one true love. I can hardly believe I am telling you this." Addie shook her head, still shocked at Rachel's confession. "Alan has been my only confidant for so long." Addie smiled sadly and briefly closed her eyes.

"But there has been another, hasn't there?" Rachel asked tentatively.

Addie raised her head. "Rachel, you're full of surprises. How did you know?"

"Don't forget, over the years you and I have written regularly, and the few times you did come home for those short visits, you made mention of a friend, Katie, if I recall correctly. You also sent photographs of you and some of your friends, and Katie was always there next to you. Even in the photographs I could see how she looked at you. Addie, what happened with Katie?"

Addie wasn't sure she wanted to discuss this part of her life in any more detail. How could she admit that she hurt Katie, that she didn't love her as Katie so desperately wanted her to? She knew there would always be that fragile twinge of remorse and guilt that she could not give her lover what she wanted. She sighed. "Honestly, Rach, I couldn't love her like she wanted me too. It wasn't fair to her...to try and act otherwise. You can't make yourself love someone when you don't."

"And Isabelle, do you still love Isabelle? God, Addie, don't answer that. I'm sorry. I'm much too nosy for my own good," Rachel said, as she breathed deeply and took a drink of her wine.

"No Rach, I think I need to say it, out loud to someone other than myself." Addie's eyes glossed over with wetness, melancholy visible on her face. "Yes, I still love Isabelle. I've never stopped...I never will."

The street was in semi-darkness, illuminated only by the soft glow of the street lights. Slowly pulling the car into the side alley, Addie let the engine idle. She noticed the ground was dry, not wet as it had always been when she had first visited Café du Temp some twelve years prior. Surprisingly, except for the absence of the black door, everything looked exactly the same. She realized she didn't know what she had expected. The tension she felt driving up LaSalle street no longer tightened her stomach or made her hands shake. She sat, strangely numb. She hadn't allowed herself to hope the door would be there, because the disappointment when she found that it wasn't would be devastating. She'd come back home to heal and to finally move on. Coming here, seeing that Café du Temp no longer existed for her, was the first step.

CHAPTER 37

Addie had been back for a little over a week. Despite her initial excitement of returning home, she was feeling the effects of the transition. The entire week had taken an emotional toll on her. The welcome home party, meetings with the university, Rachel's stunning admission, and finally, her own subsequent visit to where Café du Temp once stood, had left her drained. So, when Alan phoned her for an impromptu dinner, she jumped at the opportunity. They were meeting at The Italian Village in Chicago's Loop, one of Addie's favorite restaurants. When she arrived, she was led to the table where Alan already sat. She looked at the old Italian décor, recalling why she always felt so comfortable here. The soft lighting, charming murals of Italian cites, dark wood, and fresh flowers always created visions of what Italy must be like.

When Alan spotted her, he reached over and gave her a quick hug. "Alan, this was a fabulous idea. I'm so glad you suggested it. Despite seeing you at the party, we haven't shared more than a handful of words since I arrived home."

Alan took a sip of his lemon water and nodded. "God, don't I know it. It's been insane since you got off the plane."

Addie sat back and smiled. "Let me look at you. God it's so nice that it's just you and me this evening. You know I adore Michael..."

Alan laughed, "No, I understand. I'm glad too. Michael was happy to get me out of the house. He has his poker friends over tonight, and I am just plain lousy at cards, so I'd actually prefer to be here with you. What do you say that after dinner we cab it over to the Green Mill for an after-dinner cocktail and some jazz?" Addie clinked her water glass with Alan and smiled broadly.

They were finishing up their meal and the last of their wine when

Addie decided to share the news about Rachel. "You're serious?" Alan's face was pale, and Addie saw that he had a difficult time swallowing. She waited for the information to sink in.

Alan didn't think he could be shocked anymore, but he most certainly was. He stared at her, watching closely for any signs of anxiety or stress, any signs that Rachel's news had affected her negatively, but he saw none. He looked at her intently, taking in her skin's color, her eyes, the calmness of her appearance. All he could see was Addie, kind, sophisticated, successful, beautiful Addie. He briefly flashed to her as a teenager. She was a knockout then, but now she was the complete package. She could have her pick of any woman or any man for that matter. But he knew she was, regretfully, still in love with someone from her past. Alan shook his head and took a small deliberate swallow of his dinner wine, "So, tell me, tell me what happened."

Addie turned her eyes toward him and moved closer to avoid being overheard, "She only knows we're gay, you and I, and that I was seeing Isabelle." She lifted her eyebrows and watched him for a response. "She doesn't know about Café du Temp, about Peter, or anything about Isabelle's life in Paris. Apparently, the shock of reading that I was a lesbian was all she could handle. She could not read further, thank god," Addie sipped her wine.

"You're not upset. I can see you are...what? Relieved?"

Addie quietly lifted her glass and slowly swirled the deep red wine. "Yes, I feel less of a fraud now that Rachel knows. If I had admired her before, well now I am in awe. Her concern, if you can imagine, was that I would be angry with her for reading the journal of an 18-year-old with a broken heart. She was not appalled that you and I are gay. She only wanted to ensure that I knew she loved us and that she was concerned for our safety in a world that doesn't accept us."

Alan was stunned, more so due to Rachel's apparent acceptance of their homosexuality than her actually knowing. Alan asked for the bill. "Let's go listen to some jazz and get a nightcap. I want to get drunk tonight. I want to toast the hell out of Rachel," Alan said, "that shockingly openminded lovely married mother of twins." Addie laughed, silently thanking the powers that be for Rachel Kahlo Strieter.

Addie woke to a five-year-old playing with her nostrils. "Auntie Addieeeeee," little Addie whispered loudly, "Mama says it's time to get up."

Addie scrunched one eye open and smiled at the adorable child peeking at her from a few inches away. "Did she now?" Addie said as she lifted her niece up and put her on the bed next to her. Addie tickled her soft belly causing her niece to shriek with laughter, calling for her mother.

"Mama, Mama, Auntie is tickling me!"

Rachel walked in and leaned on the doorframe, "Ok you two, rise and shine. No lazy bones in this house."

Addie smirked at Rachel. "Okay, kiddo, you heard the boss. Up and at 'em! Go find your brother and get ready for breakfast." Addie lifted the child off the bed and gently placed her on the floor. Little Addie squealed and ran out the room, leaving both adoring mother and aunt to laugh and shake their heads.

After breakfast with Rachel and the twins, Addie left for her appointment at the University of Chicago. She had a meeting with several members of the humanities department. The current team was revamping the criteria used for their journalism courses. The University was known for producing successful award-winning journalists and authors. Addie knew that the success of her last two novels gave her credibility with the team. Still, these were serious academics and they were not going to swoon over her success, as her students often did. They wanted to know what she was bringing to the table, and she was not about to disappoint them. Her dissertation, which she had parlayed into a successful teaching method, was being successfully used in several post-graduate programs. Her goal and hope were to implement the same methods and techniques at the University of Chicago.

As she drove down Lake Shore Drive toward Hyde Park and the campus, she thought back to the seeds of her idea. Smiling, she saw in her mind's eye her 18-year-old self and Isabelle, discussing Addie's love of teaching. When she had first begun to tutor, she had enthusiastically shared with Isabelle the methods she used to help the kids grasp the information. It had made her so happy to see how impressed and encouraging Isabelle was. She had suggested that Addie write it down in her journals, just as she did with her ideas for novels. She recalled Isabelle saying, "Any idea that has a seed of possibilities can blossom into something magnificent." Addie smiled sadly and allowed Isabelle's voice to fade. She needed to concentrate fully on her meeting.

Addie stifled a yawn and looked at the clock on the wall. The meeting had already run thirty minutes over, and she could feel the beginnings of a tension headache. "Professor Kahlo, I assume you'll have the syllabus prepared for our review well before classes begin, in case there are issues or concerns." Terri Mann was an imposing figure in her sensible shoes and brown tweed dress, her steel gray eyes focused directly on Addie. She briefly noted that the stern professor could be lovely if she didn't have that perpetual scowl on her face.

"Of course, Professor Mann, you can rest assured that the department will receive everything well in advance for review," Addie responded with her most professional smile.

Steven Davis stood, preparing to close out the meeting. "Terri, Professor Kahlo has already assured us that the syllabus will be available well in advance. Do you have any other questions? Because if you do not, I would like to end the meeting." Addie immediately noticed a slight flush on Terri Mann's face. She had been shut down by the head of the department. Great, Addie thought, she will probably hold that against me too. What is her problem with me anyway, she silently thought?

"Okay everyone," announced Dean Davis, bringing Addie out of her musings, "I think Professor Kahlo has provided us with a good summary. We will get into the meat and potatoes of the program at the next scheduled meeting. Let's call it a day."

As Addie gathered her notes and was preparing to leave, she noticed the head of the department walking toward her. "Dean Davis."

Steven Davis stood with his hands casually in his pockets. "Adeena, great job today. I feel like this is going to be a perfect program for the university. We've needed something new for years, and your program is just the ticket. It helps that it's such a success at Columbia."

Addie smiled. "Thank you, Dean Davis. I really appreciate your support."

Steven Davis scratched his head and looked at Addie. He was a short rotund man with a kind face and a quick mind. "Listen, don't let Terri scare you. She's an excellent educator, and she knows your program will work. She's just passionate, and a little protective of the department." Addie looked down at Dean Davis as she stood a good four inches taller than he. She wasn't afraid of Terri Mann, just curious as to why the woman had taken an immediate dislike to her.

"Thank you, Dean. I'm sure once she has all the details, she will be pleased with how it flows." Dean Davis smiled, "Excellent, Professor, excellent."

"How'd the meeting go?" asked Rachel as she checked inventory on the clipboard she held.

Addie was at Rachel's and Mickey's restaurant helping with the liquor inventory. "Three bottles of bourbon, top shelf, two on reserve." Rachel nodded and checked off the list. "It went as well as can be expected. I had some surprising back-up from two of the professors in the department," Addie chuckled. "I think they may have read my books. Anyway, there's some skepticism by a few of the more senior members of the team, but I think it only has to do with the fact that I'm bringing something a bit controversial and new to the table. A lot of the old guard don't always like change. Five vodkas on reserve and one top shelf. You want me to add one to top?"

Rachel looked up from her inventory list, "Yeah, please. Put out whatever name brand is there, and the others can stay on reserve. But your teaching program has already been implemented at Columbia and a number of other New York universities. What's wrong with those old windbags?"

Addie laughed, "Thanks for the support, Rach, but honestly, it's just business as usual. The program is already being built into the academic year for post-graduate courses. I also have the support of the university president and the dean of the department. It's just a matter of smoothing things over with a few of the old guard." Addie looked at the shelves and checked the reserves. After another thirty minutes she was satisfied with her inventory check. "I think we're done here, Rach."

With the inventory now complete, Rachel needed to meet with their chef to go over the evening's specials. "You want to stay for dinner this evening, Ad? Roast lamb is on the menu, and we are trying out a new jazz duo. I heard them practicing this afternoon and they're really good."

Addie quickly thought about the invitation but decided instead to head back to the house, as she had plenty of work to do. "No, I think I'll just head back if you don't mind. I have to prepare for Monday's training. I am meeting with the department to review the program criteria. I should probably get started on that."

"I understand, but come back if you change your mind. No reservation necessary," Rachel winked.

The key slid into the lock smoothly, and the satisfying silence of the empty house offered the promise of a quiet evening. The lights were off and one dim nightlight cast a short shadow on the stairs. Addie breathed a tired sigh. With Mickey and Rachel at the restaurant and the twins with their grandmother Rosie, she had the house to herself. She thought of the small fib she had told Rachel, trying to justify it to her conscience. She did have work to do, plenty of it, but not tonight. Tonight, all she wanted was to simply be alone. She was happy to be back, but she needed to decompress, and she needed to just be.

Addie poured herself a Pino Noir and opened the back door. In mid-September, the air was still warm, and because Rachel's home was a few miles outside of the city, the stars were brighter in the evenings without the glaring lights of downtown obscuring the night sky. She kicked off her heels, walked to the yard, and looked around. It was nice. The space was private with tall Arbor Vitae blocking the area from the neighbor's yard. The garden still bloomed, a children's swing set occupied one corner of the yard, and there was stained wooden patio furniture on the patio. Addie sat on a lounger. It reminded her of the one she had at her apartment in New York.

She leaned back and took a swallow of the full-bodied wine. It tasted tart and mellow at the same time. It was perfect. Crickets began their chirping songs as dusk descended. She idly thought that one day she'd like a home of her own, with a nice yard, flowers, and a view of the evening stars. Would there ever be anyone to share it with, she wondered? She suddenly felt lonely, daring a small memory of Isabelle's smile to warm her heart and quell the ever-present loneliness. "One step at a time," she whispered out loud. "Take it one step at a time."

CHAPTER 38

March 1965

She was cold. Addie cursed herself for not wearing gloves and forgetting her umbrella. She knew better. Chicago in March was brutal. It could even snow in April. She half ran, half jogged the six blocks from her apartment to the university. She was running late for her first class of the day. Sighing, she silently cursed what she perceived to be a bad start to a long day. Running up the stairs to her office, she nearly collided with Terri Mann, her colleague and apparent nemesis. Since Addie had started at the university six months ago, Terri had worked hard to block her suggestions and ideas. After several attempts at extending an olive branch, Addie concluded that Terri simply didn't like her. "Oh, excuse me, Professor Mann!" Terri tutted and said nothing, but her look spoke volumes. Addie couldn't deal with the temperamental professor today, as she was already terribly late.

As Addie ran from her office with her class notes and headed for the lecture hall, she briefly thought of Terri Mann and her apparent distain for her. She realized that she needed to get to the bottom of it, but now wasn't the time. She quickly confirmed that she had grabbed the correct lecture notes for the undergrad class she was about to teach. She enjoyed this class immensely. It was a second-year course, and many students were already lining up internships for the upcoming summer break. They were enthusiastic and engaged, full of excitement and energy, eager to start their careers. She was teaching both under-graduate and post-graduate courses. She liked the full schedule. It suited her. Over the past few months she began to have inklings of ideas for a new novel. This is the way it always began for her. Last week she had cracked open a new journal to jot down notes and ideas, and characters were beginning to form. It was thrilling to see where they'd take her.

Addie was near the end of the morning's lecture, satisfied with how it progressed, when she decided to cut it short to allow for time to discuss the project she was about to assign. She was looking forward to seeing what the students could produce, given the unusual assignment. They were a bright group, and she knew she wouldn't be disappointed. "Alright everyone, attention please. I am going to now discuss your upcoming assignment project." Students grabbed notebooks and sat up as they prepared to hear the details of their next assignment. "So, the purpose of this assignment is to enhance and sharpen your research and critical thinking skills by analyzing the lives and works of acclaimed writers from history."

There were rumblings and soft groans throughout the lecture hall. Addie smiled, "Yes, yes, I know that you all have read the classics in high school, so stop rolling your eyes." Several students laughed, knowing that Professor Kahlo knew exactly that was what they were thinking. "Okay everyone, listen up and take notes. Here is the assignment. Choose an author, any author is suitable, as long as their work is from, at the very least, fifty years ago. They must be critically acclaimed and have been successful in their own time, not achieving success posthumously. Chose a novel or short stories from their best works. Your assignment is to use the material to individualize the author who wrote it. As part of critical thinking, you must see beyond the words to their meanings. Every line an author pens has a meaning to the author. Use your research to put together a picture, a personality of the author, based on your readings. Did he or she have a muse? If so, what was this individual to them? Did their political views shape the story? Or perhaps, it was their family or a lover who influenced them? Have fun with it, and use your creativity to form your conclusion."

Addie noticed more rumblings in the class. She was sure they had not received such an assignment before, as they looked like scared rabbits. "Okay, everyone, it will not be so dreadful, I promise." She smiled to try and relieve their anxiety. "I will be grading on your research and your findings, as well as your own critique and opinions, which are entirely subjective." There was an audible sigh of relief from the students, and Addie smiled. "See, not so terrible. If you have questions or require any help, please see me. My hours are posted on my office door and in the library. Enjoy your weekend."

The day had been a long one, just as Addie had expected. All she wanted to do was go home, relax a bit, and put her feet up before going to dinner. Alan and Michel were throwing a small dinner party that evening, and she looked forward to what she knew would be a great meal, interesting discussions, and hearty laughs. She was relieved after Alan had promised there would be no ambushing her with the presence of a possible "love match," as Michael referred to them. She cringed as she thought of Michael's ongoing attempts to set her up with eligible women. Dear Michael, she thought with a smile, he was sweet and meant well, but she was simply not interested. It hadn't even been a year since she ended her relationship with Katie. She was just not ready.

A soft knock at her office door grabbed her attention, saving her from delving any deeper into thoughts of how she had screwed up her relationship with Katie. Addie was readying her things to leave for the day when her colleague and friend Sarah Osterhout poked her head in. "Hey, rumor has it you scared the second-years half to death," Sarah said with a huge smile. She was one of the tenured professors, a bit older and well-respected amongst staff and students. She had a wicked sense of humor and a brilliant love of teaching.

Addie laughed under her breath, "Well, only for a moment. Then I relieved their anxiety by letting them know grading will be based purely on their own critique and opinions."

Sarah whistled low. "Hmm, interesting." Addie looked at Sarah and raised a curious eyebrow.

"What? What's interesting? Come on, spill." Sarah looked sheepish. "Tell me what's this about Sar." Sarah walked into the office, closed the door and sat down, lighting a cigarette as she made herself comfortable.

"I deplore gossip, you know that Addie, but that woman simply gets my blood boiling. I swear, whenever I'm in a room with her for any length of time, I need to check my blood pressure immediately after." Addie looked pointedly at Sarah, raising her brows, waiting for her to get to the point. "Okay, okay. I walked into the break room just as Terri Mann was giving a few of our esteemed colleagues an earful. It appears one of your students complained to Terri about the project. Terri is now on her high horse criticizing the assignment. It's appalling, Addie. She hasn't a clue about your program methods, as she refuses to even consider them. How dare she criticize you, that, that.... bovine!" Addie looked up at Sarah, shocked at her outburst, yet she couldn't help but let out an uproarious laugh. Sarah looked peevish and laughed at her own passionate response as well.

Once the two women had stopped laughing, Addie shook her head. "I can't understand why that woman dislikes me so, Sarah. I have not given her any reason, and yet, every olive branch I attempt to extend she bats away."

Sarah stubbed out her cigarette and stood, smoothing down her skirt. "I wouldn't worry about it. I'm sure it's simple jealously."

Addie looked pointedly at Sarah. "Jealously? Of what? She's tenured, she's brilliant, she's..."

Sarah put up her hand. "Stop, she's not a successful author, she's not known for her innovated teaching methods, she's most certainly not young and admired, and she is no longer the new kid in town. Listen, all I'm saying is that Terri Mann was a star ten years ago, but she never reached her potential. I don't know why. It's a shame really, as she could have done great things. Do your best to stay away from her, Addie. You're blazing a trail here, and you don't need a bitter wretch like Terri Mann in your way." Sarah squeezed Addie's arm gently and winked. "I'm off, dinner out with the poker club ladies tonight. God, I think they're attempting to set me up with someone. Heaven forbid!"

Addie laughed, "Enjoy. See you tomorrow, Sarah."

While preparing for bed that evening, Addie thought about what Sarah had said about Professor Mann. She had been the new kid in town ten years ago and full of potential. What happened? What happened to Terri Mann to turn her into the angry bitter person that Addie knew? Lying in bed, she switched off the side lamp. She didn't want to think about Terri Mann anymore. She reached toward her throat and felt the delicate rose neckless that Isabelle had gifted her so long ago, the beauty of its silver and amber colors imprinted in her memory. Drifting into sleep, she dreamed of Isabelle.

CHAPTER 39

While Addie was typing out her lecture notes, her office phone rang. As she was expecting to hear from her mother regarding this afternoon's lunch plans, she immediately picked up the ringing receiver. "Professor Kahlo."

"So, I trust you haven't been injured by stampeding cattle."

Addie grinned, "Grace! How wonderful to hear from you!"

Grace laughed. "How are you, Addie? I had a few minutes, and since I was missing my friend, I took a chance you'd be chained to your office chair just as you were at Columbia."

Addie laughed. "I've missed you too, Grace, and your snarky weirdness. No one teases me like you do. How are you, and how are little Mia, and Simon?" Addie suddenly pulled the phone from her ear as Grace yelled. "Mia! You do not feed Mr. Truffles your Malt-O-Meal! Oh shit! Addie, Mia just dumped the entire bowl over the dog's head and now he's rolling around in the entire mess! Listen honey, I need to go, but I'll be in Chicago next month for a conference. Let's meet up. I'll call you. Love you! Bye!" The next thing Addie heard was the dial tone. She shook her head and laughed as she placed the receiver back in the cradle. Not a moment later there was a soft knock on her door.

"Come in."

"Professor Kahlo? I hope I'm not disturbing you...it's Susan, Susan Marcos."

Addie turned her full attention to the young woman and smiled. "Hi, Susan. No, please come in. What may I help you with?"

Susan cleared her throat and looked a bit nervous, "Well, I was hoping I could ask a few questions about our new assignment. Oh, I'm in your second-year journalism course. The 9:00 a.m. Monday and Wednesday class."

Addie smiled and offered Susan a chair. "Please, take a seat. By the way, I know who you are. You always ask the most thought-provoking questions in class. Last Wednesday when you offered your thoughts regarding sensationalized news journalism and questioned its rise in today's most acclaimed news sources, your comments started a discussion that really got the entire class involved."

Susan's cheeks flamed red and her eyes grew wide, "Wow, you remember that? I mean, thank you, professor." Addie smiled, picked up her cold cup of coffee, and crossed her legs as she waited for Susan to ask her questions.

"Well, professor, I have been mulling over a few authors who I thought would be interesting enough to focus on for the assignment, but then I kind of went in a different direction."

Addie looked intrigued. "Go on," she said.

"Well, I'd like to focus on a different genre of literature altogether. I would like to write my assignment on the poet I. A. London. He was a critically acclaimed English poet, highly celebrated for his breathtakingly sensuous style. The imagery literally places the reader in another world."

Addie smiled. "Susan, this is amazing and brilliant actually. I myself am an admirer of I. A. London's work. What a fantastic coincidence! When I was in school, I devoured the few volumes of his poetry available, and I was mesmerized by the beauty and imagery of each word. I do know that he was very mysterious. I don't believe there are any available photographs of him, are there?" Susan was on the edge of her seat with excitement.

"So, that's a yes, professor? I can focus my assignment on I.A. London?" Addie nodded her approval and smiled. "Oh, this is fantastic, professor. Thank you so much! And you're correct, you know. I don't believe there are any photos. I have a very good friend who lives in Paris where I.A. London supposedly wrote many of his works. She thinks she can obtain a few of the volumes that are not available here in the U.S. Apparently, he was quite risqué for his time," Susan whispered.

Addie laughed. "Oh yes. Believe me, I know. As a young girl I was completely enamored of him. It was the most enthralling poetry I have even read."

Susan bit her lip and suddenly asked, "Professor, may I ask, do you still read London's work?"

Addie thought about her response, "Hmmm, I still have the few cherished volumes I had as a girl, but honestly I think that I got so caught up in my own adventures that I sadly never came back to him." Addie considered for a moment and said, "Susan, do you think your friend in Paris would be able to obtain any additional copies? I would love to rediscover his work."

Susan smiled. "I can certainly ask her, professor. I believe that after, I think it was 1913, London's body of work really took off. He became quite famous in Europe, so perhaps there are more available copies of his poetry in Paris. I have heard the theory that his most inspired work during the early 20's was due to a lost love. Isn't that just heartbreaking, professor? Pouring your heartache into your poetry for the one that you adore."

Addie smiled. "Susan, like myself, I believe you are a true romantic. Am I correct?"

Susan laughed. "Yes, professor, I am certainly that. Well, I had better leave. Now that I have the okay from you, I'm excited to begin. I plan on reaching out to my friend in Paris this week. I will see what she can find for us and follow up with you. And, thank you again, professor!"

After Susan had left her office, Addie was still reeling from the discovery that her student was an admirer of the works of I.A. London. Such an obscure metaphoric poet, thought Addie, remembering her love of his poetry. She hadn't thought of this particular poet in years, perhaps because her love of his work coincided with her time with Isabelle. Isabelle was such a brilliant poet herself, she thought. Addie, for a while, had briefly considered researching Isabelle's work. Surely her writings would be available in Europe.

But in the end, she decided against the idea, thinking that researching Isabelle would only lead to more heartache. Why torture herself? Sighing, she shook herself out of her sudden melancholy. She needed to prepare for her next class. However, she did make a mental note to pull out her copy of *Poems of Paris* from her bookshelf at home. It was time to reacquaint herself with I.A. London.

CHAPTER 40

"So, Addie, Alan tells me you are in the planning stages of another novel?"

Addie took a drink of her wine and smiled at Michael. "Well, in the planning stages is a bit premature. Right now, my ideas for a new novel are in a notebook I carry around and in my head."

Michael lit a cigarette and snapped closed his lighter. "I can hardly wait. You have such a gift, Addie. I loved your last book. It was a such a fascinating story about a family torn apart by the war and then finding each other through periods in time." Addie looked at Michael and blushed slightly. She was still a bit uncomfortable with accolades.

Michael smiled at her and then a wide grin creased his face. "You know, Addie, I still laugh at my own reaction when Alan and I first started dating, and he casually mentioned to me that his best friend was the author Adeena Kahlo. I screamed. Can you imagine his horror?" Michael laughed, shaking his head "It's a wonder he didn't walk out of the restaurant, never to return."

Addie laughed. She adored Alan's partner. She was happy that they had found each other They were perfectly suited she thought. "Hey, Michael, do you have a minute!? I need your help in the kitchen."

Michael turned toward Alan's voice. "Be right there, Alan! Talk with you later, Addie. I'd better go and help before he burns something." With that, Michael headed to the kitchen. Addie contemplated, not for the first time, how she and Alan's lives had turned out. She knew that she was fortunate; both she and Alan were. Their lifestyles were complicated and required discretion in today's world, yet they had family and friends who embraced them for who they were. What were the odds? But here they both were, with loving families and progressive accepting friends.

Addie wondered if that was what Peter had referenced so long ago when he toasted her at Café du Temp. Looking at her life now, she appreciated that she was successful and had realized her dreams. At thirty-one, she was a professor at a prestigious university and a successful author. She knew that she owed much of her success to Isabelle. Even though they were together just a little over one year, Isabelle's influence, writing, talent, and encouragement had given Addie the courage and perseverance to reach for her dreams.

"Addie?" Addie pulled herself out of her musing to see Rachel standing next to her. "Oh Rach, sorry. I was daydreaming. What is it?"

Rachel looked at Addie questioningly. "Alan announced dinner. We were all seated, just waiting for you. Are you alright?"

Addie nodded, "Oh, I'm fine, Rach. Let's go eat. I'm famished."

Dinner had been amazing. Despite Michael teasing him about his culinary skills, the truth was that Alan was a fabulous cook. As Addie drove home humming along with the radio, she thought about tonight's dinner party. Watching her parents hover over Alan as he prepared the roast and tossed the salad made her smile. They treated him like one of their sons, always wanting to help him, to mother him. He was so patient with them. She laughed to herself thinking if it had been her in his shoes, she would have banished them to the living room. Sighing heavily, she wondered how the hell she got so damned lucky.

Addie thought about that day when Rachel admitted that she knew she was gay. She had spent that night wide awake, agonizing over how she would tell her parents. She couldn't keep it from them now that she was back home in Chicago. They would know she was hiding something. Damn their steadfast intuition when it came to their children, she had thought with a smile. There was no debating it, she had to let them know. She hoped they already knew and were just waiting for her to tell them. She had reached out to both Alan and Rachel the very next day for advice, and, as she suspected, they both agreed she should do it sooner rather than later. The longer she waited, the more difficult it would be.

The day she had planned on coming out to them was probably the scariest day of her life. She hadn't slept the night prior, and she looked it. When she arrived at her parents' home, her mother had taken one look at her exhausted flushed face and immediately stuck a thermometer in her mouth. Her father had run out to buy 7 UP and soup from Stan's. In the end though, through her many tears and difficult sputtering starts, she had sat them down and explained to them that their daughter was a lesbian.

For the longest time they said nothing. Addie suspected that they knew that their daughter was different and had in their own way prepared themselves. Still, they wept out of fear for Addie's safety. It was a difficult existence after all. They wanted her to have the happiness they had, and they worried she would be alone.

In Addie's mind, she felt they were not that far off the mark. Being alone was a distinct possibility. Finally, they held her hand and hugged her fiercely, letting her know she was still loved, still their daughter, and that nothing would change that truth.

Slipping into bed, Addie reached over and turned on her radio. An old Billie Holiday tune played, and the recording sounded scratchy, as if it were plucked out of time. She smiled as it reminded her of the music that was often played at Café du Temp. She felt the beginnings of that familiar heartache that seemed to be her constant companion these days. She closed her eyes and allowed herself to remember. All these years, she thought, and she could still remember Isabelle's touch. Despite her life without Isabelle, she felt comforted because she had her family, she had her career, and she had the love and friendship of Alan, Michael, and Grace. Maybe, she thought, her sleepy eyes closing, this could be enough for her.

CHAPTER 41

It was the first week of April on a chilly Thursday morning. Addie sat in her office, the radio playing a jumpy tune as she sorted through her students' most recent quizzes. She was pleased to note that they were all doing well. The new program techniques were gradually making an improvement in their comprehension, and it showed on the most recent quiz scores. With this information, she was looking forward to providing Dean Davis with actual proof that her program was indeed working. This made her smile, and she felt vindicated, as her thoughts turned to Professor Mann.

A few days after Addie had assigned the research project, Terri had come knocking on her office door in a huff, insisting that they needed to talk. Terri entered and practically threw her assignment syllabus on her desk. She demanded to know what kind of "beatnik space cadet" project she thought she was assigning. She practically seethed. "This is the University of Chicago, not a night school class at a junior college."

Addie was offended in more ways than one. First, there was absolutely nothing wrong with studying at a junior college, you elitist bitch, she thought angrily. Secondly, her assignment was emphatically approved as part of the program. She did not need to explain herself to Terri Mann. Addie had allowed Terri to finish her rant, and then politely but firmly asked her to leave. It was all Addie could do not to tell her to get the hell out of her office. Terri had the decency to look sheepish. She knew she had overstepped her bounds. She had walked out without another word, leaving Addie to wonder what the hell that was all about.

Shaking her head at the unusual confrontation, Addie put her feet up on her desk and crossed her legs. She had decided to spend an hour or so before her lecture began, reviewing the authors her students submitted for their assignment focus. A little over two weeks had passed since Addie had assigned the research project. She was pleased to note that after their initial moans and groans, they had come to her with great suggestions and appeared to be enthusiastic about delving into the project. She was curious to see what Susan had found regarding I.A. London. Susan had approached her after Monday's class and said that her friend from Paris had managed to locate some volumes of work that were no longer in print. She had mailed what she found to Susan, and the package was expected to arrive any day. Addie recalled that when Susan asked to research the works of I.A. London for her project, she had gone home and pulled out the slim volume of *Poems of Paris.*

Addie recalled how, as she had moved her hand over the worn leather cover, memories of her time in Paris with Isabelle had come flooding back. The ache in her heart had stopped her from reading it. She had placed it on her coffee table and gone off to bed. After a few days of seeing it lying there, she told herself she was being silly and took the slim volume with her to read in bed. She had read "Paris and War" aloud, the words filling the room.

> *The darkness of her center can be the deepest black*
> *The brilliance of her existence can out shine the brightest of*
> *suns*
> *Oh, will she suffer for her beauty and decadence, to perish as*
> *an extinguished flame on a damp earth*
> *Or, will her victories of times past outlast the deeper darkness*
> *of her enemies*
> *La Ville Lumiere do not slumber, do not slumber*
> *For your brilliance is your triumph and your death.*

The rhythm and intonation of the hypnotic words brought her back to why she had fallen in love with the poetry. The beautiful imagery somehow reminded her of Isabelle, and she had gone to sleep with the book close to her heart.

It was well past 4:00 p.m. when Addie looked up at the clock on her office wall. As she had no more classes that afternoon, she decided to head out a bit early. She thought she'd give Rachel a call and drop by the restaurant. She was preparing to leave when she heard rushed footsteps outside her office door and then a sudden urgent knock. "Come in," she responded. "Professor Kahlo, I'm so sorry to disturb you. I know it's after office hours and I'm really very sorry, but..."

Addie pulled over a chair, "Sit, please. Is everything alright, Susan? You're out of breath. Did you run all the way over?" Susan sat and threw her satchel down on the floor next to her feet.

"Oh yes, professor. I did run. I wanted to catch you before you left for the day."

Addie smiled, "Well you caught me, so tell me, what has you so excited?"

Susan bent down and pulled out a small package wrapped in brown paper from her satchel. She sat up, breathed out deeply, and handed Addie the package. "This is for you, professor." Addie took the package and looked at Susan questioningly. "They're your copies of the two books of poetry by I.A. London that my friend Salena was able to locate. I already have my two copies." Susan looked slightly nervous, and Addie could tell she had something else on her mind.

"Oh, fantastic! Thank you, Susan! I'm so pleased your friend was able to find these for us. Is there something else you'd like to talk about?"

"Professor, may I close the door?" Addie's eyebrows involuntarily raised slightly, but she nodded her approval. With that, Susan stood and walked over to the door and closed it but didn't sit back down. "Professor, you're still young, right?"

Addie couldn't help herself. She laughed. "Well, Susan, I'd like to think that I have a few years left before I start that walk down the road to retirement."

Susan's eyes grew wide. "Oh no, professor, I didn't mean to imply that you're old! No, what I'm trying to say is that you are really young compared with the other professors here, so I would think that you are fairly progressive and open-minded. You seem really clued into the world and what's going on. In class you have liberal thought-provoking ideas and opinions on world events and civil rights. That's why I believe your lectures are so popular." Addie was touched by Susan's complements. It was humbling to realize that she was admired.

"Thank you, Susan. Your saying that means a great deal." Addie did not want to pressure Susan, so she asked as gently as she could, "Susan, may I ask, is there something you wish to tell me? I give you my word, I will not make any judgements."

Susan paced the small office for a few moments, and when she finally stopped, she looked at Addie and said, "Professor, I really want to focus my project on I.A. London. So please say that I may continue to do so."

Addie looked at Susan, confused. "Of course, you may, Susan. We have already established that. Has something happened?"

Susan looked at Addie and bit her lip nervously. "Professor, I.A. London is a woman...a lesbian woman." Addie stood abruptly. The realization of what Susan had just said came crashing into her consciousness. Suddenly she knew, she knew everything. It was all as easy to see now as the moon in the night sky. She looked back at Susan who was continuing to speak. "The selections of her lyric and narrative poetry from 1913 to 1924 are well...about women.

Quite honestly, professor, I believe they are about just one woman, from what I have read so far. Salena, my friend in Paris, says there are several other volumes available from her other series which she will send. But these are...," Susan pointed to the small wrapped package, "are her most famous. Professor?" Addie heard Susan's voice and was aware that she was awaiting a response.

"Susan, don't worry. There are a number of female poets and writers from history who were lesbians. This does not mean they were any less talented or acclaimed for their work. I.A. London is a literary figure, just as Gertrude Stein and Natalie Barney are. So of course, you may continue your project with her as your focus."

Susan ran over and gave Addie a quick hug, "Oh thank you, professor! I knew you'd be okay with it! I have to get going. I hope you'll enjoy the volumes as much as I do. They are rather heartbreaking, though. I think she must have lost someone very special to her. I'd better get going. Thanks again, professor!" Once Susan left the office, Addie remained standing, holding tightly to the small package that Susan had given her.

It was incredible. Everything was suddenly clear, as if a decade-old fog had been lifted. There were no coincidences for her, Addie now realized. Everything that has happened in her life has been part of the fabric of her journey. She simply had to move forward for the journey to continue.

"Bless you, Susan," she whispered. She looked down at the package in her hands, bringing it up and pressing it against her heart. Sitting down at her desk she carefully removed the wrapping, slowly sliding it off the slim volumes. As with Isabelle's other books of poetry, these were bound in leather. She ran her hand over the gold lettering of the author's name. "I. A. London." Smiling, she whispered it out loud. "Isabelle Androsko, from London. It's so obvious now." The leather was soft and worn but not torn. Whoever had owned these particular volumes had treated them with care.

Addie gently laid the first volume on her desk, and when she lifted the second volume and read the words printed in gold, she couldn't help the sob that rose up from her throat. She brought her hand to her mouth to quiet her cry, but still, tears fell. She quickly wiped them away to read the title, *The Pages of Adeena*. With shaking hands, she opened the book and slowly turned the delicate worn pages. On the inside back cover, she saw what she was looking for: a photograph of Isabelle. She gasped at the black and white photo.

Isabelle wore her favorite hat, and it looked as though she was sitting in Gertrude's salon. She had a serious look on her face, and her eyes were not looking into the camera, but it was she. It was her beautiful girl. Addie slowly lifted shaking fingers to lightly touch the photo as if she could somehow feel her.

It was very late in the evening when Addie left her office. She had stayed and read each volume slowly, carefully, meticulously, absorbing each line and each word until she knew them by memory. Driving the short distance to her apartment, she felt a mixture of nervousness and euphoria. She knew she needed to concentrate on the road, but her mind kept returning to her discovery. Isabelle, through her poetry, had written her a series of love letters over the years. From Addie's beloved copy of *Poems of Paris*, written a few months after they parted, to *The Pages of Adeena*, written in 1924, Isabelle had found a way to reach out to Addie, and there was no doubt in Addie's mind that Isabelle was asking Addie to find her way back to her.

Addie turned the key in the lock and swung the door open to her apartment. She threw her briefcase, keys, and trench coat on the couch, and walked straight into the kitchen. Kicking off her pumps, she opened the refrigerator, grabbed a bottle, and poured herself a much-needed glass of Chardonnay. Standing there, leaning against the counter, she felt numb.

She slowly raised her glass to her lips and took a long drink, letting the cool dry taste of the wine fill her mouth. She swallowed. "Oh my god...oh my fucking god," she whispered. "I need to call Alan," she said, reaching for her wall phone. Just as she started to dial, she stopped.

"No... no. I need to think this through before I say anything to anyone else," she chastised herself out loud. She began to pace, wine glass in one hand, wine bottle in the other. Taking deep breaths to calm herself, Addie waited several minutes before she could feel her heart rate returning to normal. She calmly put both her glass and wine bottle down on the kitchen table and slowly walked to her bedroom.

Lying down on the pillow-covered bed, she closed her eyes and laid the back of her arm over her eyelids. A wave of emotion hit her. Today's discovery welled up in her heart and escaped through a cry deep from her throat. "Isabelle, Isabelle, Isabelle," was all she could voice, as the pain and loneliness of the past twelve years came to the surface. Deep sobs overtook her. Curling up in a ball as if in physical pain, she continued to weep. She just couldn't stop. It was as if the years of bottled-up pain were being freed. Totally exhausted, she fell into a fitful sleep.

CHAPTER 42

Addie opened her eyes to the early morning sun, still feeling exhausted and drained from the previous night's meltdown. She sighed heavily, thinking how extremely thankful she was that she had no classes scheduled for the day. She did, however, have two department meetings in the afternoon, but she knew she could reschedule at least one. Taking a deep breath to clear her overtaxed mind, she attempted to comprehend how her excitement after reading Isabelle's poetry could have so quickly changed to anxiety.

Yesterday, after Susan had left her office, she had spent hours poring through Issie's poems. As she read each word, elation had flooded her heart. Isabelle had reached out to her through the years and through her words, and because she had, Addie knew that Isabelle still loved her, and she wanted them to be together. It was so clear to Addie now, so why then did she feel this trepidation?

Despite what she now knew, and her confusion as to what to do, she felt somewhat more in control and clearer minded this morning. She needed to get up. Ugh, she thought, looking at herself. She had fallen asleep in her work clothes. "Shit," she mumbled, "I need coffee." Dragging herself out of bed, she stripped off her clothes and took a long hot shower. The heat of the spray helped to soothe her tired muscles and clear her mind. Freshly showered and dressed, Addie stood at her kitchen counter and slowly sipped her coffee. "I have to find her," she said out loud.

It was a declaration. She had known, from the moment she discovered that I.A. London was Isabelle, that she would search for her for the rest of her life, if that's what it took. Her love for Isabelle had never wavered, had never diminished. She needed Isabelle like she needed the very air that she breathed. Isabelle still loved her, she was certain of it now, but how...how would she find her?

Addie poured herself another cup of coffee and sat at her table. She wondered, would the door to Café du Temp be there now? It wasn't there that first week she had returned from New York, but, she reasoned, it was different now. Wouldn't discovering Isabelle's messages in her poetry have changed her future? But it has been twelve years, twelve years! Addie realized that it would be 1924 in Isabelle's time. God, what if I can't find her? What if she no longer lives in Paris? Perhaps she's moved back to England. Addie stood suddenly and began to pace. She took a deep breath, realizing that she needed to calm down and think clearly.

Closing her eyes, she envisioned Isabelle's writings. She knew that the love and memories they had shared were there, written for her in her poems, and that they were real. Isabelle was real. That reality was like a drug that calmed her and reassured her. She realized that it didn't matter if she could not find Isabelle in 1924. She would find her in 1965. She knew that if the door was not there, she'd go to Paris, to England, whatever it took, but she would find her. It didn't matter what age Issie was, she loved her, and she needed to find her. The truth was, there had never been anyone else for her. Isabelle was her destiny, and the proof was here, in her words, in her poems. She was certain.

Addie took several deep breaths, calmer now that she knew what path to follow. "Trust yourself," she said out loud. "Trust Issie, trust that this is the continuation of your journey."

As soon as Addie arrived at her office, she closed her door with instructions to Mary that she did not want to be disturbed. She immediately telephoned Alan at his office. "Alan, please tell me you can meet for lunch. I have some incredible news to share with you," Addie said breathlessly. She could hear Alan shuffling papers around on his desk.

"What is it? Is everything alright?" he asked, sounding both concerned and distracted. Addie immediately responded that everything was fine, but that it was imperative that they speak in person.

Alan immediately responded. "Okay, sure, I can get away. But I need to stay downtown for a meeting later this afternoon. Can you meet me in the Loop, at the Blackhawk, say noon?"

Addie heard a knock on her door. She quickly responded to Alan, "Yes, perfect, I'll see you there. And thanks, Alan, bye."

"Yes, Mary, what is it?"

Mary had knocked a second time. "Sorry to bother you, professor. I know you didn't want to be disturbed, but the Dean would like to move the meeting up to 10:00 a.m. due to a scheduling conflict."

Addie smiled. Oh, that will actually work better for me, she thought. "That's fine, Mary. Could you please make the arrangements and notify the rest of the participants? Thank you."

As Addie was preparing for her meeting, there was another knock, and this time the door swung open. Addie looked up, surprised to see Terri Mann. She inwardly cringed. Of all people, she thought. "Professor Kahlo, do you have a minute?" Terri stood at the door appearing less confrontational than usual. She didn't want to speak with Terri, but felt, since she was already in her office, that she couldn't very well ask her to leave.

"Professor Mann, yes, of course. However, I need to prepare for a 10:00, so I don't have much time."

Terri walked in the room and gently closed the door behind her. "May I sit?"

Addie looked at her curiously, "Yes, please do," she said gesturing to a chair. What is this about, Addie thought, as nearly a minute passed without Professor Mann saying anything. Finally, Addie started, "Professor Mann, what..."

Terri stood quickly, surprising Addie again. "Adeena, may I call you Adeena?"

Addie looked momentarily shocked, but she quickly recovered and said, "Of course professor. But I don't understand, what is this about?"

Terri nodded sternly. "Adeena, I'm here to apologize." Addie's eyes gave her away, the surprise evident in her gaze. But she allowed Terri to continue without interruption. "I know that since your arrival I've been well...less than welcoming." Terri keenly noticed that Addie didn't contradict her, and she let out an embarrassed laugh, shaking her head. "Actually, I've been a total bitch, and don't try and tell me I haven't been."

Addie attempted to interject now, but Terri put up her hand. "No, please allow me to finish." Addie nodded. "Adeena," Terri said sincerely, momentarily closing her eyes, "I was wrong to be so antagonistic toward you. I'm not a cold person. Well, at least I never use to be. I'm afraid that I haven't been fair to you. You see, you remind me of someone I used to know, a long time ago. Someone I tried to forget. A young woman full of energy and spirit, with a future brilliant with possibilities and ideas. But she never reached her potential, I'm afraid. She was too stubborn and proud." Terri shook her head, the look in her eyes one of deep regret, "You see, she never went through her door, never took the chance to realize her destiny."

Addie leaned back in her chair; the shock of Terri's words evident on her face. "Terri, what are you saying?" Addie whispered.

Terri smiled sadly. "I'm saying, Adeena Kahlo, there are no coincidences for us. Your path is there for you to follow if you choose to. Your destiny awaits you. Follow your path, dear girl." Addie stood and quickly moved closer to Terri, reaching for her hand and holding it tightly.

"Terri...I don't know what to say, I..."

Terri nodded and cleared her throat. "We'll speak again, I promise, but I understand you have a meeting with the Dean. I'll leave you to prepare." Addie stood, dumbfounded, as Terri Mann reached for the doorknob. "Oh, by the way, please give Peter my best when you see him. Tell him Tereasa is doing A-Okay."

CHAPTER 43

Addie was too fidgety to drive downtown and try to secure a parking spot, so she took a taxi from Hyde Park to the Loop. As she walked into the Blackhawk, she scanned the room and immediately located Alan at a table. The maître d' escorted her to her seat and politely handed her a menu. She laid down her leather briefcase on the empty chair next to her. "Alan, thanks so much for meeting me. God, I had a rough morning, I could do with something stronger than an iced tea. Is that what you've ordered?"

Alan smiled and leaned over and kissed Addie on the cheek. "Yes, it's too early for booze, Professor Kahlo. So, what's this all about?"

Addie took a deep breath and smiled broadly, eyes shining with excitement. "I've heard from her, Alan. I've heard from Isabelle. She's reached out to me and she loves me. She wants me to find her."

Alan looked at Addie with surprise and confusion. "Ad, what do you mean that you've *heard from her*? She lives in a different time, a different world. It's been what, twelve years? I don't understand."

Addie wasn't surprised at his skepticism. She herself could hardly believe that after all these years she was coming to the proverbial fork in the road. "Alan, please listen, and I'm going to attempt to say this without sounding as if I've completely lost my mind." Addie's iced tea arrived, but Alan quickly ordered both of them a brandy. Addie gave him a sideways grin, but he only nodded at her.

Addie sat up straight in her chair and turned toward Alan, taking a deep breath. "You know me, probably better than anyone. I have not been sitting around for twelve years ignoring my hopes and dreams. I have everything I have ever strived for, Alan, my career, my family...everything except the one person in my life who will truly complete me."

Alan sighed, "Addie..."

Addie shook her head. "No, please listen. I have an amazing career as an author. It was my dream, Alan, and it happened. I have a job I love, family who accept me for who I am, and I have friends, friends like you and Michael." Addie reached out to hold Alan's hand. "But still I feel as if part of my heart is missing. So, I moved back home to reconnect with the people dearest to me and to attempt to move forward with my life, though now it seems fate has found me again. A new door has opened up to me, Alan." Alan attempted to interject, but Addie continued. "Listen, do you remember how I loved the poet I.A. London?"

Alan thought a moment. "The book you carried around with you all through senior year? Yes, I remember. You were constantly reading me lines and asking me what I thought they meant."

Addie smiled, "Yes, that's the one. About two weeks ago I assigned my students a project in which they would choose an author from the past, and utilizing one of that author's works, analyze and attempt to identify the person behind the writing. Well, one of my students, a gloriously brilliant girl, asked if she could focus her project on I.A. London. This of course brought me back to my love of that poet. Well, it turns out that I.A. London's work is out of print in the U.S., so my student reached out to a friend in Paris who was able to send two sets of volumes, one for my student and one for me.

"Alan... I.A. London is Isabelle Androsko." Addie bent down and pulled her precious volumes from her briefcase. Alan looked stunned as he took the two thin leather-bound volumes in his hands and looked at Addie again. She nodded.

He read in a whisper, "*The Pages of Adeena*. Oh God, Addie. Oh my God!" He opened the book to the last page and looked at the black and white photograph of a beautiful Isabelle, circa 1924. He stared at Addie, seemingly speechless.

The waiter brought their brandies, and they both quickly took a much-needed drink. Once the waiter left, Addie quickly continued, "Alan, these poems that Isabelle wrote, they're... love letters, love letters to me." She looked intently at Alan, desperately wanting him to grasp the meaning of her discovery. "I've read each one cover to cover and I am absolutely certain she wants me to find her. She wants us to be together, and I can't think of anything that I want more." They sat silently for a moment, both contemplating the reality of what Addie was about to do.

Alan spoke first. "You're going, aren't you? You're going to try and find her."

"Yes, yes I am," she said, determination and eagerness evident in her voice. "I know this is right, Alan. When I first realized the truth, I was terrified. What if the door wouldn't be there? What if she has moved from Paris after so many years? What if she found someone else? I was driving myself crazy with doubt. But then fate stepped in again in the form of a most unlikely person." Addie thought of Teri Mann and shook her head in wonder. "That, however, is a story for another day." Alan sat quietly, slowly sipping his brandy and accepting that this is what she would do. Addie looked toward Alan, speaking quietly, "Oh Alan, please be happy for me."

Alan nodded and smiled sadly. "I don't want to lose you to 1924 Paris, but I understand that you need to go." Quickly downing his drink, he asked, "When, when are you going?"

Addie squeezed his hand, "This evening, as soon as I can arrange it."

"Let me drive you, Addie. just like the old days." Now a genuine smile creased his mouth as he held tight to her hand.

Alan picked up Addie at her Hyde Park apartment at 7:00 p.m. It took less than 30 minutes to get to their destination, though to Addie it felt as if it has taken years, twelve years to be exact. She packed a small travel bag, because she wasn't sure what it would be like in 1924 Paris, but she had a fairly good idea. These were good years for France, the years between 1919 and 1931. Post-WW I and pre-crash Paris would be jubilant. Addie wore a long cream-colored lamb's wool trench coat to hide her 1965 dress from 1924 stares and styled her long hair into a French twist.

Before she left her apartment, she had looked at herself in the mirror. She realized that Isabelle hadn't seen her since she was 19 years old. She'd been so young. Would she find the 31-year-old Addie attractive, she wondered? Pulling herself out of her thoughts, she felt Alan take her hand as he drove. Soon they would be close to LaSalle. "Ad, I was afraid to ask, but I have to...if the door is there do you think you will come back?"

Addie didn't look at Alan but stared at the road ahead as he drove.

"I want to. I really want to. I want to bring Isabelle back with me. I can't help but think of what will happen to France once Hitler is in power. I'm terrified at the thought that she would suffer through that horrible time. From her writings, I have some hope that she may be willing to make a new life with me here in our time."

Alan was contemplative "Addie, whatever happens, whatever your destiny turns out to be, I want you to know that I love you. You are, and will always be, my dearest, most cherished friend." Addie finally turned to Alan, and smiling, she placed her head on his shoulder just as he pulled up to the wet pavement of LaSalle Street.

CHAPTER 44

Addie watched as they pulled up along the narrow side alley perpendicular to LaSalle. She noticed the small pools of rain water on the pavement. The entire area had the same film noir feeling that she remembered from when she had first ventured to Café du Temp so many years ago. The evening was chilly, and the wind whipped around her as she opened Alan's car door. Alan touched her shoulder. "Shall I wait for you, Ad?" Addie turned and smiled, and touching his cheek gently, she looked in his eyes.

"Not this time, Alan. I'll be fine, I promise." He returned the smile and nodded, knowing there was really nothing else to say. Addie kissed him on the cheek and exited the car, closing the door gently. Her heels clicked on the pavement as she walked to the black door that stood imposingly against the darkness of the back alley. Alan sat, watching her as she slowly walked away from him. He could feel a kind of panic bubbling up from his chest. She was leaving, and he realized that she might never return.

The loss of his dearest friend, his confidant, seemed impossible and unbearable. He wanted to chase after her, go with her, or stop her. But then, he grinned, she'd kill him. No, Addie was her own person and that is why he loved her. All he could do was hope that she would return. It would be difficult, as he was not known for his patience, but he'd wait, certain that she would never leave without a goodbye.

Addie could hear the roar of the L trains as they zoomed by on the tracks a few blocks over. She swallowed hard and slowly reached out to rap her knuckles on the small door within the door, and it immediately swung open. She whispered the code that she had discovered in Isabelle's poetry, and the heavy door opened with an intimidating groan.

"Good evening, Miss Kahlo. How wonderful to see you again."

Addie's astonished gaze and wide genuine smile brought a grin to Alex's face. He offered her his arm. "Your usual table, Miss Kahlo?"

Addie nodded. "That would be lovely, Alex. Thank you." As Alex led Addie to her table by the bar, she could not help but admire the décor. Perhaps because she was no longer a starry eyed 19-year-old, she could really appreciate the beauty of its rich colors, soft lighting, understated elegance, and soothing ambiance. The patrons were young, as she and Alan had been, and their excitement was electric.

"Miss Kahlo, good evening."

Addie turned to see a smiling Sam. "Sam!" Addie stood and gave him a gentle hug. "It's so nice to see you," she said with genuine affection.

"And you as well, Miss Kahlo. I must say you look stunning this evening." Addie raised her eye brow and smiled her sincere thank you.

Turning when she felt a gentle touch on her arm, Addie was thrilled to see a smiling, always handsome Peter. He looked exactly as he had those many years ago. For that matter, so did Alex and Sam. It didn't surprise her that they hadn't aged. It was simply part of the enchantment of Café du Temp.

"Addie, you've made it back to us. You look lovely, my dear. The years have only made you more beautiful."

Addie reached for his hand and squeezed it with affection. "Peter, I would say you haven't aged a bit, but apparently that is the norm here at Café du Temp."

Peter laughed good naturedly. "Please sit, Addie," Peter said as he pulled out a chair for her, "and tell me how, have you been? You know that I am a huge fan of your work. Your most recent novel was fantastic. Such emotion and visualization, it was quite satisfying."

Addie looked incredulously at him, "Are you serious? You've read my work?"

Peter nodded. "Of course! There are many wonderful contributions made to the arts and literature from those who visit Café du Temp. It's an honor to be able to experience them."

Taken aback, Addie sat down in the offered seat. "Incredible. I should know to expect the unexpected when I enter these doors." Sam brought over two brandies and placed them on the table. Addie looked at her drink and smiled gently before moving her eyes to Peter. Tapping her glass, she spoke, "The last time you and I talked you toasted me. Do you remember?"

Peter nodded. "Yes, I do. You were very young with wonderful dreams of becoming an author. I am very pleased to know that your dream has been achieved."

Addie smiled softly and nodded. "Thank you, Peter. You're very kind." Peter reached out and touched her hand. "Oh, by the way Peter, a most unexpected request came from a colleague of mine." Peter watched Addie, curiosity etched on his face as he raised an eyebrow. "Yes, she and I have not seen eye to eye on a curriculum I had implemented. However, at our last meeting, she seemed to have come around. She apologized actually. But anyway, I'm getting off topic," Addie said as she shook her head slightly "Of all things, Terri Mann asked that I tell you hello for her."

Peter nodded, but his mind seemed to move quickly away. Then clarity appeared in his eyes and a sad knowing smile creased his lips. "Teresa Mann," he whispered in a soft voice. Addie said nothing as she regarded his sadness with curiosity. "Terri was very young, like you, Addie, when she first came to Café du Temp. Oh, she was so full of energy and determination, she positively oozed it. But young Terri was not one to see beyond the physical reality in front of her. She simply couldn't take that leap of faith so necessary to embrace one's life direction. We must all be active participants in our future, Addie, we must."

Watching him, Addie nodded, knowing his words were her truth. Now, seeming to be in deep thought, he closed his eyes. Addie quietly waited, not wanting to interrupt his thoughtful contemplation. With a deep sigh, he straightened his shoulders and looked at Addie. A brilliant smile appeared on his face, and his eyes shown with sincere happiness. "This is why I knew that you, Adeena Kahlo, would return one day and that you would come to claim your future. Now, Addie" he said, "I think it's time that we drink a toast to you again before you move forward to the next step of your journey."

Peter lifted his glass and gestured for Addie to lift her glass as well. "To the power and wisdom of the heart. Its strength, when filled with love, can transcend time." They clinked glasses and Addie drank down her brandy.

"Shall we?" Peter then stood and reached for Addie's hand. She smiled and laid her hand in his as he led her to the door to 1924 Paris. She was filled with nervous excitement and hope.

Addie exited through the heavy door and felt an immediate chill in the air. Paris, like Chicago, could be very brisk in March. She stopped to make note of where she stood. She looked around, identifying the boulevard she was on, and gazed toward the Champ de Mars. There, as familiar to her as an old friend, stood the Eiffel Tower.

She looked up at the sky. The night was clear, and despite the chill in the air, there were many Parisians out strolling the boulevards. She looked at her watch. It was half past nine on a Saturday evening. Would Isabelle be home? For that matter, would she still be living in Paris at her grandmother's apartments? Addie felt a momentary wave of panic, but then, just as quickly, she rationalized that this was Isabelle's Paris. Of course, she would be here. Didn't Peter confidently walk her to the door toward her destiny?

Addie steeled herself against her uncertainty and walked toward Isabelle's home. She noted the changes that had occurred in the twelve years since she had last visited. There were many more automobiles, and the only horse-drawn carriages appeared to be for tourists. The street lights were brighter, and the boulevards were cleaner. The people were dressed in tailored suits and flapper style dresses and hats. The roaring 20's had arrived, she realized with a smile. As she approached Isabelle's grandmother's apartments, she noticed several cars pulling up while others were driving away.

Well-dressed men and women were entering the building, and the lights inside were bright and festive. A party, she thought. Isabelle is having a party. Her eyes crinkled in amusement as she recalled how Issie always loved her parties. She wondered momentarily if Gertrude and Alice would be there. Surely Simone would be. Addie took a deep breath, and standing tall, with a nervous excitement and more courage than she thought she possessed, walked confidently toward the front entrance.

As she ascended the stairs, she was met by a young tuxedo-clad man who was taking coats and wraps while ushering guests into the large entryway. Addie could see maids in their crisp uniforms serving tall flutes of champagne to guests. There was 1920's style jazz being played by three black musicians in tuxedos while a striking woman with beautiful dark velvet skin sang soulfully to a rapt audience. Addie was mesmerized by the glitz and glamour before her; it looked like a Hollywood film.

"May I take your coat, mademoiselle?" offered an impeccably dressed butler. Addie turned and said, "Oh, no, thank you. I won't be staying long." She thought it better to leave her coat on, as she did not want to draw attention to her 1965 dress when everyone else was clothed in lavish 1924 gowns and elegant tuxedos. As she continued through the entryway, she took a glass of champagne from a passing maid carrying a tray full of the sparkling wine. She took a slow sip of her wine, and looking around, considered whether Isabelle would really want to trade this life for a life in Chicago with her and forty years in the future, no less.

"It is you, isn't it?"

Addie turned suddenly and stared into the stunned face of Isabelle's friend, Simone. Addie's eyes sparkled warmly as she put down her glass and clasped Simone's hand. "Simone," she said, her voice full of emotion, "how are you? It is *so* good to see you." Simone's expression went from shock to confusion and finally to a sort of enchanted wonder.

"Addie, my God!" Simone swept her startled gaze over Addie, taking in the beautiful sophisticated woman who stood before her. "How...I don't understand. Look at you, you are no longer a girl," Simone said, not unkindly but with a sort of awe, seemingly surprised to see that Addie had grown from the slightly awkward teenaged girl she remembered to the elegant American now standing before her.

Addie smiled with amusement. "Yes, Simone, I'm far from the 19-year-old you knew so long ago.

"Addie...but how is this possible?" Simone whispered. Taking Addie's hand, she glanced around, led her into the study and closed the door behind them. Simone searched Addie's face again as if she didn't believe it was her. Then, placing her hands gently on Addie's shoulders, she shook her head and then pulled Addie in for a hug. "Addie, my God! I thought I'd never see you again, but you're here!" Simone pulled back from her hug, and her look of pure amazement slowly changed to one of concern and cautious curiosity.

Seeing the change in Simone's gaze, Addie felt compelled to ensure Simone that her return to Paris was not a negative. Addie knew that

Simone's fierce loyalty to Isabelle would certainly include trying to protect her from Addie if she felt Addie was a threat to Isabelle's happiness. "Simone, please trust me," Addie said gently, with the clarity of truth and desperation in each word. "You once told Isabelle that you liked me because you could see the truth in my eyes, do you remember?" Simone nodded slowly. "Look in my eyes now, Simone, and see the truth." Simone did not respond, but her gaze softened as she waited for Addie to continue.

Addie took a deep breath and slowly moved to the French doors that led to the home's ornate gardens, memories of walking with Isabelle in that very garden flooding her mind. Turning to Simone, she said, "I know that my being here is difficult to believe, and I understand completely that you have concerns." Swallowing the lump in her throat, Addie struggled to compose herself as she shared with Simone how she had discovered Isabelle's poetry and how her words had guided her back to Paris. She wanted desperately for Simone to understand why returning to find Isabelle meant everything, and that she would choose Isabelle over any life she had, because there was no life for Addie without her. "I love her, Simone. I have always loved her. She is everything to me.

Simone quietly paced the length of the study before turning to Addie with an honest sincerity that eased Addie's growing anxiety. "Addie, I believe you," Simone said gently. "You see, *cheri, I know who you are.* I know that you are from another time. I've known since you left." Addie looked at Simone curiously, waiting for her to continue. Simone walked over to the small liquor cart in the corner of the room and poured them both a brandy.

Handing the small glass of amber liquid to Addie, she took a deep breath. "Here, drink. I think we can both use it, *oui*?" After you left, Isabelle was inconsolable. I knew that her heart was broken and there was nothing I, as her friend, could do to help her. I was angry with you at first. I had thought you used Isabelle, that you played with her emotions and then simply left to go back to your America when you were done with her."

Addie tried to interject, but Simone continued, "*Non,* Isabelle would not allow me to berate you and that is when she told me the astonishing story of Café du Temp. She explained how you and she had met and fell in love and how you both knew your love for each other was real, but that the different worlds you lived in created an impossible barrier. I found it to be an incredible story, but knowing Isabelle, I knew it could only be the truth. That is when I understood the hopelessness of the situation for you both. I realized there was no one to blame. At the time you were both so very young. Addie, I realized there was no way you two could have been together."

Looking out over Isabelle's grandmother's beloved garden, Addie felt a barrage of emotions within her. Relief, fear, nervous longing, and joy all warred with each other, making her slightly dizzy. But despite the emotional twister tearing at her, she was absolutely certain that she belonged with Isabelle. This truth she had no doubt about. She thought of how her love for Isabelle had transcended time and how it had given her the courage to walk through Isabelle's door to find her again. Addie realized now that she had never needed to move on, but had only needed to move forward. This realization filled her with the most exquisite peace. She knew that her journey had led her here, to this place in time, to this moment.

"Here you are, Simone!" The study door suddenly opened, and Isabelle entered. Addie smiled, still looking toward the garden, imagining Isabelle gliding into the room. She always knew how to make a spectacular entrance. Addie briefly closed her eyes and took a deep breath as she turned from her view of the garden to look at Isabelle, her heart pounding fiercely. She could only stare. Isabelle was stunning. Her hair, which Addie had always loved, was beautifully coiffed in the style of the day. She wore an elegant white satin gown which clung to every curve, and a long strand of pearls swung from her elegant neck as her beautiful teasing smile focused on Simone. Walking toward Simone, she playfully berated her, "Dearest, you are my co-hostess for this charity event, and here you are hiding away and..."

Simone stood abruptly when she heard Isabelle's voice and quickly looked from Isabelle to Addie. Isabelle, eyes following Simone's gaze, stopped mid-step gasping audibly as her eyes took in the elegant woman who was Addie. Tears quickly welled as Isabelle held her hand to her mouth in a surprised wide-eyed stare. It was several moments before she could speak. Her astonished gaze ran the length of Addie's body, seemingly mesmerized by the beautiful woman before her.

Cautiously making her way toward Addie, Isabelle watched as a slow beautiful smile creased Addie's mouth. She hesitantly reached out with a trembling hand to touch Addie's face as though to prove to herself that Addie was really there and she wasn't dreaming. Her hand caressed Addie's cheek as she continued to stare incredulously at the woman who stood before her. Neither woman noticed when Simone quietly left the room, gently closing the door behind her.

Addie sighed audibly at the feel of Isabelle's warm hand gently caressing her cheek, slowly closing her eyes, she turned and tenderly kissed Isabelle's smooth palm. "Isabelle," she said breathlessly as she reached out and brought Isabelle to her. She felt Isabelle melt in her arms as they held each other in a desperate embrace. Pulling back slightly, Addie smiled broadly and gazed at Isabelle's face as if still not quite believing it was actually her. "Isabelle, my darling. My God, how I have dreamed of this moment." Addie whispered as she lovingly kissed away Isabelle's tears. "I've missed you so much, my love, so so much."

I can't stop looking at you, my love," Isabelle said as she gazed adoringly at Addie. "In my mind I still see you as my sweet young Addie, full of excited new stories of books and school, all wide-eyed hazel stares full of curiosity and mischief. But you're no longer a girl," Isabelle whispered as she touched Addie's skin and gazed into her eyes. "You're a grown woman, a stunningly beautiful grown woman."

Addie smiled as she held a still astonished Isabelle in her arms. They had made their way to the window seat and were reclined and relaxed, Isabelle leaning against Addie and wrapped in her arms. "Are you disappointed, honey?" Addie teased. "I can attempt to speak teenager, but I'm afraid it would be forced and embarrassingly inadequate." Isabelle laughed heartily.

Still smiling, Isabelle pulled Addie to her and kissed her passionately, gently nibbling on her earlobe, as she whispered seductively, "Does this feel as if I am at all disappointed, darling?

Addie's eyes lit up with desire and amusement at Isabelle's breathy words. Both women were unconcerned that a lively party continued in full force just outside the parlor door as they gazed hungrily at one another. Sighing softly, Addie lifted Isabelle's hand and kissed it, then holding it gently in her own. Addie said, "I can hardly believe I'm here with you, Iss. It's surreal, it's…it's everything."

Placing two fingers under Isabelle's chin, Addie brought Isabelle's eyes to her own. "I love you, Isabelle. I have always loved you. I want to spend the rest of my life with you. Wherever life takes you, I will be with you. I will never leave you again. You are my destiny, Isabelle Androsko, and I am yours, if you'll have me."

Isabelle stared at Addie only for a moment before a breathtaking smile slowly appeared. "Oh Addie, my darling, yes…yes, I love you. It has always been you who owns my heart. I prayed that you'd make your way to me, that you would find me again through my words, and you did. I never gave up hope, my love. I've always believed that we belonged together."

Smiling through teary eyes, Addie leaned in and kissed Isabelle deeply. Feeling the sweet warmth of Isabelle's love and the urgency of Isabelle's passionate response was everything she needed, everything she wanted. She was complete. She was home.

EPILOGUE

April 1966

The sky was a pure cloudless blue, and the wind was brisk as they sped along the winding roads of southern California. "I think, my darling, that I could live here," Isabelle enthusiastically said over the sound of the wind. Addie briefly turned away from driving to smile at the love of her life. She thought Isabelle looked stunning with her blond hair blowing in the wind and her bright eyes full of fun.

"You think so, huh?" Addie said with a smile in her voice. They had rented a convertible and were now happily driving down the coast on Highway 1 toward Big Sur. It was Isabelle's first trip to California.

"Yes, I believe so. I love the Pacific coast. It reminds me of the Mediterranean. Darling, why don't we have our estate agent inquire as to what is available along the coast. Actually, a house on the beach would be marvelous!"

Addie chuckled. "Our estate agent you say, princess," Addie teased in her best haughty English accent.

Isabelle rolled her eyes and playfully hit Addie's arm. "You know what I mean, smarty-pants, and by the way, your English accent is dreadful, darling." Addie laughed heartily, put one arm around Isabelle to pull her closer, and kissed her, while the other hand skillfully held the wheel.

Isabelle grinned and kissed Addie's cheek. "Seriously, love, we can keep our place in Chicago and purchase something on the beach. It would be fabulous to visit during your breaks from university. Rachel and Mickey's children would absolutely adore it. Alan and Michael would love it as well; you know how those two love to play in the sand," Isabelle said grinning, referencing an incident a few months back, when Alan and Michael had

271

visited a nude beach in Jamaica. Addie threw her head back and laughed and then kissed the top of Isabelle's head as she snuggled up next to her.

Addie couldn't wipe the smile off her face. It had been permanently set ever since Isabelle walked through her door to spend her life with her. Addie knew she would have stayed with Isabelle in 1924 Paris if Isabelle had asked, no matter the consequences. But Isabelle was ready, ready to follow her own destiny with Addie. Addie would always remember how Isabelle had firmly held her hand, and together, with courage and excitement, they had walked through Addie's door toward their future together.

It had taken several months of planning and meetings with Isabelle's solicitor to ensure that Isabelle's inheritance and earnings were secured in a trust that would go, after her death, to Isabelle's "only living relative" in America, a great niece who was named after her famous aunt. With the help of Simone, the funds were to be managed and secure until 1965, when the American poet, Isabelle M. Androsko, would claim her inheritance. Addie would always remember how they had flown to Paris several months ago to meet with the ever elegant sixty-eight-year-old Simone. It was a beautiful reunion. Simone's joy at their happiness was mirrored only by her own, as she watched her beloved grandchildren play in her gardens.

Addie, smiling at the memory, gazed at her beloved, secure in her arm and seated next to her. She was so very proud of Isabelle. She was reinventing herself as a poet in 1966 America. Her first volume of poetry was short-listed for one of the more prestigious awards in American poetry. Addie smiled, never doubting that Isabelle would be a success, no matter what world she lived in. For herself, well, she couldn't help but believe that her life had come full circle. She would never take for granted everything she had experienced. Now, with her family, her friends, her career, and at long last, her beautiful Isabelle, she knew she had finally found her purpose and her happiness.

Isabelle looked toward Addie and lovingly touched her cheek, "What are you thinking love? You're suddenly quiet."

Addie smiled. "I'm thinking, right at this moment, that a house by the ocean with you would be nothing short of heaven.

THE END

ABOUT THE AUTHOR

C.M. Castillo, a native Chicagoan, earned a degree in Management and an MBA in Healthcare Administration. However, she has always treasured the freedom and joy of writing fiction and now, with the release of her debut novel, her dream of becoming a full-time fiction author has come true.

When not writing or reading, C.M. can be found restocking her oversized lending library or visiting any one of Chicago's many wonderful Blues and Jazz venues. C.M. lives in Chicagoland with her wife and trio of lovable mutts.

Follow her on Twitter and Instagram @castillo35@ comcast.net, and Like her on Face Book.

For updates and exclusive previews of future releases visit her at http://www.cmcastillowriter.com.